OBSESSION
FALLS

ALSO BY CHRISTINA DODD

OBSESSION FALLS

CHRISTINA DODD

ST. MARTIN'S PRESS ⚞ NEW YORK

OBSESSION FALLS. Copyright © 2015 by Christina Dodd. All rights reserved.
Printed in the United States of America. For information address St. Martin's
Press, 175 Fifth Avenue, New York, N.Y. 10010.

www.stmartins.com

Designed by Omar Chapa

Library of Congress Cataloging-in-Publication Data

Dodd, Christina.
    Obsession Falls / Christina Dodd. —First edition.
        pages ; cm
    ISBN 978-1-250-02847-1 (hardcover)
    ISBN 978-1-250-02846-4 (e-book)
    I. Title.
    PS3554.O3175O27 2015
    813'.54—dc23

St. Martin's Press books may be purchased for educational, business, or promotional
use. For information on bulk purchases, please contact the Macmillan Corporate
and Premium Sales Department at 1-800-221-7945, extension 5442, or write to
specialmarkets@macmillan.com.

First Edition: September 2015

10 9 8 7 6 5 4 3 2 1

To my friends who have coaxed, cajoled, encouraged, and most of all listened as I created the world of Virtue Falls—thank you. You deserve every good thing, and a trip to Disneyland, too.

ACKNOWLEDGMENTS

Writing a woman in jeopardy suspense posed an exciting challenge, one I could not have done without the great team at St. Martin's Press.

Jennifer Enderlin's clear-sighted guidance and editorial direction kept me from straying too far from the main story. Her comment, "Christina, sometimes you have to kill your darlings," has led to a trail of fictional characters written and discarded, leaving only the few that fascinate and beckon. We share a vision, and that is a great thing.

Anne Marie Tallberg, Associate Publisher, and the marketing team of Stephanie Davis, Angela Craft, Jeanne-Marie Hudson, and Jessica Preeg, see *Virtue Falls* in terms of a publishing event, and generate excitement every day.

The art department, led by Ervin Serrano, captured my vision of *Virtue Falls*, the beauty and the menace, and translated it to the cover.

To everyone on the Broadway and Fifth Avenue sales teams— thank you for placing *Virtue Falls* in just the right places and at just the right times.

A huge thanks to managing editor Amelie Littell and Jessica Katz in production.

I don't know what I would do without Caitlin Dareff doing so much so efficiently.

Thank you to Sally Richardson, St. Martin's president and publisher. I am so glad to be part of St. Martin's Press.

To retired Air Force Major Roger B. Bell who critiques, edits, and proofreads every one of my books, who is my source for all things military, firearm, and flight related, who nags me when I'm behind, encourages me when I'm plodding glumly through the endless middle, and is a friend I treasure. Thank you!

PART ONE

THE KIDNAPPING

CHAPTER ONE

The highway from Idaho's Sun Valley travels north into the Sawtooth Mountains with two lanes and strategically located turnouts in case a person needs to change a tire or gawk at the scenery. The road winds past shacks constructed of beer bottles and aluminum siding, past rusty mobile homes and clapboard houses in need of paint. That highway is a drive back in time, to a moment when the West opened its arms to every pioneer and misfit in the world.

Then the National Forest Service moved in.

No one ever said they did it wrong. The world deserves places of wildness, where no one logs trees that have grown since the time of Jesus, where snowmobiles and ATMs can't challenge black bears to battle and take out rare and delicate flowers. Most people want a place where hikers and backpackers can roam the wilderness, and then only in summer months when winter retreats . . . and waits.

But even the National Forest Service can do nothing about Wildrose Valley. Wildrose Valley Road turns off the main highway, and rises up and up in hairpin turns that make flatlanders clutch and cringe. The surface is gravel, full of washboard stretches that beat a woman's teeth together as she drives her rented black Jeep Cherokee toward the place where she had been born.

She tops the summit and there it is—the valley, slung like a hammock between the mountains. Ranchers had settled here in the early twentieth century, carving out tracts of land where they raised cattle and children, grew gardens and alfalfa, fought freezing cold and the Depression and bankruptcy.

But here and now, in August, the valley is wide, yellow with grass, dappled with cattle and antelope. Meadows stretch miles to the far horizon where the mountains close in. The Forest Service likes to think they protect the wilderness; in truth, the Sawtooth Mountains themselves are the sentinels and guardians of the land.

Taylor Summers had spent her first nine years roaming the Sawtooth Mountains in search of a safe place, away from her home, away from her parents' constant, bitter arguments about her father's ranch, her mother's ambitions, and Taylor, who had somehow become the heart of their conflict.

Then, on her tenth birthday, she had moved with her mother to Baltimore, and was never again to see Wildrose Valley . . . until today.

She drove slowly down the steep grade, absorbing the changes. Where small craftsman-style ranch houses had once stood, mansions now sprawled. Not many mansions, though; rich people bought wide acreages and surrounded themselves by vistas that could not be blocked.

Taylor didn't blame them. Today, when she rolled down her windows, she heard nothing but the wind through the golden grasses and the occasional call of a bird. She recognized a few landmarks: a stand of maple trees where she used to play, the unpainted wreck of a barn where she'd swung in an exhilarating ride on a rope out of the hayloft and through the wide-open doors.

And there! *There* was the turnoff to the Summers ranch, owned by her family for over a hundred years, until her mother forced her father to sell it in the divorce and divide the profits.

Involuntarily, Taylor's foot slipped off the accelerator and the car slowed.

Look! The people who bought the place had put up a phony gate, and they had the guts to put up a sign calling the place SUMMERS FOREVER.

They not only had claimed her heritage, they'd also claimed her name.

The *bastards*.

Taylor rolled up her windows, put her foot back on the gas, and drove through ruts and dust toward the end of the basin and her goal, where the mountains came together, squeezing the road like a vise.

An hour of driving too fast got her at last to the serenity of mountains. Here was the forest she sought. The air was thin, sharp, fresh with the scents of pine and earth and growth and, yes, surely . . . inspiration.

Taylor had always considered herself a true artist.

Sure, she had gone to college to study graphic design, and sure, she had segued into interior decorating. But for all that she had besmirched her talent with good jobs that made gobs of money, she hugged close a strong sense of superiority. Deep inside, she had believed that if she flung away the trappings of success and became a full-time artist, her talent would change the world.

So to celebrate the crashing destruction of her second engagement, she had flown to Salt Lake City, rented a vehicle, and driven north along the Wasatch Range. She stopped to sketch every vista, expecting that sensitive, brilliant, expressive art would form beneath her fingers.

No. Not once. Not a hint of genius, of uplifting emotion or self-knowledge or glory or pain. All these years of believing in herself, and this . . . this was it?

Drawn by the conviction that if she got home, she would rediscover her muse, she drove north, into Idaho. In Sun Valley, she rented a room, spent the night, and now here she was, heart pounding as she pulled into an isolated picnic area. She backed the Cherokee into a parking spot hidden by brush and trees. She grabbed a bottle of water, her waist pack, and her drawing pad, and climbed out. She followed a trail that wound through the trees, looking for the one spot she wished, believed, *hoped,* would reignite her vision.

In less than a mile, the forest ended and a wide, green meadow opened its arms to her, and she recognized this place. *This,* far more than the ranch, was home. Here her father had taught her to camp, to hike, to hunt. Of all her early life, those were the moments she treasured.

Taylor climbed up on one of the smooth, massive black basalt boulders abandoned by the glaciers. To her left and her right, as far as she could see, forbidding and majestic pinnacles pierced the pale blue of the August sky. To capture the grandeur of the Sawtooth Mountains required bold-hued oil paints done on a large canvas by a master.

All they had was her.

But she was here, and she longed to pay tribute to the forces of the earth.

Opening her sketch pad, she took up her charcoal pencil and gave her soul over to the vista before her.

When she had finished, she pulled back and studied her achievement.

In high school, her art teacher had told her anyone could draw a mountain, but a true artist depicted the soul of the mountain and gave the viewer a sense of glorious austerity or forbidding heights or searing cold. A true artist created not art, but feelings: longing, terror, love. Most of all, Taylor's art teacher warned her against making mountains look like ice-cream cones.

Taylor could state with great assurance the mountains she had sketched did not look like ice-cream cones.

They looked like ingrown toenails.

She rifled through her sketch pad, looking at each and every one of her drawings. How had she reduced the imperious majesty and eternal grandeur of the western mountains to such a disgusting human condition? She had dreamed of and planned for this, imagined her artistic talent would blossom in the place so long cherished in her childhood memories. Instead, she was a failure, such a failure that she was almost relieved when she heard a car bouncing along the washboard gravel road behind her. She shut her drawing tablet, slid off the rock, and headed into a stand of pines.

Not that she needed to hide. She had as much right to be here as anyone. But she was a woman alone. The car probably contained a rancher or some tourists, but wild game attracted out-of-season hunters, old gold claims dotted the creeks, and longtime residents carried guns. Up here, it was better to be safe than sorry.

When a black Mercedes came around the bend, hitting every rut as if it was a personal challenge, she grinned.

Rich tourists. She knew the type, city folks who could not believe that every road in America wasn't paved for their convenience. She wondered how far they would go before the washboards defeated them, or before they destroyed their car's oil pan on a protruding rock.

They passed out of sight behind a boulder as big as a house, where the road cut through the meadow, and there the sound of the engine cut out.

Probably they had a picnic lunch. They'd dine and head back . . .

She glanced at her watch. Two thirty. Pretty soon, she needed to return to her rental Cherokee, too. It was a good two-plus-hours' drive back to town. But first . . . she started walking deeper into the woods, looking for something less imposing to sketch. A tree, maybe. Or a bug.

On the road, two doors slammed.

One man spoke, coldly, clearly: "Get him out of the trunk."

CHAPTER TWO

Taylor stopped.

Him? Out of the trunk?

She didn't like this guy's tone. She didn't like his words.

Who, or what, was in the trunk?

"Do you think this is far enough?" The other man sounded itchy, nervous.

She started walking again. *None of her business . . .*

"How the hell much farther do you want to drive on that miserable crapfest of a trail? Jimmy said to bring him up here, find some place lonely, finish him, and dump the body—"

She froze.

"Isn't this lonely enough for you?"

"I guess—"

A thump.

"Yes!"

Finish him? Dump the body?

She felt disoriented. Birds were twittering. Above her, massive Douglas fir trees wrapped the heavens in their branches and sang a song to the wind.

And someone within her earshot was talking about . . . *dumping the body?*

"Then that's what we're going to do," the first guy said. "You want to argue with Jimmy?"

"No. No," the other guy stammered. "Not that scary bastard."

Some guy named Jimmy had hired these guys to . . .

The trunk latch opened with barely a sound.

A child's scream filled the air.

This could not be happening. Taylor could not be up here, alone in the most peaceful place on earth, trying to get back her artistic mojo, and bear witness to a murder. A child's murder.

The second man said, "Jesus Christ, he hurled all over the trunk. I'm going to have to take this to the car detailers to get it cleaned up."

"No, you're not. How are you going to explain barf in the trunk? Tell them we were hauling a kid in there? Clean it yourself." The first guy had a baritone voice, and when he rolled out the orders, he did it with authority.

Above the voices, the child's wail became sobbing, punctuated by gasps for air.

Taylor did not want to be here.

But she was.

Chills ran up her arms, and she felt like hurling, too.

She left the protection of the trees and moved quietly into place behind the boulder.

She was safe here. She was. The boulder was as big as a house. Dense. Tall. Rolled into place by some ice age glacier.

She was safe.

She was a fool.

With her back against the rough stone, she slid and looked, slid and looked. Finally the car came into view.

And the men.

And the little boy.

And the guns.

Pistols, big pistols, held with casual familiarity in the men's hands.

One guy was bulky and narrow-eyed. He was in charge.

One was thin and muttering. He held the boy by the scruff of the neck and shook him like a terrier with a rat.

The boy . . . the boy was about eight, white-faced, dark-haired, covered with vomit. Terrified.

Taylor was terrified, too. Her hands trembled. Her knees shook. Her heart thundered in her ears.

But she could still hear the casual slap Mr. Skinny gave the boy.

"Shut up," he said.

The boy sobbed more softly.

She looked again. She recognized the big guy. Seamore "Dash" Roberts, running back, Miami Dolphins, big scandal, jail time, a career that barely survived in arena football . . . yeah.

The other guy wasn't anybody. He was just, you know, sweaty.

Both guys wore suits. Up here. In the land of ranchers, Ford trucks, tourists, and the occasional tree-hugger. So these men in the suits were out of place. But they didn't care. Because they were here to kill the boy and get out.

Good. Good. She could ID these guys . . . when she got down to the police department. *After they'd murdered that little boy.*

"Where do you want to do it?" Mr. Skinny asked.

Dash glanced around.

Taylor flattened herself against the rock.

"There, by that tree stump." He pointed. "That way we can prop him up. He'll face the road and when McManus shows up, he'll see him right away."

"Let him search." Mr. Skinny laughed.

The boy's crying gave a hitch.

She glanced again.

He was terrified. Yes, he was. But he was also eyeing the men, looking around at his surroundings, like he knew he had to make a run for it. Like he knew he had to save himself.

"Christ's sake, think about it." Dash again, snappy and scornful. "There are wild animals up here. Wolves. Coyotes. We hide the body, they'll drag it away and eat it. Jimmy will be furious. He's paying, and he wants the most bang for his buck. Shock. Horror. All that crap."

"He really wants to get this dude's attention, doesn't he?"

"You don't want to get on Jimmy's wrong side. He knows how to handle business."

The child shivered convulsively. He wore a school uniform. A school uniform, for shit's sake, with slacks, a pressed shirt, and a tie. He was old enough to know he was going to die, and young enough not really to understand.

Well. Who did understand? She didn't. She wished she could help him. But there was no way. She wasn't carrying a gun. She couldn't just run at these guys, guys who were obviously professional hit men, and save the kid. All she would do was die, too. That wouldn't help the boy. She could do nothing but watch helplessly.

Even as she thought that, she was quietly, relentlessly tearing the sheets out of her drawing tablet. They were eight-by-eleven, good-sized sheets of paper with whipped cream clouds and ingrown toenail mountains.

She didn't have a plan.

Or rather—it was a stupid plan.

But the wind was blowing. The stand of trees was no more than twenty yards away. If she ran fast enough and dodged quickly enough, she could get away. And she couldn't stand to live the rest of her life knowing she didn't make even the most feeble attempt to save a child from murder by two professional killers.

Stupid plan. So stupid. She was going to get herself killed.

She heard her father's voice in her head. *Taylor, you can't outrun a bullet.*

She knew it. She really did. But the boy's crying was getting louder again, the men more silent. They were getting down to business, which was to murder the child and pose him so that guy, McManus, saw him as soon as he drove up the road.

Shock. Horror. All that crap.

When she had freed a dozen sheets of paper, she put the tablet on the ground and stepped on it. Holding three sheets high above her head like unformed paper airplanes, she let the wind catch them, heard them flap, took a breath—and released them.

CHAPTER THREE

Taylor ran.

She thought she would hear the sheets of paper as the wind carried them into the meadow. Into view of the hit men. To distract them. From the kid.

To attract their attention. To her.

To give the kid a chance to escape.

Stupid, stupid plan.

She didn't hear the flap of the papers.

All she heard was the red buzz of fear in her ears.

She zigged out into the meadow into plain sight of the gunmen, then zagged back behind the boulder.

A gunshot. She heard the gunshot. Loud. Sharp. Cruel. Close. To her.

So they'd seen her. Yay.

"Run, kid!" she yelled.

Shouts. She thought she heard shouts.

She glanced behind her.

Seamore "Dash" Roberts came around the boulder, pistol in hand. Moving fast.

She had the lead.

Good.

But he was a running back. Big guy. Got the nickname "Dash" because he was fast.

Bad. Very bad.

To beat him, she had to run straight toward the trees as fast as she could.

To live, she needed to zigzag.

She ran straight.

She ducked.

A shot rang out.

He missed.

Oh, God. Oh, God. Please, God.

He missed because he had a pistol. That was good for her. Pistols were meant for close work. Hard to aim. Best he could do was thirty to forty feet if he was skilled, and he'd have to stop to really get a bead on her.

The forest. She had to get to the forest.

Run as hard as you can.

She reached the shelter of the trees.

She'd made it!

She glanced back.

He stopped, braced his feet, raised his pistol.

She ducked behind a tree.

A shot shattered the bark beside her.

This was okay. This was good. Because if he was shooting at her, he wasn't killing the kid.

Yeah. Real good.

She ran again, glanced back.

He sprinted toward her.

No. She knew this place.

He didn't.

She took a left.

Another shot.

She should be counting. He had only six shots . . . unless that was an automatic pistol, in which case—

This was no time for math.

Run, goddamn it.

There. The foot of the mountain. She took another left, fast and hard, around the rock, and she headed up the steepest incline she'd ever seen. And she'd seen a few.

Another shot. Close.

God. Please, God.

She leaped like a mountain goat over rocks. She ducked under brush.

She couldn't zig. She couldn't zag. The path was narrow. It was curvy. It was damn near vertical. There was only one way up this mountain, and she was on it.

So was he.

She could hear him behind her, tearing up the ground as he gained on her.

She had only one way out. One way to save herself.

The cave. In the rock.

Never, ever go in that cave. No one knows where it goes. You could fall. You could break your legs. You could never be found. Never go in. Never.

Her father's voice. He meant it.

But it was his fault she was doing this. His fault he'd taught her to be responsible and do the right thing.

She dove into the crack in the rock. She wiggled on her belly in the dirt. Fast. Without a whimper. Without a fear of what awaited her.

She was too afraid of what was after her.

The kid had run, too. He'd escaped, too. Because otherwise, this was all for nothing.

Run, kid!

The farther she went into the cave, the tighter it got. Finally there was nowhere else to go except through a passage so low and narrow it was nothing more than a splinter in the rock. But she went.

Belly to the ground, head down, she crawled into darkness. She got stuck. Her butt didn't fit. She gasped. She wiggled. She pulled. She tore skin off her chin. And she was in. Inside. In a cave, unexplored, where she could tumble and break her legs and die a slow death. She shimmied in, staying low—and fell into nothingness.

CHAPTER FOUR

Not nothingness. Taylor fell five feet onto . . . something. Something hard. Stone.

Pain exploded in her right wrist. Blood trickled down her cheek. She covered her mouth and bit down on her scream of pain.

Don't scream. Don't scream. He'll hear you.

But her wrist really hurt. Her cheekbone up by her eye socket— that hurt, too. She'd struck it on the way down. Every nerve throbbed. Every sense flared.

The little boy . . . had she saved him? Had he seized his chance? Had he run away? Or was he even now lying in a puddle of his own blood, or propped against a rock for McManus to find?

Tears filled her eyes.

Dead. He was probably dead.

Because all she had been able to think to do was toss her drawings to the wind in the hopes of distracting his killers.

She cried. A little. Silently, curled into a fetal position, holding her hurt wrist with one hand, and with her fist over her mouth.

She heard nothing from above in the shadows.

Of course not. That monster would not fit. She hoped.

Okay. Okay, she was safe. For the moment, she was safe.

She worked on her breathing, trying to stop the gasping, the sobbing. She worked on her heartbeat, trying to calm the thump against her rib cage.

She had never in her life felt like this, or been in the grip of such terror. She lived near Washington, D.C., one of the most violent cities in the United States, and she had to come back to the freaking primitive Sawtooth Mountains to get shot at.

Did the boy live? Had he run away? Had he saved himself?

Oh, please, God. Let him have run. Let him be alive.

She groped around, trying to see where she was, where she had come to rest, to find a way farther into the cave, to find a safer place.

She was on a ledge. It stuck out three feet. It was five feet wide. She lay on her belly, extended her good arm into thin air.

Nothing. No way farther in. No way out.

Cautiously, she sat up.

She explored her arm. Bruised. She winced. Or cracked.

She touched her cheek. More bruising, and the blood wasn't much. Not too much. In here, there weren't any wild animals to be attracted to the smell. Maybe some bats. These bats ate insects. No vampire bats lived in Idaho. She was almost sure she remembered that.

Light trickled through the narrow opening above her. Not much light. Not enough. And with Dash out there, she didn't dare activate her phone.

In fact . . . she pulled it out of her waist pack and powered it down.

Yes, she was in a cave. Probably no one could use her GPS to locate her. But she didn't dare take the chance.

If Dash had seen her, if he could somehow wedge his broad shoulders through the hole, he could look down at her and kill her like a duck in a shooting gallery.

But if he had, surely he would have done it by now.

She scooted to put her spine against the wall. She curled up, hugging her knees, listening for Dash, wondering if he saw her go in, if he knew where she hid, if he would come after her with his pistol—or if he would go away and return with dynamite and blast the entry and she would never, ever leave this place of absolute dark and sharp chill and the rustle of creatures unseen.

CHAPTER FIVE

Finally . . . Taylor fell asleep, rolled onto her side, stretched out . . . and fell forever into the dark, onto the rocks.

She woke with a gasp, sat up, terrified and trembling.

She was fine. She was fine. She hadn't fallen at all.

It was nothing but a dream.

But she couldn't go to sleep again. Could. Not. Did. Not. Dare. It was too dangerous.

It was dangerous to stay here, too.

Her mouth was dry. Even her teeth felt dry.

She hadn't had a drink for hours. She was dehydrated. She needed water, and soon. Which meant . . . which meant she had to leave.

She could take heart in the fact Dash hadn't followed her in. She'd seen no flashlight beam pierce the dark.

Of course, she had barely made it through the crack. That broad-shouldered, muscular murderer of a football player sure as hell couldn't do it.

Seamore "Dash" Roberts. She leaned her head back against the rock. What did she know about him?

Not much. She followed football with mild interest, and only her local teams. But Dash was special. He was a celebrity . . . of sorts. He'd played two and a half seasons for the Miami Dolphins, had been one of their hottest players. Then he'd beat up his model girlfriend so brutally he put her in the ICU for over a month, and broke her face so horribly she could never look in the mirror again, much less get work as a model. *She* committed suicide, and *he* served six months of a three-year sentence—he was a sports superstar, no reason to make him pay too much for brutality and mutilation. Then he was out on parole, confined to his home for two months, which gave him time to get picked up by the Detroit Lions. He was back on the field, fast as ever, a media darling, when he got photographed betting on his own game. That was the end of his football career. After that, there were some moments of glory in arena football, but he kept a low profile.

Now she knew why. He was working for hire as a hit man, and apparently without a shred of conscience.

A little boy. He was going to kill a little boy.

And her, too. But really . . . what kind of monster killed a kid?

She wanted to look at her phone. She wanted to check the time. It had been hours—she thought—since she'd crawled in here. Was it dark outside?

Yes, because no more light leaked into the cave.

Should she try to leave?

Could she leave, or was she trapped here?

Using her hands to sweep up the wall behind her, she stood, and at about five feet up, she located the outcrop that led to the entrance.

She was five-seven. This was doable. She could climb up there. Somehow. If the rock didn't break. If she didn't fall backward and splatter her brains out on the stone ledge, or fall all the way down into whatever oblivion waited at the bottom of the cave.

What if Dash was sitting out there, waiting?

No choice. In her waist pack she carried her phone, some drawing pencils, a sharpener, a mini-pack of tissues, a fold-up cup, and an energy bar. She had more stuff in her rental car: a couple of bottles of water, a sandwich. But she hadn't come equipped to camp. She hadn't come to survive. She'd come out to sketch ingrown toenail mountains.

She was a skilled furniture designer. She was a respected interior decorator. She liked her job. She liked the money she made. So why the hell had she decided she needed further fulfillment as an artist?

She was such a schmuck.

And she was stalling.

She groped across the rocky surface. She found dust and gravel, but nothing to hang on to.

She pulled on the ledge a little, wincing when a few chunks of stone crumbled and fell at her feet.

She opened and ate the energy bar, and stuffed the wrapper back in her waist pack.

She pulled out her phone. Held it in her hand and decided that since she was deep underground no one—that would be Dash or his mysterious boss—could trace her signal. She squatted down and huddled close against the wall, powered on her phone, and blinked at the sudden blaze of light.

Three thirty-eight A.M. She had slept longer than she realized.

She powered it down again, stashed it in her waist pack. She took a breath, and tried to hoist herself up.

Pain shot through her wrist. She landed back on her feet, squatted down, and held her wrist. And rocked.

Cracked. Yeah. Cracked for sure. And it couldn't have been her left wrist. No. It had to be her right one, and she was most definitely right-handed.

So what? She still had to get out of here.

Standing, she took long, fortifying breaths, and tried to take heart in the fact that the shelf above her had held her weight. If she could work around that wrist and pull herself up there . . .

This moment was why she had been working out with Brent, the physical trainer. If she could ignore the pain that sadist made her inflict on herself, she could ignore a few bruises and a cracked wrist.

So she did it. She mostly used her elbows, whimpering and scrabbling for anything to hold on to, finding nothing, whimpering and scrabbling some more. It wasn't graceful. She was glad no one watched her. But when at last she lay there in the narrow, tight place before the narrow, tight crack that would take her out of the narrow, tight cave, she was panting, sweating, trembling. She found herself torn between relief . . . and fear. Relief because she needed food and water, and fear that she didn't have the energy to work her way out through the tiny crack in the rock. Plus, she still didn't know if Dash was out there, and she had to crawl. He could smash her head as soon as she stuck it out.

Cheerful thought.

Wiggling around, she dug a sharpened pencil out of her waist pack.

Hey. It was a weapon. Not much of a weapon, but her karate master had promised that after only twenty lessons, she would be able to kill a man with a sharpened pencil.

Too bad she'd quit karate after lesson two, when she hit the floor and got the breath knocked out of her.

She gathered her courage to make the first move toward freedom— or death.

Beneath her knee, a chunk of rock broke off.

It struck the ledge where she'd rested below, bounced off into oblivion. Her leg dangled in the air. The rest of the ledge started to crumble— and she found herself outside the cave and upright, clutching the pencil in her fist.

And alone.

No Dash.

She wiped the perspiration off her forehead with her bare arm. Put the pencil back into her waist pack. Looked around and tried to evaluate her situation sensibly.

Sensibly couldn't change the facts.

It was cold and dark. Really cold. She could see her breath. And really dark. Moonless, and the starlight could not pierce the canopy of the ancient trees.

There were creatures out here. Not just harmless animals like bunnies and mice. Wolf packs lived in Idaho, and black bears, and she was under no illusions about those predators—as she weakened, they would rip her flesh and clean her bones.

She needed to get to her car and get out of here as fast as she could. She needed to do it before dawn.

Because in the cave, she had refused to face one truth.

Every one of those drawings she had deliberately tossed to the wind—every one of those crappy, lousy, humiliating drawings—she had signed every one of them.

Dash and his murderous cohort knew her name.

She needed to find her car before they did.

CHAPTER SIX

Dawn was breaking when Taylor knelt beside a stream, opened her fold-up cup, dipped it in the freezing water, and took a long, grateful drink.

She was already so cold she couldn't feel her fingers, the icy water made her shiver uncontrollably, and she would probably get giardia from unclean water. But better that than dying of dehydration.

Gritting her teeth, she slid her wrist under the surface and let the water numb the pain and, she hoped, bring down the swelling. She'd slipped more than once in the darkness, and caught herself, and every time agony almost brought her to her knees.

But she kept going. She didn't know she had it in her, but desperation did wonderful things for a woman's stamina and courage.

When she had calmed the throbbing, she leaned her back against a tall pine, pulled her knees into her chest in a vain attempt to get warm, cradled her arm, and faced hard reality.

She hadn't made it back to her car in time. Worse than that, she had done another thing her father had warned her not to do. She had gotten lost in the mountains. The Sawtooth Mountains. Not the kind of mountains they had in the East. Not sissy mountains. The Sawtooths were steep, with elevations towering upward to almost eleven thousand feet. Every night—*every* night—the temperatures dropped below freezing. People got lost here and never came out. Sometimes an unwary hiker found the body. Sometimes no one found any trace.

For people who wanted to disappear, the Sawtooth Mountains were the place to do it, as long as they were prepared for cold and loneliness, hunger, wild animals, and winters that started early and ended late.

Taylor wasn't totally unprepared. She had a compass—on her phone, which she didn't dare power up for fear the bad guys would track her.

She knew how to use the constellations, find the North Star. Her father had taught her. But in these mountains, studded with sudden precipices, steep inclines, and unending trees, seeing enough of the sky to consistently find the Big Dipper was impossible. She could climb higher, out of the tree line, but that was going the wrong way, and she needed to eat. Which wasn't going to happen soon. And she needed to sleep. That, she could manage. Because her father had taught her how to build a shelter.

As she uncurled from the tight ball and stood, she said aloud, "Thank you, Daddy."

She wasn't going to like this bed. She wasn't going to be comfortable. The needles were going to poke her and the sap was going to stick to her skin. Inevitably, there would be bugs. But the branches would hold her up off the cold ground and provide cover to help her retain her body heat. And as the morning progressed, the air would warm and she wouldn't be so terribly, horribly cold.

Her father had taught her that anytime she went into the forest, to take a hatchet and a knife, preferably the Randall knife—which she still owned. At home. If she had that knife . . . but she didn't, so she broke branches off the trees, piled them in a sunny spot, and arranged a nest for herself. She slid down, curled up, pulled more branches over herself, and despite the needles, the sap, and the bugs, she went immediately to sleep.

She woke in the early afternoon. The sun was shining on her face. She itched. Everywhere. And something with creepy legs was crawling down her back.

She flung the branches aside, did the bug-dance, and shook a beetle out of her shirt.

She touched her nose. Sunburn. She had a rash on her arms from the pine needles. Still she felt better than she had when she went to sleep. She could think cognitively. She could make plans and know they made sense.

Okay. She had to get to her car. The Cherokee was parked off the road, hidden by trees, a good mile from where she'd seen the attempted murder. Over this rough terrain, and at night, she couldn't have walked far from that place where the child . . . well. She couldn't think of him right now. Either he was okay or he wasn't. Now she needed to make sure she was okay.

So to find her car, all she had to do was to go down.

Yes, there was a chance Dash had found the car. Or maybe he was waiting for her along the road.

But she was miles into the mountains. She couldn't walk back to civilization. She needed a vehicle if she was going to go to the cops and report this murder—or, hopefully, attempted murder.

She scattered her nest, dumping most of the branches in the creek. No use leaving evidence she'd been here.

She would follow the creek down to the basin, stick to the trees, use whatever concealment she could find. When she found the car, she would scout around before she approached it, look for signs that another person had been there. Or was there. And if she was satisfied she was alone, she would get in and drive like hell back to Ketchum and the police station.

No, wait. First she would eat the sandwich and anything else she could find. *Then* drive like hell.

"Good plan," she said aloud, and started down the creek bed. Then she answered herself, "Of course it's a good plan. You have no choice."

Great. Twenty-four hours in the mountains and she was already turning into one of those hermits who held conversations with herself. "It's okay," she said. "A couple more hours and you'll be talking to the police."

CHAPTER SEVEN

Taylor's estimate of how long the trip would take was about three hours short. The creek plunged over precipices that she could not follow and had to detour around. She kept coming back to the water, though, knowing it was headed toward the high end of Wildrose Valley. And she was dependent on that source of water. She was starving, yes, but by God, she was hydrated.

Eventually, during one detour, she lost the creek completely. Then she simply headed down, through underbrush, over rocks, around trees. When she realized she was on a trail, she almost cried for joy. Because a trail would lead her to the basin floor.

And it did. The trail still wound through the trees, but it flattened out. The walking was easier. She knew the road was here between the two fingers of the mountains. All she had to do was find it, and she could find her car.

She glanced toward the sun. Sunset was early here, the rays cut off by the peaks. She needed to hurry. And she needed to hide.

She skulked through the trees until she found the road.

She hugged herself. *Now* she knew where she was.

The relief she felt seemed out of proportion, and made her realize how frightened she had been of a lingering, hopeless death of starvation and cold.

Her car was south. Keeping the road in sight, she moved through the pines as quickly and as quietly as she could.

Pretend you're alone here, her father said, *the first woman on the continent, strong, sure, moving like the panther that you track. You see everything. You know everything. Everything fears you.*

She whimpered. *No, Daddy. I'm afraid.*

No, you aren't. You use caution.

She nodded. *Caution.*

She was hearing her father's voice in her head.

Yep. Another day and she'd be stark-staring crazy.

It was twilight when she found the Cherokee, parked right where it had been, off the road and concealed in the trees.

She ducked behind a tree trunk, then peeked at it.

She wanted to run to the SUV, embrace its fenders, kiss its mirrors, open its doors, find her backpack and that wonderful, fabulous, tasty sandwich, the baggie of crushed granola.

Her stomach growled, urging her onward.

She resisted. She had to be wise.

But it was getting darker by the second, too dark to scout thoroughly for signs of a visitor. So she picked up a pebble, leaped out from behind the tree, and threw it as far as she could, over the Cherokee's roof to the trees on the other side, to make a noise and see if she could flush out any onlookers.

Then she ducked back behind the tree.

The pebble bounced through the tree branches and landed with a tiny thud.

She waited.

No movement. No reaction.

Dash wasn't here. He was not here.

She could hear her sandwich calling her name . . .

Don't be foolish, Taylor. Another rock, bigger this time.

She hoped, when she got some food into her, her father would stop talking to her, because this was spooky. But she sighed and did as he told her, picking up a bigger rock and flinging it haphazardly toward the brush at the front of the car.

Trouble was, she didn't have the oomph to get it that far, and she watched in horror as the heavy stone sailed through the air toward the hood. She couldn't watch. She ducked behind the tree. She had the brief thought, *That's going to cost my insurance.* She squinted her eyes shut and waited for the impact.

The car exploded.

CHAPTER EIGHT

The blast wrapped around the tree and blew Taylor onto her face in the dirt. She covered her head. Flaming debris fell around her. Her ears were ringing; dimly she heard the roar of a beast behind her.

No. Not a beast. Fire. A huge fire. She felt the heat and blistering stings as burning pine needles fell off the tree onto her bare skin.

Get. Away. Forest fire. Get out of the trees!

She crawled, then got up and ran. No zigging. No zagging. She wasn't thinking about the possibility of gunmen.

She had to escape from the fire.

As she ran, she shook her head, combed her hands through her hair. She dislodged a flaming twig and more needles. She stepped on something that crunched. Her cell phone.

She kept going. If someone was shooting, she didn't know. She couldn't hear. Oh, God, she couldn't hear. Her skin was on fire. And she was running back into the mountains, seeking sanctuary where there was none.

She never looked back.

CHAPTER NINE

On day four after the car explosion . . . or was it day four after Dash had shot at her?—Taylor found herself on the ridge overlooking her old house. Her old house that wasn't there anymore.

When her mother made her father sell his family's land and the house on it, and divide the proceeds with her, it had been an act of unimaginable cruelty to Pete Summers. He had lived his whole life on the ranch, working the cattle, mending the fences, fixing the broken-down machinery, growing alfalfa. In one fell swoop, everything he knew, everything he lived for was gone, blotted from his life as if it had never been. He'd moved to Montana, Colorado, Wyoming, worked as a ranch hand, dwindled into a shadow of the father she had loved so much until at last, when she was seventeen, he'd died in a freak snowstorm.

Her mother hadn't told Taylor right away. Taylor had been graduating from high school; Mother said she hadn't wanted to spoil the occasion with bad news. So Pete Summers had gone into his grave alone and unmourned.

Taylor had never forgiven her mother for that. Not that her mother noticed, what with the new career and the new husband.

Now, as Taylor sat on a rock with the setting sun in her eyes, she gazed at the land that should have been her heritage, and thought how fitting it was she faced her death in the same spot where she had first drawn breath.

Her old home had been a drafty old farmhouse, built in the early twentieth century and added on to, hodgepodge, as the original Summers family grew. Yet Taylor remembered it well: the wide, wraparound porch where she would sit in the summer and dream, the big kitchen with the old cast-iron gas stove with one side that burned wood where she would huddle on cold winter days, the attic with its sloped ceiling, her bed with the squeaky springs, the bathroom with the worn claw-footed tub.

This new house . . . it wasn't the same. The usurpers had built to give it an old-fashioned look, put a porch on it and wood siding. But it was clearly a vacation home, an indulgence for people who had more money than sense. There was a hot tub, for shit's sake. The windows were too wide, designed to open the house to the panoramic views of unspoiled meadow and mountain. Oh, and the windows had blinds, not curtains. Clearly, the house wasn't loved, for no one wandered in and out, slamming the screen door behind her.

Taylor sniffled.

No children climbed the big black walnut tree in the side yard, or swung from a swing under the wide branches of the Douglas fir. How could a house feel life if it was always empty, waiting eagerly for—

Wait. It was empty. The house was empty.

No one was there.

For over an hour, Taylor had sat here, moped here, and seen not one sign of life.

The house was empty.

She slid off the rock. She could go down, look in the windows, see what they'd done with the place. She could . . . she could try the doors and windows and see if any of them were open.

She took a few steps down the hill.

She wouldn't go in. Not really. It wasn't her house anymore. It wasn't her kitchen . . . although inside was food she could eat. *Food.*

Even if the family was not here, there would be some kind of food-stuffs.

Wouldn't there?

Her tears dried. She firmed her wobbling chin.

Maybe some canned soup.

She skidded down the steep slope toward the yard.

Canned soup: chicken noodle or cream of tomato. And crackers. Graham crackers with peanut butter.

Her stomach growled, had been growling for hours, for days.

Going into that house made sense. Starving to death out here didn't make sense. Freezing to death didn't make sense. Hallucinating that she saw her father meant nothing except that she was dehydrated, hungry, and more desperate than she had ever been in her whole life.

She could not go down to Ketchum to report the murder, or attempted murder, of the boy. She couldn't walk that far, not in the shape she was in, and she didn't dare take to the road to hitchhike; Dash and his friend might be looking for her. Besides, she was from the D.C. area. She knew very well that sometimes cops were on the take.

A sudden thought pulled her to a halt. What if she didn't have to go down to Ketchum to talk to the cops at all? What if . . . what if the homeowners had a computer in there? And an Internet connection? She could report the crime from here. To the FBI, to people she knew were trustworthy, someone who would know what had happened to the little boy, who could tell her if he was safe.

She hoped he was. She prayed he was.

Then someone would come for her and this nightmare would be over.

Yes! This made sense. Get in, get on the Internet and report the crime.

What if the doors and windows aren't open?

She heard her father's voice in her head, but she kept walking, sliding down the old, steep trail she remembered so well. Going home.

She hesitated when she got to the yard.

By the calendar, it was still summer, even if the temperatures at night got down to freezing. What if the family were here, but they were on a day trip? What would she do if she was sitting at their table eating soup and they walked in?

Then she'd tell them the truth, beg them to give her a ride to Ketchum . . . and hope to hell none of them was the guy named Jimmy who had commissioned Dash to murder that child.

What if they had a burglar alarm? The police would come, sooner or later.

Driven by hunger and wretchedness, she stumbled as she climbed the steps. She almost kissed the stairway with her face; she caught herself.

She had to slow down. She was starving. Her coordination was shot. She needed to get into her own home and eat. She could almost smell soup simmering on the stove. She tried the front door. It was locked. She frowned—and remembered.

This wasn't her house anymore.

She made her way around the porch, trying all the windows. *Locked.*

The back door. *Locked.*

She looked out at the yard. Branches from that last thunderstorm were scattered across the grass.

These people, whoever they were, should take better care of their trees, because one of those branches had probably broken one of their windows.

She went into the yard, grabbed the longest one, and tried to lift it.

Pain shot through her wrist.

She dropped it.

She tried to drag it.

She couldn't. She was too weak, and it hurt too much.

But the smaller branches, the ones she could drag, would never break the window. She put down the big branch and tried to think. *Think.*

Going to the woodpile beside the fire pit, she picked up a short, slender log. She climbed onto the porch, eyed the tree, then the windows, picked a likely one, and used the log like a battering ram.

The window shattered.

She froze. She waited. But no screech of an alarm pierced the air.

It was the only house around. Why would they have an alarm?

But maybe a silent alarm at the police station in Ketchum?

Yet Ketchum was fifty miles away on a winding gravel road. It would take the cops hours to get here.

She inserted her arm through the hole in the glass—double-paned, how her skinny, always-cold dad would have loved that!—and un-latched the lock. Using her shirttail, she pushed up with both hands.

The window opened easily.

Now she did cry, a hard sob of disbelief that one thing, *one thing* had finally gone right. She brushed glass off the inside of the frame and climbed in.

She was in the kitchen. It wasn't as large as she had imagined it would be. In fact, the appliances were rather shabby, as if the family had built this place twenty years ago and never remodeled. But it was tidy, decorative plates hung on a metal plate rack, and rustic—and trendy—metal canisters lined the counter.

So a woman had done the decorating.

Taylor started opening cupboards. She found dishes, mixing bowls, spices, coffee, small appliances . . . "Come on, come *on*," she said. "Where's the soup?" She opened the closet door.

Not a closet. A pantry. Of course. Filled with so many cans. So many kinds.

She wanted them all.

But lingering good sense made her reach for the chicken broth. She took it to the counter and with trembling fingers popped the easy-open lid. She didn't even peel it off. She just lifted it to her lips and swallowed.

It tasted so good she whimpered.

She put it down, got a glass, ran the water from the faucet, filled the glass and drank. It tasted vaguely of pipes, but she didn't care. She wouldn't get giardia from *this* water. She went back to the chicken broth and had another slurp.

She got a can of chicken noodle soup, popped the top, put it in a pot, and placed it on a burner. She turned it on full flame, went back to the pantry and found a bottled tea. She opened it and took a drink. Sugar and caffeine took a fast track into her bloodstream. They opened her mind and eased the headache she didn't even realize she had.

Outside, the sun was descending. Temperatures were falling.

The house was warm. Newer than her childhood home, but not so fancy as she had expected. For the first time in days, the taut fear that had kept her terrified, fleeing, always looking behind her . . . faded.

Not completely. But enough that she was able to put her soup in a bowl, sit down at the table with a spoon in her hand, and eat like a civilized person.

She put her bowl in the sink. My God, she'd tracked dirt and broken glass all over the floor. She unlaced her hiking boots and removed them. She retrieved the broom and dustpan from the pantry and swept up.

She found the half bath off the kitchen and used it. Actually peed in a real toilet. And flushed it.

She pulled the honeycomb blinds down over the broken window—they cut the cold breeze.

She wandered into the living room and sank down on the couch. Nice room. It looked like the family had saved the knotty pine paneling from Taylor's old house to use on the walls. The paneling gave the space a warm, golden feel. Homey. Like her home. Like . . . she leaned her head back on the pillows, then laid down and pulled the afghan over herself.

Just for a moment . . .

CHAPTER TEN

Taylor woke up as the sun peeked over the eastern horizon.

She sat up with a jerk. How had she fallen asleep like that? After so many hours and days of no sleep, fearful sleep, freezing cold sleep, how had she . . .

Well. She had answered her own question.

She had slept the night through. She had been without sleep for so long she had broken into a family's house, slurped their soup, and fallen asleep on their couch as if she didn't have a worry in the world. Which she guessed she didn't, since the cops had never shown up to haul her ass away.

So what was another can of soup? She was *starving*.

She headed back into the kitchen, found the bathroom again, peed in the real toilet—again—and flushed it.

Man, that *never* got old.

Back in the pantry, she found a can of clam chowder *and* a can of Spam.

She *loathed* Spam. But right now, it sounded like the best breakfast ever.

Today, her hands weren't shaking so much. She made quick work of cutting the Spam and putting it in a pan to fry. She found a loaf of bread in the freezer and popped two slices in the toaster. She used the electric can opener and opened a can of peaches. And she made coffee. She sat down and ate breakfast: the whole can of Spam, the whole can of peaches, three slices of bread, a healthy helping of preserves, and a bowl of clam chowder. When she was done, she meticulously put the kitchen back into order. If anyone came in the back door now, they would notice nothing out of place except the spattering of glass shards on the tile floor close to the window.

She unlocked the door and headed outside.

With food in her stomach and a good night's sleep behind her, the air felt brisk rather than brutal, and the limb that had defeated her last night was manageable. She pulled it up onto the porch and positioned it so it looked as if it had broken off in the wind and smashed the window.

She was very aware of the crime she had committed, and also very aware that if the residents of this house returned, she would quickly have to make herself scarce. She did not want to be shot as a trespasser.

Going back inside, she shut the door behind her and felt the heat soak into her chilled skin. To be warm was a luxury she would never again take for granted.

Starting with the upper level, she took a tour of the house.

The upstairs held three bedrooms and a bath. The main floor was the living room, the kitchen, the half bath, the master suite. There, on the wide wooden desk in the bedroom, was a computer. Walking over, she turned it on. While she waited for it to boot, she checked the modem. It was unplugged. She plugged it in. The modem lights came on.

She had power. She had a way to communicate with the outside world.

She put her hand on her heart. It fluttered like a trapped bird beneath her palm.

God. In just a moment, she would be free. She would send an e-mail to the authorities, and the police would take her away and protect her until the monster who had killed—or tried to kill—that child was taken into custody.

Anticipation hummed like fine wine through her veins.

Seating herself on the upholstered Queen Anne armchair, she waited for the computer to load. The browser came up. The home page was set to *USA Today*. The headline flashed on the screen. She was connected. WHO WAS TAYLOR SUMMERS?

She shook her head. That was the headline? What the hell did that mean?

She leaned forward. Read it again.

WHO WAS TAYLOR SUMMERS?

Her name. Why was her name in a national newspaper? In the headlines?

And why . . . why were they talking about her in the past tense?

She scrolled down.

Her picture was inserted into the text . . . and a photo of her rental vehicle, charred and broken.

She read the words.

She read them again.

The article dissected everything about her: her appearance, her parents' divorce, her education, her career as a successful interior decorator. In cold, cool prose, everything about her life was laid out for the world to see. And the story continually asked—*why would a woman with so much going for her kidnap the nephew of the wealthy and powerful*

Kennedy McManus? And do so with no more motivation than to kill the child and bring misery to those who loved him?

"I didn't do that. I didn't do that!" She was talking to *USA Today*.

The article continued, *When the child escaped and she had failed, how could she have been so naive as to die in an explosion set by her killer lover?*

She shouted at the monitor, "My killer lover? Who was my killer lover?"

The picture showed the skinny guy who had dragged the boy out of the trunk, Ramon Hernandez, a guy with a criminal record stretching back to grade school. But he was dead, too, killed by the strike force that had saved the boy.

Taylor sat back and tried to absorb what she had learned.

The boy was still alive. At least her actions had helped him.

But how had the truth become so twisted? The article said the boy was unhurt. He had to know she had nothing to do with holding him.

Didn't he tell the authorities what really happened?

Or rather—*why* didn't he tell the authorities what really happened? He had been whisked away by his uncle and not seen since. Was he hurt? Had he had a mental breakdown? Was he in a coma or something?

Taylor read the article again. Yes. There it was. Kennedy McManus stated his nephew had fallen while escaping, had brain damage, and although he was recovering from the ordeal, he was not expected to regain his memory.

There was no one to bear witness to her innocence.

Worse, the article contained no mention of Dash. None.

How could they have missed Dash?

The article claimed she had been identified by papers with her name on them. Yes, that was what Taylor had been afraid of. But those papers—"They were drawings. Not sinister plotting. How could you print stuff that's not true?"

How could the reporter have researched Taylor's obscure background and nailed the facts so precisely, but not have gotten one damned thing right about the crime? How could the cops be so stupid?

Taylor followed another link and found shocked quotes from her coworkers, friends and her first fiancé . . . and tearful quotes from her mother wondering why Taylor had returned to her childhood home to commit her crime, and if Pete Summers's suicide had warped her daughter's youthful psyche.

"How can you say that?" Taylor asked the computer screen. "He did not commit suicide!" Just like her mother to transfer all the blame for Taylor's messed-up childhood away from herself and onto Pete Summers, with no care about maligning a good man's memory . . . Taylor wiped a tear off her cheek.

It wasn't simply that the whole story was wrong, reporting her as one of the kidnappers, saying she was in the car when it exploded and her body had been unrecoverable—it completely missed the fact that someone else was behind the kidnapping, some guy named Jimmy, someone who was willing to commit a heinous crime to make Kennedy McManus miserable.

Taylor had to do something.

But what?

This story made her a fugitive.

No, worse than that.

She was dead.

She didn't exist.

She had nowhere to go.

She searched and found the story repeated in every major newspaper in the country. For some reason—slow news week—this story had caught the country's imagination. Predictably, the *Idaho Mountain Express,* Sun Valley's weekly newspaper, had featured her as a local girl gone wrong, complete with her fourth-grade school photo, big teeth and crooked bangs, and a picture of the Summers's home before demolition.

She rubbed her sunburned forehead. Rubbed her cracked, blistered lips. Rubbed her bloodshot eyes. She felt as if she needed to wipe herself clean from this terrible injustice. She got up and paced away, came back and sat down, and read more articles that restated those same wrong "facts" as if they were gospel, searching for some version of the facts. The truth. But it wasn't there.

She did find that the few remains of Taylor Summers the FBI had been able to recover were now buried in a cemetery in Maryland.

Her mother knew perfectly well Taylor wanted to be buried in Idaho.

Or maybe her mother didn't. They'd never discussed Taylor's desires when it came to her death. Why would they? Taylor was twenty-nine, in excellent health, both physical and mental, although to read these articles, it was clear her mental health was now in doubt. In fact, when she made the mistake of reading the comments, it became clear she was a woman despised and reviled throughout the world. She was a pariah—or would be, if she was alive.

The comments finally drove her from her morbid fascination with her own demise and into the bathroom. She turned on the water. She peeled off her clothes and stuffed them into the trash under the sink. She pulled the plastic bag out of the can and put it by the door. She stepped into the glass shower enclosure and into the steamy warmth, and scrubbed herself hard, peeling off a week's worth of grime, scrubbing under her nails, trying to avoid the memory of the erroneous articles and the harsh comments. How dare those people, total strangers, read about her life and presume to make judgment?

She found herself talking out loud, arguing with unseen opponents, defending herself for a crime she hadn't committed.

"I was trying to help that kid. I put my life on the line for a child I didn't even know. I didn't do it blindly. I knew I was putting myself at risk. Maybe it wasn't the best plan. I mean, it was a stupid plan. But it worked! It's not like I expected any thanks. I didn't. But I didn't expect to freeze and starve and live in constant fear from every beast in the forest. I didn't expect to have my car booby-trapped and exploded, and in the process, almost get blown up. I didn't expect to descend into such desperation that I broke into my own house . . ." Her voice broke. She gave a hard, dry sob.

She washed her hair, using copious amounts of shampoo and conditioner, trying to remove pine sap and needles and dirt and tangles . . .

"I'm a criminal. I'm afraid to go back to civilization. I'm afraid they'll put me in prison. I'm afraid Dash, who is evidently as free as a bird and not a suspect at all, will find and kill me. How did this happen? No good deed goes unpunished, and all that? Winter's coming. How can I survive? I'm going to die up here."

She heard her voice echoing off the tile. She was ranting. She sounded like a crazy woman. Maybe she was a crazy woman.

She used the squeegee to clean the shower—this place had saved her life, and she wanted to leave it the same way she'd found it. She got out, wrapped one towel around her head and one around her body. She stood indecisively, then started toward the closet. She had to have something else to wear. She hoped to hell the lady of the house was approximately her size.

As she turned, she caught sight of someone in the mirror. She jumped violently, and swung to look behind her.

She was alone.

Incredulous, she turned back and stared. She took a step forward. She touched her cheek.

Who was that woman in the mirror?

Her face had been pleasantly rounded, a placid face with brown eyes and lips that smiled often.

She dropped the towel.

Her body had been curvy, with soft hips, a well-defined waist, and generous boobs.

That face was gone. That body was gone. They had vanished as if they had never been. In their place were features refined by terror, by hunger, by pain. Her chin was squared-off and determined, her cheeks gaunt, and the gash on her left cheek had barely begun to heal. Her artfully highlighted hair was growing out, showing her brunette roots.

Sunburn had blistered her pale skin, time and again, until it was raw on her cheeks, forehead, and arms. Her eyes were too big, like a starving African child's.

But those eyes contained none of the innocence of childhood; they had stared into the heart of darkness and seen her own death. The veneer of civilization had been stripped away. She was a beast like any of the other beasts in the forest; she would take whatever action necessary to survive.

Coldly, deliberately, she would survive.

CHAPTER ELEVEN

For the first time, Taylor understood who she was and what she was made of, what she would do and say and be to continue on this earth . . . and, someday, to get her revenge on the men who had destroyed her life, and find justice for herself.

The doubts she had experienced at breaking into the home of strangers, at eating their food and claiming their clothing, faded. Someday she would make it up to them, but if this was what she had to do, she would do it.

She rummaged through the drawers in the bathroom until she found the supply of Band-Aids. And, glory hallelujah, there was an Ace elastic bandage. She wrapped her wrist—it felt better—and went back into the bedroom.

A glance at the photos on the desk proved to Taylor that she was never going to wear the mother's clothes. A wedding photo taken about twenty years earlier featured a very tall, very pregnant woman in a gorgeous white gown and a man who topped her by at least two inches. Both were beaming.

These were the owners of Taylor's property.

The picture almost made her like them.

A more recent photo showed the entire family on the ski slope—father, mother, tall teenage son, and one glaring, resentful, eyebrow-pierced teenage daughter who was about five inches shorter than the mother.

The mother was the kind of person who had pewter picture frames etched with names: the father was Brandon, she was Susan, the son was Jules, the daughter was—improbably—Cissie. They were the Renners, so all-American they made Taylor's teeth hurt. Holding the photo, she sank to her knees and *stared*.

Taylor used to be like them. She used to be the kind of woman no one noticed when she walked down the street. She wore semi-fashionable clothes, changed her hair color on a regular basis, used deodorant, brushed and flossed. Now she was . . . not normal. Not likely to remain clean, deodorized, or flossed. Not all-American.

Now she wore nothing but a towel. She had nothing that was hers except for a few drawing pencils kept in a hip pack. She was even worse than poor. She was dead, an outcast, a foreigner in her own country.

She stood, placed the photo back on the desk, and donned Susan's robe. The hem probably hit Susan about mid-thigh; it hit Taylor right at the knee. She went back to the desk and contemplated the browser.

She needed to communicate with someone, to explain that she was alive and not guilty, and that she had information to provide. But to whom?

Simply to contact a random police officer or a random official of any kind seemed at best suicidal. She needed a name, someone she knew.

Kennedy McManus was the logical choice.

She went looking for a way to contact him.

She found no direct way. Not surprising—she had worked with many wealthy, powerful people and they weren't readily accessible.

She'd worked on Maryland senator Bert Hansen's home. But she was under no illusions; he was a politician first, and if he had the chance to bring a notorious criminal to justice, he would do so with all the fanfare of a magician revealing his greatest sleight of hand. While in

Eastern Europe, she had run into a CIA agent. Yes, she knew the CIA only worked outside of the States, but surely any kind of official government contact was better than none. On the other hand, she and Elsa Medcalf had not hit it off. In retrospect, Taylor should have sucked up to Elsa.

Taylor could get in touch with her mother, who was married to an executive of a company contracted for government work. But the thought of going to her mother for help, after her mother's betrayal of her and her father . . . Taylor could not. She could *not*.

She put her elbows on the table and dropped her head into her hands. This wasn't as easy as it should be. She should be able to go to the police. She should believe they were honest and trustworthy. She did not.

Which brought her back to Kennedy McManus. She needed to research him, see if she could figure out any way to . . .

She lifted her head from her hands. Outside, she heard the spit of gravel beneath wheels. She turned her head and listened harder.

A car. A car had just driven up to the front door.

Her heart started pounding, strong, rapid.

She turned off the computer. She glanced at the French doors that led onto the porch. Should she run out? But what if someone came around that direction? What if . . . what if this was Dash? She would be caught. She would be killed.

The front door opened.

She crawled under the desk.

Men's voices in the living room. Not angry, not threatening—not Dash—just chatting back and forth.

Not Dash, but still dangerous to her. *Did they live here?*

The voices got farther away, then closer.

She huddled against the wall, then forced herself behind the desk drawers. She was not invisible, but unless these men bent down and looked, they wouldn't see her. She hoped.

They came into the master bedroom. One guy said, "No sign of an intruder in here, either."

"Something tripped the sensor."

The sensors. Of course. There *were* motion sensors in this house. She should have known.

"The branch broke the window. The debris set off the sensors."

The other guy was stubborn. "Last night the branch broke the window! The monitors recorded the break *then* and the motion *then*. That shouldn't have tripped the sensors *today*."

These were the guys from the local home-security office. And it had taken them over twelve hours to arrive from town to check out the problem? The Renners should be informed. Not that Taylor was going to do it.

"There's nothing out of place here," the first guy said.

Thank God she had wiped up after herself.

He continued, "If we don't find anything, we'll send a technician. I'll tell you what he'll find—he'll find a mouse chewed on wiring and we've got a short."

Legs walked past the desk.

Heart pounding, Taylor pressed herself into a compact ball. When Dash had chased her, she had given everything to her physical reactions. She had gasped, feared, run, sought refuge. She had been an animal in flight.

Now she was an animal in hiding, frozen in place, trembling, afraid to make a sound, to allow a single panicked breath to escape her. She wanted to stand, to shout she was innocent, to tell them she had entered the house only in the most dire of circumstances, to ask what they would have done in her place.

But she knew, without having ever faced this situation before, that she did not want to deal with smug, homegrown guys who couldn't wait to bring in their first trespasser.

The second guy said, "I'm going to check upstairs again."

"Sure. You do that." The first guy walked into the bathroom, didn't shut the door, took a pee that echoed along the tile floor and back to the place where Taylor trembled.

Would he notice the evidence of her recent shower?

He flushed, walked out into the bedroom, and stood there.

Was he looking for her?

He sighed, and the bed creaked.

She couldn't believe it. He was sitting on the bed?

The mattress creaked again.

Was he getting up? Leaving?

No. No footsteps.

That guy was lying on the Renners' bed! What a creep. He was in someone else's house, and he made himself at home in the owners' bedroom!

She *hated* this guy.

He sighed. A moment of silence, then, "Hey, Brian. It's Logan. I'm out at the Renners' place. No sign of a break-in, but for sure a broken window and probably some wire damage by rodents . . . Yeah, happens when you live in the middle of a prairie. Listen, when do you think you can send someone out? . . . Sounds good. I'll let Gary know. He's searching the attic." Chuckling. "Yeah, he's still got that rookie enthusiasm." Logan clicked off.

Two minutes later, Taylor heard a faint snore. She really, *really* hated this guy. She was crammed under the desk in a bathrobe, getting chilled. Her foot kept cramping. And the ignorant jackass snored on the bed as if he owned the place. If she was in charge of security, he would be kicking shit down the street.

Five minutes. Ten minutes. Her wrist hurt. She tightened the Ace bandage. She stretched out her leg to ease the cramp, then tucked it back in. Fifteen minutes. She tried to arrange the bathrobe to cover more of her legs and closed her eyes. Twenty . . .

From the door, Gary said, "What the hell?"

She jumped so hard she bumped her head on the desktop.

Thank God Logan jumped, too. "You son of a bitch! You scared me to death."

"Quick draw on the gun. Now put it away." Gary sounded breathless.

"Sorry, but you shouldn't have scared me. Ever since that woman

tried to murder that kid and then she disappeared, I've been nervous."
The bed creaked.

I did not try to murder that kid.

"You didn't look nervous to me." Legs walked past. "You looked
asleep."

"Tough night last night." Logan yawned. "My three-year-old is
having nightmares, and when he does that, no one sleeps. One of the
women at day care was talking about Taylor Summers in front of the
kids. Can you believe how stupid that is? Now half the kids in town
are scared to death about the Taylor boogeyman, who steals children
and shuts them in the trunk, and the other half are egging them on
with stories about how she's going to get them."

"She's dead," Gary said.

A pause. "Sheriff doesn't think so."

"You're kidding."

You're kidding.

Logan lowered his voice. "You can't tell anybody this. It's top-secret
stuff. I was sworn to secrecy."

"You know I won't."

You lying assholes. But she strained to listen.

"Sheriff didn't get called to the car explosion until after the scene
was cleaned up. His deputy, Otis Sincoe, and I went to high school together, and Otis said Sheriff thinks that rich guy tampered with the
evidence. Apparently, the rich guy has a thing about talking to her himself and getting the whole story."

Would Kennedy McManus listen? Or would he blindly take revenge?

Logan finished, "He hired trackers, you know."

"So that Taylor Summers bitch is still alive?" Gary sounded eager,
incredulous, hopeful.

"No. I don't know. Maybe. The rich guy pulled the trackers, so
they must figure she's dead."

"Rough out there in the mountains at night."

"Yep." More yawning, some walking back and forth in front of the
bed—Taylor figured Logan was straightening the comforter—while

Logan said, "My mother and her mother were friends when the Summers were married, and after the big kidnapping/escape/explosion, Mom called to offer her condolences. Mrs. Summers said she felt terrible that she'd let Taylor's father drag Taylor into the mountains, just the two of them. She figures he was abusing her, that's why Taylor was so warped."

Taylor wanted to get up then. She wanted to tell them her father had never abused her. The abuse had been from her mother: the constant nagging, the subtle undermining, the resolve to make Taylor into a carbon copy of the prima donna beauty queen that Kimberly Summers Huddlestone had been and was.

But Logan was sleep-deprived, he had a gun, he would be thrilled to bring her in.

"That's rough, but it doesn't mean she had to become a killer," Gary said.

"Exactly. Mrs. Summers is going to be on *Dr. Phil,* though."

Taylor cringed.

The two men walked toward the door.

Logan said, "So, you checked the whole house? Did you find anything?"

"Nothing." Gary sounded disappointed.

"We'll kill the interior motion sensors."

Yes! Kill the sensors.

Logan continued, "Brian is sending a technician out here first thing in the morning to find the electrocuted mouse and fix the damage."

"Electrocuted mouse. Okay. Makes sense." Gary sounded relieved. "Now, tell me more about this Summers chick. What else did your mother find out?"

Their voices faded as the two men headed out to turn off the sensors. Then the car outside started up, and they were gone.

She shivered there for another ten minutes. Then she emerged and checked the front door, to make sure it was locked, and the drive to make sure they were gone.

She had to search this house, find the equipment and food she needed, and get out fast. Get out before tomorrow when the security technician came back.

And right now, she did not dare contact anyone. Not until she'd investigated every possibility, not until she'd considered every possible response.

She had to save herself.

CHAPTER TWELVE

Owning a successful business had taught Taylor to prioritize. So now, she turned on the computer and checked the weather report. A cold winter for the area. *Great.*

Next, she Googled how to pick a lock.

She learned with the right tools and a lot of patience, picking a lock was relatively simple. So simple, in fact, that she would never feel safe behind a locked door again. All she needed were lock picks and a small tension wrench, or she could substitute paper clips or bobby pins, and a small Allen wrench filed down at the end or a flathead screwdriver.

She rummaged through the desk and found paper clips *and* bobby pins *and* a cheap flathead screwdriver. Obviously, Mrs. Renner liked to be prepared.

Taylor printed out the information on the lock-picking, cleared the history, and shut down the computer. Picking up the Renners' photo again, she considered the daughter, Cissie. This girl was a midget in a land of giants. She had issues. Best of all, she was approximately Taylor's size.

Fine. Taylor went off in search of the daughter's room. She knew when she found it; the bedroom was trashed. Except it wasn't. That was the way the kid kept it. The open dresser drawers had barfed clothes all over the floor.

Cissie was nothing if not predictable. *Taylor, meet Miss Rebellious Out of Place Teenager . . . who reminds you of you at that age.*

A narrow path led to the closet. There Taylor found and acquired a worn backpack, tossed in the darkest corner, a heavy coat, tossed in the other corner, a pair of heavy socks, smelly and balled up and tossed on a shelf, a knit hat, tossed in a tangled pile of computer cords, a pair of ski pants, tossed in the . . .

Taylor knew from looking at the bedroom that the girl was so disorganized, the items wouldn't be so much missed as assumed displaced. Scoldings might follow, but for Taylor, these items were necessary winter wear.

Taylor dressed herself from the skin out, minus a bra since Cissie had not blossomed where Taylor had filled out. Tucked on the upper shelf, she found a faded Disney princesses sleeping bag. In severe conditions, it was never going to keep her warm, but she would take it until she found something better.

Although Taylor assured herself Cissie wouldn't get in trouble for the missing items, she still felt guilty, so she removed and cleaned the three milk glasses with mold in the bottom and the bowl of rotting green food matter. She refilled a glass with mints and stashed it in the bookcase headboard. She discovered and again covered the well-read copy of *Twilight* hidden under a pile of dirty clothes. No point in betraying the girl's secret obsession with the ultimate teen romance, or the passionate, scribbled love notes in the margins.

Taylor packed her extra clothing acquisitions into the backpack and turned away from Cissie's room. And on second thought, turned back.

The kid had something Taylor might need.

At the back of Cissie's suspiciously well-kept sock drawer, she found what she wanted: a clear baggie filled with weed, two rolled joints, papers, and a lighter. Taylor had first thought to let the kid keep her stash. After all, how much trouble could the girl get into up here where no one but the stars could see her smoke it?

But no matter how desperately Taylor wanted to avoid the idea, she knew that up there, in the mountains, she might hurt herself. She might need a painkiller, and aspirin wouldn't cut it.

So she stole Cissie's marijuana, knowing full-well Cissie would wonder if her brother had taken it, or her parents, and were tormenting her by saying nothing . . . or whether an intruder had sneaked in through the broken window and stolen only things from Cissie's room. In any case, Taylor figured Cissie couldn't complain.

Now Taylor searched for camping gear. What she really needed, and did not find, was dried rations, a rated-for-cold sleeping bag, and a handheld can opener. But this family was into skiing and snowshoeing, not camping. So from the linen closet, she took a down blanket. From the pantry she chose fruit roll-ups, whole grain crackers, and pop-top cans of tuna. From the package kept in the file drawer in the desk, she took one unlined legal-sized tablet.

She had managed to hang on to her drawing pencils and sharpener in her waist pack. She could make lists, jot down her thoughts, maybe take a few minutes to draw something . . .

Immediately, the memory of Dash and Hernandez pulling that child out of the trunk slammed into her mind, and she doubled over in fear. When she opened her eyes, she had to bring her racing heart under control, had to unclench her fists, had to bring herself back up into sitting position. No matter how well she pretended she was dealing with her trauma, the truth was . . . she was ruled by terror. The memory of Dash chasing her, shooting at her, dominated her nightmares. At night, the fall into the midnight cave replayed again and again.

She wiped tears from her eyes. She had no time for a breakdown. She had to care for herself. No one else would do so.

When she had obtained all she dared, she stashed Cissie's backpack by the French doors in the master bedroom—if necessary, she would escape that way with her hard-won supplies—and returned to the Internet for some hint of Dash's employer. She looked for men with the first name of Jimmy or Jim or James who were associated with Dash, and found two—his uncle, James Roberts, and the football player Jimmy Baldwin. Roberts was retired military, living in Chicago with his wife of thirty years. Baldwin was fervently Christian. Neither of them seemed likely to employ a hit man, or to inspire the kind of awe and fear Jimmy inspired in both Dash and Hernandez. But what did she know? What kind of man would employ a hit man? She'd seen the movies. She'd read the books. But in real life? She had absolutely no idea.

She researched Kennedy McManus and found quite a lot . . . and yet so little.

He was a media darling: tall, handsome, square-jawed, unsmiling. Yet although speculation ran rampant, he guarded his privacy zealously, and after Taylor had waded through speculation and innuendo, all she had was the cold, bare facts of his life.

With his younger sister, Tabitha, he had been removed from his parents' care when he was ten and she was two. They had been put into foster care, sometimes together, sometimes apart. They lived through years in the system, years when his past, and hers, was unknown and unremarked. But his forte was data analysis, and he had emerged from high school with a scholarship to MIT. He had moved smoothly into college life, had created *Empire of Fire,* a complex role-playing game that required intensive, quick analysis to play and to win.

When McManus graduated, he sold the game for a lot of money, and used the capital to finance his own data analysis company. From all accounts, McManus was intolerant of any kind of crime for any reason. He was a shark, cruising through the business waters, tracking down industrial spies, exposing embezzlers, and doing God knew what for the U.S. government. No wonder this Jimmy person hated Kennedy McManus. Somehow, in some business dealings, McManus had probably ripped the man to shreds.

But how Jimmy had managed to find and kidnap McManus's nephew, Taylor did not understand. She could discover little about the family; only that Tabitha had been about eighteen when McManus assumed guardianship of her and her two-year-old son, Miles, and they were seldom seen in public.

McManus was thirty-two and unmarried. He never had taken the plunge, nor were his carnal affairs publicized in any way. Yet no one speculated on his sexuality; he was heterosexual, obsessively discreet about his partners, and charismatic, with blue eyes fringed by black lashes, thick black hair, and the bulk of a WWE wrestler. Although Taylor stared with fascination at his picture for a long, long time, she had no desire to sleep with him.

If she had to have a man permanently in her life, she knew what she wanted: a man who would love her more than his job, put her first above his friends and family, respect her as a partner, not as decoration or a convenience.

But more than that, she wanted a man who could sweep her away with desire, with passion, with craving, who cared nothing about the proper way to make love, and everything about the rhythm of sex. She wanted lust. She wanted unbridled sexuality. She demanded a man who could—no, would—dance with her past reason, past need, and over the cliff into ecstasy.

Her fiancés had failed to fulfill those requirements. But she had met a few guys like that. Trouble was, they weren't much for her other requisite: fidelity. She expected it from her man; she would give it to him in return.

To the artist's discerning eye—and she flattered herself that at least she had that—Kennedy McManus's character was clear. Passion? No. He held contempt for passion, for flights of fancy, for desperate yearning and wild obsession. His cold gaze could cut glass. His chest was too rock-hard to cradle a woman's head. His grim expression forgave nothing. He reminded her of Dash: ruthless, uninterested, single-minded . . . selfish.

The nephew, Miles McManus, was home and safe, and she felt sorry for the kid. Hopefully his mother had welcomed him with joy and gratitude, but Taylor could not imagine Kennedy welcoming the child, holding him close, shedding a tear of joy over his return.

Scary guy, Kennedy McManus. She did not want to contact him.

But although she would look for another way out of this mess, she feared a meeting with Kennedy was in her future.

CHAPTER THIRTEEN

In San Francisco, in the executive suite of McManus Enterprises, Kennedy McManus sat at his desk, staring at the monitor mounted on the wall where a montage of Taylor Summers photographs stared back at him.

Where was the woman?

When Miles was kidnapped from his school and his phone found in a Dumpster outside the Oakland airport, Kennedy didn't call the police or the FBI. Instead, he had sat down and examined the event as reported by the children and staff. He had deduced who on the inside had cooperated with the criminals, and called Helen Allen into his office. Within an hour, she had confessed all she knew.

A man who somehow knew her financial need had contacted her and offered her twenty-five thousand dollars to deliver Miles to him. The stranger was tall and handsome, and he said he was the child's father; he had sworn all he wanted to do was see his kid. Helen Allen had told Miles about the man, told him his father wanted to meet him, and Miles had gone with her. Just like that.

The child whom Kennedy had so carefully instructed on what to believe, whom to trust, had gotten in the car and traveled to the Oakland airport because he so badly wanted to know his father.

Kennedy and Tabitha had assured Miles his father was dead.

Apparently Miles had not believed them.

And Miles was right: his father was very much alive, in east L.A., living on the streets, selling drugs, taking drugs . . .

Even now, Kennedy didn't know how much of Miles's action was foolishness, how much was blind hope, and how much was defiance of Kennedy's directives. But the results had been disastrous, and led both Miles and Kennedy to a rugged roadside in Idaho's Sawtooth Mountains.

When Kennedy arrived in the helicopter with his security team, Ramon Hernandez had been headed for the black Mercedes, keys in hand. When he saw Kennedy, Hernandez pulled a pistol and started shooting.

Kennedy had dropped him with a gunshot to the leg. At the same time, one of his team shot and killed Hernandez before he could be questioned.

Kennedy had not been pleased. Kennedy had looked into his employee's background, but saw no sign he had profited from the move. Nevertheless, he had been removed from Kennedy's security and put into a more innocuous position.

The team had at once begun to examine the evidence, to try to construct the state of affairs.

Miles's school necktie was wrapped around the inside of the trunk latch—a clear signal he had been there.

But the boy was nowhere to be seen.

The trackers on the team pointed to the skidding footprints through the meadow.

Miles was alone and moving fast, running for his life.

So Kennedy went looking for his nephew. With one tracker ahead and one tracker behind, he followed the steep trail of broken branches up the side of the mountain, calling, *bellowing*, for Miles.

Kennedy had not come this far to lose him now.

After a half mile, Miles came careening out of the brush and flung himself into Kennedy's arms. Kennedy's relief exploded in affection— he fell to his knees and hugged Miles—then exasperation—he took

Miles by the shoulders and shook him, and told him never to do anything so foolish again—then hugged him once more.

And guilt gnawed at him.

Kennedy's father had died in a prison ward in the hospital. Kennedy's mother was *in* prison. Although he made sure they had had, and his mother continued to have, the best of care, all Kennedy had in this world was Tabitha and this boy. They were his to care for, and he had failed them both.

It would not happen again.

They got back down the mountain to the helicopter, and found one of the trackers examining the other side of the road. She said, "There was another person here."

Miles's face was streaked with tears and snot, dirt and blood and vomit, but when Kennedy looked at him, he straightened like a soldier and said, "Yes! He was a long-armed, mean gorilla asshole, and I hope you kill him, too."

Tabitha would have reprimanded him for his language and his violence.

Kennedy put his hand on Miles's shoulder. "That's my boy." To the security team, he said, "We need to send people after the gorilla, in the air and on the ground. And get a sketch artist onto the plane. Miles can describe the face on the way back to San Francisco."

The lead on the team nodded and gestured to the phone. "On it. You want to take the helicopter?" Rogers already knew the answer.

"Get the helicopter in the air. Find that guy. The cars are on their way."

Rogers nodded.

Miles sagged. "I want to go home *now*."

"I know you do." Kennedy led him to a rock and hoisted him up on it, then climbed up to sit close beside him. "But we have to find that guy so he doesn't come back for you again."

"And the lady," Miles said.

"The lady?" With a gesture, Kennedy summoned Rogers. He told him, "There's a woman, too."

Rogers nodded and went back to his team, organizing and dispersing them in the hunt.

Kennedy turned back to Miles. "Tell me everything, right from the beginning."

Miles stumbled a little at the beginning, but he bravely admitted he had gone with Miss Allen because she offered to take him to his father. They'd met the two men at the airport, and they had been kind to Miles . . . until they escorted him onto a private jet. Then they overpowered him, pushed him into the lavatory, and locked him in. When they landed, they dragged him out, wrapped him in a throw, and carried him off the airplane.

"I fought, Uncle Kennedy," Miles told him. "I hit the big guy in the 'nads with my head."

"Good for you!" Kennedy refrained from exclaiming about the swollen, purple bruise on Miles's cheek. Tabitha would do enough exclaiming when they got home.

The kidnappers dropped Miles into the trunk of a car and drove him forever, in the heat and the dark, over roads that knocked him around. "And you think I get carsick in the backseat," Miles said. "I tossed my cookies all over the place!"

"I noticed," Kennedy said drily. The kid reeked. "But you tied your necktie to the trunk to leave a sign that you'd been there."

"I was trying to break through the taillight, but a Mercedes . . . they're tough." Miles was clearly chagrined.

"Well-built cars," Kennedy agreed. "What happened when you got here?"

His nephew's eyes got big and scared, and he swallowed twice before he could reply. "They pulled me out of the trunk. They had guns. *Guns.*"

"Pistols?"

"Yeah. They were arguing about . . . about whether they should shoot me there, and how to place me so you would see me. They didn't want the . . . didn't want the wolves to drag my body away before you got here. There was some other stuff, but I was . . . I was crying. And sick. I was sick. I couldn't hear . . . what they said." Miles was embarrassed.

Kennedy pressed his shoulder. "It's okay, Miles. You did good. How did you get away?"

"You told me if I was ever in trouble to not panic. You said to *think*. I was trying, I really was, but I couldn't figure out what to do."

"You did good." Kennedy hugged the boy again. "You got away."

"Only because there was this lady."

Kennedy leaned back. "I thought the lady was one of the kidnappers."

"No! No, she was just . . . I don't know who she was. I didn't see her at first. Neither did they. But all of a sudden, papers started blowing from behind that boulder."

"Papers?"

"Yeah. Big papers." Miles measured them with his hands, then looked across the road, hopped off the boulder, and ran to the other side.

Kennedy held himself back. He would not follow his nephew. He would not frighten Miles with overprotectiveness. If the boy could forget so soon, and race away from the safety of Kennedy's arms, let him go.

Miles rushed toward a flapping white sheet of paper caught on a dense clump of grass, retrieved it, and ran back. He handed it to his uncle.

Kennedy helped him back on the boulder, then examined the stained drawing incredulously. The sketch was, he supposed, of the mountains. But it was, in its way, awful. Well drawn; the effort was clear. But stiff, awkward, off-kilter somehow, with the landscape looking vaguely warped and humanoid. This landscape would certainly be almost an embarrassment to—his gaze dropped to the signature—*Taylor Summers.*

Taylor Summers. He would never forget that name.

Miles babbled on, picking up the story where he had left off. "Those men, the ones who wanted to kill me—when they saw the papers fluttering by, they stopped and stared. Then *she* ran out from behind the rock, toward the forest."

Son of a bitch. They had a witness. If she had survived . . .

"She was running like crazy, dodging and jumping. She yelled, *'Run, kid!'* The big guy said"—Miles shot Kennedy a sideways glance—"you know, he dropped the f-bomb. Then he took off after her. I thought he was going to shoot her right away, but he didn't."

"He couldn't shoot and run," Kennedy told him.

"The skinny guy ran after them, too, and I figured she was right. This was my chance. So I ran the other way." As Miles relived his ordeal, he talked more and more swiftly. "I heard gunshots and just . . . I sprinted. I couldn't stop. I was so afraid. I got away. I ran up the mountain. I was hiding in the brush when I heard you calling, and I was afraid then, too, that you'd go away before I could get to you." Miles's brown eyes grew big and brimmed with tears.

Kennedy hugged him again, and handed him a handkerchief.

"Do you think she's dead?" Miles's voice trembled. "The lady who helped me?"

Kennedy's gaze swept the meadow, observed the grim set on Rogers's face, the purposeful way his men moved out.

Kennedy never lied to the boy. He didn't lie now. "Odds are against her. But there's a chance she'll survive."

"What about . . . what about the gorilla? The big guy who ran after her? He was mean, Uncle Kennedy. He was really mean. I want him to be dead." Miles couldn't have sounded more fervent.

"We'll work on that," Kennedy assured him.

But the damned thing was—although the trackers had spent the night scouring the mountains, they'd lost both the gorilla *and* the woman. Then while Kennedy's guys were strategizing their next move, Taylor Summers's rental car exploded, starting a small forest fire.

So whoever this Jimmy was, he was vindictive, nimble, and smarter than Kennedy had first given him credit for.

Kennedy had moved swiftly to take control of the still-burning crime scene, analyzing the data himself. In her shattered cell phone and the footprints leading away from the vehicle, they found proof the woman had been there, had survived the blast, and run like hell afterward.

But they fixed their report to the police to say she had been killed. They fixed everything, and when the police deduced she must be one of the kidnappers, Kennedy did not contradict them. He didn't dare; to reveal what Miles had told him about Taylor would also reveal that Miles had not lost his memory of the events. Kennedy did not want the kidnapper to think he was in imminent danger of being revealed; Miles must be protected at all costs.

Besides, Kennedy was sure his trackers would find Taylor Summers.

They had failed. They believed she must be dead.

So he pulled those trackers off the job—no use funding those who found it a hopeless cause—and hired a small, exclusive private investigative firm. They would watch the airports and car rental agencies, observe her mother and her former fiancés, monitor the Internet, the shelters, any place and anything a woman on the run might utilize to continue her flight.

Kennedy needed to know what Taylor Summers had seen, what she had heard . . . who had taken his nephew. He refused to believe Taylor was dead.

He wanted Taylor Summers.

Yet despite all his resources, she was nowhere to be found.

Where was the woman?

CHAPTER FOURTEEN

The next day, in the early morning hours, Taylor left the Renners' house the same way she had come in—through the broken window, and wearing three layers of Cissie's warmest clothes.

By the time the Renners returned, they would have received the report from the security firm. They would be worried. Then they would look around and realize their home was in good condition. They would decide the wind had blown the branch through the glass, make a claim with their insurance, and go on with their lives without being any the wiser.

At least, that was Taylor's plan.

She went to the shed behind their garage, knelt on the small concrete pad in front of the door, and considered the padlock. According to the Internet site she had found, picking a padlock was easier than picking the lock in a door. Okay. She had patience, the correct tools— and her schedule just happened to be free.

She went to work. Forty-five painful, frustrating minutes later, the lock clicked open and she hooted with delight. She pushed the door open. The place was dark, filled with dust, cobwebs, plywood, and a lawn mower. Someone had placed a small flashlight on a shelf to the left of the door. She turned it on; the beam was strong and clear. She shone it around the shed.

Shoved in the corner, she found a collapsed one-man tent. She knelt and touched it with reverent fingers. She desperately needed this to keep the mosquitos away, to protect her from the snow when it fell, to give her the feeling of having a home. She missed that, having a home, more than she could imagine.

She could carry this size tent. She really could.

But why was it here? Did she dare take it? She hunted around for instructions; of course, they were nowhere to be found. So she quickly tried to put it together, and soon discovered one plastic support was broken. That made her pause and think. Possibly in the woods she could adapt a branch of the right length and strength . . . She would try it, and if that didn't work, she would scrounge another plastic support from another tent in another house.

Already, she was making more plans to break and enter.

If she was going to live through this, that was what it would take.

She packed the tent into its carry bag and used a bungee cord to hook it to her backpack. She clicked off the flashlight and started to place it on its shelf, then hesitated. Flashlights got carried away from their intended position all the time. Perhaps no one would notice it was gone until spring . . . and her need was greater than the Renners'.

She left the same way she had come, clicking the padlock closed behind her, and climbed the ridge overlooking her family's land. She seated herself, knees pulled up to her chest. She watched as the sun rose over the waving yellow grasses, the stands of trees, the herd of antelope grazing peacefully in the sun. She saw the earth come alive . . . and saw, too, the rise of dust as a pickup rolled up the long gravel driveway to the Renners' front door.

The security technician. Good luck to him at finding the chewed-on wire.

When he had disappeared inside, she stood.

She ran her fingers through her hair one last time, fingered it lovingly, wistfully. Then with one hand, she gripped it tightly. In the other hand, she held scissors. Scissors she'd taken from the Renners' kitchen drawer. She lifted her chin and she cut off her hair. She cut it off to within an inch of her scalp, then threw the strands into the air. The wind caught them and scattered them across the landscape and over her family's ranch, obliterating the Taylor Summers she had been.

The new Taylor Summers moved on, into the mountains, determined to find herself a home.

CHAPTER FIFTEEN

Moving swiftly, fiercely intent on staying ahead of the oncoming winter, Taylor searched for a protected place to establish her permanent camp.

She found a cave etched into a granite cliff, with a narrow mouth and a tunnel that went back twenty feet. The shelter seemed promising until she realized the smelly fur bundle in the corner held two dark glints that looked like eyes. *Were* eyes.

Taylor decided she could not spend the winter months with a bear and left at a great rate.

A day later, in a protected hollow near a stream, Taylor found a small shack, a lean-to, really, built of logs and shingles with a steep, metal roof. It was dusty, primitive, appeared to be uninhabited: her perfect winter home. She hung around twelve hours, camping close, waiting for an occupant, if there was one, and when no one showed up, she finally gathered her courage and knocked.

No response.

Feeling much like Goldilocks, she pulled open the door and called, "Hello, is anyone here?"

Something small and gray with a long tail scuttled across the floor.

She used to be afraid of rodents. Now she paid no heed, but shone her flashlight around. One room, about eight feet square, with a low ceiling, a splintered wooden floor, and two tiny windows covered with oilcloth. The place was filthy. Old. Not fit for human habitants.

"Oh, God," she whispered. "Oh, God. Oh, God." Her heart quickened with pleasure, with anticipation. In the corner, there was a stove. A cast-iron, fat-bellied stove. A stove that would heat this tiny area and keep her warm and safe throughout the winter.

The place was clearly abandoned. The primitive bed of canvas and sticks was broken. Dirty rags were shredded in one corner. The hut would take two days of cleaning to make it habitable.

But it had that stove. That beautiful, rusty, functional stove.

The flashlight's white beam picked up a glint on the wall. She walked over to a bronze plaque, rubbed off the worst of the grime, and read, *Wayfarer's cabin, built 1971 to help those lost in the woods. Welcome, stranger, make yourself at home.*

Nineteen seventy-one? No wonder the cabin was falling apart.

In very small letters in the lower right-hand corner, she read, *Young*

Americans to Help Preserve Wilderness and Fight the Oppressive Federal Bureaucracy.

Oh-kay. She'd never heard of the organization, but she loved them with all her heart. She set to work to make the place habitable, a job that took weeks of hard labor: repairing the roof, bringing in wood, using one of her precious paper clips to make a hook to catch fish . . . and then, actually catching one.

She went down to the valley and used a paper clip to pick the Renners' front door lock. She gathered supplies, food, mostly. She left no trace of her stay, but she no longer worried quite so much whether the residents wondered at their loss of canned goods.

She returned to the cabin and settled in for the winter—and six nights later, the rusty chimney caught the roof on fire. She grabbed her backpack, her sleeping bag, her flashlight, then stood in the clear, cold night and watched the cabin crackle and burn.

She was in trouble. It was early October. Winter was here, not the nightly freezing temperatures of summer, not the early snows of autumn, but winter, and in a place that frequently recorded the coldest winter temperatures in the continental United States.

Once more she descended into Wildrose Valley, and as she did, she marveled at how well she found her way now. She was becoming almost competent at survival. Once there, she scouted some of the smaller houses and chose the empty one with no security stickers on the windows. She climbed the porch roof, discovered an unlocked second-story window, and got inside. A well-ordered calendar on the kitchen counter made her hustle through the house; in four days, the family was returning from vacation. She found her cold-weather sleeping bag and portable can opener, but she had to be careful not to take too much. She might not have many scruples left, but she knew she wanted to leave each house in such a condition that the owners had no idea someone had been there.

So she would take just enough food, gather just enough gear, to get her to the next place to gather more food, more gear. If she did this right, if she planned and schemed, she would survive long enough to figure out what to do, how to clear her name, how to escape the threat of imminent death before winter truly set in.

In the attic, she found a dusty pair of snowshoes with one broken binding. With the worn jump rope tossed nearby, she could make these work. She packed food; the unopened jar of peanut butter was her blue-ribbon prize. And then . . . and then good luck caught up with her. While rummaging through the master bedroom closet, looking for long underwear or warm, thick socks or a pair of ski gloves, she pulled down an old-fashioned, padded hatbox and found . . . a pistol.

She stared at it. And stared at it. Questions chased through her mind. Why was it here? Had someone hidden it from a curious child? Had someone feared the violence it evoked? Maybe. That made sense. Would a shot from this stop a charging bear? No.

Would it stop Dash?

Yes. Yes, it would.

Cautiously she put the box on the floor and knelt. She picked up the pistol and turned it over and over. It was cold. Sleek. Black.

When she was a child, she had fired a pistol. Her father had taught her how. Up here, a pistol would be helpful. So helpful. And maybe, with this in her grip, her constant, gnawing fear of Dash would ease.

A side holster and two boxes of bullets were stored with the pistol.

She made her decision. She took the pistol, the holster, and one box of bullets. If that many bullets didn't kill Dash, she wouldn't need the second box.

Before she returned to the wilderness, she did check the weather report . . . and knew she had to save herself now, because a storm was closing in.

She trekked the mountain, found the stony overhang that she'd marked as a possible winter shelter if she discovered nothing better, and set up camp. And lived through her first winter storm.

On the first day, she plotted her strategy to contact Kennedy Mc-Manus without revealing her identity.

On the second day, she plotted again, taking notes on everything she could do and everything that could go wrong.

On the third day, her flashlight failed. She needed more batteries. Or an LED flashlight. She lay in the dark and considered how best to explain to Kennedy McManus what had happened and why she was involved.

By day four, she was sick of peanut butter and crackers, of groping in the dark, of her own company. She didn't care about Kennedy McManus anymore, or the kidnapping. Instead she planned, feverishly, her next raid on the Wildrose Valley homes. She wanted books. Novels. Anything to take her mind away from the constant sound of the wind and her own gibbering fear she was going to die. She wanted *People* magazine, packed with interviews of vacuous celebrities and photos of beautiful people. She wanted, needed, to feel connected to the world.

Then, in the night, the branch she used as a substitute for the missing tent stake broke under the weight of the snow, and she no longer cared about reading. She cared about being buried alive. She kicked and screamed until she had knocked most of the snow off the tent, and sat up for hours, holding the tent up from the inside, until her arms ached and warm tears trickled down her cold face.

She wanted to go back down into the valley, but first she had to pack everything to carry with her. While she was doing that, the snow began to fall again.

At the end of that storm, she built a fire, caught a fish, warmed her last can of soup, and ate gratefully and hurriedly. And the snow fell.

That storm was the worst of all.

After five straight days of wind and bleak cold, Taylor woke to hear a dripping sound. She couldn't figure out what it was. All she knew was that she was hot. She unzipped the sleeping bag and kicked it off.

What had she done? Hibernated through the whole winter? She could hear the world melting. She stuck her head out of the tent. It was . . . warm.

Not really, but above freezing—and dawn hadn't even begun to lighten the sky.

What was going on? It was October. Wasn't it?

She checked the date on her watch.

Yep. October. October thirtieth, to be exact.

"Trick or treat," she said out loud. "Well, almost." She pulled her clothes up from the foot of the sleeping bag—storing them there kept them warm—and scrambled out of her tent.

The hunter's moon was huge and orange, peeking through the trees as it set in the west.

She didn't exactly know what to do with this unexpected gift.

Yes, she did. She needed supplies. Lots of them.

Her gut tightened at the thought of breaking into another home. But she didn't have a choice. She needed a real winter tent. She needed food. Another storm, and what would she have done?

Starved to death.

In the light of the setting hunter's moon, she gathered her equipment and started down the mountain.

CHAPTER SIXTEEN

The abrupt break in the frigid weather had made the snow soft, and even in snowshoes, Taylor sank with every step. Before long, she wished she'd taken the time to eat, and by the time she spotted her next mark, a small, one-story log cabin, she had lost her reservations and hotfooted it to the front porch. The place was dark and quiet, with no outside furniture and no tracks in the driveway.

She knocked. If anyone opened the door, she was going to tell them her car got stuck in a ditch, ask them to call the authorities, then disappear on a search for her mythical vehicle.

But no one answered. She laughed briefly, leaned her head against the door in thankfulness, and, like a hopeful fool, tried the knob.

It turned. The door opened.

She stared at the five-inch vertical crack that led into a darkened room, and crazy thoughts leaped through her brain.

Someone had already broken into the house and was inside.

The family that owned this place had been murdered and she was going to find them.

It was a trap. Dash was inside, waiting for her.

She pulled her pistol and pushed the door open the rest of the way. She could see the dark shapes of furniture. She took a cautious step inside and groped for the light switch. The overhead came on.

No ghosts, no bodies. No Dash. Just a leather couch, rustic wood coffee table with ring marks left by beer cans, elk heads, deer heads, antler curtain rods. The television filled one wall. The computer was antiquated and relegated to a spot on the floor in the corner. Every surface was covered with hunting magazines and camping gear. A full box of dried rations spilled over on the ottoman. A two-man tent was set up in the corner. It was like an episode of *Hoarding for Tough Guys*. Best of all, a thick layer of dust covered everything. She didn't know where this dedicated outdoorsman was, but he was not here.

She sidled toward the kitchen.

More equipment: a camp stove and three lanterns on the table, bottled water and canteens in the pantry. She popped the top on a bottle and swallowed every drop of the lukewarm water. She grabbed a package of granola bars, ate one, and went back to the living room. She tiptoed toward the closed door on the other side of the room.

She pulled her pistol from its holster, held it the way she'd seen the television police hold pistols when they searched a house: shooting hand supported by the other hand, barrel pointed straight out. "Hello?" she called, and opened the door.

Master bedroom. No one there. No one was in the house.

On the bedside table, she saw a scattering of broken glass; she found a photo of a handsome couple smiling at the camera.

The picture frame was smashed. A divorce. Bitter, she'd say. That explained a lot. And this place explained the divorce.

She shut the front door, shut the bedroom door, returned to the kitchen, and as soon as her belly was full, she looked around at all the equipment, and wondered how much she dared to take. This guy had fishing gear, lots of it, knives and axes and . . . it was like being lost in the sporting goods store of her dreams.

She chose a compass, a new, sturdier one-man tent, a survival guide from its place on the back of the toilet. She almost wept with joy when she discovered four different backpacks for hiking. One fit her well—his wife's? It held a lot more equipment than Cissie's school backpack, and with that in mind, Taylor made her selection of freeze-dried foods.

Then she found a weapon that fit perfectly into her hand.

A sling. Not a slingshot, not metal and plastic tubing, but a length of braided leather with a pouch in the middle. Put a round stone in that pouch, and she was David, and anyone who tried to harm her was Goliath.

Memories stirred. Once before she had been lost up here, truly lost. She was nine, almost ten, and as the sun set, her father had found her. He had wrapped her in his coat, then sternly lectured her about wandering so far afield. When she miserably stared at him, remembering how her mother had shouted at him, how he had shouted back, how angry they had been, he saw the truth.

She couldn't stay home. Not in that place of unhappiness and rancor.

So he said, "If you're going to go out, I'd better teach you how to hunt, and how to defend yourself." One of the things he had taught her was to use a sling. He showed her how to take both ends in one hand, and with a swift underhanded swing, to propel a stone through the air and into a target.

She loved it. She practiced for a week, got pretty good.

Then her mother packed up and moved them to Baltimore. She said it was because Taylor was running wild, and if they stayed, she would get herself killed.

Taylor said she ran to get away from her mother.

Not surprisingly, that hadn't helped.

In Baltimore, Taylor had been pitifully out of place, unsophisticated, friendless, afraid. She had taken the sling and tied it around her waist, wearing it as a belt every day, practicing as often as she could. Knowing she could defend herself, knowing she had something of her father's—that comforted her.

On her thirteenth birthday, she took it off and put it away in a drawer. She had adapted. She fit in now. Her friends made fun of her for wearing such an unfashionable belt . . . but mostly, her father had not sent her a card or a present. Again. And she hated him for forgetting her so easily.

Looking back, she realized her mother probably intercepted anything he sent. And the sling had disappeared in the move to her stepfather's house, and been forgotten. But by God, she remembered now. The homeowner even had some round steel balls to use as projectiles.

She thought of Dash.

Yeah, it was David and Goliath all over again.

She tied the sling around her waist, and at last, she sat down and turned on the computer. The poor thing wheezed as it started up; she wiped the dust off the intake vent and when the monitor lit, she sighed. No Internet. Of course not. Mr. Sporting Goods wouldn't bother to connect to the modern world.

"Thanks a lot, mister," she said, and headed back into the hills with her ill-gotten gains.

CHAPTER SEVENTEEN

That afternoon, Taylor practiced with her sling, and swiftly discovered she was not as good as she had once been. But she could learn. She *would* learn.

As the sun set, she settled down to a celebration. She caught two trout, cleaned them, built a huge fire in her fire pit, put them on a spit and roasted them until the skin crackled. She ate one with a package of freeze-dried vegetables, which tasted marvelous even if the carrots never did get soft. Then she closed her eyes and wished for a shot of good Irish whiskey served in a Waterford glass. Too bad she hadn't been able to convince herself that liquor was necessary to her survival, and steal a bottle from one of the homes she had visited.

Of course, she could always indulge in a smoke of Cissie's weed.

Her eyes popped open. She hadn't smoked marijuana since she graduated from college. She'd never been a big fan. She hated the taste. She hated the fact she ate her own weight in crackers afterward. But she had liked the way weed made her feel.

Really, what difference would it make if she indulged? No one was here. And . . . by God, she deserved to celebrate saving that kid, living through a murder attempt, and surviving two months up here in the mountains. So before she could talk herself out of it, she found Cissie's baggie, pulled out a joint and lit up, and sat by the fire and relaxed. And . . . relaxed.

She was getting pretty good at this survival thing. Fish . . . she could survive on fish if she had to. Restaurants paid good money for fresh Idaho trout, and she was getting it for no more than the price of ten frozen fingers. As long as the storms stayed away, every day she'd be out by the stream with her hook in the water. As long as the storms stayed away.

She glanced up to check on the sky, and realized stars were falling, detaching themselves from black eternity to fling themselves into her fire, and then rise again as sparks. *This weed has been dusted with something.*

Then her father showed up, sitting across the fire from her, watching her with a wise affection that both warmed and calmed her.

"Daddy," she said.

Smoke wreathed his head, his cowboy hat, his rugged features. Smoke cloaked his long leather duster, his worn jeans and his cowboy boots. Only his hands were clear to her: long fingers, strong veins, blunt nails, with a lit cigarette (*tobacco,* she knew the scent) between two fingers.

"Daddy," she said again. "Mother said you were dead."

I am. Doesn't mean I'm gone. I'm a Summers. This is where I belong.

Her eyes filled with tears. She nodded. "Yes. Wildrose Valley is where I always thought you would be. But she said . . . she said they'd buried you in Wyoming."

Doesn't matter where that old carcass is in the ground. Besides, someone's got to watch out for you. You're asking for trouble out here on your own. He pulled his pack of tobacco and his papers out of his pocket, and as the first cigarette burned down to a nubbin, he rolled another and lit it from the glowing end of the first. *Do you not remember what the winters are like up here?*

"I'm doing okay, Daddy. It's been cold, but the snow hasn't buried me—"

Yet.

"—And I haven't starved—"

Yet.

"And the people who tried to kill that little boy haven't hunted me down."

They think you're dead. If they didn't, these mountains would be swarming with bounty hunters, and you'd be nothing but a pile of bones. Someone told a lie about you being dead.

"Yes. But also—surely the police up here are not good with crime scenes."

Honey, celebrities live up here. Crimes of passion. Crimes of drugs and liquor. Those policemen aren't as dumb as you hope.

She lifted the joint and took a drag. "You think I've been set up?"

I think someone's out there looking for you.

Her voice quavered. "Who?"

You'd better hope it's the good guys.

"Even Mother said I was guilty."

Don't get along?

"Did we ever?"

I was hoping she would take care of you. That you'd grow closer.

"The last time I saw her, we had a major fight."

About what?

"I broke off another engagement, and this time only two months before the wedding." Good memory.

Why'd you do that, honey?

"I couldn't stand the guy."

Why'd you get engaged to him, then?

"Sometimes it's easier to do what everyone expects, you know?" The memory of Edmundo made her toes curl. "He was a gorgeous Italian who wanted his villa remodeled. I was hands-on. He was hands-on. We got together, and he fell in love."

But not you.

"I did, too. He had the best art collection I've ever seen outside of a museum. And you know what Mother says—it's as easy to love a rich man as a poor man." She rubbed her forehead. "But he . . . he was forty. And I think he was lying about his age. I'm pretty sure he was older."

Is forty the expiration date? Daddy's raspy, smoker's voice sounded amused.

"No. I just mean . . . after the first outburst of love, he acted old. Traditional. At first it was all, 'Ooo, ahh, I'll give you anything you want.' And then it was, 'But you won't work. I need a wife and a hostess.' When I said I wanted more, he wasn't even insulted. He told me his mother had worked, too, until she met his father. Like his mother was my role model. Then he wheedled and pouted, and finally he told me it was okay if I only loved him for his money, I didn't need to try and convince him otherwise." She flung out her hands in an upswept gesture. "How pathetic is that? He didn't think well enough of himself to imagine a woman would love the man and not his bankroll."

You adore your job?

"I do." She hadn't realized how much until she'd gotten stuck up here. "I like arranging things, making things look good. I like working with the people—let me tell you, that's an art—and knowing that when I'm done, they'll be happy living in the home coordinated specifically for them. I like making them feel safe, and at home. No job is the same. I like that, too."

You wanted to be an artist.

"I did. One thing coming up here made me realize—talent isn't genius. I'm not a great artist, and honestly? I'm not willing to live in a garret. After this, I want a cozy house in an area I love, maybe with a man I love. Or maybe alone. I can make it alone."

Of course you can. You're a remarkable woman.

She paused to wallow in his praise. "Not to go all Scarlett O'Hara on you, but after I get out of this, I'll never be hungry—or cold—again."

After tonight, you'll be lucky to be alive. Look up at the moon.

She did. It was full and bright, so beautiful as it broke through the branches to light her night. She smiled.

What do you see?

"There's a ring around it." Pale ice crystals shone like a halo.

That ain't no halo, honey. I taught you what it means.

Her smile faded. "It means it's going to snow."

Boy, howdy. Is it ever going to snow. Are you ready?

"As ready as I can ever be."

So how are you living? He didn't sound curious. He already knew. But he asked anyway.

"I go down in the valley and gather supplies."

Gather supplies?

"That's what I call it. Gather supplies. It sounds so much better than breaking into houses and stealing stuff." That struck her as funny, and she laughed so hard she fell over on her side.

He didn't reply.

Abruptly she was afraid he was gone. But when she looked up, there he was, smoking that cigarette and watching her.

Slowly, one hand at a time, Taylor pushed herself back into sitting position. "That's where I got this . . ." Defiantly, she raised the joint to her lips.

You kids think you're so goddamn smart. I was smoking that shit in the sixties.

Taylor was shocked. She didn't know why. She knew her dad had been raised during the sexual revolution. But he'd lived in rural Idaho, when a tall antenna brought in two television stations and Nat King

Cole, the most popular singer in America, couldn't keep his variety show because he was African American. "I didn't know you smoked shit. Of course, I didn't know you had committed suicide, either." Her voice came out cold, accusatory. Like her mother's.

I didn't commit suicide. I went after the cows. Did my job. Someone had to, in that snowstorm. Got the first ones in, went back for the strays. Didn't make it back.

"Does it hurt to freeze to death?" Her voice quavered.

Sure does. It's not the death I'm lookin' for, for you. You don't deserve that. You did *save that kid.*

"*Thank* you! I'm glad somebody besides me realizes it." She looked at the joint, smoldering between her fingers, and tossed it into the fire. "I don't know what to do, though. I don't know how to save myself."

You can't hide forever, Taylor Elizabeth Summers. You've got to take the bull by the horns and do something to clear your good name.

"I know, Daddy. But what? I don't even know who hired Dash to kidnap the child."

God gave you your talent for a reason, and it wasn't to draw pretty pictures of the mountains.

"They weren't pretty pictures," she said sullenly.

He ignored that. *Did you steal . . . or rather, acquire . . . a drawing tablet yet?*

"No!"

No use lying to me, child. I'm not really here.

She sighed. "Fine. Yes. I've got paper and pencils. Why?"

Draw what you saw.

She bit her lip.

Draw what you saw.

Goddamn persistent ghost. "I don't want to."

Draw what you saw.

"It hurts to remember."

It's fresh in your mind. Draw what you saw.

"What good will that do?"

When the moment comes, you want to be able to show the truth.

"Those men . . . they were cruel. Murderers. That boy. He was so scared. Terrified. Sick. Yet he was looking around, trying to figure a way out. What could I do? I had to help. Stupid idea." She'd run through the whole scene so many times in her mind. "I still don't know what else I would do."

Are you sorry you helped him?

"No! But I'm sorry for myself." She hung her head and wept.

You'll recognize opportunity when it presents itself, child. Look for it, be brave, and seize the moment to get out of here when you can, as fast as you can. You'll do that, won't you?

She nodded. "Yes, Daddy."

Now . . . stake your tent, and do it twice as good as you think you need it. Rake up pine needles and branches and pile them around the base, then place rocks on top of them. The wind's going to howl. The snow's going to pile up. You don't want to be buried alive.

Frightened, she looked at her tent.

Do you? His voice sounded fainter, more distant.

She looked back.

He was gone.

She did as she was told. She staked and reinforced the base of her tent.

Then she sat by the fire and watched the clouds race to cover the moon . . . and she used all her skill to draw the scene with Dash, Hernandez, and Miles McManus exactly as she remembered it, one panel after another.

CHAPTER EIGHTEEN

Another two weeks of storms, another two weeks of lonely darkness and cold, and Taylor *knew* she was going crazy. She couldn't strategize about clearing her name and going back to her former life. She couldn't draw. She couldn't look for opportunity and seize the moment. She couldn't even fish.

All she could think of was surviving the cold, wondering where her next meal was coming from, and if she could get down the hill fast enough between storms to gather supplies. And she thought about wolves. They howled at night, coming closer and closer.

When she found herself fondling her pistol, she packed her backpack, stepped out into the storm, and headed down the hill. Better to die in Wildrose Valley than up here as wolf food. By the time she reached the road, the snowfall had eased and subzero cold had settled in. An ever-increasing number of cars slowly passed her, making the surface a skating rink.

Where were they going? What were they doing?

Ah. They were turning in there, through the gate to one of the fabulous mansions. At the far end of the winding, plowed drive, she saw the house lit up like a Christmas tree, and a long line of cars waiting to discharge their occupants.

A party.

So she walked through those gates and up the long driveway. A sign said SERVICE ENTRANCE, and that seemed the right way to go. She sure as hell wasn't a guest. The trek led to the back of the house, toward the sound of voices, the glow of light. She found herself at the kitchen entrance beside a white moving van that proclaimed, GEORG'S FINE CATERING, and in smaller letters underneath, KETCHUM, IDAHO.

She edged down the side away from the light.

A long ramp angled from the truck to the driveway. Husky men moved narrow refrigerators on wheels out of the truck and up another ramp through the open double doors and into the kitchen. A myriad white-coated waitstaff carried plastic-wrapped silver trays of hors d'oeuvres inside.

A short, skinny, excessively animated man in a dark suit and a wool coat stood in the middle of the action, giving orders in short, clear, concise sentences that held all the more authority for his quiet tones.

Taylor watched the activity with all the longing of Lancelot for the illusive Holy Grail. These people had food. She was hungry.

But even more than that . . . they were human. She hadn't spoken to another human being in over two months, unless she counted her father, and she knew it was nuts to have seen him. She absorbed the babble of voices like the parched earth soaked in a sudden rainstorm. After so much silence, she almost couldn't distinguish one word from another.

Suddenly, she realized the officious man in charge had turned on her like a rabid dog. "Are you from the employment agency?"

She stared at him, mute.

"God. Another idiot." In a slow, clear voice, he asked, "Did the employment agency send you?"

"No."

Her voice was apparently too faint for him to hear, for he shouted, "Do you know how to serve food?"

"I've waited tables," she said. *Almost ten years ago when I was in college.*

"Good. Go inside, put on a black servers' outfit." He looked her over and sighed loudly and ostentatiously. "No, wait. First, take a shower in the servers' bathroom. Wash . . . your . . . hair."

Bewildered, she touched her head.

"Wash? You know, with shampoo?"

She didn't answer, but stared at him wide-eyed.

"Are you on drugs?" he asked sharply.

"No."

"If I weren't desperate . . ."

Taylor saw him wavering, saw her opportunity fading, and seized the moment. In a clear voice, she said, "I'm out of practice, but I can do it. I promise."

He chewed on his lip, then nodded. "You'd better do it. After you *wash . . . your . . . hair*, get dressed in the servers' clothes. Then come back into the kitchen. When I say it's time, you take a tray, go up, and offer an hors d'ouevre and a napkin. Can you do that?"

"I can."

"Hurry. We don't have all night."

She nodded. But she didn't know where to go.

He sighed again, walked up to her and took her arm, and led her toward the house. He parted the bustling stream of humanity like Moses parted the Red Sea. At the door, he took her face in both his hands and spoke directly into her face: "Through the kitchen, down the hall, to your right. That's the servers' bathroom. Shower. Use soap. Don the servers' outfit, the *black* outfit." He scrutinized her further. "The people they send me." Raising his voice, he said, "Sarah!"

A woman's voice came from the depths of the kitchen. "Yes, Georg!"

"Feed this thing before you put her to work." He gave Taylor a push.

A broad, cool-eyed woman looked her over, picked out clothes from a cupboard on wheels, and handed them over. "Come back," she said, "when you're clean and dressed."

Taylor found herself prodded around mobile refrigerators and marble countertops, around cooks wielding knives and long spoons, past stovetops filled with boiling pots and sizzling pans, and into a dim hallway and the servers' bathroom. She'd taken enough speedy showers in strange bathrooms; she knew what to do. She stripped out of her grubby clothing, leaped into the shower, used a scratchy loofa with scented soap, leaped out, covered herself with hand lotion—sure, she was in a hurry, but her skin was parched and cracking—and dressed herself in black slacks, a black shirt, a black vest, and a red bow tie. She picked up the black jacket and carried it with her as she returned to the kitchen. She didn't know what to do about shoes; her boots wouldn't work here, but somehow she thought Sarah would have a solution.

Sarah did. She pointed at Taylor's feet. "What size?"

"Eight."

"I need a size eight black oxford!" she shouted.

Someone else's shoes were shoved into Taylor's hands. Taylor donned them, grimacing at the feel of used bowling shoes. But the plate of food Sarah placed in her hands distracted her.

"Sit." Sarah pushed her toward an empty corner of the long table surrounded by yet more slicing, dicing sous-chefs. Placing her hand on Taylor's shoulder, she pressed her into a chair in front of a plate overflowing with a variety of cheeses, breads, hors d'oeuvres, and exotic tidbits. "Eat. It's bad advertising for Georg when his server looks like a starving child from a third world country."

Taylor nodded. She sat. She ate. She looked up.

Sarah was watching her shrewdly.

"The crab cakes are oversalted," Taylor told her.

"You're not from around here. I didn't think so." Sarah turned, chins jiggling, and shouted in her deep voice, "Griffin! Pull the crab cakes apart and start over, and this time, put down the saltshaker!" She turned back to Taylor. "Anything else?"

"Everything exemplary, especially the steak bites dusted with dried morels and peppercorns."

"My creation," Sarah said with satisfaction. "And kudos to you for recognizing the morels. What's your name?"

Taylor should have thought of this, but getting hired, actually talking to people . . . when she walked up the driveway, she hadn't dreamed *this* would happen.

"Come on. *Come on.* You're going to make me think you're an escaped convict." Sarah was far too shrewd for Taylor's comfort.

"Summer. My name's Summer." Not much of an alias, but one Taylor would respond to.

"All right, Summer. Finish your food. We've got another fifteen minutes before we have to be out there with the trays."

Taylor slowed down. It was all delicious, and rich with flavors she hadn't tasted for too long. She didn't dare overindulge. And, she suspected, refreshments would be provided throughout the evening. These caterers—they fed people.

She put her half-finished plate on the counter by the dishwashers, and joined the lineup of servers beside the array of silver platters.

To her surprise, Georg himself handed them out, telling each server what was on the tray, making them repeat it back. "This is the first big event of the holiday season. Mr. and Mrs. Brothers were my original clients. You will not fail me." His dark gaze swept around the waitstaff.

Everyone murmured, "Yes, Georg."

Taylor felt a tremor of stage fright. She was going into a party. With people. Would someone recognize her?

Georg paced before them, never still, gesturing deliberately, pointing at one server, then the other, snapping his fingers for emphasis. "Whatever you do, keep moving. You look for guests to signal you, you offer the tray when you get a chance, but you glide through the crowd. You are unobtrusive. You dress alike. You look alike. You are alike. You are Georg's servers. After the party, no one even remembers you were there."

"Right," Taylor murmured. These were wealthy people. She was staff. No one would even look at her. She followed the others up the stairs, down the corridor, and into an enormous ballroom of shining hardwood floors, crystal chandeliers, and lofty flower arrangements. A band played background music from the stage in the corner. This room, this home, was arrayed as gloriously as any in a formal Washington, D.C., event.

On the other hand, the guests wore western chic. The men wore black leather dusters, black cowboy hats, and big belt buckles. The women wore fringed leather dusters in jewel tones with fur trim and snap-front shirts. Everyone wore jeans and cowboy boots. Expensive jeans, and expensive cowboy boots.

The bar was busy. Servers with champagne were hopping. And Taylor found her tray of chicken satay emptied almost at once. She returned to the kitchen and this time brought out nacho bites with fried oysters. Then Brie served on croissants smeared with butter.

After the first rush of consciousness at being in a room with so many people, Taylor settled down to work in the crowd. She overheard broken bits of conversations. She gathered that this was the annual fund-raiser for the local rodeo given by Mr. and Mrs. Joshua Brothers of the Brothers Resorts and Dude Ranches, and for the first time Taylor realized how dangerous her appearance here could have been. She had once bid on the redecoration of their western-style luxury hotels. At the time she had cursed the loss; now she thanked her lucky stars she hadn't won the contract. If she was recognized . . . her skin crawled on the back of her neck, and she turned to see who was watching her.

It was an old man, out of place in his formal tuxedo, and he beckoned her.

She hurried to his side.

Once he had been much taller, but now he had shrunk until he was about her height. He was fragile and bony. His shoulders were bent; he looked as if he were about to fall over. And he sported a mass of white curling hair and overgrown white curling wizard eyebrows over bright, inquiring blue eyes.

She liked him. "Can I help you, sir?" she asked.

"Yes. What's that on your tray?"

"Bacon-wrapped jalapeños stuffed with shrimp and cheese."

He hummed with delight as he helped himself. "Are you allergic to shrimp?"

"Not at all."

"Then sit down and eat the whole tray." He waved the jalapeño in her face. "My God, you girls. Always dieting to within an inch of your lives. How are you going to catch a man, looking like that?"

She couldn't help it. She grinned. "They already fed me in the kitchen, and I don't want a man."

"Are you gay?"

"No, sir."

"Divorced?"

"No, sir. I'm currently unattached, and happy to be that way."

He clicked his tongue in disgust. "Don't be ridiculous. All women should be married." He took a hearty bite, chewed, and swallowed. "I shouldn't be eating this. Heartburn will keep me up all night. But I love 'em, used to eat 'em by the train-car load. Goddamn, that's great. Don't tell my wife."

"I won't." Taylor offered him a napkin.

He took it. "So . . . you were disappointed in love."

"Several times."

"It's like riding a horse. Gotta get back in there. You don't want to die alone."

She didn't know what to say to that. She'd faced death too often lately to be able to joke about it.

The old man saw something in her face, because his blue eyes narrowed. Then he looked past her and said, "No, I am not allowed to eat such spicy food, but thank you for offering." He shoved the half-eaten jalapeño into Taylor's hand.

She slipped it into her vest pocket.

A woman's strong voice came from behind Taylor. "Joshua, do not try to bullshit me. After so many years, I know exactly what you're up to before you even think to do it."

"Pain in the ass," he muttered, and dabbed at his lips.

"I told you not to harangue this child." The brilliantly gowned old lady slipped her hand through her husband's arm. "Don't pay attention to the old coot," she said to Taylor. "He's always trying to save the world."

"It could be worse. He could be trying to destroy it." Two months without making polite chitchat, and already Taylor had lost the knack.

Joshua elbowed his wife. "See there? This young girl likes me."

"Even if you do tell her she's too skinny."

"Too damned much dieting these days. I like a woman with meat on her bones. Like Lorena." He patted his wife's rump.

Lorena calmly removed his hand and held it in hers. "What's your name, dear?" she asked Taylor.

"Summer." The lie came more easily this time.

"Beautiful name," Lorena said.

"You know," Mr. Brothers said, "before we hit it big with the resorts, Lorena here used to be a hairdresser. You might get her to cut your hair. I'm not trying to be mean, gal, but you look like you backed into a lawn mower."

"That was rude, Joshua. True, but rude. And I am *still* a hairdresser.

Never know when this being wealthy thing might take a header and I'll have to go back to work." Lorena glared at her husband.

He glared back at her.

Taylor could tell they'd gone over this ground multiple times, and their fight was nothing more than affectionate sparring. She started backing away. "I should go back to work, too, before Georg fires me."

"If he tries, tell him to speak to me," the old man said gruffly. "Anyway, it looks like they're hailing me to do my little song and dance, and start the auction." He straightened his coat.

Lorena straightened his tie.

He walked toward the stage to increasing applause.

Of course. He was Joshua Brothers, the host of the party and the owner of the house. All the clues had been there. Taylor had simply become so socially inept she hadn't recognized them.

Mrs. Brothers patted her arm. "When the party's over, come and find me and we'll trim that hair of yours. It'll improve your chances to find steady work."

Mr. Brothers took the microphone and announced Lorena's name in proud tones.

"There's my cue," Mrs. Brothers said.

Taylor watched her walk toward the stage. *Keep a steady job.* Is that what she should be doing? Tonight, no one had recognized her. Instead of skulking in the mountains with no plan and no future, should she go into Ketchum and see about becoming a . . . a waitress?

Yes. She could continue to work. Because no one ever looked at the servers. But for any kind of work, she needed a first and last name and a Social Security number. Not everyone was going to look at her and assume she was registered with an employment agency, nor would they be willing to hire her with no documentation. Georg had been reluctant, and Taylor had no guarantee she would receive money for her stint tonight. On the other hand, she'd had a hot meal and a shower, so it was worth taking the chance.

At the party, cocktails, hors d'oeuvres, and the auction gave way to dancing, and then a generous buffet and circulating trays of dessert.

Summer carried the bite-sized lime cheesecake in a chocolate cup, and found herself very popular. She was serving two women, smiling and saying, "I'm sorry, if you're lactose intolerant I'm afraid the cheesecake is not your best choice. But the cotton candy cups are not far behind, and—"

Behind her she heard a man say, "You know the Renners had a false alarm on their security system, right? Now Dick Harbo insists his place got broken into."

CHAPTER NINETEEN

Taylor froze like a statue, tray balanced, expression fixed. "—and I tested them myself," she finished in a hurry, and turned to offer the cheesecake bites to the three couples behind her. "Lime cheesecake bites," she said, and willed the man to keep talking.

"How would Harbo know? Since his divorce, that place is a junkheap." The female speaker could not have been more disdainful of Dick Harbo, or more enthusiastic about the cheesecake. She took two.

"Maybe so." The man spoke; Taylor recognized his voice. "But he knows everything he has and where it is. He's missing a one-man tent, a survival guide, some dried rations, his ex's backpack, some other stuff." He waved off Taylor and her tray.

Now Taylor knew the name of the guy she'd stolen the tent from, that he was obsessive-compulsive about his possessions, and her suspicions of his divorce were confirmed. Great.

"Did the burglar destroy anything?" another man asked.

"How could you tell?" the first woman asked.

Everybody laughed.

Everyone except Taylor, who hoped she didn't have that deer-in-the-headlights expression.

A third man said to Taylor, "Sure, honey. I'll take one of those." Then, "Was anything messed up?"

"Clean as a whistle," the first guy said.

"What kind of burglar breaks in and cleans up after himself?" the third guy asked. "Sounds to me like Harbo is drinking too much."

Another woman came from behind and joined the group. "Yes, but *we're* missing our pistol."

With a jolt, Taylor realized that everybody here knew each other. These were the neighbors in Wildrose Valley.

Taylor offered the new woman the dessert tray.

"I already had one, thank you." This lady was impatient, determined to speak her piece.

Everyone in the group had either taken cheesecake or refused. Taylor was supposed to move on. So she turned away and pretended to be offering her tray to the same group as before.

"Since Valerie shot Macalister with the BB gun, we have been absolute freaks about keeping guns in the safe. But this was a brand-new Glock I had bought for Peter for Christmas. I hid it in the—"

"Excuse me, could I have one of those?"

It took a minute for Taylor to register that the tall woman to her left was hovering, waiting for dessert.

"Of course!" Taylor handed her a napkin, and waited for her to make her choice from among all the identical desserts.

"These are low calorie, right?" The woman winked. She was tall, blond, in her forties, with a pleasant expression.

". . . finally thought it was me . . . I'm so absentminded . . . had to ask . . . everyone denied . . ."

Taylor smiled. "Calories are relative, aren't they?"

"They're my relatives, for sure. At least, they hang around like they are!" The woman laughed and stroked one hand down her hip.

Taylor laughed, too, and wished this woman would shut up and move off. She could only hear bits and pieces of the conversation behind her.

". . . but one box of the bullets was still there, so I wasn't mistaken!"

Murmurs of dismay rose from the group.

The newest cheesecake-desiring woman swung to face them. "What are you talking about? Carolyn, is there something missing from your house? Because Cissie swears she did not take my screwdriver or the scissors."

My God. That was Susan Renner. Taylor had been so intent on the conversation behind her, she hadn't recognized . . .

She glanced toward the edge of the ballroom.

Georg stood there, arms crossed, glaring at her.

She glided away, offering her cheesecake bites until the tray was clear.

By the time the party was winding down, voices had grown loud and stories expansive, Mr. and Mrs. Brothers had raised over half a million dollars for next year's rodeo scholarships, and Taylor's feet and back hurt.

At a signal from Georg, she made her way back to the kitchen.

Servers were collapsing in chairs around the table.

Taylor started to take a seat next to Jasmine, a vivacious, pretty young blonde, but Jasmine turned her shoulder and said to the girl beside her, "Georg is too nice. He is always picking up the trash."

Taylor jerked back. Jasmine was talking about *her*. Which shouldn't matter. This kid looked like she just got out of high school. The trouble was, Taylor hurt like a teenager, reborn into a world that didn't understand her, where only the fittest survived—and she didn't yet know if she was one of those fittest.

Then she remembered who she was, how successful she had been with her business, that she had survived a murder attempt and the harshest of conditions . . . and she seated herself next to Jasmine and smiled. She could take this kid out with one hand tied behind her back. She needed to remember that. The kid needed to realize it.

Sarah shouted to the assembled staff, "Quiet! Georg wishes to speak."

A hush fell, and the chefs moved around the table.

Georg stepped into the center and sadly shook his head. "You all did as well as can be expected." He pointed his finger at them, one at a time. "But next week, we have a cocktail party for a thousand on Friday, and on Saturday, a sit-down dinner for two hundred. The cooks must be brilliant." His gaze lingered meaningfully on Taylor. "The servers must be swift and unobtrusive."

She looked down.

He continued, "Next week, get a good night's rest before work, and prepare to shine!"

Heads nodded.

Taylor nodded.

"Sarah will divide the leftovers among anyone who wants them," he said.

Taylor almost jumped for joy.

"The remainder will go to the homeless shelter in town. Now." Georg smiled. "Mr. and Mrs. Brothers would like to personally thank you for your efforts."

Hand in hand, Mr. and Mrs. Brothers stepped into the kitchen. In the ballroom, Mr. Brothers had been the charmer, the chatter, the speech-giver. In here, Mrs. Brothers was in charge, handing out envelopes with substantial tips, and inviting any who were too exhausted to risk the icy roads to stay the night in the barracks inside (females) and the bunkhouse outside (males).

Most of the servers headed home; Taylor supposed if she had a home, she might do the same. As it was, she was grateful not to face the climb up the mountain to her tent. She stashed her leftovers in her backpack, and stashed that in the massive Sub-Zero refrigerator. She crashed in the barracks along with five of the other women. Jasmine stuck around, too. Perhaps the kid wasn't the hotshit bully she pretended to be.

Taylor slept the sleep of the warm, full, safe, and exhausted.

She did not dream about her father.

In the morning, the Brothers's cook made them a hearty breakfast. At her place under the napkin, Taylor found a note. She waited until she went back to the dormitory before she opened and read it.

I owe you a haircut. Collect now.

The note was unsigned. But really, it didn't need a signature.

As the others left, Taylor lingered behind. The cook led her to a small sunroom on the east side of the house.

Dressed in a blue button-up shirt and black slacks, Mrs. Brothers worked at a desk spread with papers. She looked different in the sunlight: not so much older, but shrewder, less a lightweight arm-ornament and more in charge. When Taylor stepped in, Mrs. Brothers said, "Come in, Summer, and sit on the stool. I'll let Joshua know you're here, then I'll get my razor."

Taylor eyed Mrs. Brothers. "Razor?"

Mrs. Brothers had a tremor in her hands. Yet she seemed confident and unconcerned. "A razor cut will give you a sharper edge on the top. As young as you look, as thin as you are, and with the bone structure you have, you need a severe shape to make you look less like a waif and more like a punk. It'll help fend off predators. A lot of them prowl these parties."

"Oh." Taylor sank down on the stool. "I don't feel young or easy."

"It's all about image," Mrs. Brothers assured her. Picking up the house phone, she pressed a number and said, "She's here, dear. Don't hurry, she'll be here a while . . . fine, hurry if you want to."

Considering that Taylor was already ready for a nap, and the Brothers had been up as late as she had . . . they were extraordinarily energetic.

Mrs. Brothers ran her fingers through Taylor's hair and along her scalp.

Taylor wanted to stretch like a cat. It had been months since anyone had touched her in any way, so she wanted to sink into the warmth and the comfort.

Mrs. Brothers clipped a towel around Taylor's shoulders, picked up the razor, and set to work.

Taylor sat very still, waiting for a nick on the ear. But Mrs. Brothers overcame her tremor with no problem, and Taylor closed her eyes and relaxed. She almost dozed . . . until she heard a man's footsteps in the corridor.

Her eyes popped open.

She was trapped. Dash had hunted her down.

But no, the footsteps were slow, with a slight shuffle.

"Here he is." Mrs. Brothers took the razor away. "Hello, darling."

Mr. Brothers smiled at them both. "What a lovely sight on this bright morning!" Going to Mrs. Brothers, he kissed her on the cheek, then patted Taylor on the shoulder. With a groan, he seated himself on the couch. To his wife, he said, "I'm too old for such late-night carousing."

"You're the one who insisted the band play for another hour."

"Why did you let me do that?"

"As if I could ever stop you from doing anything, you bullheaded old fart."

Taylor bit her lip on a smile. "How long have you two been married?"

"Fifty-two years of happy wedded life." Before Taylor could offer her congratulations, he added, "But we've been married sixty-three years."

Taylor laughed, as she was supposed to.

"I'm done with the left side. What do you think?" Mrs. Brothers turned Taylor's face toward him.

Mr. Brothers stared at Taylor without speaking long enough to make her anxious. "Is it bad?"

"No, he's thinking. Can't you tell by the vacant expression in his eyes?" Mrs. Brothers was obviously irritated by his silence.

Mr. Brothers shook himself. "It's a good haircut. I didn't mean that. It's just . . . here with the sun on your face, you remind me of someone."

CHAPTER TWENTY

Shit. "Who?" Taylor asked.

Mrs. Brothers turned Taylor's face back toward her and studied it. "Yes, who?"

"I don't know," Mr. Brothers snapped. "When you get to be my age, everyone you meet looks like someone you've already met. Summer, where'd you grow up?"

"In Baltimore," Taylor said. *Mostly.*

Mr. Brothers shook his head. "Never lived there. Never even spent too much time there. Too close to D.C., too full of politicians and bureaucrats."

"Yes, it is." Taylor was afraid she wasn't going to like the answer to her question, but she had to ask. "Where did *you* grow up, Mr. Brothers?"

"Right here in the valley," he said. "My father and mother had a ranch. They lost it in the thirties—Depression hit here hard. I went into the navy in World War Two, but I always retained good memories of the place."

Taylor nodded. She retained good memories of the place, too. She also harbored a terror of the place, both because of Dash and his attack and now, because . . . did Mr. Brothers remember her family? "So that's why you bought a house here?"

"We bought the land years ago, donated most of it to the Forest Service, and developed a few hundred acres for us and a few other folks who had more money than sense." Mr. Brothers chortled. Then he stopped laughing and stared at Taylor again. "You look like . . . that kid . . . who lived on a ranch up the road."

"Who?" Taylor kept her smile.

"His name was . . . ." Mr. Brothers squinted as he tried to remember. "Walter, I think."

Taylor broke a sweat. Walter was her grandfather.

"Walter . . . can't remember the last name. Family lived there forever. Walter was a few years younger than me. He went to the war in forty-four, to the South Pacific, got shot in the hip, was in the hospital for a damned long time, then got mustered out."

She barely remembered her grandfather, but she did remember his limp. Now she knew how he got it.

"After the war, in South Carolina, I met Lorena, got married and settled down." Mr. Brothers scratched his chin. "Walter was thin as a rail, just like you. You sure you're not related?"

"Anything is possible, of course. But I'm not naturally thin." Taylor felt as if she was tap-dancing through a minefield. "I've recently lost weight."

He frowned. "Too much sushi. You should eat a steak."

"I'll make a note of that." She smiled at him, deliberately using her charms to beguile him, distract him.

It worked, too, although Mrs. Brothers sighed. "He is such a sucker for a pretty face."

Mr. Brothers scowled. "You women are so smug." Mrs. Brothers and Taylor both smiled at him, and finally he smiled back. "Eat a steak," he repeated.

"I confiscated some of the leftovers." Taylor had confiscated a *lot* of the leftovers.

Mrs. Brothers finished with her razor and turned Taylor to face him. "What do you think?"

"Charming. Gamine." His blue eyes twinkled.

Taylor accepted the handheld mirror from Mrs. Brothers, looked at herself, and looked again. The cut gave lift to her face, made it less oval and more angular, and shaved about ten years off her life. She looked very much like the teenage member of a street gang. "I like it. I like it very much. Thank you, Mrs. Brothers."

"Come back when you need a trim," Mrs. Brothers said.

Not in a million billion years. Not with Mr. Brothers trying to remember the ranching family up the road. "Thank you."

"Honey, you forget," Mr. Brothers said, "we're leaving on Tuesday. We're off to a stockholders' meeting in New York."

Mrs. Brothers sighed. "I didn't forget. I was ignoring it. Why don't you go and I'll stay?"

"You have to go. You charm them into submission." He stood up, came over, and put his arm around his wife. To Taylor, he said, "They think she's a sweet little old lady. They don't see the spine of steel underneath."

"You're giving the girl the wrong idea about me." But Mrs. Brothers smirked. Then she whipped around to face Taylor. "We're alike, you and I. I don't know what you're going through, but you're going to figure it out, or die trying."

Taylor didn't know what had clued Mrs. Brothers to her plight, but she did know better than to admit to anything. "How right you are." She slid off the stool. "Thank you both for the work, the food, the shelter, and the haircut. I'll be going now. Enjoy your trip." Even though her neck prickled with the knowledge that they were watching her, Taylor walked out of the room with an air of confidence. She paused just within earshot.

Mr. Brothers said, "Why did you say that? What do you think's going on with the girl?"

"I don't know, but she looks haunted."

"Ghosts?" Mr. Brothers asked.

"Maybe."

"We gave her an opening if she wants to come back and ask for our help. That's the best we can do."

"I wonder if we'll see her again."

It depends on what I find out when I check out your profiles online. Silently, Taylor continued toward the kitchen. She grabbed her backpack out of the refrigerator and walked out the door. It wasn't until she got back to her camp that she discovered someone had removed all the food she had stashed inside the pack. She felt the color drain from her cheeks. Nothing else was disturbed . . . good thing. She kept her drawings in here at the bottom of the backpack.

She knew better now. She would never leave her backpack anywhere it could be searched.

And Jasmine, that little bitch, was going down.

At 3:00 A.M., Joshua Brothers sat straight up in bed. "Goddamn it!"

Lorena came instantly awake. "Is it your heart?"

"No, you old worrywart! I'm fine!"

Lorena struggled up on her elbows. "Then . . . what did you forget?"

"It's not what I forgot. It's what I remembered. The ranching family, the one down the road from me, the one that girl looks like—their last name was Summers." He clicked on the bedside light. "You know, like Summer, like—"

"Like that woman who kidnapped Kennedy McManus's nephew."

The two of them considered the ramifications.

Lorena put her feet over the edge of the bed, padded into the bathroom, used it, came back and got in bed. "They said she was dead."

"Did she look dead to you?" He got out of bed, padded into the bathroom, used it, came back and got in bed.

"Just because she said her name is Summer . . ." Lorena said.

"I don't believe in coincidence."

"No . . . Do you think she did it?"

"No," he said with irritation. "But like you said, I'm a sucker for a pretty face."

"I'm not, and I don't think she did, either."

"Either she's the best con artist either of us have ever run into, or she's innocent. We should report this to the police."

"Honey, with our short-term memories, we won't even remember this in the morning." She reached across him and turned off the light.

"Right." He pulled her into his arms. They rested together, silent.

She asked, "Where do you think she's staying?"

"No place that serves burgers, that's for sure."

She laughed.

They went to sleep.

But in the morning, they both remembered.

PART TWO

THE MURDER

CHAPTER TWENTY-ONE

Taylor worked the next weekend, and the next, and the next. She settled into Georg's team, got to know the staff, to work with them in a rhythm. She learned the finer points of serving, then under Sarah's direction, she moved on to the work of an under-chef, chopping vegetables, sautéing meats, boning fish. She absorbed the knowledge, seeing a different part of working a wealthy household than she had ever seen before. She ate well, and she was warm on a weekly basis.

She took her backpack to every catering event, and hung it in a tree out of sight of the house, and brought it in to fill it with leftovers when she knew it would never be out of her sight. She began to feel as if she had done as her father instructed, as if she had seized the moment.

Then Taylor lost two weeks of work to the snow, and when she at last dug herself out, she was desperate and starving . . . again. When she managed to get to the gates of the party house, she hung her backpack on a high, broken limb in a pine grove at the far end of the massive yard, and trudged up the drive. She made her way to the kitchen door, and stood at the back of the catering truck waiting to be recognized.

Georg gave orders to everyone else, and pretended he didn't see her.

His staff took their cue from him, and walked past her as if she didn't exist.

Only Jasmine took the time to smile smugly.

In the battle between the two of them, Jasmine was the winner.

Taylor wanted to sit down and cry. But she didn't dare. She needed this work. She needed this food. She needed the warmth and the human companionship. When Georg tried to walk into the kitchen and leave her out in the cold, she grabbed his arm. "Please . . . ," she whispered.

For the first time, he looked at her. Closed his eyes as if the sight of her was painful. Gave a mutter of disgust. "All right. Go in. Eat. Get dressed. We really need you to serve, but in this condition"—he waved his hand up and down as if to illustrate her terrible appearance to the world—"you'd scare the guests. So you'll work in the kitchen."

She nodded and started inside.

He grabbed her arm and brought her around to face him. "But listen to me. I need a steady staff. I don't know what's going on with you, but leave that bastard who locks you in the basement and starves you, come down to Ketchum and get some counseling. I'll take you down. I'll help you. I'll give you a job. Just . . . grow some self-respect and leave him." He swept into the house ahead of her.

She stared after him.

The bastard who locked her in the basement? Georg . . . he thought she was involved in an abusive relationship. She had been so worried about going into town, being identified as a murderer and thrown in jail, she hadn't considered that it was possible to go somewhere—a woman's shelter—say as little as possible, get a job, and use their resources to figure out her next move.

This could work. She felt pretty certain no one would recognize her—no one had so far—and even more sure that once she IDed herself as an abused wife, everybody would take care not to look directly at her. Oh! And she could keep her head down as if she were ashamed and afraid . . . "Thank you," she called.

Energized, she hurried into the house. She showered and changed into black slacks, a black shirt, and a red bow tie, then topped it with a white chef's coat and a white chef's hat. She grabbed a plate of food and ate like a ravenous beast, and went to work. The first flurry of setup was done, and the cooks had settled down to a steady rhythm.

Georg stood alone, surveying his crew, and Taylor walked up to him. "I'll do it," she said. "I'll go with you tonight."

He glared at her fiercely, and with his typical candor said, "You should have done it long ago. Now chop the onions."

She did. She chopped onions; the other cooks mocked her for the tears that ran down her face. She listened to the servers complain about the size of the house, the number of guests, the wealth of their host. The women talked about their host, too—Michael Gracie was apparently a handsome devil in an Armani suit with a real Rolex on his wrist, and a top model and a French actress were fighting over him. He got a big thumbs-up for ignoring them, offering his arm to an aging actress, and taking her in to dinner.

As the courses progressed, the frenzy in the kitchen grew ever more intense, and Taylor's adrenaline raced as she fought to keep up with the chopping. Her blade flashed, over and over, slicing through cilantro, fennel, parsley, oregano. Nothing halted her fierce attack on the vegetables and herbs . . . until someone collided with her knife arm.

She dropped the eight-inch chef's knife, yanked her vulnerable hand away, and examined it. It happened all the time, the sous-chef cutting off the tips of their fingers with a sharp blade. Even Georg sported a shortened index finger.

But by the grace of God, Taylor had done no more than cut off the end of her thumbnail. She turned in a fury. "Be careful!"

Jasmine shrugged, all innocent and airy. "Oh. Did I bump you?"

The simple bitch had done it on purpose.

Taylor grabbed her and yanked her around. "Listen to me, kid. I'm not going to let a pouty brat like you hurt me, and if you're smart, you'll toe the line or Georg will toss you out on your ear. It's not an accident you're down here working the kitchen tonight instead of upstairs, where you can look for a rich husband."

Jasmine's eyes got big, and for the first time, she seemed aware that Taylor could be dangerous. "What do you mean?"

"Outside, Georg saw you walk past me and smirk."

"Georg doesn't care about you!"

"Amazingly, he seems to. But more than that, he makes the decisions for his team and doesn't like people like you thinking they can play him." Taylor put her face right into Jasmine's. "Tonight, if not for you, he would have ignored me, and I'd be outside freezing and starving."

"You're not really starving." But Jasmine's gaze swept Taylor up and down, and Taylor could see her narrow little mind working, computing the fact that maybe Taylor *had* been starving. And maybe . . . that Taylor was tougher than Jasmine could ever imagine.

"Keep your opinions to yourself," Taylor said. "And don't you *ever* bump me again."

From directly behind Jasmine, Sarah spoke. "Is there a problem, girls?"

"Not at all." Taylor let go of Jasmine's arm, picked up the chef's knife and the sharpening steel, looked Jasmine in the eyes as she drew the blade across the shaft—top to bottom, top to bottom—to hone the edge.

Jasmine eyed the motion and edged away. But she was dumb enough to mutter, "Nut case."

Sarah stared, narrow-eyed, as the blade sang on the steel shaft, and didn't move away until Taylor wiped her knife and went back to work.

Then, at the moment between the entrée and the dessert course . . . sound died. Motion stopped. The only movement and noise in the kitchen was the bubbling of pots. And a deep, warm voice said, "I wanted to take a moment to thank everyone for your efforts. Dinner is a triumph and I will be making my appreciation known."

Taylor turned, a slow swivel from the cutting board. She didn't need to hear the whisper that ran around the kitchen to know . . . this was Mr. Gracie.

CHAPTER TWENTY-TWO

Wow. Yes.

Taylor groped on the counter behind her. She put down her pastry tube stuffed full of whipped cream. She straightened her white chef's coat and her white chef's hat, and stood at attention, her gaze fixed on the wonder that was Mr. Michael Gracie.

Maybe she had been too long away from the sight and sound of an honest-to-God rock star hot guy, but the impact of his sensuality rocked her back on her heels. He was tall, athletic with a swimmer's body, broad in the shoulders, narrow in the hips, and with long, strong legs. He oozed old-world charm, outrageous wealth, beauty in body and soul. His mussed, curly, ash-brown hair tumbled around his forehead, and his olive skin seemed to glow with days of past sunshine. His dark gaze touched on each one of them, and when he looked at Taylor, he smiled.

At least . . . she thought he smiled. She felt a little giddy.

His gaze wandered on, then returned to her, sharp and enigmatic. His eyes narrowed. He looked her over. Definitely looked her over. And this time, he *did* smile, a warm and charming smile.

She couldn't look away. Not until he did.

He turned to Georg. "Could you help me pick out a very special wine for the dessert course? I would like to give my friends a present."

The way he said it, as if he knew what it was to give, sent a thrill down Taylor's spine.

"Of course, Mr. Gracie. I'd be glad to lend you any small expertise I have in the matter," Georg said.

The two men walked toward the back of the kitchen where a set of stairs descended into the basement. The whole kitchen released its collective breath.

Charlene, one of the servers, was waiting to transport the first round of sweets up the stairs to the dining room. "That man can pick out my dessert wine any day," she announced.

"Amen," Taylor said.

"And Summer, he liked you." Charlene glanced at Jasmine.

Jasmine's cheeks were red, and she looked like a cobra about to strike. "Why would he bother with her, skinny and no makeup with an overgrown thatch of a haircut!"

Charlene waited until Jasmine flounced away. "Yep. He definitely liked you."

Taylor's hands shook as she picked up the pastry tube and returned to work piping flourishes of freshly whipped cream onto the individual *pots au chocolat,* then adding a small, decorative sprig of mint. She smiled a secret smile.

Within five minutes, Georg was back in the kitchen. He leaned close to Taylor. "Give that to Jasmine to finish. Get rid of the chef's jacket and hat. Pick up a black serving jacket and a *black* bow tie. You're going to help me."

Jasmine glared.

Taylor could see Georg make a mental note, and knew Jasmine had just condemned herself to an eternity in the kitchen. Honest to God, that kid needed to learn subtlety.

Taylor changed, and waited for Georg as he collected Brent, the new guy they used for carrying heavy loads; Allison, the most attractive member of the team; and Charlene.

While Brent and Allison donned serving clothing, Georg stepped close to Taylor. "Mr. Gracie specifically asked for you."

"He did?" *He did?*

"Mr. Gracie pays well, and I don't speak ill of employers who pay well. But in general, I find it's best if my female servers are unnoticed by hosts and guests." Georg looked into her face. "Especially a woman in your circumstances."

"My circumstances?" Taylor deflated. "As a battered woman, you mean." Because having a good-looking guy check her out was fun, but Taylor needed to concentrate on survival.

When Brent and Allison joined them, Georg lined everybody up, looked them over, and told Brent to button the collar button on his shirt.

They now looked, in Taylor's opinion, like a family of funeral directors.

As they descended into the basement, Georg told them, "Mr. Gracie already knew which wine he wanted. He simply wanted me to deal with transporting the bottles. Which is where you come in."

"We're the muscle," Brent said proudly. At twenty-one years old and six and a half feet tall, Brent *was* the muscle, if lacking in brains or tact.

Georg viewed the big, brash boy with disfavor. "Right."

The basement was bare, sparse, cool, and set into the hill, but as they entered a small anteroom, Taylor saw a narrow, arched, solid oak door set into the wall.

"The wine cellar," Georg told them, and opened the door.

It opened silently and inside, a motion-activated light flipped on.

Taylor took a deep breath. The rich, fruity aroma of wine perfumed the air.

Georg ushered his staff inside the dimly lit cavern, and the door whooshed shut behind them.

"Fabulous." Allison did not so much speak the word as breathe it.

In her line of work, Taylor had seen, and decorated, some excellent wine cellars, but even she had to admit this was impressive. Like everything else in the house, the cellar was the largest, and the tallest, she had ever seen lined with bottle racks from floor to ceiling. The walls appeared to have been carved from solid rock, and the far end disappeared in the shadows.

"Why is it so dark and cold?" Brent rubbed his arms.

"Light and heat are the enemies of wine," Georg said.

"Oh." Brent seemed amazed. "These are *all* bottles of wine?"

"Yes," Georg said.

"Don't they drink beer?" Brent asked.

Georg was getting annoyed. "If they wish to. But they don't keep it in the *wine* cellar."

"Oh. Right." Brent nodded in approval. "Do they have a beer cellar?"

Taylor took over to spare Georg's sensibilities. "No. They do probably have a beer cooler, though."

Touch-screen monitors had been set at intervals into the walls.

"What are those for?" Brent pointed.

"They're the catalog of wines and the locations," Taylor answered.

Georg sent her a sharp glance. "Our Summer is right."

Taylor shut her mouth firmly. She did not need to give herself away with her knowledge.

Brent reached out a finger to tap the screen.

Georg snapped, "Do *not* touch that."

Brent pulled back his hand. He said, "Yes, sir," but his gaze wandered back to the monitor.

"Do not touch anything." Georg's stern gaze swept his staff of four. "Not any of you. Mr. Gracie would view any mucking with his possessions with displeasure, and you do *not* want to displease Mr. Gracie. You're here to carry cases of wine, so stay close and keep your hands to yourself." He pulled a folded printout from his pocket. "We're serving a Seghesio Old Vine Zinfandel, port, and an ice wine from Mr. Gracie's personal winery, three cases of each. Each of us will carry one case, except Brent, who will carry two."

Brent puffed out his chest.

Georg continued, "We will *gently* transport these into the dining room and stand at attention while Mr. Gracie presents the wines to the guests and they applaud his generosity. Then we will take the bottles to the staging area beside the dining room, where they will be uncorked and allowed to air. We will return to the kitchen at a rapid clip since, due to this disturbance, we are now behind schedule. Brent, don't touch that!" The last was in a sharp, staccato voice.

Brent pulled his finger away from the dusty bottle. "I was going to wipe it off."

"Do. Not. Touch. Anything." Georg's face turned the dusky red of annoyance. "You do understand what *anything* means, right?"

Brent nodded.

Georg went to a cubicle, where long, narrow bottles of golden wine glistened. "Summer make sure each bottle is correct, pack it into the case and"—he sighed again—"can you lift this?"

Taylor locked eyes with him. "Of course."

Going to another cubicle, Georg repeated the instructions to each of his staff, saving Brent until last. He hovered over Brent, checking each bottle himself to make sure it had the proper label.

When the wine was packed, the staff lifted their cases and followed Georg, but not back toward the door where they had entered. Instead they took a left into a completely different section of the wine cellar. This second room was long, wide, and lined with rows of bulky old-fashioned oak wine barrels against each wall. The barrels were three feet apart and had been placed on carved wooden racks that held them two feet off the cool, flagstone floor. Small carved wooden plaques hung from narrow chains, identifying the varietal inside: CABERNET SAUVIGNON, BARBERA, MOURVÈDRE.

Taylor had seen this kind of setup in some old, respected European wineries—but only to impress the tourists. Yet here, the careful attention to decorative detail, combined with the scents of aging wine and new oak, made her think this was an actual working cellar. She asked, "Georg, does Mr. Gracie keep wine in these barrels?"

"He does. Idaho wineries produce some fine wines, and Mr. Gracie owns one of the wineries. For his own pleasure, he transports his best vintages and ages them here in this controlled environment. When he has guests he wants to impress with his European heritage, he brings them down and taps a barrel." Georg sounded . . . *off* . . . as if he didn't want anyone to know his real thoughts.

But Taylor suspected those thoughts were not complimentary. Yet . . . why? Mr. Gracie appeared in every way to be a man admired by his colleagues. And God knows she admired him. "What *is* his background?" she asked.

"He's an orphan. He says his family originally came from southern France." Georg was careful. Too careful.

She moved back toward the end of the group, and realized Brent was lingering, nudging one of the casks with his shoulder. "What are you doing?" she whispered. "Trying to get fired?"

"I can't believe it. All this wine, waiting to be drank."

"Drunk."

"Yeah, I imagine everybody gets drunk. How much do you think is in each one of these?"

"A regulation-sized wine barrel holds sixty gallons and weighs about six hundred pounds." She eyed the barrel. "These are custom wine barrels, probably half again as large."

"Whoa." He nudged it again. "Feels like it weighs a ton."

"Not that much. Including the weight of the barrel, it's maybe a thousand pounds."

Brent was clearly impressed. "How do you know all that?"

I've decorated a winery in Cenorina. I dated the vintner. It was fun and I learned a lot. I even learned he was a lying, cheating bastard. "I once visited the California wine country and took a tour. Now, let's go." She stepped away.

Brent bumped the barrel again.

It settled more securely into place. The supports groaned.

And Georg whipped around and stared forbiddingly.

Brent looked guilty.

Unfortunately, so did Taylor.

"Don't! Touch!" Georg thundered.

Taylor hurried to rejoin the group.

At this end of the cellar, two massive oak doors awaited them under an arch decorated with an ornate carving of vines and grapes intertwined with the name Gracie. Georg pushed against one of the doors; like the other, smaller door where they had entered, it whooshed open silently. He held it with his shoulder and waited while his servers exited. Then he let it go and took the lead again, and walked up the wide, ornate stairway toward the main floor.

Taylor took her place in the line as number three server, and as she walked, the hum of conversation from the dining room grew louder.

Outside the doorway, Georg turned to his servers. "You'll follow me single-file. When I tell you to stop, you'll place the wine at your feet. You stand against the wall, look over the top of everyone at the table—don't stare!" He glared at Brent. "And smile. Mr. Gracie will make a speech about the wines he is offering. When he's done, you'll pick up your box and we will exit at the other end of the dining room, into the serving area. Got that?" He glared at Brent again.

Brent nodded and grinned.

"My God." Georg rubbed his forehead between his index fingers, then he straightened. Taking Brent by the shoulder, he shoved him into line directly behind him. "All right, let's go." He hovered in the doorway, then at a signal from inside, he gestured to them and led the way.

Taylor walked in second to last, put her box down on the signal, straightened, and gazed over the tops of the heads of the guests.

She had never in her life felt so naked. Yes, her hair was cut. Yes, she had lost twenty pounds. Yes, it had been three and a half months since she'd disappeared into the mountains.

But three hundred wealthy, influential people were gathered at a series of elegant round tables. Taylor had been a high-end interior designer; she had probably worked for some of them, creating warm and inviting interiors for their homes. If one of them recognized her . . .

She couldn't resist. She skimmed the faces, never allowing her gaze to linger, but checking to see if anyone was staring specifically at her.

And two of them were, both men, both middle-aged, both openly lustful. Were they the kind of men who sensed vulnerability and swooped in for the kill?

Euw. Thank God that tonight she had been chopping onions and not serving tables, as so many of Georg's female waiters had been. Now those women stood against the back wall, waiting to be summoned to top off a glass or remove a plate.

She concluded her survey of the lesser tables and slid a glance at Mr. Gracie.

He really was a gorgeous man, well groomed, with a marvelous physique and a deep, resonant voice.

He was saying, "These two aperitifs are jewels of flavor and color, precious gems in the world of rare wines and exclusive ports, moments of sunshine and grapes from summers past."

Polite applause.

Taylor didn't care what Georg said. Michael Gracie wasn't all flash and show. He was eloquent, intelligent, and obviously had a good palate. Maybe someday, when her life was back to normal, she'd see if he needed a home decorated and they could . . .

"Look. Look!" Allison whispered out of the side of her mouth. "It's Colin Sebastian, from the new Bourne movie, and he's with Melissa Clarkson, the one who won all the gold medals in swimming. I heard they were dating, but they denied it." She chortled softly. "Yeah, right."

Taylor didn't care. Not really. She was intent on her own survival, not on the trivia of celebrity dating. But . . . Colin Sebastian . . . he was such a great action actor . . . She didn't turn her head, but she was looking. "Where?"

"Head table. Behind Mr. Gracie."

Her gaze found the head table, larger, grander than all the others, filled with men in expensive suits and women in sequined dresses.

She saw Colin, as beautiful in person as he was on the screen, and Melissa, tall and sleek in a dress that bared her swimmer's arms and shoulders.

Seated at the table next to Melissa, she saw *him*—Seamore "Dash" Roberts. In the flesh.

CHAPTER TWENTY-THREE

Dash looked exactly as he had on the highway at the north end of Wildrose Valley: large, smug, dressed in an expensive suit and impatient with the proceedings.

He wasn't looking at Taylor. He seemed oblivious to Taylor.

She yanked her gaze away and stared down at her toes, then collected herself and looked over the heads of the diners at the far wall. She did not want to attract attention. Obviously. She wanted to blend in with the other servers.

"Are you okay?" Allison whispered. "You look like you're going to faint."

Taylor took a long breath. "Colin," she said. "I'm woozy. Too close to him."

"God, yes." Allison understood rampant hormones.

Georg looked down the line of servers and glared fiercely.

What was Dash doing here? Was he a guest of Mr. Gracie's? Yes. Yes, he was, because now Mr. Gracie was introducing the celebrities at the head table. Movie stars, two, Colin and a British grande dame. Singers, two: a rap star and an opera star who introduced programs on PBS. Politicians, four: one senator, two big-city mayors, and a Chinese dignitary. And athletes: two, Olympic swimmer Melissa and former football star Dash.

Taylor slid a glance at Dash when he stood up and waved, then sat down and adjusted his tie.

How ironic that she had made the decision to come to the dining room on the ridiculous belief that to do otherwise would be remarked on in the kitchen. Who cared about *them*? None of them had chased her up the mountainside, shooting to kill. None of them had the ability to murder her with his bare hands.

Her face burned so hot she feared she would burst into flames, yet her hands were icy. This felt like a police lineup; she was caught, held, exposed with a light on her guilty face.

She'd been here for hours. Hadn't she?

Yet Mr. Gracie was still talking. "I'm pleased to have celebrities among my guests who honor me by visiting my home, and I'm proud to announce you have raised over one hundred thousand dollars for breast cancer research!"

More applause.

"I'd like to introduce the head of breast cancer research at the American Center for Cancer Control, Carolyn Romano, who will fill us in on what your money will do to fight this terrible disease."

A woman standing at the back of the room came to join him, and spoke earnestly about the efforts to treat and eradicate breast cancer.

Taylor didn't hear a word. She was sweating too hard, concentrating too much on being invisible, hoping with all her heart she wouldn't faint from fear.

A burst of enthusiastic applause brought her back to the moment. "That's cool," Allison said.

"What?" Taylor barely moved her lips.

"She says Mr. Gracie is matching the donation. Over one hundred thousand dollars." Allison sounded hungry. "So he's gorgeous *and* generous."

Taylor wrenched her attention to Mr. Gracie as he stepped up to the microphone.

"I'm not a good man," he said.

A spattering of applause interrupted him.

He shook his head. "No, I am not a good man. But my mother died of breast cancer. She was such an intelligent woman, dynamic, alive, and even the short time I knew her, she taught me so much about people. I have never forgotten . . ."

Taylor needed to keep her attention on Mr. Gracie. She needed to appear fascinated by him, as so many women here were fascinated by him. And in fact, the way he spoke, the way he looked—he was fascinating.

Mr. Gracie continued, "That last time when she held me, even as young as I was, I felt the life slipping from her body, and I fought to keep her with me. I begged her to stay. I was helpless."

Taylor couldn't stop herself. She slid a sideways glance toward Dash. She expected to see him looking bored. After all, a man who would hire himself out to murder a child seemed unlikely to care about breast cancer.

Dash scrutinized Mr. Gracie with the cool calculation of a running back studying the game play.

A chill ran down Taylor's spine.

Why? What possible interest could Dash have for Mr. Gracie except as a meal ticket?

She looked again at Mr. Gracie.

He was still talking, a vital, handsome man exposing his vulnerabilities for the good of a charity. "So I donate to breast cancer, because I cannot bear to think of another child having to face those bleak moments when he is irrevocably alone, and forever after, there is no one who understands him . . . the boy he is, and the man he grows up to be."

If Mr. Gracie was acting, he was doing a hell of a job, because he tugged on her heartstrings. Every woman at the tables had her linen handkerchief pressed to her damp eyes, and every female server was surreptitiously wiping tears off her cheeks. Men groped for their credit cards, resigned and even eager to donate more.

She looked again at Dash.

He was not moved. His credit card remained tight within his wallet. Yet still he watched Mr. Gracie intently, as if struck by Mr. Gracie's refinement.

She did not for a moment believe Dash knew a damned thing about refinement.

For a long moment, Mr. Gracie stood in silence, his mobile face drawn and pale with the effort of speaking with such emotion, and he looked to his right, as if seeing a beloved ghost. Then he shook himself free of his old heartache, and nodded to Georg.

Georg signaled the line.

The servers picked up the wine and with dignity followed him toward the serving area.

Mr. Gracie said, "Georg's servers will be pouring for you. If you would hold the wine until everyone is served, so I may make a toast to salute you, my guests, who have honored me with your friendship and support, and to salute your generosity."

"And to your mother," Taylor murmured.

Michael Gracie's head swung toward her. His brown eyes lightened with warm flecks of amber, and his kissable lips grew tender.

He had heard her. Somehow, he had heard her.

For a moment, she feared he would acknowledge her in front of the room. In front of Dash. But no—he faced the room again. "And yes, let's toast my mother, and the end of the dreadful disease that took her too soon."

Men like Mr. Gracie and Mr. Brothers reminded Taylor that there was good in this world. Both were leaders of industry. Obviously, they succeeded with a combination of intelligence and ruthlessness. But both men hid depths of emotion, and when Mr. Gracie spoke of his mother, Taylor could see beneath the polished façade into the young boy he had been . . . and she wanted to protect him.

When the servers were out of the dining room, Taylor felt almost light-headed with relief. She put down her box while Georg directed the table servers on how to decant and fill the glasses. Then she, Charlene, Brent, and Allison left by another door, to the stairs and back down to the kitchen.

For one wild moment, Taylor considered fleeing out the back door, never to return.

But the memory of her father stopped her. *What are you going to do to get yourself out of this mess? You can't hide forever, Taylor Elizabeth Summers. You've got to take the bull by the horns and do something to clear your good name. You'll recognize opportunity when it presents itself, child. Look for it, and seize the moment.*

Going back to her station, she took her pastry tube away from Jasmine, who flounced off, and began once again to decorate the *pots au chocolat.*

Was seeing Dash the opportunity of which Taylor's father had spoken?

Or should she run before it was too late?

She viewed the tremor in her fingers.

Running looked pretty good.

But she couldn't return to the mountains. She'd barely escaped death too many times to believe that was a viable option.

She knew one thing; whatever else Dash was—athlete, abuser, hit man—he was not an actor. If Dash had recognized her, she would have known. She had been, as Georg hoped, invisible to that particular guest. So her best bet was to go into town with Georg tonight. Stay in a shelter until she could move on. And figure out her next step in bringing Dash to justice.

As Taylor worked, as she thought through her options, as no Dash appeared in the kitchen to kill her, her hot face returned to a normal color. She relaxed her hunched shoulders and rolled her neck. She finished her stint in desserts and began the cleanup, scrubbing the pots until they shone, gathering Georg's treasured knives from the workstations, sharpening them, washing and packing them in edge guards and carrying cases.

The dinner rush wound down. The kitchen staff began to relax, to chat, to high-five each other and laugh a little. Sarah came by and picked up the white jackets and chefs' hats, and stuffed them in a laundry bag. Georg came by with the cash. The volume of voices increased and became decidedly more cheerful.

Taylor tried to join in. Everything was okay. The memory of her father gave her comfort. She would do as he instructed; she would seize the day and extricate herself from this nightmare of endless winter and gnawing hunger. Yet in the logical part of her mind, she knew she couldn't depend on the advice and foresight of a man who hadn't really been there.

A change in the rhythm of the kitchen caught her attention.

"Heads up," Allison whispered. "It's *him,* and this time, he brought friends."

Taylor looked around.

Mr. Gracie and Dash walked through the kitchen. Three men in black suits surrounded them.

Mr. Gracie spoke animatedly to Dash.

Dash smiled a cold, satisfied smile.

As Taylor stared, she could think of nothing else but Dash's cold capacity for murder. He was totally selfish, completely immoral, unable to comprehend another person's pain, willing to snuff out a life. He didn't even notice the serving staff that surrounded him, or the men in suits who accompanied them. Yet he listened to Mr. Gracie, observed Mr. Gracie, as if everything depended on Mr. Gracie. As if everything depended on . . . killing Mr. Gracie.

Dash was going to kill Mr. Gracie.

No. No, she had to be wrong. Mr. Gracie was an intelligent, sophisticated man. This was his home. He was safe here.

Yet the specter of Jimmy lurked in the background, directing Dash's actions. Who knew if Jimmy might hold a grudge against Mr. Gracie? Or might want to take advantage of the schism in the business world his death would cause?

Mr. Gracie met her gaze and lifted his eyebrows questioningly.

She looked down, then up at him in appeal.

He walked over to her, slid a light finger over her cheek. "Smile." His large, brown eyes warmed to a deep amber. "It's not as bad as all that."

His eyes . . . so beautiful, so kind, so perceptive. She felt as if he saw into her soul. She shouldn't have asked, but the way he looked at her . . . She blurted, "Do those men work for you?"

"They are my friends," Mr. Gracie said.

"Oh." Now what was she supposed to say? *Don't trust them?*

Head tilted, Mr. Gracie watched her. "You are a funny girl. How old are you?"

"Older than I look," she said.

"Right." His eyes cooled. "So you're underage. When the party is over, make sure Georg takes you home to your mommy and daddy."

She looked to see if Mr. Gracie's consideration had brought Dash's attention to her. It had; he flicked her a disgusted glance and followed Mr. Gracie into the corridor that led to the wine cellar.

Immediately she was ashamed. What kind of self-centered coward feared Dash would harm Mr. Gracie, and at the same time feared more for herself?

If only she knew those other men were truly Mr. Gracie's friends, and not Dash's new accomplices. But they didn't act like friends. Their stolid expressions, their deliberate movements made them look like bodyguards. Or assassins.

"What's the matter with you?" Allison asked. "You get Mr. Gracie to talk to you, and instead of being happy, you're clutching that knife like you want to murder someone."

Taylor looked down at the knife in her fist. She had been sharpening a narrow, four-inch boning knife, and she still held it . . . but now she held it point out, cutting edge up, ready to stab and slash.

Michael Gracie didn't realize what he was getting into. He was probably like the rest of the world, interested only in Dash's athletic record and paying no attention to his criminal record. Mr. Gracie could be walking into a trap.

"Are you okay?" Allison said urgently. "You look sick."

Yet Mr. Gracie didn't look like the kind of man who would foolishly trust a man like Dash. In fact, he looked quite the opposite: a man to be feared and respected. Perhaps, this time, Dash had made a mistake.

The trouble was, Taylor remembered Mr. Gracie's vulnerable appeal for cancer funding, and the touching tale of his mother's death. He didn't realize he was associating with a killer. He didn't know someone—someone with no scruples, someone named Jimmy—might have hired Dash to eliminate him. If Taylor did nothing and Mr. Gracie was killed tonight, Taylor would never forgive herself. "I'm feeling faint," she said to Allison.

"Did you cut yourself?"

"Yes." Taylor slid the boning knife into the pocket in her black slacks. She folded her hand into a fist, as if to hide the wound. "A little."

"I'll tell Sarah." Allison started toward the kitchen dictator.

"Don't! I'm fine. I'll go clean up." Taylor headed down the utility corridor. When she was out of sight, she hooked a right and found her way back to the main corridor, then to the service entrance of the wine cellar. She stared at the narrow oak door and contemplated what lay within: a long cellar filled with bottles, then to the left, a wider, shorter cellar lined with wine barrels.

Mr. Gracie could take care of himself. She was not obligated to save a grown man as she had been to save a young boy. Yet she intended to do nothing but walk in quietly and, if all was well, pretend to look for her knife, pretend to find it, and leave. If violence was being done, she intended to flee, screaming, out the door, up the stairs and into the kitchen, and give Dash what he deserved.

That was all. That was easy. She could do this.

The door was stuck. With a feeling of relief, Taylor tugged at it—she would not have to go in at all.

Then with a silent *whoosh,* the door gave way.

Damn. Now she was committed.

She crept inside. The door shut behind her, silent and weighty.

This part of the dim, L-shaped cellar was empty. She heard nothing, no voices. She tiptoed forward, one timid step at a time, past the long walls filled with bottles. The cool air washed across her hot cheeks, and she took big breaths to ease the constriction in her lungs. Nothing helped; the closer she got to the second cellar, where the wine barrels lined the walls, the more afraid she was.

At last, at the left-hand corner where the two cellars met, she knelt and contemplated what to do next. She could go forward, creep along the wall behind the wine barrels, look between and below the stands that supported them, assure herself no one was there, then return to the kitchen.

But her jangling nerves told her someone *was* there . . . and she should get out as fast as she could. She was about to back away when from somewhere unseen, Mr. Gracie said, "Dash, I've been meaning to speak to you about your performance last August."

"Oh. Yeah, Mr. Gracie." Dash sounded alert, concerned, ready to report.

Taylor relaxed. This wasn't a hit. They were discussing Dash's showing in arena football. These guys were doing nothing down here except chatting and tasting wine. Taylor had made a big mistake.

But this mistake was not fatal. All she had to do was escape without being detected. She started to ease away, back around the corner, toward the door and back to the kitchen.

Then Mr. Gracie said something that froze her in her tracks.

"So, Dash, tell me again about how you lost track of Taylor Summers."

CHAPTER TWENTY-FOUR

At the sound of her own name, Taylor's mouth dried. She slid down until she squatted on the balls of her feet. Pure instinct told her she needed to make herself as small a target as possible. Because the world had just tilted on its axis.

"What? Why?" Dash sounded wary. Concerned.

"Because none of the reports said anything about Taylor Summers being a self-defense expert." Mr. Gracie's voice was coolly interested.

Taylor slid, inch by wary inch, toward the shadow under the closest of the wine barrels.

"The reports all said she was a crazy bitch," Dash said.

"They did that," Mr. Gracie acknowledged. "But *you* said she was a karate expert. You told me that's how she got away from you."

Taylor put her cheek on the floor, and looked through the spindly supports of the barrel stands. She could see men's shoes, five pairs, all black, all shiny, and the hems of black, pressed, suit pants.

"She attacked. I was surprised. Maybe she wasn't an expert, but she took me out and escaped." Then Dash turned aggressive. "Anyway, why do you care? I fixed her car up good, and she died in the blast."

"That was a smart move." Mr. Gracie sounded approving.

He approved of Dash killing her.

Which meant . . . he had hired Dash to kidnap and kill Miles McManus.

My God. Taylor had made such a mistake. The biggest mistake of her life. Maybe the last mistake of her life.

She had to get *out*. Out of this cellar, out of this house, and no matter what it took, as far away and as fast as possible. She started to crawl backward.

Dash wandered into Taylor's view, framed by wine casks.

She froze, a hunted animal that had roamed into the wrong den.

"I'm concerned that you didn't check in that whole thirty-six hours. That's not like you, Dash." Now Mr. Gracie wandered into view, too.

Two men. One had tried to kill her. The other . . . the other now demanded an accounting of Dash's failure.

As blood drained from her head, Taylor wobbled. She slid her hand up the leg of the cask support, and clasped it firmly to hold herself still.

Dash was a massive hulk who looked suddenly diminished by the tall, slender gentleman beside him. Yet Dash smiled, showing the gap between his teeth, and said, "Jimmy, my man, I told you. After she attacked me, I was unconscious until the next morning. Then I headed back down the road and found her car. I knew I didn't have much time before the cops found it, too. So I came here, picked up the explosives, and did the job."

Why was Dash calling Mr. Gracie . . . *Jimmy*? His name was Michael Gracie.

But of course it wasn't.

Michael Gracie was a pseudonym. Michael Gracie was fooling the whole world about his identity and his activities.

Mr. Gracie—Jimmy—said, "Like I said, it's not like you not to be in touch . . . how did you get to the house?"

Dash flexed his shoulders. "I hitched a ride with a rancher."

"I thought you stole a pickup."

"No! Who told you that?"

"I found a police report saying a pickup had been stolen, then found a couple of days later in town. I thought that sounded like you."

The two men were slapping words back and forth at each other.

The other three men were ominously quiet. She had been right about them. They were bodyguards. Or assassins. But they didn't work for Dash. They worked for Michael Gracie, and she thought—no, she knew—Dash was in trouble.

"Okay. Yeah. That's what I did."

Mr. Gracie acted bewildered. "Why lie?"

Dash answered swiftly, "You wanted it clean. I hated to admit it got messy."

"Stealing a car isn't messy." Mr. Gracie threw an arm around Dash. "We used to do it all the time."

Dash looked him in the face, and visibly relaxed. "Yeah. Yeah, we did, when we were kids back in Chicago. Good times, huh?"

"Good times," Mr. Gracie agreed. "And you pulled off this robbery without leaving any evidence."

"Didn't do anything to that pickup except use some gas," Dash muttered.

"That's using the old noggin." Mr. Gracie grabbed Dash's chin and forcibly waggled his head.

Dash let him do it.

Dash was afraid of Michael Gracie.

That made Taylor afraid, too. More afraid. She gripped the barrel support even harder.

What was she doing here? Hadn't she learned her lesson even yet? Michael Gracie was the big bad, he had his own hit man, he ordered the murder of children—and she was trapped here in the shadow of a wine barrel, praying no one looked her way.

Dash spread his hands palms-up in appeal. "I'm sorry, Jimmy. I can't believe that bitch ruined your kidnapping. That kid should be dead, and Kennedy McManus should know it was his fault. If you give me another chance, I promise I won't . . . I promise nothing will go wrong."

Mr. Gracie looked into Dash's eyes.

Dash stared back, sweating, pale.

Mr. Gracie smiled. "I was pissed that you screwed up, Dash, but this was the first time ever. Right?"

"First time." Dash sounded breathless. "I've never failed you before."

"Never. Too bad, but I can't try the same trick—stealing the kid—because McManus is on the lookout. So let me think of what I should do next." Mr. Gracie walked away, out of Taylor's line of sight.

"Thank you, Jimmy. You're good to me," Dash said humbly. "You've really got it out for McManus. What did he do to you, man?"

Mr. Gracie paced back toward Dash. "I gave him my friendship. I gave him my trust. And he betrayed me."

Dash laughed incredulously. "No one does that. The bastard is dead meat."

"No. That's too easy. I'm going to destroy his family, his friends, his business, everything he's fought for and loves."

Mr. Gracie's unemotional voice chilled Taylor to the marrow.

Dash nodded. "I get it. You want him to suffer."

Mr. Gracie paced away. "If he was a friend, I'd still kill him for what he did. But he wouldn't ever see it coming." He paced back. He shook his head as if surprised. "Dash, did you hear that?"

"Hear what?" Dash glanced around.

"I thought I heard something moving . . ." Mr. Gracie gestured toward the empty part of the cellar.

Taylor bent her head down to hide her pale face. She peered up through her lashes, held her breath in terror. She hadn't moved. She hadn't heard anything. But she was going to get caught.

Mr. Gracie relaxed. "It was probably a rat. I'll get the exterminators out here . . ." He cocked his head again. "No! Listen!"

Dash turned his back to Mr. Gracie. He looked around the cellar. He glanced toward Taylor, crouched twenty feet away, a small dark ball of dread and nerves. He didn't see her. Then he looked again, and he did. He raised his arm to point, and said, "Jimmy, there's something—"

At the same time, Mr. Gracie lifted his hand, the one holding a Glock, and fired a bullet into the back of Dash's head.

CHAPTER TWENTY-FIVE

The blast ripped through the silence of the cellar.

Blood and brains spattered.

Taylor jumped so hard she slammed the wine barrel support with her shoulder.

The gunshot echoed back and forth against the bare stone walls and floor.

Dash crumpled, nothing but a body and an empty skull.

The barrel settled on Taylor's hand. A thousand pounds of wood and wine crushed her little finger. Flesh, fingernail, bone, two inches of agony.

Taylor bit down on a scream.

Mr. Gracie lowered the pistol. He spoke to the body at his feet. "My friend, you should know I don't tolerate even so much as a first failure."

Taylor would not faint. She could not throw up.

One of Mr. Gracie's bodyguards, a white guy with a barrel chest and a smashed nose, walked over and looked down at Dash. "Boss, that was real nice of you to let him think he had a second chance."

"He was a friend," Mr. Gracie said simply, as if he'd done Dash a favor, and he handed his bodyguard the pistol. "Barry, make sure you get rid of that."

The two men walked away, out of Taylor's sight.

Taylor tugged at her hand.

It wouldn't come out. She was trapped by the first two joints of her littlest finger.

She tugged again.

She didn't think she could make the pain any worse. But the tendon and muscles were still connected, and when she pulled, she felt everything move all the way back to her wrist.

She couldn't get out.

She had to get out.

She braced herself and yanked.

Agony.

"Clean up the mess," Mr. Gracie said. "After the dinner guests depart, I want to bring the overnight guests down here, give myself an alibi."

"Right, boss." Barry stood over Dash and asked one of the other bodyguards, "So, Norm, what do you want off him?"

Norm said, "His tie. Does it have blood on it?"

Barry used his size-fourteen foot to roll Dash over. "Tie looks pretty good. The shirt's ruined, though."

Terror beat in Taylor's veins, in her ears. *What were they doing?*

"I don't care about the shirt or the jacket, just the tie." Norm knelt and stripped the tie away from Dash's throat. Then he removed his own tie. He dropped it on the body, and casually knotted Dash's tie around his neck. Taking his white handkerchief out of his pocket, he dabbled it in the blood, and held it to his forehead so that it half covered his face. He faced toward the door, toward Mr. Gracie. "How's that?" His voice changed, blurred, became an intoxicated imitation of Dash's voice. "I drank too much, tripped on the way back up . . . I'm a clumsy ox of a football player."

"That's good, Norm." Mr. Gracie said. "Make sure the guests see you, and see the blood."

"I know." Norm nodded. "I'll fool 'em."

"Say your piece, then I'll send you to the hospital for stitches." Mr. Gracie's voice was so matter-of-fact. "You'll arrive in town, go to a bar, have witnesses . . . then Dash vanishes, never to be seen again."

Taylor observed the scene through a glaze of pain and misery, and she understood. *She understood.*

This whole scene had been a setup. They had brought Dash down here with the intention of killing him.

Norm looked enough like Dash to be able to fake people out, at least from a distance. He was going to walk out of the wine cellar with Mr. Gracie, allow the guests to get a glimpse of him, claim he'd had an accident, leave, and then Dash would disappear, and Michael Gracie would never be suspected.

But if Taylor didn't get *herself* free, she was going to disappear, too. These men . . . they were cleaning up the mess. They were going to see her, find her, kill her. She had to do something.

She couldn't move the barrel. She couldn't force her way free.

She was trapped. *She was trapped.*

Mr. Gracie asked, "Is the shipment ready to go to Washington?"

"Of course." Norm sounded vaguely insulted. "We pulled the shit from one hospital in Pocatello and one in Salt Lake. We've got a physician who's cooperating . . . he was stealing drugs before, selling them himself. He's not anxious to have the law involved."

"Good work." Mr. Gracie allowed a note of approval to color his voice. "We have hallucinogens coming into the Washington coast from our cookers in Canada. We'll make the exchange and fly the stuff into our airstrip in Ohio. Good market there, especially in the middle schools."

Taylor wanted to gasp, to bring air into her lungs and drive away the fainting sensation, to gain control of her pain so she could think her way out of this trap. She did know a way. She did. But she couldn't bear to think of it.

She had a boning knife in her vest. Sharp. So sharp. She knew how to wield it. Georg had taught her.

But . . . oh, God . . . her finger.

Barry walked away.

She thrust her right hand into her pocket, wrapped her fingers around the handle of the knife. Then she hesitated. She didn't want to do this. There had to be some other way . . .

Barry returned with a tarp that he spread on the floor next to Dash. He rolled the body onto it and wrapped it up, and tucked the top over Dash's head like gift wrap, and fastened the loose ends with broad silver tape.

The third bodyguard came into view. He hoisted Dash's body over his shoulder and headed to the other side of the cellar.

Barry pulled the end of a small barrel loose.

It was empty. Together they wrestled Dash's body inside.

"Load the barrel on the plane. A visit to Washington State will be a nice change for Dash. After he's been there for a few days, the helicopter can take him up and drop him into the Olympic forest."

Taylor felt sick. She didn't want to be dropped out of a helicopter over the wilderness area. All she wanted was to get out of here before they found her.

She faced facts. Her finger was ruined anyway, crushed beyond saving.

In one smooth motion, she pulled the boning knife from her pocket, pressed it against the mangled joint closest to her hand, and with swift, expert savagery, cut off her own finger.

Blood filled her hand, ran up her sleeve.

But she was free.

She kept the knife in her right hand, thrust her left hand into her pocket, hoping that would contain the bleeding. She rose slowly, slid back around the corner, and retreated, step by silent step, along the wall of bottles.

Had she made a sound? Had Mr. Gracie seen a hint of movement? Or did he sense an unknown presence?

Because she heard him say, "I'll make a sweep of the cellar." The hard *snap* of a man's black dress shoe on the flagstone sounded in her direction.

She moved more quickly, reached the narrow exit door. Pushed it open a crack, slipped out, pushed it shut.

She wanted to lean on it, give herself a moment to recover.

No time.

She knew where to go. She knew what to do.

Still holding the knife like a weapon, she strode out of the anteroom, up the stairs, into the noisy, hot, steamy kitchen.

Allison called, "Are you okay?"

Taylor ignored her. Ignored the faces craning around at her. She slipped the knife into her vest. Picking up a clean white dishcloth, she wrapped it around her fingers. She walked toward the outside door, then backtracked and grabbed two oven mitts.

As she pushed the door open, she heard Georg shout, "Summer, if you go out, don't come back!"

But she never stopped moving.

She was in pain. She was without hope. She had hit rock bottom.

But she wasn't afraid anymore. What else had she left to fear?

Adrenaline carried her out into the freezing weather, where the white stars shone in a heartless black sky and the temperatures hovered barely above zero.

About a mile behind the house was Mr. Gracie's private airfield. She had spotted it from the hill. Now she headed in that direction, swift and sure, pulling on the oven mitts for warmth and trusting the black uniform and the dark night to hide her from curious eyes.

There on the field, she saw the two private airplanes. One was large, sleek, ostentatious. Obviously, that must be Mr. Gracie's. It held his precious "shipment" and soon Dash's body would join it in the cargo hold. No one stood guard; why would they? No one was crazy enough to be out tonight—no one except one woman fleeing mutilation and murder.

The other plane was a small Cessna huddled against the side of the runway. The stairs were down. Thank God.

Taylor crossed the runway. She climbed the stairs.

The plane was empty. Frigid. Her breath froze on the still air. And the bleeding slowed . . .

A few lights glowed in the cockpit. One single light lit the rear of the passenger compartment.

Toward the front of the cabin, two luxurious leather seats faced each other, backs to the windows. She passed between them, checked the lavatory, and figured no way she could hide in there—even if she was lucky and was undetected before the plane got off the ground, the pilots would sooner or later need to hit the head. On one side, metal storage lockers were stacked beneath the windows. They were various sizes, all locked. The top locker was long enough and wide enough for a corpse.

An ugly suspicion poked at her brain.

This was not a regulation Cessna. It had been customized for . . . for Mr. Gracie's smuggling needs.

She glanced out the window.

A forklift was crossing the runway, holding a wine barrel on its tongs. One man drove, the other rode along. Barry and the other body-guard, coming with the corpse.

She had miscalculated. They were headed her way.

CHAPTER TWENTY-SIX

Taylor didn't have a lot of time.

She rattled the latch on the body locker; it was locked. She glanced around. Across from the door, a cabinet door hid the galley. She dropped low—she didn't want them to spot her through the windows—and rushed over. She opened the cabinet. Liquor, food from the party, blankets . . .

She helped herself to a blanket and slid into the cockpit.

Here she was luckier. A man's leather jacket hung over the back of one seat. A small pocket screwdriver was clipped to the pocket. He had a small notepad with a pen, too, but the screwdriver would do a better job. Stripping the oven mitt off her good hand, she confiscated it.

Outside, she heard the forklift drive up and stop.

The guys had to get Dash's body out of the wine barrel and lug it up the stairs. She had time. Not a lot, but enough. It had to be enough.

She stayed low, crawled back to the locker, placed the oven mitt and the blanket atop the body locker. The pocket screwdriver had two metal bits; using her right hand, she inserted the flathead into the handle—and picked the lock.

She laughed in triumph.

Okay. She was way too relaxed, and probably in shock.

But thank God for the time she'd spent breaking into houses. Who knew she'd have to pick a lock so she could hide in a traveling coffin? Of course, if this didn't work the way she was hoping, she could be trapped and murdered all the more easily. Especially since she could hear the two men outside the plane, grunting and cursing as they labored up the stairs.

Taking the mitt and blanket, she flung them into the storage locker and climbed in after them. She shut the lid, and in the dark, she groped for the lock. She jammed the flathead screwdriver into the mechanism, pushed up on the handle with the palm of her hand . . . and prayed. Prayed that the small metal screwdriver wouldn't break when the guys tried to open it.

The metal in the box was thin—and why not? The corpse wasn't going to try and open it. Through the metal she heard, "Fuck!" "Son of a bitch is heavy!" "Goddamn, jammed my finger!" "Turn him this way." "No, this way." "Get the lock."

She held her breath.

A key scraped. The end slammed into the screwdriver's flat head. It turned partway.

But the screwdriver held.

"What's the matter with you? Open the fucking coffin!"

The lid jumped. "It won't open."

"Turn the key."

"I did."

"Do I have to do everything around here?" Something thumped on the floor.

Dash's body.

Taylor closed her eyes and fought nausea.

The key slid free, then came back with a vengeance. It twisted hard, and she realized . . . if Barry broke the key off in the lock, she was trapped.

But he cursed, punched the lid, punched the lid again, and pulled the key out. "Fucking goddamn lock, fucking how the hell are we supposed to fucking get this body—" He slammed his body into the whole row of lockers.

She had a vision of him pulling a gun and shooting the lock off. That was what they did in the movies.

But no. He kicked the lockers again. "Dash will have to ride on the goddamn fucking floor, and fuck the pilots if it makes them sick. I don't give a fuck. Make sure someone fixes the goddamn lock when the plane gets back."

"Okay."

And that was it.

The two men stomped off the plane, leaving Taylor in the box and the corpse on the floor.

She stayed there for about three minutes, listening as the forklift drove away and silence returned. She thought a lot of crazy things, mostly that this was a trap. But that really was crazy, and she knew it. Carefully she extracted the screwdriver from the lock—it took some work, because it was bent, and slowly lifted the lid an inch.

Except for her and . . . and Dash, the plane was empty.

She lowered the lid.

Taking the blanket, she wrestled it around to cover as much of herself as she could. She inserted the screwdriver into the lock again. And she dozed.

She came to when two pilots came aboard, male and female, speaking quietly and in civilized tones . . . right up until the time when they started their preflight inspection and found the body.

"What the hell?" The male pilot stood toward the front. "I told those goons I wasn't going to fly with another body rolling around the floor. It's a fucking safety hazard."

Amazing how guys sounded alike when they were mad.

"Yeah, it is." The female laughed. "But you just don't like it."

"Do *you* like it?"

"No, but Mark—it doesn't creep me out like it creeps you out."

"Ha. Ha. Great. *You* do the inspection back there."

Footsteps.

Tense moments spent listening while the female pilot checked doors, windows, rattled the lid on the body locker. "It's locked," the female pilot said.

From the front of the plane, Mark called, "I don't care if it is or not. I'm not lifting that body inside."

"Me, neither. That's where I draw the line." A murmured, "Ick, there's blood all over," and the female pilot joined Mark at the front.

Blood all over? Yeah. Probably from what was left of Taylor's finger.

As Taylor began to realize she had stowed away, that she was escaping Wildrose Valley at last, tears of relief, of pain, of sorrow, seeped from beneath her lids.

She stayed awake as they took off, and no matter how much she tried to sleep, to shake off the constant, grim, debilitating pain of her own amputation, she stayed awake until they landed, two hours after takeoff.

The two pilots deplaned, leaving the body behind.

Someone would come and get it. Someone she did not want to meet.

She wrestled her way out of the blanket, walked to the cockpit, picked up a clipboard and a baseball cap. She looked at the man's worn leather bomber jacket tossed carelessly across the back of the pilot's seat. She laughed, said, "Even a blind pig finds a truffle sometimes," and pulled it on, inching her wounded hand through the sleeve and out the cuff. She zipped it up, and strode with feigned confidence off the plane into a bitter cold breeze.

As she stepped onto the asphalt, she caught a glimpse of tall pine trees. Then the runway lights went out.

The door opened on a small, dimly lit building. The pilots and two men exited, got into a car and drove away; at once, the forest swallowed their headlights.

She followed the car away from the airfield, down a narrow gravel road, hearing nothing but the low moan of the wind announcing an oncoming storm. But this storm was different from the ones that assaulted the Sawtooth Mountains. The air felt thick and damp, cold in a way that struck right to the bone.

She got to the highway, stood uncertainly, not knowing whether to go to the left or the right. As she hesitated, she heard a new sound—the splash of icy rain hitting the pavement.

Of course. The ordeal in Wildrose Valley was over.

Another had begun.

Taylor turned right, and walked.

PART THREE

NEW GIRL IN TOWN

CHAPTER TWENTY-SEVEN

Virtue Falls, Washington

Kateri Kwinault woke early, and grumpy. She had taken a pain pill last night. Usually when she got desperate enough to do that, she slept eight hours and woke refreshed. But damn. It was six in the morning and here she was, staring into the dark and listening to ice hit the window.

Vile day. No one could blame her if she didn't go down the cold, dark, empty street and open the Virtue Falls library . . . except the Norton kids would make the trek in no matter what the weather, and she hated for them to see darkened windows and return to a cold, empty house to wait for their single mother to come home from work.

So Kateri would go in. But first, she'd go back to sleep for another hour.

Determinedly she closed her eyes. And found herself flexing her hands, her feet, turning her head. She felt pretty good, even with the weather, even after the accident. Her joints, both real and artificial, seemed to be working easily, and this morning she was not haunted by memories of that turbulent blue tsunami that had smashed her Coast Guard cutter and almost killed her . . .

Her eyes popped open.

For God's sake. Might as well get up.

Moving like an elderly woman, which she was not, she sat up. She, who had always moved swiftly over the earth, who had studied and worked to exceed her beginnings . . . she had been reduced to using first a wheelchair, then a walker, and now her canes. Doctors called it a miracle; they had told her she would never walk again. She called them fools—although not to their faces. Never tell a medical professional who wields a needle and a scalpel that he, or she, doesn't know what he, or she, is talking about.

Holding on to the bedrail, she stood and, as she always did, took a moment to relish the sensation of the floor beneath her feet. Groping for her canes, she began to get ready for work. She found herself dressing in a breathless rush, as if she were late to an important appointment. "What do you suppose is happening?" she asked Lacey.

Lacey was the dog equivalent of a prom queen, a girly blond cocker spaniel who pranced and twirled and was popular with everybody. For Kateri, Lacey was an ambassador of goodwill, for like any good prom queen, Lacey hid her intelligence and alpha bitchiness beneath an amiable and seemingly obedient disposition.

Now the dog danced up and down, her blond ears flopping madly, urging Kateri to hurry.

"I know. We'll go." Kateri wrapped up warmly and pulled on a waterproof poncho. She fitted another, small, pink waterproof and sequined felt coat around Lacey; one of Lacey's dedicated fans, the trucker, John Rudda, had brought it to her from Las Vegas.

Kateri thought it looked silly.

Lacey adored the coat.

A glance out the window at the shiny streets made Kateri mutter, "I'll take the walker." She hooked her bag onto the bars and headed out.

Her apartment was new, built since the earthquake two and a half years earlier, and her unit had been tweaked to accommodate her handicaps. Once she returned her wheelchair to the veteran's organization, she didn't need the tweaks, but she did need that ground-floor access and proximity to her job.

The Virtue Falls library was housed in the old feed-and-seed store, a sturdy building that had withstood the earthquake and the aftershocks when the "new" library, built in the 1970s, had collapsed like a house of cards. The store was a temporary shelter for the books, or so the Virtue Falls City Council claimed. Actually, Kateri hadn't seen any movement toward building a new library. Thus far, the city council had not deemed a new library to be necessary or vital to the community.

To the city council, Kateri had cited the number of children who arrived every day after school to listen to her read Harry Potter or *Charlotte's Web,* and the preschool kids and their parents who arrived every day to examine her small menagerie of gerbils and fish while Kateri told the legends of her tribe about the earth, the sea, the gods, and the animals. She presented the statistics about the number of books, movies, and audios checked out every week, and spoke eloquently about the various reading groups that met at the library. In return, the city council raised her salary by one dollar an hour—she was now working for more than minimum wage—and increased the library buying budget by one hundred dollars a month to . . . one hundred dollars a month.

They were politicians. And they were idiots. But that was redundant.

What she couldn't quantify, and would not try to, was how the library served as a community center. She always knew when a marriage was in trouble. The wife would avoid Kateri's gaze while she checked out *20 Ways to Keep Your Marriage Healthy* and *How to Heal a Broken Relationship.* When Irene Golobovitch won her gazillionth blue ribbon for quilting, Kateri invited the elderly woman to set up a frame in the corner, and on Thursday evenings, to teach anyone who wanted to learn how to assemble and stitch a community quilt.

Thursday evenings had turned into a huge success. Ostensibly, the women were performing the traditional female task of sewing. In truth, they were talking. Talking about their kids, their husbands, their families, their jobs. They complained. They laughed. And sometimes the conversations roved into deeper territory; abuse, hunger, loneliness, depression.

Kateri had been the commander of the local Coast Guard station. She didn't have the training or the knowledge for this kind of female-bonding crap. Yet here she was, threading her needle, passing the box of Kleenex, making sympathetic noises while some woman she had known her whole life sobbed her guts out because the husband she'd married in high school was having an affair with a goat. Or something.

As the result of one massive earth movement, Kateri had found herself tossed out of the testosterone-laden world of the military and into the thick of Virtue Falls female bonding. As her mother had said on one of the few occasions when she was sober—*Life ain't fair.* Kateri counted herself as the living testament to that.

Now it was December twelfth, close to the winter solstice, eight o'clock in the morning, and still dark as midnight. The town was shut down. Ice hit the streets, coating them with a slick glaze that shone blue in the streetlights. Kateri leaned heavily on the walker; she did not intend to fall and break *anything.* She'd had enough surgeries to last ten lifetimes . . . her face looked pretty good, but her body looked like a road map, the old-fashioned paper kind that had to be folded and refolded until the corners fell apart.

Lacey bounded ahead, skidded, got her feet under her again, and glanced reproachfully at Kateri as if she'd caused the problem, then bounded ahead again.

Despite the slicker, the gloves, and the boots, the icy rain managed to touch Kateri's face, drip off her chin, slither down her neck. She almost turned back, but like Lacey, she desperately wanted to reach the library. The closer she got, the more her sense of urgency increased. She turned the corner and looked across the street toward the entrance.

By the light of street lamps, she could see that someone had left a pile of clothes on the concrete steps. People in town did that sometimes, figuring she would distribute them to the needy. And of course, she always did.

Yet Lacey barked and ran across the street, and she didn't do that for a pile of old clothes.

So Kateri followed as fast as she could, squinting through the rain and darkness.

No. Definitely not clothes. Someone was huddled in a fetal position against the door.

God, the whole town was like a skating rink, and this person was out in it?

Lacey reached the pile of clothes and nosed at it, and the person, a woman, probably, turned her head and looked at the dog, then with difficulty extended a hand for the dog to sniff.

That was invitation enough for Lacey. She crawled into the person's lap and stretched out, trying, Kateri thought, to warm her.

Kateri reached the steps, stood on the sidewalk, and said, "Excuse me? Are you all right?"

Stupid question, but this person should be dead.

The woman looked away from the dog she was petting and directly at Kateri. She was white, young, twenty-five, maybe, and her face was so pale Kateri thought she must be frozen. "I'm fine, thank you," she said. Her voice was thready, and she enunciated carefully, as if she was having trouble moving her lips.

"I'm Kateri Kwinault, the librarian." Kateri climbed the stairs. "Come in."

"Thank you." The woman *really* was polite. "This was as far as I could go, so I was hoping someone would come along." She scooted aside to allow Kateri access.

"Of course. And this is far enough." Kateri got the door open and switched on the lights. It was chilly inside, but nothing like the biting cold outside.

Lacey leaped from the woman's lap and toward the library, inviting her in. When the woman was slow to respond, Lacey bounced back to her, bumped her, then spun around and dashed back into the library.

Kateri said, "I can't assist you. Can you come in, or should I call someone?" She knew the woman could now clearly see her crumpled, crooked, broken body, but that was all right. Sooner or later, everyone heard the story about the tsunami ripping Kateri out of the cutter. The massive wave had crushed her, drowned her, taken her to the depths of the ocean. There she had met the god her people believed caused the earthquake. Kateri didn't talk about the Frog God—everybody freaked out, Native Americans and whites and anybody else who heard—but she knew what she had seen. She knew the pain he had caused her, and the power he had granted her. She knew sooner or later she was going to have to figure out what the Frog God wanted from her. But not now.

The woman tried to stand. She collapsed, then half-crawled, half-rolled inside, as if her limbs could not quite comprehend the commands of her brain. She held one arm close to her chest.

As soon as she cleared the entrance, Kateri hurriedly shut the door and locked it. "I'm going to turn up the heat," she said. "What's your name?"

"Summer. I'm . . . Summer."

CHAPTER TWENTY-EIGHT

Kateri appreciated the irony of the name. "Well, Summer, it's good to meet you. Can you get yourself out of those clothes?" Summer wore a uniform of some kind, all black with a black bow tie. "I've got blankets and throws. The kids come in wet and cold and when the old furnace breaks down . . ." It didn't matter.

Summer stared fixedly at the dog as if Lacey's enthusiasm fascinated her.

"I've got a floor cushion." Kateri got towels out of the cupboard, the ones she used to wipe up. "Take off your hat," she said.

Painfully, Summer pulled off her cap and dropped it beside her. Then she halted, as if more was beyond her.

Kateri sat on her walker seat and dried Summer's short hair and face. She tossed the wet towel aside and covered Summer's head with another dry one.

"Yes, I can undress." Summer answered the now-old question by holding up her right hand, encased in a black oven mitt. "If you would get me started by removing that."

Kateri pulled it off. It was damp; Summer's fingers were white and looked frozen. She hurried to the thermostat, turned it up, and heard with relief the old furnace wheeze to life. "Can you move them?"

The woman stared down at her.

"Your fingers. Can you move them?"

Summer did, and winced.

"They hurt?" Kateri lowered the seat on her walker, then eased herself down.

"Yes. So badly."

"Good. They're not frozen." Kateri called Lacey, removed the pink, sequined coat, and dried the squirming spaniel.

"Right. I knew that . . . Water?" Summer whispered.

"Of course." Kateri let Lacey escape her. She used the handles on her walker to support herself as she struggled to her feet. She went into her postage stamp–sized office, got a bottle out of her private stash, returned, and opened the lid.

Summer took it, tried to put it to her mouth, but her hand trembled too much. She lowered the bottle in defeat.

Lacey trotted to her side and nudged her, encouraged her.

"What a nag," Summer told her. "Okay, okay." She lifted the bottle to her lips again, and this time she managed to drain half before taking a breath. "Better." She sighed. "It's weird. Water was falling from the skies, and I was dying for a drink."

Kateri liked this Summer person. She spoke to the dog as if Lacey were a person, with good humor and appreciation for the dog's concern. As Kateri gathered blankets from the cupboards and cushions from the kids' section, she chatted, trying to keep Summer's attention on something besides her condition, trying to warm her from the inside with conversation. "I found Lacey in a garbage heap on the edge of town. I don't usually go there, but I was out walking and headed in that direction. No reason . . ." *Except that, like today, I felt some great need nipping at my heels.* "The dog had been hit by a car, was half dead, but she managed to lift her head when I spoke to her. When I dribbled some water from my bottle into her mouth, she nudged me like she's nudging you."

"She is so beautiful." Still, Summer's words were stiff, as if her face were frozen. "I would never have known she had been hurt."

Lacey *had* been hurt. She had been nearly dead, until Kateri had touched her, had felt Lacey's blood on her hands, felt the sad ebb of a life that was ending too soon, and rebelled against the injustice. Kateri had refused to let Lacey die. Now Lacey lived, thrived.

Summer moved her left hand away from her chest. She didn't have an oven mitt on that hand; she had her fingers wrapped in a spotted white rag. Spotted with . . .

Kateri shouldn't have been shocked, but she was.

Blood.

"Shit!" Kateri grabbed her first aid kit and pushed her walker close. She sat down on the seat and took the poor, abused hand in hers. "Let me see," she said.

"Careful. Careful!" Summer winced, whimpered, cradled her wounded hand in her other hand, turned her face away.

Kateri unwrapped the rag slowly, noting that it was a kitchen dishcloth, that the amount of blood increased as she got closer to the skin (duh!), and that, thank God, the blood flow seemed to be stopped. She finally wound the cloth down to the point that she could see it was stuck to the end of Summer's little finger.

And she knew.

She got the scissors out of the first aid kit and began to cut away the extra material. "Who did this to you?" she asked fiercely.

"I did it." Summer leaned against the wall, no longer blue with cold. Now she was almost green with pain and horror. She pulled a small, sharp, blood-stained knife from her pants pocket, and dropped it beside her. "I was trapped. They were going to find me. *I did it.*"

"My God. Oh, my God." Kateri chanted the words like a prayer. "Listen. My experience here at the library allows me to kiss a boo-boo and make it better. I can put on a Disney princesses Band-Aid." She dug in her bag for her phone. "I'll call nine-one-one—"

With her uninjured hand, Summer caught Kateri's wrist. "No! No emergency personnel. No doctors, no forms, no names."

Kateri stared at the young woman. Summer was half dead, but still she managed to be both ferocious and insistent. "You've lost a lot of blood."

"Not a lot. I've been cold from the moment it happened. Slowed the flow. No hospital. No." Summer's hand slipped away. "Promise."

"I promise. But we've got to have . . . somebody . . ." Kateri eased herself from the seat onto her knees. She knocked the ice off the man's bomber jacket that Summer wore, unzipped it, then slowly, so slowly, peeled it down one arm, then down the other and over the poor, wounded hand.

Summer cried, and at the same time said, "Thank you. I'm so cold it doesn't really hurt. It's just . . . it's so horrifying I can hardly stand to—"

Someone knocked on the library door.

Kateri couldn't believe it. "Who the hell . . . ?"

"Kateri! Kateri! It's Mrs. Branyon. I need that new book. That one . . . with the guy . . . and the girl . . . and they do the wild thing and kill each other?" Eagerness quivered in Mrs. Branyon's voice.

Kateri and Summer looked at each other in horror.

"She's like a hundred years old," Kateri whispered.

Mrs. Branyon banged on the door again.

Kateri shouted toward the door, "The library doesn't open for two hours!"

Of course, Mrs. Branyon, the most hateful old woman in the world, went into one of her harangues. "Kateri Kwinault, I pay for your salary, and you better let me in and give me that book, or I'll report you to the mayor!"

Kateri couldn't believe the gall. In a rage, she shouted, "No! Go home! The library opens at ten."

Outside, a moment of startled silence was followed by a huff of astonishment and indignation. "I will tell . . . I will tell the mayor *and* the city council," Mrs. Branyon said.

"You do that! And I'll tell them you came out in the middle of an

ice storm to get a pornographic book filled with bondage and hot sex."
Kateri's voice got louder and louder. "What do you think about that?
What will your daughter think about that?"

"Insolent Indian. You're probably drunk and imagined the whole
thing," Mrs. Branyon roared back.

They listened to the grumbling noise as Mrs. Branyon wandered
away.

"Bitch," Summer whispered.

Kateri found herself laughing. "She is. She sticks with the classics.
The traditional drunken-Indian insults. They never grow old."

"Where am I?" Summer asked.

"Virtue Falls. In Washington State. On the Pacific Coast."

"Oh." Summer nodded. "I'm going to lay down now." That was
all the warning Kateri got; Summer slid sideways on the wall to the
floor.

Shit. Summer was looking worse and worse. Kateri threw three
blankets over her, figuring she needed the heat more than she needed
to be jerked around to get her out of the damp clothes. "Now . . . listen. No hospitals, no medical assistance, but Rainbow is the waitress
here in town and she's a genuine earth mother. I'm calling her. She'll
know what to do."

Summer nodded, swallowed, shook in a sudden bout of shivering.

Lacey whimpered and crawled close.

Kateri shoved a pillow under Summer's head, and called Rainbow.

Rainbow answered, sounding as cranky as Kateri had been to be
awakened. "The café is closed. I'm supposed to be sleeping in. So this
better be good."

"You know about losing the tip of a finger, right?" As Kateri talked,
she scooted down by Summer's feet, unlaced her soaked black leather
shoes, and eased them and her socks off.

On Rainbow's end, the pause was long and profoundly confused.
"Yeah . . . a few of the cooks I've worked with have cut off a fingertip,
and I did a pretty good job chopping my thumb when I was about
twenty. Why? You cut off your finger?"

"I got a lady here. She needs help."

Rainbow said, "This lady lost her fingertip? You called me because some cook cut off her fingertip? I don't think so. Kateri, what's going on?"

Kateri held the phone away from her mouth and spoke to Summer. "Can you move your toes?"

No response.

"*Summer!* Can you move your toes?"

The toes wiggled reluctantly.

Kateri dried them, covered them with a towel. "It's not just her fingertip. It's . . ." She scooted away from Summer and lowered her voice. "Listen. You know I wouldn't call if it wasn't an emergency. I'm afraid she's going to . . . Can you come to the library?"

"What crazy shit are you into now?" But Kateri heard Rainbow throw off the covers. "Goddamn it, Kateri, it's cold in here. It's cold outside. Have you looked out the window? Have you seen the ice? You want me to come out in that?" As Rainbow got dressed, she was huffing like a steam engine. "My God, *you* went out in this, didn't you? Have you no sense?"

"Not much."

Rainbow took a long breath. "All right. Tell me. How bad is it, this woman's finger?"

"Amputated down to the joint below the nail. She managed to pull some skin over the top of it. It . . . it doesn't look good."

"Call the EMTs."

"I can't. I promised."

"She's off the grid, huh?" Rainbow understood that right away. Respected it, too. "Okay. I've got some painkiller. I'll bring it."

Thank God for Rainbow. "Just come." Kateri smelled cigarette smoke. Heard Lacey bark. "This is way beyond my experience. She's got hypothermia and she looks like . . ." She glanced at Summer.

Summer, who lay still and quiet, her face pale and her brown eyes wide as she looked into the next world.

"She's dead!" Kateri cast the phone aside.

The old cowboy who knelt beside Summer turned his head and looked into Kateri's eyes. *She's not dead. Not if you help her.* He stood and walked away, giving Kateri room.

Lacey crawled close to Summer's side and rubbed her head against Summer's unmoving arm.

Kateri ignored the frantic squawking from the phone. She scooted back to Summer and put her fingers on the pulse on her neck.

It beat faintly. But it still beat.

"Come on. Come on!" Kateri embraced Summer, a whole-body embrace, willing her own life into the still form. "You didn't come this far to quit now. Come on! Live!" She put her ear close to Summer's mouth.

Summer wasn't breathing.

The cowboy said, *Help her. You can save her. That's why she came to you.*

Once again, the faint scent of tobacco smoke touched Kateri's senses, compelling her to believe in him. To believe in herself.

So she put her mouth to Summer's and breathed her breath into her lungs.

CHAPTER TWENTY-NINE

Taylor wandered through green fields touched by mist, where time did not exist and life was weighed in tastes of golden joy and seen in blossoms of yellow despair. She would stay. She wanted to stay. *Please . . . life had been so difficult.* She would stay. She needed to stay.

Then . . . someone touched her arm.

"You son of a bitch." She lunged at her attacker. "Leave me alone!"

A woman's hearty voice: "Kateri, tell me why I do stuff like this for you."

"Because I can't do it for myself." A woman's soft voice.

"Yeah, yeah. Hypothermia is a bitch, and so's she." Another touch, this time on Taylor's foot.

Taylor kicked her attacker as hard as she could. "Are you going to kill me? I dare you to try."

Someone coughed, gasped. Hearty Voice again: "Okay. We're not going to play nice." She sat on Taylor's hips and unbuttoned her shirt.

Taylor's rage faded, and she tore at the shirt. "Get it off. Get it off!"

The weight disappeared, and Hearty Voice said, "What's she doing now?"

"I looked it up," Soft Voice said. "Wanting to rip your clothes is one of the weirder signs of hypothermia."

Taylor got her shirt half off. Tore at the waistband of her pants.

"What about trying to kill me?" Hearty Voice asked. "Is that a sign of hypothermia?"

"Half the people in Virtue Falls want to kill you." Soft Voice laughed.

Taylor paused to listen. Familiar voice . . . She strained to hear it.

Soft Voice spoke again. "Yes, Rainbow, rage is a symptom of hypothermia. You're a big girl. She's half dead and she cut off her own finger. So dry her off. She's shivering."

They rubbed Taylor with what felt like a wire scrub brush.

She fought, but she didn't have the strength. So she cursed.

Someone licked her face.

She struck out.

The dog yelped.

She tried to open her eyes, to say, *Nice dog.* And, *Sorry.* She managed to open her eyes and whisper . . . something.

A pretty blond cocker spaniel crept forward and placed its head on the pillow next to Taylor's. Taylor lifted her hand, inch by painful inch, and stroked the soft head. Somehow, that made her feel calmer. She closed her eyes and let them wrap her in blankets . . .

Taylor couldn't speak. She couldn't think. She couldn't remember where she was or why she was here. Her skin hurt.

Hearty Voice said, "It's her pulse and breathing that scare me. She needs to be in the hospital. Can you imagine the scandal if she dies in the library?"

Again the soft voice. "She won't."

This time Taylor knew that voice. "Kateri," she whispered. Kateri, the angel who had appeared out of the blue, frozen world.

"Wow." Hearty Voice. "You must have impressed her. She knows you."

Kateri said, "Yes, and we'll keep her alive."

"We? You're assuming I am going to help you."

"No, I meant Lacey and I."

The dog barked.

A moment of surprise, a loud laugh, and Hearty Voice said, "That's putting me in my place."

"Someone has to." The creak of wheels as Kateri moved her walker across the threadbare carpet. "I'm going to call Dr. Watchman."

Taylor shouted, "No doctors! You promised!"

"She's mumbling something." The woman with the hearty voice leaned close. "Nope, can't tell what she wants. Kateri, why are you going to call that old horse doctor?"

"Dr. Watchman knows what she's doing—she's always treating the Families when they go out and get drunk, cut, stabbed, shot, beat up." Kateri sounded farther away.

Hearty Voice said, "But Dr. Watchman's not supposed to treat humans. She's a veterinarian, for shit's sake."

"People are very much like horses," Kateri replied in a prosaic tone.

"A lot of them are very much like horses' asses," Hearty Voice said.

Kateri chuckled softly. "True . . . More important to the case at hand—Dr. Watchman doesn't report stuff to the authorities."

Taylor relaxed.

"Dr. Watchman doesn't report stuff to the authorities because *she's* Native American and *her patients* are Native American."

"And *I'm* Native American, so she won't tell on me," Kateri said.

"Half Native American," the hearty-voiced woman said.

"*And* I'm god-kissed."

"Yeah, yeah." Rainbow scoffed, but beneath that, Taylor heard caution.

God-kissed. What did that mean? Taylor tried to ask, but again, no one paid any heed. *Why wouldn't they listen?*

Danger. They were in danger. Michael Gracie was after them. They were going to die, and it was Taylor's fault.

She fought again. She needed to run. *They* needed to run.

Hearty Voice restrained Taylor by wrapping the blankets tighter.

Lacey whined and rubbed her head against Taylor's face.

"The doctor's on her way." Kateri was close again. "Summer can't stay out here in the main room. The children will arrive soon. I've made her a bed in my office. If we use blankets as a stretcher, can you drag her in there?"

As Taylor bumped along the floor on the makeshift stretcher, pain racked her joints. She screamed. And screamed.

The dog barked. And barked.

Kateri and Rainbow tried to hush them both.

They got Taylor into the office and shut the door.

"Wait until she's had some painkillers," Rainbow said. "Then we'll make her more comfortable."

Taylor drifted off, then woke in a panic when someone put a needle in her arm.

Michael Gracie. He was going to kill her.

Taylor fought until the sedative took effect.

When she came out of it, it was dark. She was cold. She was in pain. She fought again.

The third time she woke, daylight shone from the high windows in the cement-block cell. Three women slept sprawled in chairs around her.

Who were they? Where was she?

Who was she?

Taylor silently cried until the dog snuggled with her. She slept.

On day three, she knew who she was. She knew where she was. She knew who these women were. And she wanted to cut off her finger again. It made sense, because if she got rid of her finger, she wouldn't be trapped here anymore, and Michael Gracie wouldn't get her. *He was going to get her.*

Taylor heard Rainbow say, "She's really crazy," in a voice of awe.

"No, she's not," Kateri said. "She's had hypothermia, and she's got an infection. She'll come out of it."

Another needle. More sleep.

Taylor woke and met Rainbow. Rainbow was tall, raw, with broad shoulders and big hands. She had recently shaved her head, and her salt-and-pepper hair was a quarter-inch long from ear to ear. She had a long, uneven, jagged scar behind her left ear where no hair grew. Taylor vaguely thought that if she had any sense, she would be afraid of Rainbow.

Taylor met Dr. Watchman, a Native American who wore her black hair in a long braid that dangled down her back. She smelled of peppermint, and handled Taylor as if she *were* a horse, efficiently, briskly, and without allowing any struggle. Somehow, Taylor expected her to sing Indian medicine chants. But she never chanted. She never said a word.

The nights were the worst, but Kateri was always there, her lilting voice singing the chants the doctor did not. For Kateri, Taylor always quieted down.

Yet Taylor could not bring herself to eat until Rainbow shook her roughly and said, "Kateri didn't save your skinny ass so you could die of starvation in her office and leave her to explain that to the cops. Eat this soup, damn it!"

The dog barked disapprovingly.

But Taylor ate.

More pain, more days, and the distant sound of children's voices singing Christmas carols . . .

Christmas. She had survived to see Christmas. She thought her father would be proud.

Kateri explained that they had to transport Taylor out of the library and to Kateri's apartment, and they had to do it this week, between Christmas and New Year's, while the library was closed for the holidays.

Taylor didn't want to move.

She wasn't given a choice. On the day after Christmas, when the early night had fallen and rain blurred the streets, Rainbow wrapped Taylor tightly in blankets, covering even her face, then wrapped her again in a rug. With many a grunt, she hoisted Taylor over her shoulder and carried her outside. The cool, damp air slid through the layers. Kateri warned her there would be a jolt. There was, as Rainbow placed her onto the tailgate of her Volvo station wagon and slid her in like a package.

Lacey leaped up and settled herself on Taylor. Then the little dog growled, a surprisingly deep, menacing snarl.

Taylor heard a vaguely familiar, screechily unpleasant voice say, "So you're stealing a rug from the library?"

"Mrs. Branyon! How good to see you! Actually, it's my rug. I used it in my office, and next week I'll be replacing it with a new one I ordered from Ikea. But thank you for asking!" Butter would not melt in Kateri's mouth.

Why did Taylor remember Mrs. Branyon?

The woman said, "Likely story. Thieving Indian doing nothing except reading books to kids and taking money from the city for it. Should be ashamed . . ." Her heels tapped on the sidewalk. Her voice faded.

Taylor remembered now. "Old bitch," she said.

She didn't think anyone had heard her until Rainbow laughed and agreed.

The transport into the apartment was as wrenching as the removal from the library, leaving Taylor exhausted and semiconscious.

But here it was quiet, warm, and comfortable. Time had no meaning for her, and Taylor let herself drift—for days—through blessed nothingness. Everything had been so difficult for so long, she had been so afraid, so hungry. She had dredged up the last coin of courage and then spent it to get to Virtue Falls. Now she couldn't bring herself to sit up and grasp reality. And she didn't want to try—until the day she heard voices in the living room.

Kateri . . . and a man.

CHAPTER THIRTY

Taylor tried to stand. Her knees buckled. She slithered off the bed, crawled to the open door, leaned against the wall beside it, and listened with all her might.

"It's not as bad as you think." A man's voice, deep and warm, with a hint of a Spanish accent. Not Michael Gracie's voice.

"You're a lousy liar. It's twice as bad as I think." Kateri's soft voice wasn't soft anymore. Instead, it crackled with such authority Taylor was reminded of her first-grade teacher, Mrs. Williamson, a stern disciplinarian and the terror of Taylor's young life.

Automatically, Taylor sat up straight and squared her shoulders.

Kateri continued, "I work in the library. You think I don't hear everything that happens?"

"You're too damned smart for a woman." He spoke with affectionate humor.

A light slap, then Kateri said, "Landlubber doesn't know what he's doing, and he's too arrogant to learn. I cannot believe he was promoted to commander of the station. No one is less qualified to lead men anywhere, much less onto the Pacific Ocean to bring in a boat full of drug smugglers. Did he figure because they were in a sea kayak with no motor they wouldn't know how to handle firearms?"

"I believe he said something to that effect, yes." The humor was gone from the man's voice. "That smuggler shot Ensign Morgan in the chest. The bullet hit his lung, rattled around in there. Until the helicopter got there, I thought we were going to lose him. We might still."

Abruptly vicious, Kateri said, "It's too bad the bullet didn't hit Landlubber."

"He's good at hiding." The man's voice dripped with sarcasm. "Fast, too."

"Put your men into the line of fire, then duck out of the way. Oh, Luis." The despair in Kateri's voice broke Taylor's heart. "I screwed up, man."

"Because of the cutter? You didn't overturn it. The tsunami overturned it. And it was Adams's fault that you didn't make it through the breakwater and into the open sea. He blocked you. There were witnesses."

"I can't pass the buck on this one. *I* was in command. *I* was at the wheel. That cutter, and the lives of my men, were my responsibility. Instead of playing poker with Adams, taking his money and making fun of him—"

"He deserved it."

"Yeah, he sucks at poker. But that's not the point. I could have made him listen." Kateri sounded flatly certain. "Then at least he would know something now and I wouldn't be waiting every day to hear he's *accidentally* killed one of you. Or all of you."

Taylor peeked around the door.

Kateri and Luis sat on the short couch in the tiny living room, facing each other and looking at each other . . . earnestly.

Luis was Hispanic, with black, close-cut, curly hair, dark eyes, a brown complexion, and a bone structure that looked like those of the statues on Easter Island. His dark blue Coast Guard uniform was rumpled and his face was lined with exhaustion, as if he'd put in a long day and wanted, needed, comfort.

"He lived through that earthquake. He saw that tsunami." Luis's voice shook as if the memories frightened him even now. "He almost got you killed, and he hardly seems to recall any of it. He's determined that what works on the East Coast should work on the West, and sometimes, he wants to prove he's in command and I can't . . . we can't do a damned thing with him." Luis thrust his hand through his hair. "If his uncle ever gets voted out of Congress again, maybe we'll have a chance to dump him. As it is, he keeps applying for commands back East, but his reputation precedes him, and no one will have him."

"It's the military, the Peter Principle. Everybody gets promoted until he's in over his head, then that's where he stays."

"Ha." Luis couldn't even work up a decent chuckle.

"It's not funny, because it's true. I'm so sorry." Kateri put her hand on his arm. "You know if I could, I would still be there at the station, bossing all of you around."

"You'd be good at it, too." Luis looked down at her fingers. Loneliness and longing etched his face. "For God's sake, Kateri, if you'd let me help you!"

Kateri took her hand away. "I'm fine on my own."

"I know you are. But we could be better together."

At the tone of his voice, Taylor's toes curled, and she ducked her head back into the bedroom. She leaned her back against the wall, and thought she shouldn't be eavesdropping. Not on this kind of talk. Not when they were being so intense, so personal.

At the same time, she couldn't stand to move away.

"Come on, Luis. We can't be together. You know that. I can't . . . do . . . that . . ." Kateri's voice trailed off.

"There are all kinds of ways to do . . . that . . ." He laughed.

She laughed back. "Pervert." Then she sobered. "Why would you want this body anyway?"

Bam. Like that, he sounded serious again. "Do you think it matters to me that you got beat up in the ocean? I mean, you had a great body before, and I wanted you, but it's not about your body. It's about *you*. I want *you*."

"I appreciate that. I really do. But there are so many women out there who loves some Coast Guard officer. Go find one. Make love. Get married. Make babies. You deserve the best."

"I know. Which is why I deserve you."

A silence followed, one that made Taylor peek into the living room.

Luis held Kateri's face between his two hands, and he was kissing her so sweetly, it brought tears to Taylor's eyes.

He lifted his head. "Kateri, I love you. Let me take you to bed and show you."

Kateri hesitated.

For the first time, Taylor realized she was in Kateri's apartment, a one-bedroom apartment, in the only bed. Kateri was sleeping . . . where? On the couch?

Guilt rolled through Taylor. While she had been nursing her depression and lethargy, Kateri, battered and broken, had been sleeping on the worn love seat.

Taylor dropped her forehead against the wall.

The sound was louder than she expected.

She froze.

Luis said, "What was that?"

"Must have been the dog," Kateri said.

"Yeah. Listen, Kateri . . ." He tried to get intense again, but the moment was over.

Taylor didn't know if Kateri was tempted, if she would have yielded. But with Taylor in there, Kateri couldn't let Luis take her to bed to prove anything.

Damn it to hell.

Taylor *had* to drag herself out of her lethargy. She had to face life again. *Now*. She had to find a job. *Now*. And she had to start . . . *now*, with a new name and a new purpose.

Her name was Summer, and for the rest of her life, that was who she would be. Summer . . . forever.

PART FOUR

THE GAME

CHAPTER THIRTY-ONE

In Virtue Falls, September was Sheriff Garik Jacobsen's favorite time of the year. The rush of summer tourists was gone, to be replaced by the less frenetic influx of whale-watchers, who arrived to observe the migration of the great gray whale. The locals began to relax from the frenzy of tourist season, and put their minds to enjoying the last golden, warm days when summer eased aside to allow autumn to splash garish color all over the leaves and the sky. Sometimes, this time of year, when the sun skipped across the top of the fog, the whole world turned pink and swirled in tiny, intoxicated water droplets.

Yep, September made Garik want to do a little undignified jig in the middle of the square.

Of course, school started, too, so the number of car wrecks increased as a new batch of high schoolers got their driver's licenses. Garik spent every afternoon handing out speeding tickets to sulky, defiant teenagers.

Garik had done his duty for the afternoon. Now as his reward, he opened the door of the Oceanview Café and was enveloped in a rush of heavenly odor: fish and chips with coleslaw; doughnuts fresh from the fryer, shaken with cinnamon sugar and served with homemade blueberry preserves; and coffee, a local Washington grind, smooth, hot, and black.

"Hey, Sheriff. You can't stay away from me, can you?" Rainbow batted her eyes at him, picked up the coffeepot and a mug, and sashayed to his usual table.

He followed and slipped into the chair against the wall. One thing a career in law enforcement taught—always keep your back against the wall. "How could I stay away? You're the second most beautiful woman in Virtue Falls."

Rainbow laughed, loud and hearty. "Having Elizabeth move to town destroyed my chance to be Little Miss Virtue Falls. Want a piece of blackberry pie? Dax made it this morning."

"Just coffee."

"What? There's no coffee at the courthouse?" Rainbow filled the mug.

"Mona makes it."

"Mona." Rainbow grimaced. "You know, she's a lousy human being and a POS secretary—"

"Personal assistant." Garik took care to be politically correct.

"—a POS personal assistant, and Sheriff Foster's the one who hired her. If she can't even make a decent cup of coffee, why don't you fire her ass?"

He looked at Rainbow.

"Oh, yeah." She nodded as if she was just now recalling that she remembered all along. "Mona's blowing City Councilman Viagara Venegra, and I hear she's got sequined knee pads."

Garik did *not* grin. But it was a struggle. "I can't address that issue."

"You don't have to." Rainbow patted his shoulder. "I'll bring you a piece of pie on the house. We at the Oceanview Café appreciate law enforcement gifting us with your patronage. Saves us from getting robbed."

Visiting the Oceanview Café was tough on the diet. "When was the last time this place was robbed?"

"Never. See how good you are?" She walked away.

Some people might say—did say—that he must be bored with his job. After all, he hadn't really wanted it. He'd inherited it when Sheriff Foster had resigned in a very final way.

Some people might say—did say—Garik wasn't fit for the job. Those were the people who remembered him as the scrawny orphan Margaret Smith took in, the one who got to live at her Virtue Falls resort and get waited on by her staff, who graduated from high school with a degree in smartass and moved to the big city.

Most of those people conveniently forgot that Margaret made him work at the resort, that he finished college, and from there, went right into a career in law enforcement with the FBI.

The FBI career had been exciting, cool—and had got him divorced and battling nightmare memories. He'd managed to win his wife back, but because of his time at the FBI, he still carried a burden of guilt heavy enough to crush a man's soul.

He was working through that. Elizabeth helped him—Elizabeth was a scientist with a way of looking at the world that always gave him a fresh perspective.

Margaret helped, too. His adoption mother was almost ninety-four, and as sure of herself as ever. He drove her to church every Sunday morning. He made confession, did penance, received absolution, and knew Margaret was on her creaky old knees praying for him, too. If he was going to get into heaven, he would do it with Margaret's help—and by taking care of Virtue Falls.

Rainbow appeared at the table, put down Garik's pie, then turned to face the door as the afternoon group of whale-watching tourists filed in, chatting excitedly about spotting a huge gray whale doing its routine of surfacing, blowing, and submerging.

"Did you hear them?" she asked out of the side of her mouth. "They actually used the word *huge*—like there is any other kind of gray whale."

Garik chuckled and picked up his fork.

She whipped over to take their orders.

One thing about Virtue Falls—Garik had a pretty good idea what was going on in the community if he visited the Oceanview Café, and drank coffee while half the citizens of this fair metropolis came by his table and tattled on their neighbors or gave him hell for doing a lousy job or told him his wife was one smart woman, because they didn't understand a word Elizabeth said.

Yeah, him, too, at least when she was talking about her work at the geological study. And she did that a lot, at home and on television. Still, he was learning . . .

If the tattling neighbors didn't come through, all he had to do was stop by the tables where the senior citizens had set up camp and ask what was up. They knew *everything*.

Across the square, the newcomer in town, Summer Leigh, came out of the courthouse.

One March day this spring, she had appeared, strolling down the street with Kateri Kwinault and Rainbow Breezewing. When he introduced himself, he thought Summer had all the hallmarks of a battered woman: she was skinny, jumpy, unable to meet his gaze, seemed uncertain about her own name, and was missing at least one body part.

Within a month, she had become a part of the community. She recovered from whatever her ordeal had been. Not that she was bossy or talked a lot. Mostly, she was private. Yet when the spirit moved her, she spoke her mind in a tone that left no room for doubt; this woman had at some point led a successful life. She'd been in charge.

She started her own business, Summer Homes. She called herself a housing concierge, and she cared for vacation homes around the area. She did whatever the homeowner needed: she decorated, arranged for repairs, coordinated security upgrades. She even worked for Tony Parnham, a hotshot Hollywood director, as the construction inspector for his new home. In her spare time, she house-sat for the Virtue Falls residents who were on vacation. Folks who wanted to, "Buy local," rushed to use her, especially since in a town this size, people gifted with her abilities were thin on the ground.

She had found a need and filled it. Whatever job she had done previously had amply prepared her to open this business. Yet she had pulled a stunt that almost landed her in jail; to prove one homeowner had purchased shoddy security, Summer had broken into her house.

Garik had been called. Mrs. Westheimer had calmed down and decided not to press charges, and to give Summer the job of maintaining her security. But when Garik privately asked *how* Summer had learned to pick locks, she'd shrugged and said she had looked it up online. When he asked her *why*, she hadn't answered at all.

Every Saturday afternoon, at the library, she taught Eva Rivera how to read. Every Thursday night she attended Kateri's quilting club. And whatever help Kateri had given Summer, Summer paid back by utilizing Kateri whenever she needed help with her business. Garik had seen not only an easing of financial pressure on Kateri, who lived with the constant stress of medical expenses. Oh—and Summer drove Kateri anywhere she needed to go.

Yes. Garik found Summer Leigh an interesting anomaly of sophistication mixed with wariness. In Garik's experience as an FBI agent, an interesting anomaly always bore watching . . . although Elizabeth said that calling Summer *interesting* in that tone of voice proved his suspicious nature.

Now, as she got her keys out of her small cross-body bag, he noted that she'd gained a little weight. Her appearance was casual but put-together: short brown hair, subdued makeup, a pair of comfortable flats, slim-fit blue jeans with a worn and braided leather belt, a black T-shirt, and a tan linen jacket . . . which covered a suspicious bulge at her side.

The woman carried a piece. She *always* carried a piece. Not that that was unusual in western Washington, where the whole place was a weird combination of Wild West bravado and organic foods/politically correct mentality. But twice a week, she lifted weights with Kateri's trainer, and she ran at least five miles a day, up and down hills, ran as if someone were chasing her.

He'd like to know what man had scared her so thoroughly.

She headed for her car, a 1969 Pontiac GTO two-door hardtop she'd somehow cajoled out of the crankiest old fart in town, Mr. Szymanski.

Since Garik was sixteen, he had been begging Mr. Szymanski to sell him that car. It still had the original paint job, for shit's sake. The old guy had bought it new, treated it like a beloved child, always kept it in a garage. It had four on the floor, a 389-cubic-inch engine, three two-barrel carburetors, and dual exhaust. And that woman had landed it.

Damn, that pissed Garik off. And *damn,* he wondered what the story behind Summer Leigh truly was. He'd find out someday.

And *damn,* he wondered how much Mr. Szymanski had charged her for the car. She hadn't visited the bank, so . . . did she pay cash? Or did Mr. Szymanski hold the loan? Or had he handed over the keys because he was a fool for a pretty face?

Garik finished his coffee and pie.

Between all the gossip he'd collected, all the problems he had to solve, and all the caffeine he'd taken in, he would definitely be up all night.

A car with California plates sped past the café's front door—yeah, it was definitely speeding. It whipped a fast right, drove past the windows where he sat, flipped an illegal U-turn, and ended up parallel parking across two angle-in spaces. The driver and the passenger didn't get out. They just sat there and stared out the front window.

Rainbow flitted over. "Bet they don't know the sheriff is watching them."

"Probably not." He stood up. Definitely time to go out and say a few words to the folks who had possibly had too many early afternoon vacation cocktails.

"Backpackers," Rainbow told him. "Young couple. Experienced hikers. They left yesterday morning, drove up to the Wilderness Creek trailhead, were supposed to be gone three days. Wonder what happened?"

That changed the way he would go approach them. "Somebody got hurt?"

"Maybe. You'd think they would have gone to the hospital."

At last the car doors opened, and a guy and a woman got out. They looked around as if bewildered, then they started toward the courthouse.

Garik caught up with them as they reached the steps.

The woman spotted him first, then grabbed the man's arm and brought him around to face Garik. "Ethan, it's the police," she said. "Thank God."

Their complexions were gray, and both seemed wobbly on their feet. Something had truly horrified these people. In his calmest tone, Garik said, "I'm Sheriff Garik Jacobsen."

The woman seemed incapable of saying more.

The man stared at him accusingly.

Garik prompted, "Can I help you?"

"You have . . . do you know what you have out there in the woods? In the Olympic National Forest? Pristine wilderness . . . mountains . . . streams . . . snowy peaks?" The man pointed a shaking finger. "Do you know what we saw?"

"I don't know." Garik hoped it wasn't a Big Foot sighting. "Why don't you tell me, Mr. . . . ?"

"Salter. Ethan Salter." He wiped his forehead on his sleeve. "All we did was go off the trail so we could . . . all we did was walk off the trail for about fifteen minutes, just . . . we were just going to . . ."

"That's fine, Mr. Salter." Garik didn't care if they'd gone off the trail to have sex, as long as they didn't get lost. "Tell me what you saw."

"A head," the woman burst out. "A man's head. By itself. Sitting on a rock. A hole in the back of the skull . . . and the face bones were shattered. This bird was sitting on the jaw and pecking at the insides of . . ." Covering her mouth, she looked around wildly.

"Lady's room is down the corridor to the right," Garik told her.

She ran.

Ethan Salter watched her helplessly. "She's sick," he said unnecessarily. Crossing to the stone balustrade, he leaned against it and crossed his arms over his body as if he were holding himself together. "A body, a man's body. Rotting. Most of it was hanging way up in a pine, up on the branches, but animals and birds had eaten . . . parts. Bones and . . . bones had fallen here and there on the ground. And that head . . . someone shot him, didn't they?"

"I haven't seen the evidence, so I can't say." Probably. The last skull they'd found had definitely been a shot to the back of the head with a blast that destroyed the facial bones, making dental identification impossible.

"I suppose you see this stuff all the time, but we were . . . we wanted to . . . We knew we shouldn't leave the trail, but we never imagined . . ."

"Come inside." Garik took his arm. "We have a map of Olympic National Park and Forest. You can show us the approximate location and we'll see what we can do to solve the mystery."

As they climbed the stairs, Ethan Salter said, "Does this happen around here a lot?"

"No." Not a lot. Only one other time. Which meant more were possibly waiting to be discovered, the National Forest Service rangers were not equipped to handle such a gruesome and possibly far-reaching investigation . . . and Garik had better get his information together and give his ex-boss at the FBI a call.

It would be good to know if bodies were landing in other parts of the country, or if Washington had produced another nut case for Garik to investigate.

He could hardly wait.

CHAPTER THIRTY-TWO

Moving like a bat out of hell, Taylor Summers, alias Summer Leigh, drove the winding road to the Thackers' vacation home.

She loved her GTO, the one that would be forever known as the Judge. She loved the Ram Air III engine, the Rally II wheels without trim rings, the Hurst shifter with the T-shaped handle, the wide tires, the decals, and most of all, she loved the rear spoiler, which kept the vehicle from leaving the ground at high speeds. She'd driven the Judge at some killer speeds, put it through the gears, performed some amazing maneuvers, and never once had the rear wheels lifted off the road. So she guessed the spoiler worked.

Even more, she loved how enviously every male citizen of Virtue Falls watched when she got in and turned the key. Even the sheriff had desperately wanted her car; that dear old man Mr. Szymanski had told her so. But, as Mr. Szymanski had said with a chuckle, having Garik Jacobsen beg wasn't nearly as much fun as having Summer flirt, so *she* got the Judge, and for a good price, too.

She pressed on the accelerator, ran through the gears, then whipped through the hairpin turns up to the Thackers' mountain home. When she parked in their circle drive, she checked her watch: twenty-three minutes and forty-two seconds. That was a full thirty seconds off her original time and about seven minutes less than it took most people. One thing about living in Virtue Falls—there wasn't enough law enforcement to cover the miles of highway, country roads, and gravel tracks, and so far, she'd managed to avoid trouble—or at least the police-giving-her-a-ticket kind of trouble.

Now she eyed the two-story New England–style mansion. Outsized windows on every level faced the panorama of mountains and lakes. A long deck crowned the length of the front porch.

She hadn't won the contract to care for the Thackers' house. Pissed her off that Mr. Thacker had taken the word of the Seattle electronic-security guy rather than hire a Virtue Falls resident to make sure his home stayed safe. She was pretty sure he'd made his decision based on gender, and that pissed her off even more. Mr. Thacker had made a mistake when he hired City Security, and another when she asked him whether he would be willing to give her the contract if she proved to him City Security wasn't so secure. "Sure," he'd said. He had been deliberately off-handed and confident in his decision.

Which was why she was going to break in. She was taking a chance here. But what else was new? And why not? The only way she was going to succeed as a vacation home concierge was if she was bold, weighed her options, and fought for the business.

Besides, Mrs. Thacker had privately told Summer that she despised

Clarence Kibble, the arrogant jerk who ran City Security, and she would support her in her efforts to win their account. Since Summer had judged Mrs. Thacker to be the true power in the family, she was willing to give this a try.

Summer loaded her cross-body bag with her kit of lock picks and her iPad, unfolded her aluminum ladder and placed it against the second-story deck, and climbed up. There she evaluated the security at the master bedroom French doors and windows. All were wired with a motion sensor.

Yeah. Getting in there would have been too easy.

Next she shinnied up the downspout, onto the shingled roof, and all the way to the top, where a decorative widow's walk crowned the house. She was betting it wasn't merely decorative. When Mr. Thacker had handed his home over to City Security, he had told her he'd done it because he was a practical man, and the people from Seattle had years of experience, which she did not. Okay. A practical man would not waste a means to climb out onto his roof and clear the moss away, or inspect the shingles after a windstorm.

Sure enough, the widow's walk included a small door, and sure enough, City Security had cut corners and left it unwired. She picked the lock and was in the attic in less than a minute. She lowered the recessed ladder, descended into the master bedroom closet, walked into the master suite, and stood on the thick Oriental carpet next to the Thackers' king-sized bed. Laughing softly, she pulled her phone out of her pocket and dialed the Thackers' Southern California home.

Mr. Thacker answered.

She took care to erase any amusement from her tone. "This is Summer Leigh of Summer Homes Vacation Concierge Associates."

"Oh. Yes." His voice turned wary. "What can I do for you?"

"It's what I've done for you, Mr. Thacker. I've proved your security system is lacking."

Now he became indulgent. "And how did you do that?"

"I'm standing in your master bedroom, and you'll note I arrived without City Security's knowledge."

A stunned moment of silence, then, "I don't believe you!"

"I thought you might say that, so let me live-video my surroundings." She pointed the camera around the room, then brought it back to her and waved and said, "Hi, Mr. Thacker."

"How did you . . . ? How did you get . . . ?" He was gasping.

She hoped he didn't have a heart attack. "I came in through the unsecured portion of your home. What I'll do next is go out onto your deck. That should set off the City Security alarm, and they will call the police, and then they will call you." As she opened the door and walked outside, she said, "I hope I've convinced you to give me the chance to work with you on keeping your vacation home safe. Not only can I make sure a break-in is almost impossible for anyone but the most expert burglar—"

"Like *you*?" he said.

"I assure you, Mr. Thacker, I am not an expert burglar." Although she continued to sharpen her skills. "I can pick a few locks—which, when my clients locked themselves out of the house, is a useful skill—and I'm knowledgeable about the vulnerable entrances of a home. What you and so many homeowners don't realize is that a determined burglar can always find a way to enter your house, and that every safety precaution should be taken."

"Then why are you better than anyone else?"

"I live close, in Virtue Falls, and should someone set off the alarm, I can be here before law enforcement. If the burglar does damage, I can repair it before your next visit."

"The police will be there soon enough!" Mr. Thacker's voice was rising.

Okay. He was really angry. Perhaps this hadn't been such a successful gamble after all.

"Actually, if you'll hold for a moment, I believe the sheriff is calling me now." She went to the other line. "Sheriff Jacobsen?"

"Did you break into the Thackers' house?" He sounded exasperated.

"Yes, but I left a message with Mona telling you I was going to do so."

"She forgot to pass on the message."

"Mona's not very reliable, is she?"

Summer thought she heard him mutter something about sequined knee pads. Then he said, "You have got to stop this or someday I will end up arresting you." He sounded as if that would make him unhappy.

It would make her unhappy, too. She didn't need Sheriff Jacobsen poking around in her business. On the other hand, landing the Thacker job would make it possible for her to justify hiring office staff for twenty hours a week. "I've only broken into one other house." *In the state of Washington.*

"Which is two more than most people!" Sheriff Jacobsen's voice rose. "My actual concern is that you may break into the wrong house and get shot."

She touched the Glock she kept holstered under her jacket. "I will endeavor not to have that happen. Now, if you'll excuse me, I must get back and smooth Mr. Thacker's ruffled feathers."

"Not quite yet," the sheriff said crisply. "My mother, Margaret, would like to meet you. Elizabeth is out of town at a geological conference, so you're the ideal person to distract Margaret from her loneliness. Is Thursday night at seven all right with you?"

Astonishment gave way to outrage. "You're blackmailing me. If I don't visit, you'll arrest me."

"Yes."

"Blackmail is illegal."

"Report it to the local authorities. You can do so Thursday night at the resort at seven." Sheriff Jacobsen hung up.

Huh. She had realized he was suspicious of her. But she'd never expected blackmail. On Thursday night, she would have to watch her every word.

She clicked back into the call with Mr. Thacker.

And found Mrs. Thacker was also on the line. She was laughing.

Mr. Thacker was not, but he wasn't quite as huffy, and by the time the call ended, Summer had obtained the promise of a signed contract that would allow her to handle the security of their home and property. Mr. Thacker even promised to send her a key so she wouldn't have to break in every time. They finished the call when City Security buzzed in, undoubtedly to inform the Thackers they had an intruder in their vacation home.

At that point, Summer had been inside for over thirty minutes. She wouldn't want to be the person at City Security who spoke with Mr. Thacker now.

Seating herself at Mrs. Thacker's dressing table, Summer took deep breaths to calm herself. *She had won.* She had won the account, she had a viable business, she could afford to hire Kateri. *She had won.*

After a big scene like this one, she always realized how much she had risked, and how much she could lose. At the same time, she knew she needed to properly establish herself in the community before trouble hit.

And trouble was coming.

She would bring it on herself.

Reluctantly, she pulled the drawing out of her inner pocket and spread it on the table before her.

When she'd run from Wildrose Valley, when she lost her backpack, she had lost the catering money that would have made her start in Virtue Falls so much easier . . . and she also had lost the drawings she'd been making of the kidnapping. Over the past months, in her spare time, she had re-created them, slashing them down in harsh black-and-white, usually in the wee hours of the morning when the nightmares woke her.

This drawing . . . this drawing held particular meaning for her. This scene was the beginning of her descent into hell.

With Kateri and Rainbow's help, and utilizing the skills she'd learned as a decorator—and as a housebreaker—she was making a life for herself. But there was not one moment when she wasn't afraid.

Placing her left hand on the table, she stared at her little finger, pale pink and mutilated.

If only she could see the way out.

As she had done so many times in so many other houses, she started the Thackers' Wi-Fi and computer, connected her iPad and uploaded the scan of her drawing, and attached it to an e-mail on their account. She typed in a message, to Mr. Joshua Brothers, thanking him for his help all those months ago, expressing her sympathy on the loss of Mrs. Brothers, and asking for a favor. If he knew Kennedy McManus, would he forward the attachment, unopened, to him?

Quickly, before she could change her mind, she pushed *Send*.

The answer came back almost at once. Mr. Brothers thanked her for her condolences, said he was glad they had helped her, and that he would be delighted to pass this on to his pal Kennedy Mc-Manus.

She noticed he did not promise to leave it unopened.

Ah, well. It wasn't like she'd had any other choice. She had tried to contact Kennedy McManus herself; he was wealthy, a corporate head, and guarded by a legion of assistants. Sending the drawing through Mr. Brothers was a chance she had had to take.

She stood. She didn't want to be late for tonight's quilting session at the Virtue Falls library. She was a lousy quilter, but she liked to go. She listened to the stories, to the gossip, to the mumbled pleas for advice. She helped Kateri with refreshments. After all those months in the mountains, she had learned how to make friends again, and those friends were precious to her.

And now that her message was sent, she needed distraction.

For all she could do was wait.

Mr. Brothers stared at the attachment. "Well, dear, what do you think? Should I do as she asks and pass this on to McManus without looking at it? Or should I go ahead and open it?" When no one answered, he glanced around.

He would never get used to having Lorena gone.

He enjoyed few pleasures these days. Might as well indulge his curiosity. He had no one to tell about it, anyway.

Popping the attachment open, he stared. His eyes widened. "Damn, Lorena. The shit is going to hit the fan."

CHAPTER THIRTY-THREE

A hot summer at Gracie Vineyards in southern Idaho had ripened the grapes early. For the field workers, the workday started in the predawn hours. They cut grapes until the heat of the day changed the sugars in the fruit. Then they rested. For Pete Donaldson, the Gracie Vineyards vintner, the hours were longer, harder. Harvest was his busiest time of year.

Yet here he was, in the third week of September, on a raised platform in Michael Gracie's wine cellar in Wildrose Valley, praising Michael's palate, his decorating, and his method for storing wines in his own home. The vintner had taken time personally to supervise the transfer of older barrels from Michael's cellar to Gracie Vineyards, where the wines would be bottled, as well as the transfer of this year's vintages into Michael's cellar. And to fill the time, Donaldson was sucking up.

Michael was fine with that. He enjoyed being complimented. Brazen flattery was but another way to tell that people were afraid of him.

Bodyguards Barry and Norm, both tall, both brawny, watched as a dozen winery workers fastened chains around a barrel and, with a lot of grunts, rolled it off the supports and onto the pallet. The forklift picked up the pallet and headed out the broad double doors and toward the ramp that led up to the truck.

"As soon as the wines settle down, I'll get them bottled with the Gracie label," Donaldson said. "I personally picked out wines I think will be the top of our line when they are bottled."

"Gold medal winners, I expect." Michael had hired Pete for his inborn talent and his exclusive UC-Davis Viticulture and Enology degree.

He paid him well, and in return, he expected awards and high ratings for each bottle of Gracie Wines.

"It's been a difficult growing year. I don't know . . ."

Michael turned his head and stared at Donaldson.

Donaldson hastily added, "The wine you store in your cellar will be award-winners."

"Yes," Michael said.

The vintner feared losing his lucrative and prestigious position.

Yet, in the cellar's cool atmosphere, the workers were sweating, probably because they speculated about the one barrel kept empty for Michael's use. Maybe they recognized the bloodstains that never quite came out of the flagstones.

Pete Donaldson did not comprehend how fragile life could be.

The workers did. Brutal reality held no surprises for them.

They fastened a chain around the last barrel to be replaced and hoisted it onto the pallet, then high-fived each other. All the old barrels were on their way to the truck; half the job was done. Now they had only to place the new barrels onto the empty barrel stands. Two workers stretched and groaned. One held his pack of cigarettes and glanced Michael's way, as if wondering if he dared light up. One leaned a hand on the barrel support to lower himself to the floor. He grimaced, snatched his hand back, and looked down.

Then he screamed, shrill and high. He wiped his palm against his pants, then screamed again.

Men gathered around him, exclaiming in wonder and then horror.

"What in the world?" Donaldson hurried down the stairs.

Michael gestured to Barry, who intercepted him, spoke quickly, directed him back toward Michael.

Michael opened the door and gestured Donaldson out. Cold with rage and a lurking fear, he said, "We've had problems with an infestation of rats." *One big rat named Dash.* "We've had them exterminated, but I'm afraid that worker might have found a rotting carcass."

Donaldson glanced back. "But these fellows are used to filth and vermin. Certainly Cesare is—he's from a poor section of Panama City!"

Michael grasped Donaldson's arm and firmly guided him into the corridor. "Poor devil."

The door closed behind them.

Donaldson glanced at Michael's face, and seemed to quake. "I should return to the winery and to work. Crush is ongoing."

"You'll join me for dinner." Michael put his arm around Donaldson's shoulders. "After we have thoroughly enjoyed each other's company, my helicopter will take you back." For whatever the worker had found, there was no covering it up now. Michael would remind Donaldson who paid his salary, would deliver a warning to keep his mouth shut, and gently explain that once a man went to work for Michael Gracie, he quit only when Michael said he could quit.

One dinner and a helicopter ride should do the trick.

CHAPTER THIRTY-FOUR

Kennedy McManus sat on a folding chair in the small auditorium in St. Francis Catholic School in Bella Terra, California, and watched Miles perform his lines for the grade-school version of *Pirates of Penzance*. Like his mother and his uncle, Miles had an appalling voice, off-key and unsteady, and his part was mercifully short. But deep beneath the pain of listening to the boy screech like a tortured violin— *really* deep beneath that pain—Kennedy felt an uncle's pride.

In the year since Miles had been kidnapped, he had grown taller, of course, but he was measurably more mature. For a kid, he was thoughtful, and viewed the world around him with an adult's perception.

Tabitha hated that Miles had lost his innocent trust in people.

Kennedy figured better now than during his teenage years, when he would be a total screwup anyway.

Reaching over to take his sister's hand, Kennedy squeezed it until she uncurled her fingers from the tightly held fist and squeezed in return, and when Miles finished and left the stage, Tabitha turned to him and smiled. "Thank you for coming."

"Thank *you*," he responded. "If not for you and Miles, I would have no one."

She nodded. "Yes, and then you'd be . . . alone."

Alone was not the word she had been going to use. *Alienated,* maybe. Probably she was thinking that he would be even more divorced from the human race than he already was. Probably that was true.

In a distant way, he worried about it sometimes. He felt few of the emotions that roiled through the people around him, setting them alight or depressing them or giving them strength or taking it from them. At the same time, he didn't understand why his sister thought him deprived. He said what he thought; people listened. He focused on a goal; nothing distracted him. He spent time with his friends, lovers, and colleagues, evaluated their needs versus their abilities; he always got their best efforts in any endeavor. To him, life was not a heated mishmash of whims and desires, but a well-balanced and forward mobility.

Only Miles's kidnapping had yanked him from his calm contemplation of life and into a welter of unwelcome reactions. Not only had the emotional turmoil interrupted his work, but he had not enjoyed himself at all. Clearly, the whole feelings thing was oversold. Although it created clever musicals performed by children's off-key squeaky voices, emotion was not fulfillment, it was agony.

And it left ashes in its wake . . . because every day he wondered how Taylor Summers had slipped past his team and vanished. Where was she today? Hiding in a city? Married to a country bumpkin who asked no questions? In some foreign country living under an assumed name? Or rotting in some deep valley in the Idaho mountains?

Logically, the last scenario was the most likely. But he didn't believe it. The man who computed probabilities for every situation believed that if Taylor Summers, was dead, he would intuitively know.

Irrational and embarrassing. He did not admit it to anyone.

The play ended. The kids took their bows. The parents, grandparents, and relatives stood up, talking and laughing, and headed into the cafeteria for refreshments.

St. Francis was a good school for Miles, not because the Mc-Manuses were Catholic—they were, but neither he nor Tabitha were active—but because Jesuits ran St. Francis and they were strict and suspicious of outsiders. Kennedy believed the brothers would keep Miles safe. In turn, Kennedy paid the absurdly high tuition and tithed the same amount again to the parish church.

Hey, whatever worked.

Now he stood, holding a cup of punch and listening as Miles's math teacher told Tabitha what she needed to do to help him sharpen his skills. Kennedy smiled as he listened; Tabitha's brain, like his, was razor-sharp and analytical, and for all that she had never graduated from high school, she had a clearer understanding of higher mathematics than most Nobel prize winners.

When Kennedy's phone vibrated in the pocket of his jacket, he excused himself and stepped to the side. He opened it to an e-mail from Joshua Brothers . . . how very odd. He hadn't heard from the old man since he'd sent his condolences on the sudden death of Mrs. Brothers. Kennedy read:

Hi, son,

I'm the conduit here, passing this on to you.

Hope it helps.
JB.

Hmm. Enigmatic. Kennedy hoped the attachment wasn't a chain letter. He opened it, and even before he recognized the scene, he recognized the style.

Taylor Summers had drawn this sketch.

Driven by a gust of that despised emotion, his hand shook briefly, violently. *She* was *alive.*

He didn't want anyone else to see this. Not until he'd had the chance to examine it himself. So although it hurt to do so, he shut the attachment. He looked to see if anyone was paying attention to him—in fact, several single mothers viewed him as if they were starving carnivores and he was an untasted pâté of fatherhood. He sidled away and returned to the empty auditorium. He once again opened the attachment.

In the spare strokes of a black pencil on a white background, Taylor had reimagined the moment when the kidnappers pulled Miles out of the trunk. The passion with which Taylor re-created her memories made the sketch painful to view. The meadow, the road, the trees, the Mercedes, the steep slope Miles had scrambled up in his escape, were nothing more than a backdrop for Miles's terror, the kidnappers' indifference, and unseen, but still pervasive, the horror of the innocent onlooker. This drawing had been conceived and generated by the woman who had seen everything and moved to take action.

Yet . . . where had she been for the last year? Why was she contacting him now?

What did she want?

He called Mr. Brothers, heard his quavering voice, and felt a pang. Mr. Brothers had always been loud, brash, impatient, and now, since the death of his wife, he sounded old. But he was still amused. "You called to see what I knew about Taylor Summers, huh, boy?"

"I did, sir."

"I don't know a goddamn thing. She was up here for a while, working for a caterer. Lorena and I met her at our party a couple of months after your brouhaha . . . Girl called herself Summer—"

Kennedy filed that away in his mind.

"—and she looked rough. Life had not been good to her." Mr. Brothers sounded sad. "It's only because I knew her family that I figured out who she was. Then she disappeared."

"No communication until now?"

"None. I figured she was dead."

"No. I knew she wasn't dead." Kennedy looked again at the drawing. "You think she was living in the woods all that time?"

"I don't know how she could have been. It's cold here, not like your namby-pamby central California cold, but *really* cold. But for sure she was starving . . ." Mr. Brothers's voice became gruff. "She did you a favor, and she paid big for it. I expect you'll be wanting to return that favor."

"I do. I will. No matter what, I will repay her."

"Good boy. Let me know how it all comes out."

"I promise." They clicked off, and still Kennedy stared at the drawing.

He understood Taylor Summers had been unjustly portrayed by the media. Yet he had examined her life and found nothing particularly admirable about her. Her mother said Taylor was ungrateful and defiant. She had a good mind, but what had she done with her intelligence? She had become an interior decorator, a silly occupation. And with two broken engagements behind her, she seemed to be one of those women who passionately attached herself to a man and then, when love became routine, she broke a heart and walked.

Yet for all that, Taylor Summers fascinated him. Had she felt so passionately about injustice that she had risked her own life for an unknown child? Or had she seen in Miles and his kidnapping a chance to feed the excitement she craved?

He opened his photo app, and found his album with the photos of Taylor he had collected, and as he had every day for the past year, he wandered through her pictures from the day she was born until the day she had disappeared.

She had hidden from him so well. Now at last she revealed herself. She knew something. She offered the information. Yet she had sent no message, just the drawing. He could only assume she wanted something. He had only to discover what she wanted in exchange . . . and decide if he would give it to her.

A hand fell on his shoulder.

He jumped, and clicked off the phone.

Too late. In her scolding, overbearing, motherly voice, Tabitha said, "Honey, what are you doing, looking at her again? Taylor Summers is dead."

"No, she's not." Knee-jerk reaction. *Shut up,* he warned himself

Tabitha continued as if he hadn't spoken. "She did a wonderful thing. Every night, I get down on my knees and thank God that Taylor was there to help Miles. But that doesn't change anything." Tabitha rubbed his back as if she wanted to soften the deathblow of his dream. "She's dead, she's gone, you can't find out what she knows, and this fixation on her is not healthy."

It would be better if Tabitha didn't know what he had received, better if she didn't get her hopes up that the kidnappers would soon be brought to justice. Better if she didn't know that the woman he had obsessed over for the past year was now making contact . . . for whatever reason.

He put his phone away. "You're right, I'm sure. Now—if we don't get back in there and get some of the carrot cake, it will be all gone."

He didn't fool Tabitha. She looked into his face. Then she sighed. "You're never going to give up, are you? In fifty years, you'll be an old, friendless man with no wife and no children, sleeping alone with the picture of a dead woman."

"You're dramatic." He put his arm around her shoulders and turned her toward the cafeteria. "Let's find Miles, get our cake, and for the love of God, don't you dare leave me alone with any of the mothers."

"Some of them are very nice women, and would be a welcome change from the type you usually are involved with."

"What kind of women are those?"

"Dead women."

Once his sister got the bit in her teeth, there was no stopping her. Or . . . almost no stopping her. "If you leave me, I swear I will leave you to suffer through these programs alone."

She grimaced. "You win."

"I know. I always do." As Taylor Summers would soon find out.

CHAPTER THIRTY-FIVE

It was midnight before Barry stuck his head in the entrance of Michael's office. "It's not what we thought it was."

Michael Gracie looked up from his paperwork. "Barry, come in and let's speak in private."

"Right." The big bodyguard glanced behind him, stepped into Michael's second-story office, the one with the all-encompassing view of Wildrose Valley, and shut the door. He walked over to the desk, put his hands behind his back, and waited stoically.

Michael put down his pen and leaned back in his chair. "What did we think it was, Barry?"

"Some of Dash's brains." Barry was not the brightest star in Michael Gracie's constellation, but he could always be depended upon to speak the truth.

Michael hoped it didn't get him killed one day. "Then, what was it?"

"Somebody's finger."

Michael waited a few beats. "How did somebody's finger get under one of my barrel supports?"

"That's what we're trying to figure out. That, and whose finger it is. Some white person's. It's mashed pretty badly—fingernail and bone broken all to hell. Rotted, too."

"So it's been down there for a while, but how long is tough to tell because it's cool in the cellar and that would slow decay."

"Right." Barry scratched his head. "I didn't think about that. Good point. Anyway, we recovered a partial fingerprint. We're running it through the federal database right now."

"You used my software to get into the federal database, did you not?"

"Of course."

"Good. I wouldn't want you to try on your own."

"No. I don't do that computer stuff." Barry stopped, seemingly overwhelmed by the thought.

"The finger?" Michael prompted.

"Oh. The finger. Only problem is, I'm pretty sure it's a woman. Either that or a kid. It's pretty skinny."

"Why is that a problem?" Michael knew the answer, but he liked to walk Barry through every problem step by step. It increased the chances Barry would move from one problem to the next without undue confusion.

"If it's a man, there's a decent chance he was in the military, or worked on some federal or state program, or was arrested or went to prison. Then the feds would have his prints. Women and kids—not so much."

"Let's say this was a woman. That seems most logical. What was she doing in my wine cellar? How did her finger get caught under a wine barrel? How did she escape?"

"Oh. I know how she escaped. The finger's been cut off right at the joint." Barry lifted his hand and with the other hand showed Michael where and how.

"So a woman got her finger stuck under a wine barrel and cut it off rather than wait for someone to find her." Michael allowed his simmering anger to heat. "What would make her do that?"

"She wasn't supposed to be down there."

"That goes without saying. But to cut off her own finger . . . what did she see that scared her so much she was willing to mutilate herself?"

"I guess . . ." Barry stared at Michael as if he couldn't look away. "I guess she saw you shoot Dash in the head."

"I guess she did."

Barry paled.

Michael knew why. In prison, he'd been told that when he was enraged, his brown eyes turned black, and gazing into them was like looking into hell. When that happened, violence occurred.

Michael was beyond rage now. He was livid.

Barry's broad chest expanded. "I made a mistake, boss. Are you going to shoot me like you did Dash? If you are, could I ask you to do it in the heart? My wife's going to want to have a body to be the widow of, and I need a face for that."

Michael found himself shaken by sudden, unholy amusement. My God, the man was a simpleton. But loyal as the day was long to both his wife and to Michael. For that, he got a pass on this one mistake. "As if I would shoot you," he crooned. "If it hadn't been for you, I would have been killed in prison. I owe you."

"Ah, boss." Barry's battered face lit up, and he dug his toe into the rug.

"Now, what's next?" When Barry looked confused, Michael spoke slowly. "What is our next move to find this fingerless person?"

"Oh. I've got guys looking at the security stream for the entrances to the wine cellar. It would be easier if we had security video in the cellar. Not that many people get a tour of the cellar. But we don't have it in there because we use it for . . . you know."

"I know." Michael held himself very still, kept his face calm and serene. "But now we know exactly when to look for this intruder."

"When?"

"When I shot Dash. And we know who she could be."

"Who?"

"A guest. One of the caterers. One of my housekeeping staff."

"Right." Barry pulled his phone out of his pocket. "Let me tell the video guys we have a date to work with."

Michael waited while Barry conveyed the message, then asked, "How are our winery workers?"

"They won't be a problem. They all got a big bonus, a nice dinner, good liquor, and I suggested that unless they wanted a fast trip across the border in a body bag, they'd keep their mouths shut."

"Good." Michael wasn't really worried about them. They had come from rough circumstances. They understood what could happen if they displeased him. It was Mr. Hotshit Winemaker who still didn't have a clue. "Did Donaldson get back to the winery without incident?"

"You made him uneasy, boss."

"The screaming in the cellar made him *uneasy*." Michael smiled unpleasantly. "*I* scared the piss out of him."

"I don't know how you do it, without violence and all. I guess you've got a gift." Barry was in awe. "But even with that, he wasn't smart enough to know to stuff a sock in it. On the ride back, he asked the pilot a lot of questions."

"What kind of questions?"

"Where you were from. How you made your money." At one time, Barry's nose had been smashed in a fight. Now the tip turned red with disapproval. "So the pilot showed him the Sawtooth Wilderness area, a close-up tour and low to the ground, and by the time they landed at the winery, Mr. Donaldson seemed convinced he didn't want to know anything and he should get back to work."

"Monitor his outgoing for the next year. If he calls the wrong number—"

"You mean like the cops?"

"Exactly. If he makes that call or sends that e-mail, stop it before it gets anywhere and let him know that's inappropriate behavior." Michael picked up his pen. "The exorbitant salary I pay him buys loyalty as well as fine wines, and as a good employee of Michael Gracie, he needs to remember that."

"True that. But there's one other thing." Barry went to the door, opened it, and brought in a filthy, battered backpack. "I don't know if this has anything to do with anything, but last week while the gardeners were cleaning up for winter, they knocked this out of one of the trees."

Michael put the pen back down. "It was in one of my trees?"

"In the grove of pines out there"—Barry waved a hand at the darkened windows—"dangling from a broken branch about ten feet up."

"Who put it there?"

"Dunno."

"How long has it been there?"

"Dunno. A while. It's damp and mildewy." Barry viewed it

distastefully. "I thought maybe this belongs to *her*. The one in the cellar."

"Unlikely." Although perhaps not. "Why would one of the staff hang a backpack in a tree?"

"I didn't think about staff. I thought a paparazzi chick had been sniffing around with her camera and all, trying to get footage of you because you're rich and famous, and ended up getting her tit caught in a wringer."

Michael allowed himself a small smile. "Most amusing."

Barry looked surprised, then pleased. "That was funny, wasn't it?"

"Barry, you have potential." That thinking did show an advanced sort of logic. "I like the paparazzi idea. Have you looked in the backpack?"

"The gardeners said it was mostly empty. I squeezed them to see if they'd stolen anything. Scared them. One of them put back the snow-shoes that had been hooked to the outside, then they both started digging cash out of their pockets. Since cash was the last thing they were going to give up, I figured there wasn't much else. The side pocket had socks and gloves. There were some drawings at the bottom." Barry rattled on, not realizing what he had said. "The paper got all wet and the pencil bled so there's not much—"

Michael held out his hand. "Give me the backpack."

Barry looked at the backpack, then at Michael. "What? Why?"

"Give it to me, and go away." Michael never changed expression, but Barry put the backpack on the desk, lifted his hands above his head, and eased toward the door.

When the door shut behind him, Michael caught the backpack's metal frame and tilted it toward him. It was, as Barry said, damp and mildewy, and empty except for the papers wadded at the bottom. Michael brought them out and spread them on his desk.

They were wrinkled, water-stained, most of them almost illegible. But on one sketch, he could see enough. A car, two men, a child dragged from the trunk . . .

It wasn't signed, but then, it didn't have to be.

Taylor Summers. This was Taylor Summers's backpack.

CHAPTER THIRTY-SIX

Michael crumpled the drawing in his fist.

Taylor Summers was still alive. And she had been in his house.

His intercom buzzed.

He pressed the speaker button.

Barry said, "We've got the girl on the security cameras, boss. She's dressed in a caterer's outfit."

A memory sprang to life, of a woman standing in his kitchen, staring at him, her big eyes wide with distress. Michael turned to his monitor. "Show me."

At once the security video took over the screen, and Michael recognized the corridor that led from the kitchen to the wine cellar. A woman dressed all in black walked toward the door. She pulled on the handle, hesitated, looked around, then pulled again. She slipped inside. Michael asked, "How did she get into a locked wine cellar without tripping the alarm?"

The video paused.

"I wondered the same thing," Barry said, "so I went down and checked the latch. The door automatically locks, and the alarm works."

Michael did not like that answer. "So the alarm was not functional that night?"

"I'm working on that now. I believe"—Michael could almost hear Barry squirm—"we may have had a wine theft."

Michael did not like that answer, either. "On that night, we had a wine theft, and a woman who saw me shoot Dash? Are the incidents linked?"

"No. No, I'm pretty sure not."

"Pretty sure?"

"Very sure."

"Then perhaps the wine theft involves my security team?"

"No!" *That* Barry sounded relieved to report. "They're reviewing the video, and they found one of Georg's staff, some big dude, strolling into the cellar after the party was over. Just walked in. He was inside for five minutes and came out with a case under his arm. He, um, turned and waved at the camera."

"Insolent bastard." *Nobody* laughed at Michael Gracie. "I have some very expensive wines in there. Or rather . . . I had."

Barry talked faster. "Security found an earlier glitch in the computer program. They suspect before this guy arrived, he hacked the system, took a trip to the cellar, did surveillance, then came and got what he wanted."

"Do we know the man's name?" Michael asked.

"According to our records, he's Brent Kenney, an Idaho farm boy. But while there's a Brent Kenney living on a farm outside of Pocatello, it isn't this guy. This guy is a hacker, and a thief, and he's *good*."

"Track the illegal sale of my wine. Find the seller. Kill him." Michael was finished with the subject. "Now—show me a close-up of the woman's face."

The video reversed. Taylor came backward out of the wine cellar, paused at the door, and looked around. The focus zoomed in, then sharpened.

Yes. His instincts were correct. That was the woman he remembered in the kitchen.

"Skinny female. She could almost have slipped through the crack in the door." Barry was making excuses.

Michael wanted no part of that. "She didn't, though. Tell my computer security team I will personally go through records and find out how my system was hacked and why we weren't alerted." He made his voice softer and deeper. "Before I do that, they might want to make sure it never happens again."

"I'll tell them."

"Now—get Georg in here. Let's have a conversation with my dear caterer." Michael clicked off the speaker.

He had spoken to Taylor Summers. He had touched her.

He kept a computer file on the McManus kidnapping; from

inside that, he brought up a photograph of Taylor Summers, taken three years earlier. He divided the monitor and placed the two pictures side by side, one for her career portfolio, and this one, a close-up from that night at the party.

In the professional shot, Taylor's blond hair was skillfully styled and expertly colored. Her rounded cheeks blushed and her skin had been made up to give her a perfect matte finish without a hint of shine. Yet not even the most assiduous of photographers could completely hide her character. Her full, smiling lips hinted at a passionate soul. Her head tilted as if she could hear the winds calling her to adventure.

In the video still, Taylor was thin, *gaunt,* her face bony and un-attractive. Her brunette hair had been shaved close at the sides and cut short at the top. Her lips were chapped. Her skin was rough and shiny, as if she was sweating with nerves.

Yet for all that, in the kitchen, something about her had caught his attention. He remembered thinking she was interesting in an odd, wild, waifish way. He remembered being fascinated by the girl, speaking to her, accusing her of being underage and thinking she was too much of a fledgling for him.

Part of her youthful appearance had been the haircut. Part had been her wary, terrified gaze, as if she had suddenly realized the world was full of peril and predators, and she was a tasty morsel.

He supposed that was exactly what Taylor Summers had realized, and when she sneaked down into the cellar and seen him shoot Dash . . .

But he had good reason. Did she understand that?

Yes, he thought she did. He didn't know what hardships she had suffered, but the soft, sweet, ultra-civilized Taylor Summers of the first photo had been transformed into a woman who would do, *had done,* whatever it took to survive. That woman had cut off her own finger to save herself.

He stood and walked to the large, gilt-framed mirror hung over the bar, and he scrutinized his reflection.

Long ago, he had gone through a similar transformation.

He traced the barely visible white lines down the length of his nose, over his lips and chin, under his eyes and across his forehead.

Scars. Scars from a day that had changed him from Jimmy Brachler, farm boy, small-time drug dealer, and sometime pimp, into Michael Gracie, a man to be feared.

Jimmy Brachler had been so fucking cocky. He had been a college student, paying his tuition by running MIT's drug and prostitution rings. It hadn't been hard to set up the system; he had the brains for it, and he knew how to hide his tracks. Only one man could have caught him—Kennedy McManus.

But Jimmy hadn't worried about that. Kennedy was brilliant, yes, an upperclassman, lofty and noble. Kennedy had offered his friendship to Jimmy. He had admired and encouraged Jimmy's computer knowledge, Jimmy's head for strategy, and the speed at which he learned and adapted to change. Kennedy and Jimmy's online game battles were legend among MIT students.

So why would Kennedy bother to look into the successful drug and prostitution rings Jimmy had set in place?

Because MIT officials asked him to.

And why would Kennedy betray his friend and worthy opponent without a word of warning?

Because he was so lofty he refused to have anything to do with anything ignoble. When Jimmy went to him, to demand an explanation for his treachery, Kennedy had been scathing in his condemnation, called Jimmy's scheme illegal and immoral. When Jimmy pointed out that someone was always going to sell drugs and sex, so why not do it right, Kennedy had turned his back.

But when Jimmy stepped through the doors of the federal prison, he had not yet resolved to take revenge on Kennedy McManus. He had been pissed about going to prison, but he had also believed he could run things there the same way he'd run things at MIT. After all, he knew he was smarter than everyone else at the penitentiary.

What he hadn't been was wise. He'd never experienced the kind of vicious ruthlessness that ran like a sewer beneath the prison system. In the first week, he'd made his moves to take control of the market.

In retaliation, the prison's drug dealer, Shel Baranyi, had his men capture Michael in the men's toilet. They raped him, broke his legs, sliced his face with a rusty box knife, pissed on him, and left him to die. The prison guards hadn't found him for hours. By the time Michael had arrived at the hospital, he was DOA.

No one cared.

Somehow, he revived.

No one cared about that, either. No one except his grandparents, and all they did was pray for his soul.

According to them, he was already damned to hell, so why bother? What he had needed was a doctor with skill at plastic surgery, and when he'd revived in Emergency, no such doctor was available. By the time the available doctor finished sewing him up, his appearance sent the nurses backing out the door. He'd sent a message to Kennedy McManus, begging him to come and help.

The silence was deafening. And damning.

Three months later, he was back in prison, walking the halls with a stiff gait and wearing Frankenstein's face. Even Shel Baranyi had shrunk away. And for good reason—Jimmy now understood what it would take to win.

Within a month, Shel Baranyi died, strangled by a garrote.

One by one, Baranyi's men were murdered in various and vicious ways.

Prison officials suspected Jimmy Brachler.

Nothing was ever proven.

Seven years later, when he got out of prison, Jimmy Brachler disappeared as if he had never existed.

After three surgeries to his face, not even his grandparents recognized him . . . and Michael Gracie was born. Michael Gracie, with his noble pedigree and his expensive homes and his quietly successful organization. He traced people who didn't want to be traced, hacked governments and industries that didn't want to be hacked, organized prostitution rings, and moved supplies of drugs and guns around the world and into the hands of anyone who had the money to pay.

Yet no one suspected him of anything, for everything he did, he did with originality and flare. No detail escaped him; for him, discovering new and unique ways to circumvent the system provided endless entertainment. When he finished setting a procedure in place, no one in law enforcement ever had a clue. Well, sometimes some smart cop stumbled into one of Jimmy's organizations by accident. But then s/he either joined . . . or died. Mostly died.

Kennedy McManus had gathered the information to send Jimmy Brachler to prison, and because of that treachery, Kennedy had had an extra seven years to build his company.

But Michael Gracie had caught up, surpassed his former friend, and now was poised to crush Kennedy in every way possible—by destroying his company, his family, his confidence, and ultimately, his life. Michael would never have been so cold-blooded if not for his years in prison. For that, he owed Kennedy thanks.

As for Taylor Summers . . . she had ruined his first move in the strategic game Michael played with Kennedy.

She deserved death.

And she either was dead, or out there somewhere plotting . . . what?

Yes, what? After hearing what had passed in that cellar, she most certainly now knew he was behind the kidnapping, yet nine months later, she hadn't betrayed him.

Probably she was dead.

Yet . . . he returned to his desk and again stared at the two photographs on his monitor. He admired the new Taylor Summers. She was like him. She lived when she should have died. She had transformed herself into a formidable survivor. She had done what she had to do to discover his identity, and she was willing to sacrifice anything to stay alive.

Maybe, in his kitchen, he had subconsciously recognized her as a woman of strength and determination . . . and a worthy opponent. He had never met a woman who could match him. Taylor Summers could very well be that woman.

"That was a waste of time." Barry stripped off his bloodied rubber gloves and tossed them in the plastic trash can. They landed with a moist *plop*. "He didn't know much."

"I wouldn't say that." Michael dispassionately surveyed the broken body on the table. "We learned a few things."

The wine cellar was cool and, at last, quiet. No echoes of screams had worked their way into the walls, no desperate pleas hung on the air. It was always that way. When someone was dead, they were gone. Ghosts did not exist, the afterlife was an empty promise, and all that mattered was winning, here and now.

Georg had not won, not here, not now, nor would he ever again supervise a feast or be kind to the help, or visit his female wife or lay with his male lover. He was gone.

But he had given Michael a few valuable chunks of information. "We learned Georg thought Taylor Summers was an abused wife, that he was going to take her to a shelter, that the last time he saw her was the night of my party. She walked out the door and she never came back."

"Remember right after the shot, you looked around the cellar?" Barry scratched the dark stubble on his chin, leaving a bloody mark. Probably he'd cut through his glove with the scalpel. "Why'd you do that, boss?"

Michael did remember. "I thought I heard something. But I didn't really have that sense of someone watching me. I wonder why not?" No one observed him unaware; his instincts had been honed by seven bitter years of training in the penitentiary, where failure to remain alert ended in pain and death. How had this woman sneaked past all obstacles to view him in the act of murder? He should have been more aware, not less.

"Why didn't she go to the cops and report the crime?" Barry removed his butcher's apron and stuffed it in the trash can. "She's dead. Or she's smart. And afraid."

"For safety's sake, let's assume she's alive. She found out *I* kidnapped Kennedy's nephew. She saw me kill Dash. She's afraid I'll find her, too." She would be right to hold Michael in terror. "So where did she go? How did she get there?"

"Hitchhike?"

Michael's mind flipped through the vehicles in the parking lot, the helicopters that had ferried guests in and out, the private planes at his airstrip . . . "I'll look for her. If she's alive, I'll find her. Then I'll put her through her paces. She lived through months of winter in Wildrose Valley and the mountains. She survived somehow . . . you have to admire that."

"*I* don't have to," Barry said truculently.

"I do. It's not often somebody ruins my plans and lives to tell the tale. How did this woman survive her encounter with Dash, and the winter, and manage to maneuver herself into place to find out everything she needed to know about me?" The drawings proved she remembered everything, too. So many details, all safe within her head. "Taylor Summers bears further examination."

At the same time, he wanted to laugh. No one ever thwarted his plans, much less a high-end interior decorator with artistic aspirations.

"Sure, boss." Barry grimaced at the blood that had splashed his white, rolled-up sleeves.

Michael spread his arms wide. "Did any of the blood spatter hit me?"

Barry looked him over. "You stood back. You're clean."

Michael glanced at the table. "It really is too bad about Georg. He was a great caterer, and up here, it'll be tough to replace him."

"Someone will step up to take his place."

Michael started toward the door. "Yes, but will they serve those cotton candy cups?"

Barry joined him. "They will if you tell 'em to."

"Yes. They will." Michael stopped Barry. "Clean up the mess. Get rid of the body. And this time—make sure no one's hiding behind a cask."

CHAPTER THIRTY-SEVEN

Kateri shooed the last children out of the library, and shut and locked the door behind them. Turning, she slumped against the door. "Some days are longer than others."

Mrs. Dvorkin plugged in the vacuum cleaner. "Not really. Every day has the same number of hours. It only seems as if one day is longer than another."

Kateri didn't know whether to laugh or groan.

Their cleaning lady was literal to a fault.

She watched Kateri walk across to the door. "What are you doing tonight?"

"Garik—Sheriff Jacobsen—asked if I wanted to come to dinner at the resort. But it was a long week, so I told him I'd take a rain check."

"You should go. You could use a treat." Mrs. Dvorkin was a thirty-something widow, tall and thin with close-cropped brown hair. Life had not been kind to her, but she walked the streets with her shoulders back and her head up.

"We could all use a treat. But not tonight. Don't work too late!" Kateri walked out onto the porch and used the handrail to get down the stairs. She didn't really need her cane anymore—her improvement had been, in the words of her doctor, miraculous.

She liked being miraculous. But she used her cane anyway, for those moments when weariness overcame her and balance was illusive.

She walked toward her apartment, enjoying the crisp air, the bright leaves, the last few dribbles of sunshine before autumn stole them away. In the distance, she could hear the faint drumbeat of the waves pounding against the land, the rhythm synchronized with the pump of her heart and the breath of her lungs. Morning and night, sleeping and waking, she was part of the ocean, and the ocean was part of her.

In the shadows ahead a man slouched, leaning on the iron handrail that led to her apartment. Luis Sanchez.

She had not been kind to him. She had sent him away, had not seen him for over two months, not an easy thing in a town the size of Virtue Falls. But she would recognize him anywhere.

When he'd first arrived in Virtue Falls, he had been four years out of the Coast Guard Academy and had worked assignments in the Gulf for the Port Security Unit. He had walked with a swagger, smirked with a know-it-all attitude, been heart-stoppingly handsome and conceited as hell.

One mission on the water during a Pacific winter storm had knocked the know-it-all out of him. He'd come back to port quiet and thoughtful, and she watched him, wondering if he was now too scared to be of use to her. But the next time out, he had been magnificent, working the rescue. Even better, she could never forget how, when they turned to go back to port, he had faced the wind and howled with delight.

Until that moment, she had never loved a man, but she loved Luis then.

And now, unfortunately.

After the tsunami and during the long months of surgeries and rehab, Luis had been a faithful friend, visiting, encouraging, helping, holding. At some point his swagger had become a man's quiet confidence, his know-it-all attitude, actual knowledge . . . and he was still heart-stoppingly handsome. Damn it.

Kateri joined Luis and kissed his cheek. "How're you doing?"

"*Hola*, my darling." He straightened up from his slouch, and viewed her with an appreciative eye. "You're looking lovely and strong. You are taller."

"Think so?" She straightened, pleased at the idea. She'd come into the Coast Guard at five-ten and 140 pounds. One of her politically incorrect boyfriends had told her all she needed was a tomahawk and some leather fringe and she would be the primitive American goddess of love . . . and savage execution.

When she'd first met Luis, she had topped him by two inches. Since the surgeries, she'd lost her height advantage. And stupidly, now she would like to be taller than him again. "What's up?" Because she didn't think he was lurking around, waiting for her for no reason.

"I thought you ought to hear it from me—Ensign Morgan has been honorably discharged."

Her brief euphoria at seeing Luis faded, leaving her standing on the sidewalk in the deepening dusk and wishing she could do something: change the past, fix the present, push Landlubber off the cliff . . . "How's Morgan taking it?"

"His lung capacity is greatly reduced. He has to have breathing therapy a couple of times a day. Can't run or play sports with his kids. He's depressed. His wife is tearing her hair out. The family is moving back to Ohio to be close to relatives." Luis shrugged eloquently. "I don't think the marriage will make it."

"I hope Adams is proud of himself." Actually, she hoped he felt guilty.

But Luis shook his head. "The sad thing is, he is—real proud of himself. His uncle the senator is visiting."

"I'm sure that makes Adams the hotshit in town." Her sarcasm bubbled hot and right to the surface. "So Adams is going to get his promotion?"

"Yep. More money for incompetence."

"I don't care, as long as he's leaving for a command at a bigger station on the East Coast." She waited for confirmation.

Luis said nothing.

"Come on." She smacked her cane against the railing. "His uncle didn't come to visit merely to tell him he got a promotion!"

Luis leaned closer and lowered his voice. "I *accidentally* got a glimpse of the paperwork. Landlubber doesn't know it, but he's staying right here. I'd guess his uncle came to deliver the news himself, and soften the blow."

"If his uncle thinks that's going to make any difference with Lieutenant Sulkypants, he doesn't know his nephew."

"Maybe Lieutenant Sulkypants's mama insisted. All I know is we're stuck with him for at least another two years and another couple of dead seamen."

"Because this is a small Coast Guard station, and yeah, he's been responsible for the loss of a cutter, and destroyed the health and career of Ensign Morgan—"

"And your health and career."

"—but those are small losses compared to the damage he could do in a big facility. They won't transfer him because here he has less chance of making visible and serious mistakes."

The two stood there in the gathering darkness. Streetlights flickered on. The shadows beyond deepened.

She said, "Someone's got to do something about that guy."

"The military frowns on revenge."

There was nothing more they could do. Or say. Not about Adams. Not without descending into futile anger, anguish, and heartache.

So Kateri looked up into Luis's brown eyes, trying to communicate her sympathy and her sorrow. And she allowed herself to be distracted. "Luis . . . it is not fair that you got eyelashes like that."

He batted them at her. "*These* lashes?"

"Yeah. You've got the most beautiful eyes . . ." She touched his chin, ran her fingers over the harsh black burr of his afternoon beard.

He leaned in and kissed her. His lips were warm, and he moved them like a Latin dance, smoothly, rhythmically. His breath eased into her, scented with hot coffee and rich cream and bold experience. He slipped his hands around her waist and pulled her into him until they touched, top to bottom, and his body heated her by slow degrees, bringing her to life in a way that was new . . . because since the tsunami, *she* was new, broken and put back together in a different way.

He stretched back, then leaned in again and rested his cheek against hers.

Tears gathered in her eyes. He was so good, so sweet, and he wanted her despite the scars, the cane, and the handicaps. She had fought him, fought the need and the feelings. He was a good man. He deserved a whole woman, one who could roll wildly on the bed with him, who could bear his children and live a full life every minute of the day. What he wanted was not what he deserved, yet maybe she should trust him . . . "Come in," she said. "Luis, come into my home."

She felt him startle. His arms tightened on her. "Kateri, *mi amor* . . ." Then he let go of her, stepped away, fast, lifted his hands and held them as if she had burned him. "I can't. I have a date." His voice was reluctant. And he looked guilty.

She . . . she didn't know what to say. How to respond. Dating was what she had wanted him to do. Or so she'd said.

He said, "I could call and cancel."

"No. No, that"—she waved a hand as if her plea still hung in the air—"was a momentary weakness on my part."

He moved closer, filled her senses with Luis. "I like you when you're weak."

"All the reasons we shouldn't be together are still there."

"They were always your reasons." He was bitter now, rejected and angry.

God. She hated this. "Luis . . ." She touched his shoulder.

He shrugged her off. "I'll let you know how the date goes, shall I?" He turned and walked away.

She watched him, watched his straight back and broad shoulders and fine ass, and all the perfect parts of him as he strode away from her and disappeared into the gathering dusk. She was glad he had moved on. She really was. But . . . She pulled out her phone, pressed a number and said, "Garik? If that invitation for dinner still stands, I'd love to go."

CHAPTER THIRTY-EIGHT

Summer parked her car in the Virtue Falls Resort's parking lot and sat for a few minutes to rehearse some possible imaginary conversations with Sheriff Jacobsen, and his adoption mother, Margaret Smith. In these imaginary conversations, she was charming and evasive, and answered every question without revealing too much. If only she could pull this off . . .

She glanced at the resort, ran through her imaginary conversations again, then reluctantly removed the holster and pistol from around her chest and locked it in the glove compartment. It wouldn't do to carry a firearm into dinner with Sheriff Jacobsen. He might demand to see her nonexistent permit.

Getting out of the car, she locked the doors, something few people bothered to do in Virtue Falls. But few people who lived in Virtue Falls had witnessed a kidnapping and a murder, cut off their own finger to escape certain death, and feared that moment when Michael Gracie came hunting for them.

And few people in Virtue Falls had contacted Kennedy McManus and now waited to hear what he would do.

Virtue Falls Resort perched on a cliff overlooking the Pacific Ocean, a little too close to the edge for Summer's comfort. The building looked like a giant, four-story log cabin with a covered, wraparound porch. The wooden door stood open; she opened the screen door, walked into Virtue Falls Resort and into the past.

The cavernous great room reminded Summer of the classic log-and-limb architecture of Old Faithful Lodge in Yellowstone Park. Massive rustic Douglas fir beams supported the high knotty-pine ceiling. A fire in the tall stone fireplace gave out warmth and a sense of intimacy, and attracted a group of guests. They chatted quietly, seated comfortably in a grouping of carefully maintained early twentieth-century furniture.

Cool place, this resort.

No one stood behind the check-in desk, so Summer walked over, rang the bell . . . and inhaled deeply. The air was rich with scents of grilled meats, roasted garlic, red wine reduction sauce, and something prepared with bacon. Or prosciutto. Or some other smoked pork product.

A woman's voice spoke from the shadows. "Miss Leigh, welcome to my resort. Most people comment on the architecture first. I can tell you're a girl after my own heart—you're more impressed by the food."

Startled, Summer looked more closely, and realized a tiny, bent, bright-eyed old woman watched her from an oversized chair set against the wall. Summer walked forward, hand extended. "You must be Mrs. Smith."

"Mrs. Smith was my mother-in-law. Call me Margaret."

Summer heard the slightest wisp of an Irish brogue. "I do appreciate the beauty of the resort. The architect was brilliant, and you've obviously cherished the building as it deserves."

Margaret took Summer's hand in both her own, cupped it, and looked her over. "You simply appreciate the more tactile pleasures of food. I find that those of us who have at one time or another been truly hungry share that trait."

Margaret's insight startled Summer. Apparently not much got past her.

Great. This evening just got more difficult.

"Hang your jacket." Margaret indicated the vintage oak coatrack. When Summer had complied, Margaret used the arms of the chair to push herself to her feet. She gathered her cane in one hand, and put the other through the crook of Summer's elbow. She pointed toward the elevator. "We'll have drinks in my suite on the fourth floor. The view is excellent, and we must enjoy these lingering, beautiful days of autumn, don't you think?"

Summer pushed the up button. "I confess I am not fond of winter." She flexed her fingers, remembering the numbing cold of the Sawtooth Mountains, and her icy introduction to Washington State.

"Virtue Falls Resort has already celebrated its hundredth birthday. Built in 1913 by Noah Smith, Senior, this elegant boutique hotel and spa perches on a rocky precipice over the Pacific Ocean, and was a profitable addition to the immense Smith fortune, which consisted of a thousand wooded acres, a sawmill, and the mountaintop mansion in which the family lived." Turning to Summer, Margaret said, "I'm a raconteur. You appreciate that, do you not?"

"I do." Summer laughed. "It's a gift."

"A gift of blarney, my father always said." Margaret got that look the elderly got when they saw things long ago and far away. "He would know. I got it from him."

The door opened, they stepped in, and the elevator began its majestic ascent to the fourth floor.

"I'm so glad you accepted my invitation to come to dinner," Margaret said. "You've made quite an impression on Garik and Elizabeth. Elizabeth, of course, likes you because you don't bother her with nosy questions about her past, but you do ask intelligent questions about her work."

"What she does is interesting. Her past is her own."

"And *that's* what Garik finds interesting about you. Most people *are* nosy. Why not you?" Margaret touched her button nose. "He used to be an FBI agent, you know."

"I had heard that." From Virtue Falls locals who thought every stranger needed to be sternly warned to behave.

"Now he's the sheriff, and *he* says people follow patterns. For instance, when he expresses interest in someone, he expects them to spill their guts. His term, not mine." Margaret watched Summer with bright curiosity. "Your guts remain unspilled."

"I do my best not to bore anyone."

The doors opened and the two women moved with majestic deliberation into the suite.

"Ah . . ." Summer had stayed at many fabulous spas and resorts, but still she was impressed. This single large room held a massive bed, a small fireplace, comfortable chairs, and a round dining table. The floor, the walls, the drapes, glowed with color, luxury, and that indefatigable, hard-to-define attribute—comfort. "I love this."

"Truth to tell, so do I. It's a good place for little Maggie O'Brien of Dublin, Ireland, to rest her weary bones." Going to the French doors that led onto the deck, Margaret flung them open and gestured out. "If we're lucky, before the sun sets, we'll catch sight of a gray whale on its southern migration."

Summer walked out and stared across the Pacific Ocean toward the whales and waves and horizon, where the sun would soon dip below the edge of the ocean. "How do you ever look anywhere else?"

Margaret settled into a chair. "The view gives wings to the soul."

Reluctantly, Summer turned her back, and on the far wall of the room, she saw a wood and glass case lit by a small, discreet spotlight, and inside . . . "My God, look at that!" Forgetting every bit of manners she had ever learned, she hurried over to look more closely.

An exquisitely crafted piece of jewelry rested against a black velvet background.

"Is that . . . ," she wanted to say, *real*. Instead she said, ". . . an heirloom?"

"Indeed it is. That's the Singing Bird, commissioned in the early twentieth century by Mr. Smith as a gift for his wife after the birth of his first son. From Tiffany's, of course. The plumage is emeralds and rubies, the eyes are aquamarines, and the bird, a phoenix, stands on the legendary seventeen-carat Smith emerald."

"Seventeen carats?" Summer couldn't take her gaze away.

Margaret chuckled. "When I first saw the brooch, I was a chambermaid in Dublin. Mrs. Smith's oldest son had been killed in World War One and was buried in France, and she was on a journey to visit his grave."

Summer faced Margaret. "She brought you back to the States?"

"She was alone in the city. I had a large family and a lot of connections. I did her a favor." Margaret's eyes twinkled. "When I arrived here I met her second son, Johnny, and we married. And that is how Maggie O'Brien became Margaret Smith."

From the wry twist of Margaret's mouth, Summer suspected there was more to the story than that. But Margaret said no more, so Summer turned back to the case and let her fingers hover over the glass above the glittering, deep green emerald. "Do *you* ever wear the Singing Bird?"

"No! I am only its custodian. The case is bullet-proof, impact-proof, and the brooch is protected by the most up-to-date security in the world."

Summer snatched her hand back.

Margaret laughed. "It won't get you as long as you don't try to take it. I can't really imagine you as a thief, yet Garik says you are quite the expert at breaking into houses."

Garik was a mouthy bastard. "I only break into a house when I want to illustrate to the homeowner how easy it is to do. Then I take their protection in hand and everybody's happy." Except City Security, who had been profoundly *un*happy.

"One wonders how you learned such a skill, and what drove you to the brave and foolish act in the first place." Margaret put her hand to her chin and looked thoughtful. "Of course, I did note that you had at one time been hungry. And you suffered a grievous injury to your hand."

Summer seated herself, and looked down at the pink stub of her finger. "It could have been worse."

"Of course. It could always be worse."

Sheriff Jacobsen rapped on the casement. "Margaret, look at who I brought you."

Elizabeth Banner Jacobsen and Kateri stepped inside the room.

"My darling girls, I didn't expect either one of you!" Margaret Smith embraced them. "Kateri, Garik told me you couldn't come."

"I discovered I most definitely could." Kateri held her cane in one hand, and her smile held a sharp edge.

"Wonderful! Now sit down here"—Margaret indicated the chair on her right hand—"while Garik pours us all a drink."

Everyone gave their orders. Garik served Margaret her whiskey, Kateri a glass of red wine, and Summer and Elizabeth took a bottle of water.

He took water, too.

"Elizabeth—I didn't expect you back until tomorrow night." Margaret kissed her cheek again.

Elizabeth flopped down in an armchair. "I couldn't stand the conference for another day. Geologists are boring, the food was lousy, and everyone was drinking every night."

Garik perched on the arm of her chair. "And the old farts were hitting on you."

"Yes," she said grumpily. Elizabeth Banner Jacobsen was one of those women other women hated on principle. Her blond hair, guileless blue eyes, and curvy figure sent every straight man into a frenzy of desire. More important, Elizabeth was oblivious to any competition; she was gorgeous, she knew it, yet didn't seem to value her beauty. Maybe Garik did, but he couldn't be all about the beauty, because Elizabeth overflowed with brains and was honest to the extreme. Living with her could *not* be good for any man's ego.

Of course, he was a handsome man, too, and even better, he had that competent air about him that law officers often had, as if he could, and would, protect a woman with his life.

"I am glad to be home." Elizabeth touched Garik's arm, then looked at Summer. "Also glad to know Summer gave in and came to the resort. I thought for a while Margaret was going to have to issue the invitation."

"What does that mean?" Summer asked.

"That few people have the guts to refuse a ninety-four-year-old woman," Garik said.

Summer conceded with a nod. "The whole family is into blackmail, I see."

"I learned from the best." Garik went over, kissed Margaret on the cheek, returned to Elizabeth, took her hand, and kissed it.

He looked charming and carefree and not at all like the narrow-eyed sheriff Summer had come to expect. In here, he was nothing but a guy in love with his wife and at home with his family and friends.

"Successful blackmail is the only advantage of being my age," Margaret said firmly.

"So, Summer, how are you doing with the Judge?" Garik sounded casual.

Summer wasn't fooled.

He was green with jealousy.

"My car?" she said. "I manage okay. That little beast really moves. Hugs the curves. Accelerates like no car I've ever driven. I'd never driven a stick before, so Rainbow taught me."

Garik blurted, "Rainbow? Rainbow Breezewing taught you how to drive that car? I can't believe I haven't given you a ticket yet."

Margaret laughed. "You were so worried, Garik, that little Summer Leigh wouldn't be able to drive the Judge the way it deserves to be driven, but she's got it under control."

"Yeah. I'm so happy." Garik did not *sound* happy.

The women exchanged grins.

"Speaking of Rainbow," Garik said, "has anybody seen her lately?"

"She's gone walkabout again?" Kateri asked.

"Looks like it. She hasn't been to work in three days. Dax had to bring in a substitute waitress, and he's cursing Rainbow up one side and down the other." Garik turned to Summer. "She disappears periodically, is gone for a while, then returns and goes back to her routine like nothing happened."

"No one knows where she goes?" Summer asked.

"I've always thought she went out wandering in the woods," Garik said. "But it's late in the year. At any minute, that first winter storm could come roaring in."

Great. Garik was concerned about Rainbow. In Summer's book, that made him more likable. And it was so much easier to watch her words around a stern law-enforcement officer than a friend. She *knew* she shouldn't have come.

"There's no use worrying about Rainbow. She can take care of herself." Kateri finished her water.

"I'm not worried, exactly." Garik took Kateri's bottle and placed it on the bar. "But let's say I'm cautious . . . ever since we found the bodies in the forest."

CHAPTER THIRTY-NINE

Summer flinched.

She glanced around.

No one had noticed. They were all intent on Garik.

She took a breath, brought her voice under control, and said, "I must have missed some good gossip. What bodies in the forest are we talking about?"

"Someone dropped two dead bodies into the Olympic National Forest, figuring no one would ever find them, I guess," Elizabeth said. "Creepy, huh?"

"It's impossible to open a sealed airplane in flight," Kateri informed them. "So probably they were tossed from a helicopter."

Garik nodded. "That makes more sense. Because where would a plane take off and land without anyone noticing?"

Summer knew the answer to that; when she had stowed away on the plane from Idaho, she had landed on that isolated, forest-bound airfield about two hours' drive from Virtue Falls. When she had walked away from the airfield, down a lonely one-lane road to the highway, she had been barely conscious, surviving on instinct alone. She had walked through wind and icy rain until that moment when a farm truck drove up behind her. The old couple inside had offered her a ride, and regardless of the fact she had never hitchhiked in her life, she accepted gratefully. She had no choice. She could not have gone much farther. She climbed in the back beneath a tarp, and by the time she got to Virtue Falls, she had been half dead with hypothermia.

She didn't know where the airfield was. And she wasn't about to say what she did know. That would lead to unanswerable questions. "Were the people killed first?"

"Shot. Both of them." Garik waved a hand in the general direction of the mountains. "The Olympic Range is a big national park—almost fifteen hundred square miles. We figure there are more. Somewhere."

Elizabeth asked, "Did you talk to Tom Perez?"

Garik explained to Summer, "Tom Perez was my supervisor at the FBI, and he's still my contact. He said this is the first he's heard of bodies being dumped in a national park."

Summer took a few deep breaths, a sip of water, a few more breaths. "Do you have any ID on the bodies?"

"The most recent body is a winemaker from eastern Washington. According to the police report, he was behaving oddly, said some things that made people think he'd had a mental break. He disappeared, and everyone assumed he'd flaked out. Turns out he was in the Olympic Forest." Garik looked somber. "His parents don't understand what happened or how he got here."

"A winemaker from eastern Washington?" Not Dash, then.

"Name of Pete Donaldson. He had recently changed jobs. He used to work for a winery in Idaho . . ."

The sound of Garik's voice faded into the background.

A vintner from Idaho had been murdered and dropped into the forest. If she looked up Pete Donaldson, she would bet he had worked for Gracie Wines.

How had she dared imagine she could escape Michael Gracie? She had been on his plane. It had landed on an airfield somewhere on the Olympic Peninsula. Smugglers brought their goods in from Canada, using the convoluted Washington coast to hide their activities. She had heard Michael Gracie discussing his part in the business. She knew he had connections here somewhere. But she had never seen him, or his thugs, in Virtue Falls, and she had relaxed her vigilance.

What a fool she was.

The house phone rang.

She recoiled.

Garik answered, spoke to whoever was on the other end, hung up, and came to offer his arm to Margaret. "They're ready for us in the dining room. Shall we?"

• • • • •

Kateri had always thought the dining room at the Virtue Falls Resort represented the epitome of graceful elegance. Mirrored panels decorated the burnished gold walls. The tables, covered by starched white cloths, gleamed with crystal and silver. Formally clad waiters and busboys moved smoothly and unobtrusively. And the wide swath of windows overlooked the ocean, where seagulls, coaxed by treats from the kitchen, swooped and danced in the outward-facing lights.

When Kateri had been the Coast Guard commander, she had dominated this room. She had been a force to contend with, strong and proud. Now she was just proud. Maybe, if a man looked closely, he would still see beauty behind the ruins. But no man cared to bother except Luis, and Luis . . . was on a date.

The maître d' showed them to a round, five-person table set in the corner.

Margaret seated herself where she could survey the whole room. "I like to be able to watch over operations in my restaurant," she told Summer.

"I understand completely. I also like to see what's going on." Summer took a seat beside her, her back against a wall.

Garik sat on Margaret's other side.

Elizabeth took her seat next to Garik without even noticing the shuffling.

After a single glance at the large, centerpiece table, Kateri turned her back to the dining room. She couldn't stand to watch Senator Jensen, the mayor, City Councilman Venegra, and their wives; the Thirteenth District Coast Guard commander, Rear Admiral Richard Ritchie; . . . and Lieutenant Landon "Landlubber" Adams, all spiffed up in his Coast Guard dress blues.

She wished she'd never come. What a fool she'd been for not thinking of this—where else did she think the senator and his nephew would eat? At the only five-star restaurant in the area, at Virtue Falls Resort.

Kateri allowed the maître d' to pull out her chair. She seated herself, then handed him her cane. He leaned it against the wall with Margaret's. With a flourish, he placed Kateri's linen napkin into her lap.

She smoothed it across her thighs. "I always enjoy myself at the Virtue Falls Resort Restaurant. I know I will tonight, also."

Margaret reassured her with a pleasant, "We'll make sure you do."

Waiters swarmed the table, providing water and wine and menus.

Margaret said, "Today I heard from Tony Parnham."

Kateri picked up the conversational ball. "The movie director? Cool. What does he want?"

"He wants to host a Halloween party at the resort. He'll invite friends, colleagues, and guests from town."

"Guests from *this* town?" Garik pulled a disbelieving face. "Who does he know in Virtue Falls?"

"He is building that home on Eagle Road." Summer seemed not at all surprised at Margaret's news. "He hopes to join the community. One might think he is a hard man, but he's an artist, interested in the story, not the cash box."

"On the phone, he seems very agreeable; he told me to bring in the Virtue Falls folks I thought would add to the festivities. He wants everything to be top drawer. He's sending in a party designer." Margaret's eyes sparkled. "We'll have a good time."

After that, the conversation flowed comfortably.

The resort manager, Harold Ridley, came by to ask about their comfort. The waiters were attentive, the food was excellent, and as they moved from appetizers to the main course, Kateri's tension began to ease.

Then Garik muttered, "Heads up."

At her right shoulder, Adams's hateful voice drawled, "I'm glad to see you here, Kateri. I didn't know you got out much anymore."

She looked up slowly.

Adams was like the quintessential preppie on the planet. Pale, fair, blond, with capped teeth and hands calloused from lifting weights in the gym. His upper-crust Boston accent and attitude had set her teeth on edge the first time she saw him. But back then, it hadn't mattered what she thought of him, because she was in charge. She outranked him, outsmarted him, and knew she would outlast him.

Conceit and vanity, ground into the dirt by cruel fate.

Adams was flushed, his eyes vicious; he must already have received the bad news about his assignment.

So Kateri said, "This is an occasion, indeed, when we have a U.S. senator in town. Did he come to deliver good news?"

"Only that I'm going to receive a promotion to lieutenant commander." Adams puffed up his chest.

"So you'll be leaving us for a new command?" Kateri smiled, all teeth.

"Not at all! I am promised that I will be here for a very long time." He smiled back at her, pissed and at the same time grimly triumphant.

All Kateri's pleasure in taunting him vanished; she had been secretly hoping Luis was wrong, that Adams would go somewhere else. She wanted him to become some admiral's aide, and fetch and carry, take messages, go to formal dinners, and never do harm to another Coastie as long as he lived.

She ought to know by now she couldn't wish bad news away.

A big hand landed on her shoulder. "Kateri? Kateri Kwinault? I thought that was you. How good to see you looking so well!"

She looked up into the face of Thirteenth District Coast Guard Commander, Rear Admiral Richard Ritchie. "Thank you, sir, I am well."

Her court martial had been a matter of naval custom, convened not because of any assumption of guilt, but to make the circumstances surrounding the loss of her clipper part of the official record. Then the government had listened to Landon Adams's testimony, she had been accused of incompetence, and Admiral Ritchie had had a mess on his hands. She was pretty sure he hadn't believed her responsible, but she also knew that with the pressure from Adams's uncle brought to bear, the admiral had been hard-pressed to keep her out of military prison.

Then witnesses had come forward to say Adams had obstructed her race out into the open ocean. She had been acquitted. Adams had never been charged of deliberate sabotage, of which he was most certainly guilty, or of falsifying his testimony . . . also guilty.

In Kateri's next life, she intended to be born into a family with political power. From what she had seen, influence really made your life easier.

Now she faced the admiral, a man who had spent the evening with the U.S. senator who was Adams's uncle, various dignitaries, and Adams himself. She supposed, if she was being fair, Admiral Ritchie deserved kudos for acknowledging her.

She prided herself on being fair. "Congratulations on your new grandson, sir. You must be thrilled."

The conversation became emptily social, and when the senator's party left, Kateri felt as if the whole dining room heaved a collective sigh of relief. Harold and the waiters rushed out with complementary chocolate truffles for every table.

Elizabeth picked one up, took a single bite, spit it back into her hand, and sighed gustily. "I must be sick. I'm tired, the chocolate tastes funny, and every time I try to drink wine, I want to throw up."

Silence fell over the table. Every head swiveled to face her.

She looked around. "What?"

"Dear," Margaret asked in even tones, "have you thought that you might be pregnant?"

Elizabeth's expression went from disbelief, to indignation, to nausea, to disbelief again, to anger, and back to disbelief. "That's impossible!"

Garik shook his head. "Elizabeth . . . *think*."

"Theoretically, it's possible, sure. But . . . but I've been taking . . . pills . . ." Elizabeth looked around at the way everyone was trying to keep a straight face. "This is not funny!"

"I'm sorry, but it sort of is," Kateri said. "You had strep throat. You took antibiotics. You're a scientist. You know what antibiotics do to the effectiveness of oral contraceptives."

"Yes. But I didn't think . . ." Elizabeth seemed honestly indignant. "It was only once!"

This time, no one could quite smother his or her laughter.

Margaret leaned across and squeezed Elizabeth's hand. "Don't you want children?"

Elizabeth thought as if the idea had never occurred to her. "I suppose. Yes, we could have children." She turned to Garik. "Don't you think we could?"

He laughed softly. "I think perhaps we *are*."

"But this would be badly timed," she said. "I'll be pregnant when the dig is at a standstill for the winter, and have an infant in the summer when it's busy!"

"In my experience," Margaret said, "children are the definition of inconvenient."

Garik stood up and took Elizabeth's arm. "Let's go talk about it."

Margaret watched them leave the restaurant, then looked at Summer and Kateri. "*Talking about it* is how they got in this situation to start with."

Summer laughed, and stood. "Thank you, and please thank Sheriff Jacobsen and Elizabeth for me. The food, the surroundings, and most of all, the company made this an incomparable evening."

"Come back, then. You, too, Kateri." Margaret put her hand on Harold's arm, and he helped her out of her chair and escorted her out of the room.

"So are you glad you came?" Kateri asked.

"I guess. Looks like your ride got distracted by the news he is going to be a father. You want me to take you home?"

"Thanks, that would be great."

But when Summer came back into the dining room with their jackets and Kateri's cane, Kateri was nowhere in sight.

One of the waiters nodded toward the deck. "She's out there."

Summer slid out into the night. The fresh, salty wind blew in her face, tossed her hair around, raised goose bumps on her arms. "It's chilly," she said as she joined Kateri at the railing.

Kateri stared steadfastly, silently into the night.

Summer pulled her jacket on, then, unbidden, tossed Kateri's over her shoulders. She faced the invisible horizon, tucked her arms tightly around her middle, and asked, "What are you doing?"

"Listening."

Summer listened, too. She heard the seagulls cawing, the snap of the American flag on the roof, and the raw, constant roar of the waves crashing against the cliff.

"What do you hear?" Kateri asked.

"I can hear the first autumn storm far to the north, taking form. I can hear the power of the ocean. It's awe-inspiring. And terrifying."

Kateri turned her head and looked at Summer, and in the light from the resort, her pupils were distended, her eyes like holes drilled into an old, weary soul. "Most people look at the mountains and think they're pretty. They hear the ocean and talk about sandy beaches and date palms. They don't understand that nature carries its own death sentence."

"I didn't understand. Before."

"Nor did I. Before." Kateri hooked her hand through Summer's arm. In a voice fraught with humor and pathos, she said, "I occasionally come out to the sea to ask the Frog God what the hell he plans to do with me. Surely he had a reason for destroying and transforming me. These trials could not possibly be purely the capricious whim of a god. Could they?"

Summer closed her hand into a fist, and felt the smooth, scarred end of her little finger. "I like to think there's a meaning for all this."

The two women turned away from the Pacific, massive and relentless, and headed through the resort and the parking lot toward the car. Summer unlocked the doors and the two women climbed in. She started the Judge and put it in gear, turned onto the coastal highway between the resort and Virtue Falls, and drove carefully, watching for cars, for headlights moving too fast, for anything out of place. Nothing illuminated the way except the patches of dense white fog.

Then, about halfway to town, she saw flashing red and blue lights in her rearview mirror. She pulled to the narrow shoulder of the road.

Sheriff Jacobsen's patrol car whipped past her.

On her way home from cleaning the library, on a Virtue Falls side street, Mrs. Dvorkin had been hit by a speeding car.

The driver did not stop.

CHAPTER FORTY

One golden day of autumn slipped by, then another, then a week, and Summer waited. Waited for the rain to start, waited for Kennedy Mc-Manus to appear . . . waited to be murdered. But a whole bunch of nothing happened, and that, paradoxically, made her tense enough to cause Rainbow to comment that some *person* needed to remember who had saved her ass. By which Summer understood she had been snappish. She reined in her frustration . . . and waited some more.

Now Summer drove the coastal highway to Eagle Road, then to the circle drive. She turned in and parked at the rear of the Hartmans' house.

Over fifty years before, the broad, one-story ranch home had been built with wide windows that faced the ocean. At a mere four thousand square feet, it was puny for a wealthy family's vacation home. The charm lay in the location. A lovely stand of cypress, twisted and gnarled by the constant winds, surrounded the home. A long, winding path led through water gardens to a narrow set of rickety stairs. Those wandered down and around to a wide, private beach where the family played, picnicked, and walked.

The Hartmans were Summer's first clients; yesterday they had contacted her to let her know they had loaned out their vacation home and to ask her to get it ready. Which was odd, because one bad experience had taught the Hartmans to never allow strangers to stay. But perhaps this was a friend, coming to Tony Parnham's Halloween party.

Virtue Falls was buzzing about the guest list: celebrities, movie stars, and Hollywood power brokers were converging for the event. The invitations had become the objects of envy and gossip. A catering service had been brought in from San Francisco; they were hiring extra waitstaff from town, and everyone under the age of twenty-five who had acting aspirations applied.

Summer was lucky; she held one of the coveted invitations. Tony

Parnham's Halloween masquerade would be the first social event she had attended as a guest in over a year, and she intended to enjoy herself.

At the Hartmans' back door, Summer sorted through her keys, let herself into the laundry room, and punched in the security code. Once she was inside, she reactivated the alarm. She adjusted the whole house thermostat to seventy-two. The sheets and towels were stored in a dehumidifier, so necessary in the damp marine climate. The Hartmans had been unsure about the number of residents who would be staying, so Summer counted out five sets of sheets, one for each bed. After she had prepared the bedrooms, she would return for towels.

The house was quiet, and she missed Mrs. Dvorkin, not merely because she would have to do the cleaning Mrs. Dvorkin normally did, but for her company, too.

But Mrs. Dvorkin was barely out of the hospital, covered with abrasions and recovering from a concussion. If not for her own quick thinking, she would have been hurt much worse, but at the first sound of the accelerating car, she had run for the alley. The car had made a sharp left turn and followed, hitting the brick wall first, then knocking her off her feet and into the air. She had slammed into a plastic garbage can, then bounced off the pavement. People hurried out of their apartments. The car backed out of the alley and sped away. A description of the car, a brown Subaru Forester, and the first three Washington license plate numbers yielded nothing; the make of the car was common in Washington, and Sheriff Jacobsen believed the plates to be stolen.

So until Mrs. Dvorkin was back on her feet, Summer would prep the house. To fill the silence, she entered the living room and headed toward the stereo system. She reached toward the controls—and heard a sound behind her.

She dropped the sheets and turned, smoothly pulling the pistol from the holster under her jacket. She pointed it at the man who had risen from the easy chair beside the fireplace.

He raised his hands to show they were empty.

She took a long breath to slow the pounding of her heart, and lowered the pistol. "Kennedy McManus. You are here at last."

Kennedy McManus. He had found her. He had come for her. And looking at him in the flesh, seeing him alive and breathing, his blue eyes steady and fixed on her as if he would absorb her, body, mind, and soul . . . well. Summer didn't know if she was glad this moment had finally arrived, she only knew she would behave as if this moment was expected and normal. Not that it wasn't expected—but nothing could ever make this meeting normal.

She said, "It's a good thing I've been waiting for you to turn up, or you would now be sporting a hole in the middle of your chest."

"Taylor Summers." His hands were steady as he let them fall to his side. "You're quick with that pistol."

She had listened to him online; his voice was exactly as she expected, yet to have him say her name, the name so few people knew, sent another terrified jolt through her system. "Summer. My name is now Summer Leigh."

"Summer Leigh," he repeated.

"You're a friend of the Hartmans?"

"A friend of a friend."

Kennedy had connections. Of course. "You got my e-mail?"

"Joshua Brothers passed it on."

"How did you find me?"

"I am good at what I do, and one of the things I do is strategic data retrieval. I needed a place to start, and your e-mail to Mr. Brothers provided that information." Kennedy's dark hair was trimmed and neat. He wore a black suit, a white shirt, a burgundy tie. He dressed like a businessman attending a stockholders' meeting.

Yet the trappings of civilization were nothing but a disguise. Beneath the tailored jacket and starched shirt, his body was that of a dockworker, a wrestler, a warrior. Any smart woman would note the contrasts, and handle him with care.

Summer was a very smart woman. She fastened the safety on her Glock 26 Gen4, slid it into the holster, and straightened her jacket over the top. "It's like a knit scarf. Pull one thread and the whole thing un-ravels." Leaning down, she started to pick up the sheets.

Without warning, he was standing right in front of her.

She straightened.

He was tall, muscular, with big hands and big feet. How had he moved so quickly, so quietly?

He took her shoulders. He looked down into her startled face and fiercely asked, "Where have you been?" He didn't give her a chance to answer; he pulled her into his body and hugged her, as if . . . as if she were a vanished lover, a wife believed lost at sea, the most precious mem-ory of his life brought back to life.

She stood stiffly, cautiously, as she tried to judge his mood, the rea-son for his actions. Did he intend to surprise her? Hurt her? Was he nuts?

But he simply . . . cradled her. The heat of him surrounded her, eased into her bones, let her relax in slow increments. And that spelled trouble, because she hadn't touched, hugged, loved anyone in over a year. Her body was starved for affection. "What are you doing?" she asked cautiously.

"A year. A year I've believed you were alive, wondered where you were, what you were doing, and now you're here and you—" His voice caught as if snagged by a great emotion.

"We do not know each other." She spoke definitively, wanting him to hear, to realize the truth. "We have never met before."

"I do know you." He slid his hand up the back of her neck and his fingers into her short crop of hair. He pressed her head, urging her to rest it on his shoulder.

She let him, testing his strength.

But it was her strength that was lacking. "So you don't believe that stuff they said about me in the news?"

His snort was a masterpiece of derision. "That you had anything to do with kidnapping Miles? Why would I be so stupid?"

"I don't think you're stupid, but the news said Miles had fallen and had brain damage, so I didn't know if he could clear me."

"Not true. He was superficially hurt. We gave out the story about brain damage to assure the kidnapper Miles could not give us pertinent information that would lead to an arrest."

"I'm so glad your nephew is okay." She had worried.

"The important information which he was able to give me was that you were innocent." He massaged her neck.

That felt good. "I'm glad he did that—but why did you then allow me to be destroyed in the media?"

"For Miles's own safety, I had put out that he had no memory of the events. I could not contradict the police's theory that you were involved. I hoped you would realize that I did believe in your integrity."

"The reports drove me into hiding."

"And drove me crazy with wondering where you were and what had happened."

Sarcasm bubbled right to the surface. "Poor you."

He hesitated, adjusted, changed his tactics. "I'm sorry. I know it must have been difficult to see your character destroyed."

"Difficult?" An understatement. "I could not believe it was happening. I couldn't believe the lies . . . my own mother. So she could go on *Dr. Phil.*" That was a relationship broken beyond repair.

"I am sorry. When this is over, we will do damage control."

"You bet we will."

"Why did you finally contact me?"

"Everything I read about you said you were a man who listened to reason, who was impeccably honest. I thought I could convince you I was innocent, and if by some chance you refused to see reason, I could make a deal with you to protect me, and you wouldn't break it."

"I never break my word."

"I know." Before her backbone disintegrated, she asked, "Don't you want to know who took your nephew?"

"Yes. Of course I do. Will you tell me?"

"I will. When we have come to terms."

"Okay." How could he sound so . . . so reasonable? So willing to let her make the decisions?

Damn him. She had looked at his online portrait and decided that he was relentless, ruthless, analytical, cold, and the kind of man with whom she never, ever wanted to be involved. She was right about everything . . . except when he embraced her, he didn't feel cold. And if this display of fondness wasn't passion, it was a ploy to . . . to do what? What did he hope to gain?

He smelled good.

She took a cautious breath. Like pine and citrus, like the promise of Christmas with gifts waiting to be opened and long-anticipated surprises.

Not important. What mattered were his intentions and his strategy.

He leaned his cheek against her head.

She closed her eyes and sighed.

If he had bad intentions and an evil strategy, he was cleverly disguising them with warmth, gentleness, and that alluring scent of sin.

He tilted her chin and kissed her. He took her quick breath of surprise as if she owed it to him. He sank his tongue into her mouth, dominated, explored . . .

Wait a goddamn minute.

She shoved him away. She backed up as fast as she could. She wiped her hand across her mouth. "No." Because being hugged was one thing. Friends hugged. Friends did not French-kiss. "Who do you think you are?"

He stood with his chest heaving, his eyes intensely blue, his hands outstretched in appeal. "I'm the man who never gave up on his search for you. I always believed you were alive."

Which was either charming or creepy, depending on your point of view.

She looked at Kennedy, at his businesslike demeanor interrupted by that one strand of dark hair that hung carelessly over his forehead, and those brilliant, persuasive eyes.

So . . . a vote for charming. "No matter." She spoke to herself as much as him. "It doesn't follow that within two minutes of our first meeting, you get to put your tongue down my throat." She retreated toward the entry, the front door, and an escape route in case this guy turned out to be a rapist or a nut case.

Or . . . a man who thought she could be controlled through seduction.

Yeah. That had to be his scheme. Gain control by using her loneliness against her. "Do you try to sleep with every woman who sends you a drawing?"

"No. Only you."

She bet he had a beautiful singing voice, all deep and baritone. "Well . . . well, we're not lovers."

"You liked my kiss."

He made her knees shake, and she leaned her hip against the side table. "That doesn't mean I'll sleep with every guy who grabs at me."

"I know that."

But she didn't trust him. She already knew when he chose, he moved quickly. "How do you know so much?"

"For the past year, I have stared at your picture every day and every night. I've read your e-mails, your work notes, your texts. I know who you slept with, who you didn't, why you broke it off with your fiancés. Although you didn't attend your father's funeral, I suspect that his death broke your heart and your spirit."

She expected him to research her, yes, but not like this. Not so that he could poke his finger at her emotions. "How dare you presume—"

Kennedy watched her; his blue eyes were brilliant, deep, intense. "I've read your high school diary." He hadn't moved.

She hadn't moved. She still leaned against the table. But she felt stalked, trapped by his words, his height, his attitude. "Where did you get my diary?"

"From your mother. I paid her."

She felt more betrayed by him for destroying her privacy than by her mother for taking the payment. Because she expected nothing different from her mother. "I thought *you* had standards."

"I couldn't meet you, yet I knew you the first time I saw your photograph."

"Then you realize that I know how to be alone."

"You may know how to be alone." His voice had that deep, persuasive tone that made her knees buckle. "But you don't know how to be with me."

"All I need from you is safety." Anything else was too dangerous.

"I will give you safety whether or not we have sex. But let me tell you this." He paced toward her, taking his time, allowing her to flee. Or not.

She did not. Would not.

He said, "There are only two things I don't know about you—where you've been for the past year, and whether or not we will set each other on fire when we have sex. I don't know if you're going to ever tell me about your lost year. But I'm betting yes on the second."

"You're obsessed." Which sent a chill through her . . . and a most inappropriate heat.

"Yes." He took her hands in his, put them palm to palm, intertwined their fingers in a slow, sensual tease. He leaned close, so close his lips were right above hers; his breath filled her nostrils, and heat rolled off him in waves. "Let me show you what obsession means."

CHAPTER FORTY-ONE

Summer closed her eyes.

If she took this step, if she let Kennedy McManus make love to her, she would have ceded control to him. She had not come through hell for that.

She opened her eyes. She shook her hands free of his. She pushed him away. This past year had taught her to adapt, to think on her feet. Events did not shape Taylor Summers. She shaped events.

So she clasped him around his ribs and looked into his eyes. In as prosaic a tone as she could manage, she said, "My drawings are on my iPad."

She saw the flash of some emotion in his eyes. Fury, swiftly subdued? No, more likely irritation that his seduction plan had gone amiss.

"Let me get it." She retraced her steps back down the corridor, through the laundry room, and out the back door. She unlocked her trunk, got her briefcase and duffel bag, and turned back to the house.

Kennedy stood in the door, his black hair rumpled by her hands. He watched her with the grim expression she had seen in so many of his photos.

"What?" But she knew what. He thought she had run.

He didn't understand. She was done with running . . . unless Michael Gracie was chasing her.

She strode steadily back toward the house, toward Kennedy.

He moved aside.

The return to the living room was oppressive and silent.

She put her briefcase on the coffee table, pulled out her iPad, unlocked the hidden files, and passed him the tablet. "Here. Look through my drawings. I'll go . . . wash my hands."

She went back to the guest bathroom and used the facilities and, as she said, she washed her hands. Repeatedly. While staring into the mirror and reminding herself that spontaneous sex was always a disaster. At least . . . for her it always had been.

But still she wanted. Her body, starved for far too long of all but the most superficial of touches, needed to be held, to feast on passion and get drunk on the taste and the scent and the feel of a man.

Kennedy McManus smelled like memories of innocent love, looked like the stripper at a bachelorette party, and yes, he would be a banquet to the senses.

This stirring in her body was his fault, and she hated him for that.

Thoroughly she dried her hands. She opened the door. She walked back down the hall, stepped into the living room, and—

There he stood, holding the iPad, and gazing at her with narrowed eyes. He turned the tablet toward her. "You expect me to sign a letter of agreement saying I will get you your old life and good reputation back?"

He was so sure of himself, she couldn't help but mock him. "Can you not do that?"

His eyes kindled with rage. His chest heaved—and by God, she could see enough to know it was a very impressive chest. "Damn you," he said. "You've got me by the balls."

She didn't follow at first. Then she understood. "Because *you're* responsible for letting your nephew get snatched? Yeah. Okay. I didn't have to try and save him. I could have hidden behind a tree, pretended it had never happened. I could have reported it to the police and been guilty for the rest of my life. So don't tell me you're responsible. I made the choice." Her voice caught. "*I* did."

"I know that. You *chose* to help my nephew. That's gold." He paced toward her, picked up her left hand. He took her little finger between his thumb and forefinger. "And it would appear helping Miles cost you more than even I imagined."

She extricated her hand from his, and closed her fingers into a fist.

At the time, losing her finger had not felt like a sacrifice. It had felt like survival. But now, she felt almost embarrassed, as if she were trying to guilt him. "I want my life back. I want my reputation back. I want to live without fear. I am charging you for my choice."

He got in her face, nose to nose, compelling her to believe him. "I will pay." He plucked a stylus out of his shirt pocket and signed the letter, then placed the iPad on the coffee table. "To the best of my abilities."

"You're Kennedy McManus. I expect that will be satisfactory." She dangled a tempting tidbit. "And you'll figure out who Jimmy is. You know, Jimmy—the guy who had your nephew kidnapped." She headed out toward the car again.

He followed. "Jimmy. My God, I know a dozen Jims and James and Jimmys, and not one of them has any reason to want to hurt me."

That was naive. "You're successful. For some people, that's enough."

"That's ridiculous."

Even more naive—and very Kennedy. She had read enough about him to know he understood the intricacies of any technological problem, and not much about human nature. She also knew she would get nothing but frustrated by arguing with him. She opened the back door and set the mechanism to hold it open. "Trust me on this. You pissed this guy off big-time, somehow . . . he said you were friends, and you betrayed him."

He followed her out to the car. "Where are you going?"

"The Hartmans told me to prepare the house for guests. I have a cooler filled with the essentials to stock the refrigerator."

"No point. We're not staying here."

Like she hadn't seen this coming. "*I'm* not. I've got an apartment in town."

"I can't guarantee your safety in Virtue Falls. We'll go to California, where I'll put you in the hands of my security team."

Fat chance. "I didn't ask you to guarantee my safety. I'm doing that." She glanced at her watch, then at him. "In two hours, I've got a building inspection to perform, so if you don't want me to load the refrigerator, let me know now. I've got other stuff I can be doing."

He stood there like the proverbial immovable object. "You said you wanted your old life back. Why bother with your business here?"

She placed her hand on the car and leaned toward him. "I like what I've got in Virtue Falls. I like being a vacation home concierge. I like being a construction coordinator. I work for myself, there's a demand for what I do, and over the next few years, I expect to expand the business to include other areas of the coast, probably into Oregon and Northern California. When I say I want my old life back, I mean that I want to be able to use my own name, or if I wish, legally change it to Summer Leigh. I want to travel by plane without being afraid someone's going to spot my phony ID. To see my former friends and not have them scream and run away from the murderous kidnapper. I want a life without fear."

"You say I don't know what we're up against. That's true. But no matter who this Jimmy is, California would be safer for us both."

"Yeah. No one's tried to kill me lately, so I'm not going to California." She smiled without humor. "Now—are you staying? Do you want your refrigerator stocked? Or do you need to return to California to find Jimmy and figure out how to nail him for his crimes?"

"No matter where I am, I can find him."

She maintained eye contact.

He gave up first. "I'm staying."

"Okay." She leaned into the trunk and pulled out the cooler. "Grab those bags of groceries. We'll get you fixed up."

He got the bags and followed her toward the house. "I'll go with you on your inspection."

"You most definitely will not." She went inside, put the cooler on the counter and waited while he came in.

"You can't be alone, and as a man of wealth, I've taken courses to guard against terrorists."

"I've read the books on safety, and I've taken classes, too. Online, but I learned a lot." She shut the door after him, and locked it. "Look. If Jimmy figures out I'm alive, he'll have a sniper kill me. There will be nothing you can do."

Kennedy paced, his fists clenching and unclenching in frustration.

"What's more, having you here increases my danger. He's probably watching you, wondering why you came to Virtue Falls."

"I came without fanfare."

"He's watching you," she repeated. "And he's smart. He knows you're here. Hopefully he thinks you came for vacation or to work out a project. So let's not give him notice I'm alive by having you tag along after me." She headed to the kitchen. "Anyway—I won't be alone. I'm going to be on a construction site with framers and concrete guys and roofers. The basement and foundation are finished, but after the fact, the homeowner decided to install a wine cave. You know? Concrete poured to look like the walls are hollowed out of rock? That takes skill, my friend. It's a big cave for a vacation home—when it's full, it'll hold two thousand bottles. I have to go. With concrete scheduled for this afternoon, the construction supervisor needs approval to complete the pour."

Kennedy didn't bother to fake it. "I have no idea what you just said." She opened the cooler. "I inspect the rebar—you know what rebar is?"

"Those long iron bars they place in concrete to make it strong."

"Right. Reinforcement bars. Before the builder pours the concrete, I inspect the rebar size and spacing to make sure the contractor didn't try to cheap out." She loaded the refrigerator and turned to face Kennedy.

He put the groceries in the cupboards in some proper, methodical order only he understood. "This is a seismic zone. Isn't . . . cheaping out . . . dangerous?"

"Exactly. Lots of earthquakes, some serious, so placement and amount of rebar is imperative. Same with the framing. It's got to be right. The landscape architect has heavy equipment out there moving and removing some big trees, too. When this place is done, it's going to be a great estate." Which gave her a thrill; the Parnham home would be the first that she had guided from foundation to finish.

Kennedy folded the bags and handed them back to her, then glanced at the clock. "If you're leaving in two hours, I need your information now. Start from the beginning, and tell me every detail about that day Miles was kidnapped. Why were you there? What did you see? What did you hear? What made you interfere? How did you escape?"

CHAPTER FORTY-TWO

Kennedy saw Summer's glow of enthusiasm visibly dim.

"Right. Come on, then. Let's get down to business." Turning on her heel, she walked into the living room.

He followed. "I don't understand. Why would a woman who has traveled, seen Paris, Tokyo, and the Taj Mahal, and worked for the fashion world's foremost interior designers . . . why would you enjoy the thought of pouring a concrete cave of fake stone, or be thrilled about studs, trusses, and connections?"

"You don't have to understand. I don't understand what thrill you get from digging around and tracking stuff in people's computers, either. That doesn't mean I think *you're* nuts."

So he'd said something wrong, although he didn't know what. "I didn't say I thought you were nuts. I asked for an explanation."

She seated herself in the easy chair, and folded her hands in her lap. "I suspect any woman who tried to make you understand anything would be doomed to failure. Your understanding is limited to what's logical to your mind, and that is a very limited comprehension."

He intended to point out that what was logical to his mind *was* what was logical, but Summer distracted him by launching into a speech that covered the events of Miles's kidnapping as she had seen them.

As she spoke, Kennedy walked off to the side. Her severe haircut flattered and revealed her features. Resolution, horror, and fear marched one by one across her mobile face. Yet while she remembered the events clearly, she was also able to separate her emotions from them.

That surprised him. He had told her he researched her thoroughly, and he had. He had come to a few conclusions: the Taylor Summers who had saved his nephew was flawed, a woman trapped in a career that did not fully engage her, a woman given to extravagances of emotion that led her into passionate love affairs and, later, broken engagements. The divide between her mind and heart seemed narrow and constantly changing.

Unexpectedly, he had been swept up in the pleasure of seeing her move quickly and with ferocity, of hearing her voice correct him about her name, of realizing that the Taylor Summers he had studied for so long had been burned in the fire, and Summer Leigh had risen like a phoenix in her place. He had taken her into his arms and . . . well. He had kissed her. If she had yielded, he would have had sex with her. Now he had himself back under control. But he still wondered at his own madness, and worry twitched in his mind. What spell had she cast on him?

She interrupted his reverie. "The man in charge of the kidnapping was Seamore 'Dash' Roberts," she said. "Do you know him?"

He stepped into her peripheral vision. "I do. Are you sure?" The Taylor Summers she had been seemed frilly, girly—an interior decorator—definitely not the type of female who followed football.

"Dash was a running back," she said. "This guy ran faster than any person I've ever seen. If he hadn't been intent on shooting me, he would have had me."

"Why would Dash Roberts kidnap my nephew?"

"Because his boss told him to." Serious as a heart attack, she looked at Kennedy. "I don't know if you've heard, but Dash has disappeared. With Jimmy as his employer, it's not smart to fail."

Kennedy had not heard. "You mean you think he's dead?"

"I know he's dead. I saw him killed."

That surprised him. "Killed. You saw him killed?"

"Shot in the head execution-style." Her voice was cool. "Months later . . . on my last day in Wildrose Valley." Gently she cradled her little finger in the palm of her right hand.

"By Jimmy?"

"That's what Dash called him. Jimmy."

Who was this Jimmy? What kind of thug had she—and Kennedy—run afoul of? What kind of man terrified her so thoroughly she always carried a pistol? And wore a leather belt that looked as if it could double as a weapon? "It's all right. Don't jump ahead. We'll get to that part of the story soon." He thought he sounded comforting.

But she shot him an annoyed glance. "I didn't jump ahead. I merely answered your question. But I'll take care not to deviate from the prescribed chronological path again."

She got aggravated about the strangest things.

She described her wild flight up the mountain, her dive into the cave—and stopped.

"Go on," he said.

She opened her mouth. Shut it. Took a breath and tried to speak.

Her voice caught. Her eyes filled with tears, and she shook her head repeatedly. Finally she said, "Sorry." She croaked the word.

"Did Dash follow you?"

She shook her head again.

"Were there bats or blind fish or—"

She put her hand to her throat as if to ease the tension. "Was safe. Stayed . . . overnight. I got out. But dark. Just . . . dark."

He supposed, after her ordeal, she had the right to suffer PTSD. Yet how odd, to describe the violence and fear of the kidnapping, yet balk when describing the safety of a cave. He glanced at his watch. Probably her fear of the dark was a good thing to skip, since they had little more than an hour left. And with Summer, he was already in too deep, entangled in passions and emotions he didn't understand or imagine he would ever experience. "We'll skip the cave. You got out of the cave and went to your car . . ."

She took up the tale with the explosion, her flight into the mountains, and her fear that Dash would find and eliminate her. "But he never found me again. I found him, and he did not see me until . . ." She cradled her mutilated hand again. "I think he saw me right before the bullet entered his brain."

"When was that?"

"Early December."

"You survived in the Sawtooth Mountains from August to December?"

She stared straight ahead. She nodded.

"It's brutal up there." He asked the question that had been bothering him like a stone in his shoe. "*How* did you survive until December?"

"I changed careers." She smiled faintly. "I became a burglar."

Cold crept from his gut and from the old, jagged memories of his childhood. He looked down at his hands, at his sensitive fingertips, so gifted at lifting a wallet or opening a combination-lock safe. "You became a burglar. You . . . stole things."

"Food and survival gear. Yes." She laughed.

Her hilarity made him ill.

She continued, "Actually, I broke into the first house with the intention of going to the law. I mean, after I ate, which was my first priority. But when I turned on the computer and saw I'd been blamed for Miles's kidnapping . . . I was trapped. I didn't know what to do, so I thought I could just . . . stay alive until I figured it out." She shook her head. "No one can stay alive up there in the mountains. Not without shelter, without food, without human contact. The loneliness drove me insane. I was . . . crazy. I . . . hallucinated."

She would not distract him with excuses. "You said the *first* house. You broke into more than one house?"

She nodded.

"It takes skill to be a successful burglar. It takes training."

"You can learn anything off the Internet." She slipped off her jacket. She had broken a sweat. She was nervous. From guilt?

God, he hoped so.

She said, "Breaking into houses was the only way I could survive."

"No, it wasn't the only way."

She faced him, eyes flashing. "What would you have suggested?"

"You could have contacted me."

"*Really?* I could have?" Her voice slashed him with sarcasm. "Because you're a wealthy man, protected by your staff. After a couple of months in Virtue Falls, I did try to call your office, but they wanted to know why I should be allowed to talk to you. I hung up, fast. I thought about e-mailing you directly, through the corporate e-mail account, but I didn't know who would vet your mail, or if Jimmy might have tapped into your account."

Offensive suggestion. "No." Yet this Jimmy had corrupted a decent woman, Helen Allen, with a bribe tailored just for her. So no matter how repugnant the idea, Summer might be right.

"I have information you need," Summer said, "but more than once I was almost killed for involving myself in your business. I *do* learn from my mistakes. I knew better than to give away my location or any personal information, so I held back until I was satisfied I could contact you in a way that was likely to get *your* attention without getting *me* killed or arrested. I wanted guarantees that I will not end up as roadkill in this battle you're waging with your enemy."

"My enemy. Jimmy." Kennedy paced across to the window and looked out at the ocean. "Mortimer would be a better name."

"*What?*" Summer's voice rose.

"Too many Jimmys."

Summer came to her feet, and faced him, chin up, arms straight by her side, fists clenched. "I know the name Jimmy is using now."

Kennedy swung to face her. "What is it?"

"Michael Gracie. Do you know him?"

Kennedy opened his mouth, then shut it. Was this a lie? If so, it was so tremendously huge it bordered on the ludicrous. "I met him a couple of years ago at a stockholders' meeting for a company I was considering as an investment." He watched her face to see if she had second thoughts about her accusation.

"The research I've done on Michael Gracie has been cautious. I didn't dare probe too deeply for fear he had a watch set for his name. But he seems to be what he says he is—a billionaire of wide-ranging government and industry interests." She relished her delivery of the knockout punch. "But his real name is Jimmy and he hates your guts."

"He has no reason to hate my guts."

"Maybe he does. Maybe you just don't remember." Leaning down, she picked up her jacket and pulled it on. "There. That's all the information you need. You don't need me anymore, so you can go back to California to get your team started on the search."

Wait. He might have his doubts about Summer. But he wasn't prepared to leave her. Glibly, he said, "I can't use my people. The person who kidnapped my nephew—Jimmy or Michael Gracie or whoever he is—has already proved a remarkable ability to corrupt good people." God. He now realized he needed to be aware of further treachery, deliberate or inadvertent, in the company. "Such a move could put him on alert. I'll have to do this by myself."

She struggled between the answer she wanted—*go away*—and the fair answer. At last she grudgingly said, "Won't it take you a lot longer?"

"It will take longer," he admitted. "But I am still the best at what I do. I can discover the truth, no matter what the circumstances."

The fact she had hoped he would find a way to take Michael Gracie down, and do it quickly, reassured Kennedy that she truly believed Michael Gracie was their villain. "Cool." She turned to go. "Let me know when you've got this whole business figured out and I'm once more free to go on with my life."

"No!" He moved to intercept her.

She lifted her fists.

He supposed he should be glad she didn't reach for her gun. "I need your help, and I'm not convinced you don't need mine."

He read skepticism in her face. And how was such an insight possible? He was a powerful man, used to having others read his thoughts and anticipate his needs. He did not bother to read theirs. But some kind of compromise was needed, and he guessed it had to be him. "Go to work, but come back. Please. Come back."

Her chest heaved. She stared at Kennedy as if she wanted to shove him, or slap him, or kiss him. "All right. I'll do my inspection, and I'll return here. But remember this—I've lived this long without you. If I die today, you can smugly tell yourself you tried to help me, but I was too stubborn to listen."

"Yet you'll still be dead." Even before he met her, he had cared about her. Now, with his hands hovering inches above her arms, he leaned in. "I need you," he whispered, and kissed her, a lingering kiss that wordlessly begged her to stay.

When he lifted his head, she swallowed. Her eyes fluttered open. She stared at him.

For the most part, his relationships with women were defined by sensible distance, carefully preserved.

No matter what doubts he might have about Summer's character, still he wanted no distance between the two of them.

"We have nothing in common," she said.

"Except bad parents who damned us both to a never-ending relationship hell of trusting and not trusting, wild emotions and rigid control."

She looked stunned.

He felt a little stunned himself. Perhaps insight was a matter of caring enough to bother.

She stepped away, straightened her jacket as if it had been mussed. "You—stay here and work. But be careful. Michael Gracie is a genius when it comes to espionage."

"Just because I don't use my gifts for espionage doesn't mean I don't know how to play that game." He told himself he wanted to reassure her. But actually he wanted to impress her. "I have a way to work the Internet . . . while I hide in plain sight."

"Right." She wet her lips. "Don't go into town."

He did not appreciate the warning. "You'll need my phone number. Let me give you my card."

She plunged her hand into the pocket of her jacket.

They exchanged business cards, like two cautious strangers rather than what they really were—unwillingly passionate and daring partners.

"How long will you be?" He thought he had the right to ask.

She must have thought so, too, for she answered, "Three hours. Four. The construction is only a couple of miles down the road. I'll get some more clothes from my apartment, and bring back a pizza or something."

"I can cook."

She stopped and stared.

"Simple stuff," he admitted.

For the first time, she smiled at him. Really smiled.

He almost staggered with pleasure. "Be careful."

"I always am." She fluttered her fingers and she was gone, driving like a bat out of hell around the circle drive and onto Eagle Road.

He might as well go to work. Not only did he need to discover who Michael Gracie really was, he also needed to distract himself from the worry of knowing that like a naiad, Summer might disappear again and he would spend his life searching for her . . . again.

CHAPTER FORTY-THREE

Summer looked around at the rebar cage that would set the concrete in the walls of the wine cave. "This is going to be cool."

The construction superintendent, Berk Moore, shuddered. "After it's finished, I wouldn't be caught dead in the damned thing. I hate caves. Not enough wine in the world to make me like one."

Summer grinned and kept her own counsel. No use announcing to every person she met that she hated caves, too.

He continued, "I prefer a beer any old day. In fact, if you like, after work I'll buy you dinner and a beer at O'Hara's Pub."

The invitation was so unexpected Summer answered before she thought: "I don't drink." Then she realized—she'd just been asked on a date. Which threw her into a welter of emotions: surprise that she hadn't noticed he was interested, horror because she most definitely wasn't interested, embarrassment at the memory of this morning's scorching kiss with Kennedy, and a swift need to smooth over the relationship with Berk. "But thank you," she added hastily. "I've heard O'Hara's makes a great fish and chips."

"They serve their crab cakes with a cabbage cilantro salad on the side. I never get enough of that stuff." He rubbed the belly that bulged over his belt and went back to business as if nothing personal had ever happened. "So we're cleared for the pour, and I need to get on the framers."

"About every third stud needs more nails."

"It's that lazy bastard Peter Paxton. I don't know why I keep him. I always have to send him back to fix his screw-ups."

"How many kids has he got?" Summer asked shrewdly.

"Too many." Berk led the way out of the hole into the basement, and up the stairs to the first level.

They stepped out of what would be the back door and surveyed the site.

It was, as Summer had told Kennedy, going to be a great estate. The three-storied skeleton of a house perched on a precipice overlooking the Pacific Ocean. On the north end, a fanciful round tower rose a story above the rest. Everywhere on the lot, Summer heard the boom of the waves and knew, if she looked down from the cliff, she would see giant rocks sticking up like granite teeth, with birds, and seals, and sea lions. "Have you heard from Tony Parnham? He's going to be in town, and I figured he'd want to see the progress."

"He's going to be in town? Shit! I haven't heard a word. I'll bet he's going to drop in just like that." Berk shook his head in disgust. "Hey, listen, thanks for the heads-up. It helps."

"No problem. I'm surprised he didn't call. He seems like a nice guy."

"Some homeowners are weird like that. They think they're going to show up and catch me sitting in my Barcalounger, drinking a beer."

Five acres of woods surrounded the house, and as Summer watched, a huge excavator puttered across the lot, its tracks moving ponderously toward the fringe of cedars on the east side of the lot. "What's he doing?" she asked.

Berk gave the John Deere a cursory glance. "I don't know. Taking out those trees, I guess."

Summer frowned. "Tony Parnham wanted the cedars."

"Cedars," Berk said scornfully. "Talk about allergy makers."

She looked at him.

"But you're right," he said hastily. "Parnham is paying for them, and if he wants them left in place, they'll stay in place. Still, that's Jack Aarestad in the cab. He's good. We're lucky to get him. He just got out of prison."

"Lucky?"

"Nothing to worry about," Berk assured her. "Unless you were married to him. His ex wanted everything. Jack got belligerent. She got a restraining order. He got drunk, took a baseball bat and smashed the windows in their house."

Summer was horrified. "Was he trying to hurt her?"

"He said he was trying to destroy the value of their home so she wouldn't get much when they sold it. Didn't work out too good for him. He spent a few months in the can. Now he owes *much* money to the ex, damages and settlement, so he'll work any hours I ask." Berk watched the excavator bucket bite into the ground in front of the cedars. "You got the landscaping plans?"

"Here." She waved her iPad.

"Good. Let's check them out and . . . wait. Hear that?" He cocked his head and turned it toward the road. "We got done with the inspection barely in time."

The first concrete truck rumbled up the drive and headed toward the wine cave.

Berk smacked Summer on the arm. "They're early! Let me know what you find out about the trees. I'll talk to Jack when I get done with this." He took off at a jog toward the truck and the wine cave.

"But . . ." But when Berk got done with the pour, it would be far too late for the cedars.

Summer shivered. The day was not getting warmer; it had started out at fifty-two degrees and stuck there, with a raw breeze and a gray overcast sky. If she hadn't been in such a hurry to get away from Kennedy, she would have borrowed a coat from the Hartmans' stash. She really ought to text him to see if he'd made any progress . . . But no. She'd see him soon enough, and it rankled that he lectured her about how she could have survived more efficiently. He'd never looked death in the face, or he wouldn't have the guts to be so judgmental.

Of course, she was pretty damned sure Kennedy McManus would be judgmental no matter what the circumstances.

She shouldn't care.

But she did.

She adjusted her hard hat and headed for the GTO, parked on the edge of the driveway with two pickups, the roofer's new Ford 350, and a Dodge Ram 1500. She unlocked her door, climbed into the driver's seat, and started the engine. The heater blew cold air across her feet. "Warm up," she muttered. "Come on, warm up."

But if Kennedy was such a genius, he might have this Michael Gracie mystery wrapped up by the time she got back, and they could go their separate ways and never see each other again and good riddance to . . . well, Kennedy *and* what probably would have been some great sex.

She glanced at the excavator.

In the cab, Jack was staring at a piece of paper he held in his hand. His hand looked like it was shaking. Was the excavator vibrating?

She found the landscape plans on her iPad, but the screen was too small to see the details, and when she expanded the view, she lost the landmarks around the edge of the property. She got out, popped the trunk, and dragged out the roll of blueprints.

Jack wasn't digging at the roots of the cedars anymore. He was moving the excavator toward the edge of the clearing, toward a massive bigleaf maple. Bigleaf maples were tall, with thick, spreading branches; they crowded out the evergreens and made a mess when they shed their leaves, so the tree probably *was* scheduled to come out. Or not. Tony Parnham lived in the desert around L.A., and was fanatically fond of the greenery that covered the Washington coast.

She could see the marks where Jack had already been excavating the roots of the maple. All it needed was a good solid push with the bucket and it would fall backward into the forest.

She hopped back into the driver's seat. The heater was warming up, yay, and her poor frozen feet began to thaw. She flexed her hands, then unrolled the landscape plans against the steering wheel. Yeah, the bigleaf maple was supposed to go. But the line of cedars was most definitely not.

She looked up and made eye contact with the guy in the excavator. Maybe she could talk directly to Jack. She raised her hand and waved.

He stared at her forbiddingly.

She broke eye contact. She looked back at the blueprints and pretended to study them. The scars from that divorce must have turned him into one of those men who held a grudge against all women. She'd better leave the discussion about the landscaping to Berk.

From the house, she heard the crew shouting. She looked up and saw the framers on the third floor waving their arms, pointing at her, then beyond, yelling as loud as they could.

She looked to see what they were having a fit about.

Jack had moved the excavator into position behind the maple, stuck the bucket into the back of the trunk, and was pushing the tree—right at her.

CHAPTER FORTY-FOUR

The tree descended slowly, the roots ripping out of the ground. Then gravity took over and it fell faster. And faster.

For one long, foolish second, Summer gaped. Then she reacted. She flung the plans aside. She slammed the car into gear, popped the clutch, and peeled out, spitting gravel behind her. She fishtailed, straightened out, roared along for twenty feet.

She was out. She was safe!

Then one branch of the tree slammed down on the trunk, lifting the front wheels off the ground. Summer bounced off the roof. The Judge got traction and leaped forward. She came down on the steering wheel, racked her ribs, then thumped back into the driver's seat. Somehow, through the bucking bronco of a ride, she managed to cling to the wheel, so as soon as her foot made contact with the accelerator, she floored it again. The tree let her go with a reluctant screech of wood against metal. She blasted forward another twenty feet, and stopped.

The tree was down—the trunk had smashed the cabs on the two pickups that had been parked beside her. She looked to the side. Jack was climbing off the excavator. As she watched, he hopped to the ground, took one look at her, saw her staring. He lifted his hand and took a menacing step toward her.

Her breath locked in her throat.

Then he looked beyond her car. His eyes widened. He turned tail and ran into the woods.

She sat shaking in shock and horror. She was safe now. Safe.

The guys at the site raced toward her, still shouting, but she couldn't hear them for the ringing in her ears.

Two workers went past, full-tilt boogie, roaring with rage.

Oh, yeah. They owned the pickups.

Berk ripped open her door. He shouted at her, she figured some question about her health.

"I'm okay." She wasn't dead, she meant. She took off her hard hat. "But if I hadn't been wearing this . . ."

Berk ducked down and looked in the car.

She heard him clearly enough this time.

"Oh, my God," he said. "You dented the roof."

Stupidly, she repeated, "I . . . dented the roof?"

"Look at it! What a heartbreak. Add that to the damage to the exterior . . ." Something about the way she stared must have penetrated his grief over the car. "You sure you're okay? You look sort of green."

My head hurts. My neck hurts. My hands hurt. The steering wheel mashed my boobs up around my throat. "Scared me," she said, and climbed out of the car.

One of the construction guys said, "No shit it scared you. But you didn't sit around. That was the fanciest driving I've ever seen. Lady, you rock."

Obviously, she'd won his eternal admiration. She stood on shaky legs and let the damp, chilly air wash over her hot cheeks.

"Listen." Berk gently took her arm. "I don't want you to look. You'll just be upset."

At the pity in his voice, her knees gave way. She leaned against the car and tried to brace herself for more bad news. "Now what?"

"The branch pretty much totaled the trunk of your car."

"The trunk?" Red dots danced before her eyes. She thought she was going to faint.

"I know," he said. "I know. It's a crime what that bastard did to this fine piece of machinery. But listen, my cousin runs a body shop in Aberdeen. He's good. Really good. He'll fix the Judge. None of this Bondo crap. He'll hammer out the dents and paint it and make it as good as new."

She breathed deeply, tried to keep herself from pitching face-first onto the gravel.

Berk leaned closer. "This car is so famous up and down the coast . . . he would almost work on it for free. Don't tell him I said that, just keep it in mind when you take it in."

She numbly nodded.

"That's the best I can do for you. Now, excuse me. I have to see if I can figure out what happened to Jack. The little asshole." Berk walked away saying, "You give the guy a chance, and what does he do? He destroys a classic car."

She leaned against the hood. The cool of the metal soaked through to her skin. She supposed she *should* go look at the trunk to see if the car was still drivable. She wished she could collect her thoughts enough to understand what had happened, because right now, she couldn't figure out why . . . why this had happened . . . to her.

The men milled around.

"What was Jack thinking?"

"He ran away."

"No shit he ran away. Did you see Orrie and Chuck? They were carrying their hammers when they went after him."

"Drunk."

"Drugs."

"Divorce."

"But why try to kill *her*?" Accompanied by a nod of the head at Summer.

That was what snapped Summer out of her stupor.

Because that truth she hadn't quite faced.

Jack had tried to kill her. He had looked right at her, seen her, then deliberately aimed a tree at her.

In the months since she'd come to Virtue Falls, she'd begun to relax her vigilance. She was cautious, yes, but no longer paranoid about everything and everybody. But now, someone *had* tried to kill her. Tried in the weirdest way, but tried—and almost succeeded.

Michael. Gracie.

No. No. He couldn't have found her at the same time as Kennedy McManus. Unless he followed Kennedy. Unless he was smarter than Kennedy.

Gently, she shook her head to clear it, then as it throbbed, she held it in her hands. When she looked around again, she was alone.

The construction crew were over looking at the downed tree, at the wrecked pickups. One or two of them were headed back to work. It wasn't that they didn't care. But they were used to her being one of the guys. When she said she was okay, they believed her.

She wasn't okay. She was scared. She was in shock.

Why not fire a bullet?

She remembered what Michael Gracie had said about hurting Kennedy: *That's too easy. I'm going to destroy his family, his friends, his business, everything he's fought for and loves.*

Had Michael decided to hurt her in the same way?

Orrie had chased Jack into the forest.

Chuck was headed back toward her. When he met her, he said, "The lousy little coward pissed himself and ran."

"I know." Jack probably wouldn't stop until he got to Canada. But did he take the paper he'd been reading?

She shook off her pain and terror, and limped toward the excavator. She climbed up on the track and looked inside the cab. The space stunk like a dirty ashtray; the floor was awash with crumpled coffee cups. In the narrow space beside the seat was a piece of white paper, twisted into a hard, stained spiral. Leaning in, she pulled it out and with shaking hands, she spread it out.

Her photo stared back at her, taken recently in Virtue Falls.

Underneath it was printed two words: *Summer Leigh.*

CHAPTER FORTY-FIVE

"I can't believe the construction crew was dumb enough to believe you were okay." Kateri paced across her tiny living room.

"The guys saw no blood, I said I was okay, ergo . . ." Summer shrugged, and winced.

"Men are simple creatures," Kateri said.

In unison, the women nodded: Summer, sitting in a straight-back kitchen chair, no top, only her bra, and Dr. Watchman, who was examining Summer's ribs, back, and neck. And of course Lacey, who watched them with a worried brow.

As Dr. Watchman poked her ribs, Summer held herself very still. "The construction crew cheered when my car started and I was able to drive it off the site. It was the car they were concerned about."

Kateri rubbed at her hip, and paced to the window. "How did you keep the trunk closed?"

"They hooked it with bungee cords."

Even Lacey snorted.

At four o'clock, the clouds hid any hint of sun, the wind whipped in from the ocean, and the people on the streets kept their heads down. That first winter storm was getting closer; every joint in Kateri's body ached, even the artificial joints. Which made no sense—artificial joints had no nerves—but the doctors were philosophical, speaking of phantom pain and the mind playing tricks.

Yeah, yeah. Kateri said, "I wish Rainbow was back."

"So do I," Summer said. At Dr. Watchman's unspoken urging, Summer tilted her head to one side, then to the other. "I'm worried about her."

"Pfft." Kateri waved away Summer's concern. "Don't worry about Rainbow. She's capable like nobody I've ever met, and telling her that she could get hurt alone out in the forest just makes her belligerent."

Dr. Watchman hummed in agreement.

"But Rainbow hears everything that goes on in this town, and she'd know why we've had two 'accidents'"—Kateri used air quotes—"that harmed two women within two weeks."

Dr. Watchman seldom spoke, but when she did, it was worth listening to. She spoke now. "Two women who are Summer—or look like Summer."

Summer stiffened.

Kateri stopped pacing.

Dr. Watchman ran her fingers firmly up Summer's spine. "What? That never occurred to any of you?"

"No, but if someone is after Summer, that is not good, either." Kateri stared at Summer, and inevitably her gaze came to rest on her little finger.

Dr. Watchman massaged Summer's stiff shoulders. "No concussion. You'd know if you had broken bones, but you've got a lot of bruising. You're going to feel worse tomorrow. Take some over-the-counter pain pills, apply ice and heat alternately. A skilled massage would help the stiffness. Call Dr. Frownfelter if you get dizzy or have any abdominal pain. Promise me you'll do that. Promise."

"All right. I promise," Summer muttered, and got to her feet. "I'm staying out at the Hartmans' place, keeping an eye on it. I don't have to tell everybody here to be careful, huh?"

Kateri and Lacey followed Summer out the front door and onto the tiny, low porch. Kateri pulled the door shut to give them a measure of privacy. "That guy you're afraid of? Michael Gracie? He's found you."

Summer stood round-eyed and horrified. "How do you know his name?"

"When you got to Virtue Falls and you were so sick, you shrieked his name in terror."

"Oh, God." Summer knelt and fondled Lacey's ears. "I shouldn't have come to you, but I—"

"Of course you should come to me. I've already been dead once, drowned and eaten by the Frog God. How much worse could it get?"

Summer smiled as if she found the humor painfully amusing. "I wasn't responsible the first time you died."

"If some human guy tries to kill me, he's responsible. Anyway"—Kateri pointed one finger toward the Pacific—"I've been through so much pain it has lost its mystique. I don't enjoy it, but I can survive it. Don't you feel that way? That you've already been through such an ordeal, you can face anything now?" Kateri thought that of all the people in her life, only Summer would understand.

"Yes. Yes, I do. But it's also why I train and watch and anticipate." Summer gave Lacey one last scratch under the chin, then used the iron railing to lever herself to her feet.

Lacey took her place at the edge of the top step and surveyed the street.

Kateri realized that Summer stood on the cusp of a change, a change she had planned since the day she stood up in Kateri's living room, declared she refused to quiver inside any longer, and she went out to greet Virtue Falls.

Summer watched Kateri bend and rub her knee. "You're in bad shape today."

Kateri rocked her hand back and forth. "Kind of."

"What's the doctor say?"

"That my recovery has been miraculous, there are bound to be setbacks, and take two aspirin and call him in the morning."

"He didn't really say the part about the aspirin, did he?" Summer asked.

"No, he wants me to take pain pills, the heavy-duty stuff, the stuff I could sell on the streets. And sometimes I do take them, but I can't stand the thought of growing dependent on them."

"Oh, my dear." Gingerly, Summer enfolded Kateri in a hug. "I think I have problems, then you make me realize at least I have the possibility of an out."

"Maybe so, but you're not *out* yet."

"I can't hide from *him*." From her enemy, Summer meant. From Michael Gracie. "He's not the Frog God, but he's crafty and cruel. He's handsome and compelling. So handsome. So . . . he's fascinating. Riveting. Everywhere he goes, he leaves broken bodies and shattered souls."

"Except for the handsome part, he *sounds* like the Frog God." Kateri didn't like the way Summer talked about him, as if he enthralled her.

"Now that he knows where I am, he won't let me out of his sight." Summer gripped the black iron railing with both hands, and her eyes glowed when she spoke of him, glowed with fear or infatuation. Or both.

"You escaped before."

"Only because he didn't know I was there and what I'd seen." Summer stuck her hands in her pockets and wrapped the jacket tightly around her middle. "Anyway, I survived today, and I plan to survive tomorrow." She grinned, as if the act of living was an amusement not to be trusted. "Are you going to the Halloween party?"

Kateri grimaced. "No. Margaret Smith invited the Coasties."

"Sure. A bunch of virile young military men will liven it up. I know you don't want to see Landlubber, but don't you want to see the rest of the men?" Summer peered at Kateri through the deepening gloom. "See Luis Sanchez?"

Kateri wanted to kick the railing. She would have, too, but she didn't break bones on purpose. "Does everybody in town know I've got a thing for Luis?"

Summer hesitated.

Kateri knew what that meant, and she did kick the railing. But softly. "Damn it!"

"You kissed him on the street."

"I wondered if that would come back to bite me on the butt."

"I don't know that everyone believes it. I mean, I've heard people gossip about how dedicated he was to you after your accident, but no one seems to think that—" Summer stopped.

"No one seems to think that a handsome, fit guy would bother to want crippled little ol' me." Kateri understood. Oh, boy, did she. "That's the problem. Not too long ago, I could have walked into that party and *dominated*. I was tall, smart, tough, and beautiful. Now, if I go, most people will glance at me and look away. People who do talk to me will either be old friends or people who pride themselves on winning their politically correct points."

Summer, God bless her, didn't deny it. "But to forgo the food, the music, the spectacle, because of your vanity—that's dumb."

Stung, Kateri said, "Yeah, but vanity's all I've got." She sighed. "He's got a girlfriend."

"Luis's got a girlfriend? You're kidding! He loves *you*." Summer's honest astonishment salved the wound a bit.

"A man has needs. So do you want to sell our party tickets to Mrs. Branyon and use the proceeds to go on vacation? Mexico? Hawaii? Bella Terra? Tuscany?"

"Sadly, my dear friend, that is the best offer I've had all year." Summer gave Lacey one last pet and headed for her car. A few steps away, she turned. "There's only one problem."

"What's that?"

"Getting her hands on our tickets would make Mrs. Branyon happy."

Kateri's pleasure deflated like a busted balloon. "That sucks."

For five days, Rainbow had camped out, keeping an eye on the old, abandoned World War II airport. The weather was getting progressively cooler, the wind livelier. She had decided that tomorrow morning she would give up, knock down her tent, and head back to Virtue Falls. She'd seen enough suspicious stuff to give a report to Garik Jacobsen, and she knew he would take action.

Then, right after sunset, a truck rattled down the road, bringing two men dressed in black coveralls who headed inside the ramshackle old building and shut the door behind them.

Rainbow figured she was too tall to flit, but she could dash, and she did, from tree to tree, getting close enough to see inside the windows while one man talked into a radio and the other fiddled with some switches.

Across the treetops, she heard the roar of a plane.

The guy flipped the switches, and long rows of lights illuminated the edges of the runway. The jet came down steep and fast, landing lights glaring. It landed hard, thrust reversers engaged before touchdown, then slowed swiftly, taxied up to the small building, and shut down the engines.

The man who had been talking on the radio walked up to the side of the plane as the stair door opened.

A smooth, handsome, well-dressed gentleman and two pilots descended and headed toward the building.

Rainbow lost sight of the gentleman. Then she heard a sound off to the right, swung around, and saw a man-shape silhouetted against the lights, taking aim at her.

She flung herself to the ground.

A bullet whistled past.

Then she was up and running, dashing, flitting, and all round getting the hell out of there.

It looked like her hunch about the airport had panned out.

CHAPTER FORTY-SIX

Summer parked the Judge in the Hartmans' driveway and gathered the cardboard Chinese food containers out of the passenger seat.

She didn't really want to go in. She was bruised and sore, she didn't want to explain what had happened today, and worse, she felt guilty for being late, like she was a straying wife who'd stopped at the bar for a drink after work. This morning, she had stormed out of here in righteous indignation. Kennedy had been an asshole who doubted her integrity.

Tonight, she was feeling sorry for not feeding him dinner on time. And she knew he could cook.

She was so screwed up.

No. *Women* were so screwed up.

Yes. Blame it on the whole gender rather than on herself. It wasn't fair, but it made her feel better.

Sluggishly, she climbed out. She wouldn't even have come back, but she could see him showing up in town, searching out her apartment, outing himself to the population of Virtue Falls. For the most part, she wished he would go back to California to do his research. She didn't know why he wouldn't, unless he figured he was going to convince her to do the horizontal tango.

Man, did he have the wrong girl tonight.

The back door flung open.

She swiveled on her heel.

Light from inside the utility room flooded the drive, and there he was, Kennedy McManus, a perfect silhouette of a perfect man: broad shoulders, narrow hips, long legs, big hands he used with the skill of a concert pianist. "Need help?" he called.

"No! I'll get this." She did *not* want him to see her car. She suspected he would say stuff like, *I told you so.* After the day she'd had, she didn't need that. Even if it was true.

But he ran down the steps, then like a husband of long-standing, he leaned in and kissed her.

She had never had a husband of any kind, but if that deliberate, hot, lingering kiss was any indication of what married life was like, she had been missing a lot. If she hadn't been creaking like an old woman, she would throw the Chinese food on the ground, flung herself at him, and have used him until he made her forget her fear and her pain. But she *was* creaking.

Gradually he pulled away. He looked down at her. He used his thumb to wipe her lower lip, and smiled. In an absentminded tone, he said, "It's incredible how pretty you are."

Pretty? With no makeup to start with, a few tear stains, and a thorough battering today? The light out here must be bad. Or good, depending on how she looked at it.

He took three of the containers. "Wait until I tell you what I've found out about Michael Gracie." He headed toward the house.

Kennedy McManus had a reputation as having a one-track mind, and now she believed it. He hadn't noticed the car at all—the first male who hadn't freaked out about the damage. Points to him.

She shook the kinks out of her legs and followed. "What?"

"Nothing." He held the door for her. "His background is impeccable. Everything he says about himself is true."

She bristled as she walked into the house. "Except that I know his name is Jimmy." Was Kennedy doubting her?

"Everything is so smooth. Normal people can be caught in self-serving lies. They spin their stories to prove they're not to blame in a dispute, not at fault during an accident, . . . to make themselves look better. Everything Michael Gracie says about his flawless self appears to be absolutely, positively the truth." They headed into the kitchen. "Which makes me doubt every word."

She relaxed. "That is pretty shady, isn't it?"

"Almost impossible." Kennedy put down the containers and started opening them. "What did you get?"

"I don't know what you like, so I got a little of everything. I figured there would be too much, but you could have it for lunch to-morrow."

"I like it all, and this ocean air gives me an appetite. When I got tired of looking at the computer, I took a run on the beach."

Immediately her brain stripped him down to his shorts and sent him sprinting across the sand, the waves crashing behind him, seagulls sailing overhead, as the sun set and cast a golden glow over his rippling chest. If her business didn't pan out, she could have a career creating commercials for orange juice or insurance or dog food. Or female erectile dysfunction . . . too bad that didn't exist.

She cleared her throat. "Did you get a lot accomplished?"

"Accomplished? No." He got out plates and silverware, and loaded them and the food boxes on a tray. In one day, he'd certainly made himself at home.

He said, "I brought up Michael's photograph and then compared every James/Jim/Jimmy in my corporation. I started about a year ago, the time of the kidnapping, and worked backward. I included men who have moved on." Kennedy headed for the living room.

She trailed behind. Again.

"Did you know that during the years my company has been in operation, there have been fifty-two men who have some variation of James in their names? And two women." He put the tray on the coffee table and turned to Summer. "Should I run the women?"

"You mean you think Michael Gracie could be a transsexual?" Remembering him and his almost visible sexual aura, she laughed. "No. He is most definitely a man, born with package in place."

Kennedy scrutinized her as if seeing something he did not like.

In the brief time she'd known him, he'd done that too often. She met his gaze, and smiled tightly. "He's unself-consciously male, and attractive."

"Got it. Not gay, not a transsexual." Kennedy waved her into the armchair and seated himself on the closest corner of the couch. "When I expand the search to include men I've ever worked with in any corporation who have the names of James, it gets exponentially larger and more difficult."

She browsed through the containers, found the pork fried rice and the black pepper beef, and filled her plate. "Sounds boring."

"It is like strolling through a garden of businessmen in white shirts and dark suits, and looking to see which one is different. The conclusion—none of them are. It's made me rethink my business attire."

She laughed out loud.

He looked surprised, then pleased. Apparently he didn't make people laugh often. "After I got done with that, I set up a facial recognition program to compare the faces. It's running now, and should pick up our man."

"Should?"

"If Jimmy has had enough plastic surgery, it's possible that the parameters for the facial recognition software need to be tightened." Kennedy didn't pay attention to what was in the containers, he just loaded up and used his chopsticks to attack the food. "This is good," he said in surprise.

"Try the mu shu shrimp," she advised. "But only if you like garlic."

He looked right at her. "Do you?"

"Love it."

"Then I'll eat it."

He was telling her . . . they were on a date. Emotions. Relationships. She wasn't ready for all that. "So—why don't you make the parameters tighter anyway?"

"The search takes longer, and to my mind, it seems unlikely that any man—any person—would go to such extremes."

"Not to fool you, but maybe for other reasons." She remembered Michael Gracie so clearly, his form, his grace, his mobile features, his eyes glowing with an inner light. When she first caught a glimpse of him, she thought he looked like a god. Then she saw him shoot Dash, and realized he was more like Lucifer, the dark angel. She feared him for his power, his intelligence. She sank back in her chair, and flinched at the bruising in her ribs. "I think he's as smart as you are."

"It's possible. Looking at the complete and brilliant cover-up of his past, I would say even probable." Kennedy put down his plate. Lifting Summer's feet from the ottoman, he sat and placed them in his lap. He started a slow massage, thumbs in her arches, then running to her heels and toes, each spot receiving its own massage.

The sensation was so intimate, the silence so intense, she wanted to object. Then, as she relaxed into the massage . . . she didn't want to object.

His voice was hushed and gentle. "You're moving with caution, and your car is crunched. Tell me what happened today."

CHAPTER FORTY-SEVEN

Kennedy had let Summer think that she could pick her time to tell him about the tree and the car and her injuries and who and why and what were they going to do. He'd eaten with her, talked to her, listened to her, soothed her into a state of relaxation, and then dropped the bomb right in her lap.

She wanted to squirm in her chair. But squirming would hurt too much. "Someone felled a tree . . . on me."

Kennedy's expression did not change. "On purpose?"

"The guy leaped out of his excavator and started running, and to the best of my knowledge, he hasn't stopped yet." To say it out loud made it so real. "The only explanation is that Michael Gracie has found me."

"Have you been to the doctor?"

"She suggested ice and heat, pain relievers, and a massage." It seemed unwise to mention that Dr. Watchman was a veterinarian. "But aspirin is all I'll take. *He* will not come at me when I'm drugged and helpless. And I won't go in for a massage." *Except for the one you're doing on my feet . . . don't stop.*

"Why not?"

"I'm not going to lay facedown on a table, naked and vulnerable."

"No. I wouldn't like you to do that, either." He stood up and went into the kitchen.

She dug the paper with her photo out of her bag.

He came back with a Costco-sized bottle of pain reliever and an ice bag wrapped in a towel. "Where do you need the ice?"

"My ribs." She took it from him and started to slip it under her shirt.

But he seated himself on the ottoman, unbuttoned her shirt and examined the purpling bruises. He set his jaw, but placed the ice bag gently on the worst of the marks, handed her two aspirin and a bottle of water, and asked, "What do you have there?"

She gave him the paper. "I found this in the cab of the excavator."

"He tried to clumsily kill you." Kennedy's face looked as it did in his off-putting online photos: distant, unemotional, analytical.

At this moment, having that formidable logic working for her was a comfort. But at the same time, it was hard to reconcile the passionate lover with the rational brainiac. "All this time, I have feared a sniper's bullet." She took the aspirin. "I've thought that every moment on earth could be my last. Why . . . why this? Why the hit-and-run?"

"The hit-and-run?"

What was *she* thinking, to mention Mrs. Dvorkin's accident? "I suspect he hired someone to run over me last week, someone who looked like me. But Michael Gracie is an efficient killer. So what is he thinking?"

"Without knowing who he really is, I can't successfully speculate on his motivations." She could see Kennedy's mind at work, assessing, organizing, deciding. "Give me the rest of the information. How did you end up seeing Gracie murder someone?"

Her head hurt, and she rubbed her temples with her fingers. "In the Sawtooths, winter was setting in, and breaking into houses wasn't cutting it. But I lucked out. I showed up at a party, and I got a job. I worked for Georg's, the catering firm in Sun Valley."

"Doing what?"

"Waitstaff. Kitchen staff. He paid me, too. Cash. But you know what? When you're living in a tent in the mountains, there's nowhere to spend the money. What he gave me that I needed was the leftovers. If not for Georg, I wouldn't be alive." She laughed a little. "He thought I was an abused wife. He was going to drive me down to the women's shelter, and I was going to go. I thought I could move from that position to somehow contact you and get back to reality. Man, did that plan fall apart."

"You met Michael Gracie."

"Right. I worked a party at his house. And I saw Dash. He was palling around with Mr. Gracie, and I thought . . . I thought Dash was going to kill him."

"And you cared?"

She had cared. She had thought she saw something great and noble in Michael Gracie. In a few brief moments of conversation, she had been captivated by his charisma. When she thought of him, she was afraid, but also . . . something stirred in her, some emotion that buzzed with delight at the memory of his face and his voice. She looked down and moved the ice bag to a different bruise. "I didn't want to see him dead."

"Why would you care so much about a stranger?"

Nothing on earth could make her tell this cool-eyed man about her hallucination of her father, his prophecy that she would die if she didn't seize her opportunity and his urging her to do so. She could only imagine what Kennedy would say about *that*. Anyway, that wasn't the only reason she had found herself in that wine cellar. "Don't we all have some kind of obligation to do what we can to save a life, even a stranger's life?"

"You believed you were saving Michael Gracie." Kennedy picked up her hand and held it before her eyes, so she was forced to look at her mutilated finger.

"I was an idiot. He shot Dash in the head. I saw it. I was trapped. I had to cut off my finger to escape." There. She had said it.

He hesitated as if he really would like to spend the evening harping on her imprudence. "Give me the details."

She told Kennedy everything she could remember from the moment she had followed Dash and Michael Gracie down to the wine cellar to stowing away in the body locker in the airplane. "He knew what he was doing. He has a system set in place to dispose of the bodies. Yet he has a spotless record. He's after you. He's after your family." She grasped Kennedy's fingertips. "Get him, or we will all die."

Kennedy turned his downturned hand and held her palm to palm. "Please go to California."

"It's too late for that." She leaned back wearily. "He's found me, and the only way I'm going to get away is to take him out. You have to figure out who he is, what he does, and how to pin these crimes on him."

"I have the resources to protect you in California."

She shook her head. "If I believed that, I would go. But I don't, and if he's going to kill me, I want it to be here. Virtue Falls took me in."

"You'll endanger your friends."

"He won't make another mistake. Any other murder attempts will be more precise." It was up to her now to inspect every event and every occasion and weigh the percentages that Michael Gracie had engineered a trap . . . and a killing.

Standing, Kennedy paced across to the desk and his computer.

She watched him, then closed her eyes. Her head hurt. Her body hurt. She was tired: tired of being afraid, tired of hiding, but mostly just tired. She wanted to go to bed and sleep, and wake up to sunshine and singing birds and a world that looked like a Disney movie.

She must have drifted off, because she started when Kennedy sat down on the ottoman again. She opened her eyes and looked at him. He wasn't as noble as a Disney prince, but right now, he looked pretty good. She smiled.

He didn't. "I just now looked up your caterer. I thought he might be a source of information."

"You don't want to involve him. He could get hurt."

"He disappeared about two weeks ago."

She started feeling sick.

"In Ketchum, Idaho, a dog found a human thigh bone and brought it home. Yesterday, they found what was left of the remains, not much, apparently, but his hands were the hands of a chef."

She remembered. "Georg was missing a fingertip."

"Law enforcement is testing the DNA, but his assistant in the business has IDed the body as Georg."

CHAPTER FORTY-EIGHT

To her horror, Summer burst into tears.

Kennedy leaped into action—picked her up, put her in his lap, and sat down in the chair. He handed her his clean white handkerchief, which he just happened to have in his jeans pocket—who even carried a handkerchief anymore?—hugged her, and rubbed her back.

She tried to speak, to tell him that she never did this. But every time she opened her mouth, she sobbed so loudly she was embarrassed. Finally, she crunched herself into a little ball, grabbed his shirt in her fists, and bawled like a newborn calf. Her grief about Georg, her fear, her sense that she was trapped in a never-ending nightmare . . . it all came pouring out in unrestrained emotion that, despite her attempts at control, lasted far too long. And worse, oh, God, the very worst thing was—she had to blow her nose. On his handkerchief. Loudly.

He simply hugged her.

When she gradually hiccupped to a stop, she didn't dare lift her head. Because like Kateri, she was vain enough not to want to display herself when her face was as red and swollen as a birthday balloon.

"I'm sorry." She spoke into his shirt.

"Don't cry much?" he deduced.

"No." She sniffled.

"You needed to."

Okay, that was unfair. He was caring and civil about her snotting all over his shoulder? If he kept up the cherishing, he'd make her fall in love with him.

Red and swollen or no red and swollen, the thought brought her head up. She stared at him in shock.

He stared back. "What?"

"I should leave."

"No, you shouldn't. You should stay here and sleep with me."

"I can't have sex."

He smiled, his mouth half-quirking as if he was amused. *About no sex.* "Despite the rumors of my prowess, I can abstain. But don't tell anybody. I've worked hard to establish those rumors."

He had a sense of humor. *About no sex.* Who was this guy? "Okay," she said faintly.

He helped her to her feet. "I made the bed in the master bedroom. There's a gas fireplace in there. I thought we would light it." He put his arm around her and helped her walk. "I'm from California, you know. We grab any chance to light a fireplace."

He made the bed. He wanted to light the fireplace. Next he would say he liked to cuddle. "Have you been reading one of those books on the right thing to say to a woman?"

He drew himself up, magnificently insulted. *"Me?"*

"Right. Sorry." She smiled as she limped into the bedroom.

Dr. Watchman was right.

The next morning, Summer woke to the smell of coffee and the knowledge that when she tried to get out of bed, it was going to suck.

It did. Every joint in her body ached. She hobbled into the shower and let hot water pound on her back and shoulders. It helped. Some.

Her ribs were marvelous shades of purple. Any eggplant would be proud to be her. Yet . . . she'd enjoyed a good night's sleep. She'd had to wake up every time she turned over, but Kennedy was there, helping her, holding her. Even better, he always had an erection, which reassured her that he deeply felt the no-sex deprivation. She needed that reassurance even more than she needed breakfast and aspirin.

She pulled on her workout clothes and padded barefoot out into the living room, to find Kennedy staring evilly at his monitor.

He barely glanced at her. "I've run through my whole life, every Jimmy I've ever met. No matches. I'm going to have to tighten the parameters."

"How long will that take?"

"Two days, give or take. Once I've set up the program, I'll know for sure."

"I'm sorry." She headed into the kitchen and poured herself a cup of coffee. "Do you want me to freshen your cup?"

No answer.

She walked out with the coffeepot in her hand. "Kennedy?"

He didn't notice her. "I've got two ways to go at this, and neither is working. I'm looking for a Jimmy I know. And I'm researching Michael Gracie. I'm good at finding the loose thread in a cover story, and then it can be unraveled. But with Gracie, I cannot locate where the truth begins and the lie ends."

She went back into the kitchen, set the pot on the burner, and returned. "Did you find his family?"

"He claims to have been orphaned as a child and raised in Chicago by wealthy, elderly, now-deceased relatives who shielded him from the public eye. It's easy to fake a cultured background when there's no one to contradict you."

Impulsively, she said, "You never bothered to create a cultured background for yourself."

Kennedy's mouth curled unpleasantly. "No. I come from a family of thieves and scam artists."

She knew that. His unregistered birth, his felon parents, his childhood edged with crime, were no secret. She had discovered the details in a few brief moments on the Internet. But a single glance at his face, frozen with distaste, showed her the truth. He hated his past.

She pulled up a chair facing him, and sat. "So it's possible for you to erase all trace of your past, but you never did it?"

"It's not possible to erase all trace. Somewhere someone will know something. Somewhere there's a photo or a newspaper clipping or a speeding ticket. I will discover the facts about Michael Gracie. As for me—when the truth is unexpectedly revealed, it can cause great trouble. My past is there for all to see. No one tries to blackmail *me*." In a rare display of disquiet, he ran his hands up and down the arm of the chair. "Except for my own mother, of course, who does on occasion try."

A big, loud relationship warning alarm went off in Summer's head. "What does she want?"

"Out of prison."

"You won't help her?" Summer didn't know what she thought of that.

"That's not an option. She tells me she and my father *had* to steal to survive, that the world was against them, and that they had to make a living any way they could. No matter how successful I am as a strategy analyst, no matter how much money I make as a businessman, she still believes that if I had continued to participate in the family business, my father would be alive today."

"She blames you for your father's death?" This was getting real. Gritty. "How did your father die?"

"One Friday night about ten years ago, he climbed onto a roof to rob a school, stepped on a skylight, and fell twenty feet into an empty classroom. Broke his legs, his back . . . he lay there all weekend until the janitor found him on Monday morning."

Summer covered her mouth in horror.

"The police took him to a secure ward in the hospital. He took a week to die." Kennedy showed no emotion: not embarrassment, and certainly not sorrow. "My mother was grief-stricken. I believe she truly was. I believe she did feel affection for him, although perhaps that affection was driven by how easily she could manipulate him."

"She . . . manipulated him?"

"She manipulates everyone."

With bone-dark certainty, she said, "Not you."

"Most certainly me. For most of my childhood, I observed my father and mother. I saw how she handled him with a combination of charm, guilt, and misdirection, and I despised him for it. I was unaware of her machinations in regards to me. Until . . . until I saw her with my little sister. By the time Tabitha was two, Mother had taught her to steal wallets from purses. Mother believed in early training, and Tabitha was good, as I had been." He moved his pen and notebook around the desk, lining them up in different directions, then parallel to each other. Then he stopped, looked at his hands, and gripped the edge of the table. "Tabitha was caught, as I had been. I saw my mother pretend to be horrified, apologize, tell the kind lady that Tabitha would be going to our church and speaking to the minister."

"You had a church?"

He laughed shortly. "Not at all. That was my mother, stage-managing her way out of police action. But for Tabitha, the incident was her first realization what we did was not a game. That lady whose wallet she lifted cried because she was poor, because she desperately needed the money we would have taken. Tabitha was tiny, but she saw the lady's children, she saw the poverty, and she didn't want to steal more."

"Your mother forced her to—"

"Not forced! Never forced. Manipulated her. Told Tabitha how disappointed she was in her, how we all had our jobs in the family, how if Tabitha didn't put her own family first she would be our downfall." Kennedy hated admitting this, hated admitting who and what his mother was. "I'd heard it before. I heard it when I rebelled, when I felt compassion . . . when I said I wanted to attend school."

Summer released her in-held breath. "You didn't go to school? At all?"

"I was *homeschooled*." The man knew how to use sarcasm.

"You went to MIT. You had to be able to test in."

"My family is blessed with high IQs and technical brains. Once I was no longer in my parents' custody, I caught up quickly."

Summer nodded. "I can see you would." She could also see why he had become so successful. He had the motivation only the child of a misfit could have, and a mind that had grown outside the bounds of conventional education.

"I will never forget the blistering humiliation I felt when I realized I was as much a creature of my mother's machinations as were my pathetic father and my baby sister." Kennedy touched Summer lightly on the shoulder. "Whatever affection I felt for my mother died long ago. But I know my responsibilities. I fulfill my responsibilities without fail. But I will not help Mother get out of prison. If I did, whatever damage she did, whoever she hurt with her scams . . . I would be accountable."

"I see that. And I'm sorry." What else was Summer supposed to say? "I'm sorry." Reading about his early life had given her insight into the reason for his successes. But it hadn't given her the details, or a glimpse of the pain that had formed him. Putting down her forgotten coffee cup, she leaned in and hugged him.

He didn't return her embrace. But he allowed her the gesture.

"How did this affect your sister?" she asked.

He gripped her arms and set her back into the chair. "I don't talk about Tabitha."

"Okay." Summer understood his reluctance. But she also knew she had been put firmly in her place.

"As I stated, I always fulfill my responsibilities. Which is why I will now do what must be done." He showed all the granite-jawed lack of emotion he had while talking about his parents.

"What's that?"

"I will marry you."

CHAPTER FORTY-NINE

"What?" The injury to Summer's brain must have been worse than she realized, because she was hallucinating.

"I will marry you. Right away. We can fly to Las Vegas and be done with it. We can even stay the night if you like."

Obviously, it wasn't *her* brain that had been affected. Kennedy was crazy. "Michael Gracie?" she said. "Remember him? Despite everything I've said, you don't believe he can track us?"

"You give him too much credit. Or perhaps you don't give me enough. I can distract him, lose him."

"Why am I even discussing this with you?" She threw her hands into the air, then winced at the thoughtless gesture and the pain it caused. "The whole idea is . . . absurd. Why would you want to marry me?"

"As you know, I have quite an uncontrollable desire for you, and you seem to react to me with similar fervor."

"Fervor?"

"And as I know, you have the need for security. You want to be married."

"What?"

"The other men—"

"Other men?" She felt the hair rising on the back of her head.

"Your other fiancés. They let you think about it too long."

"It?"

"Marriage. You realized the dangers inherent in a lifetime relationship. I don't blame you for that, the divorce rate proves they are certainly there, but I think we can agree we're two intelligent people who can work out any problem, even going so far as to take that problem to a marriage counselor." He was pontificating. Oblivious to her rising fury, he continued, "You search for fulfillment imprecisely, for you fear commitment. The abrupt loss of your father scarred you, made you a coward, and your mother's disinterest taught you the sense of maintaining a shelter around your emotions."

She contemplated the various shades of red that colored her vision. "So you know what I'm thinking, huh? What I'm feeling? Better than I do?"

"As I said, I have studied you. I may not be right in every instance, but my hypotheses are usually correct."

In a voice she thought sounded reasonable, she asked, "Excuse me. While I'm flattered you give me credit for *some* intelligence, I'm obviously not up to *your* standard of intelligence, because I don't understand how we got from, *Summer, you should go to California where you'll be safe* to, *Summer, we have the hots for each other so let's get married.*"

"I'm sorry, I'm not making myself clear." He looked concerned, as though being unclear was a carnal sin. "That's unlike me."

It didn't escape her attention that he had also tacitly agreed she wasn't up to his standard of intelligence. She flailed her arms around, and winced again. "This is bullshit! My former fiancés are none of your business. Nor do you know anything about my reasons for ending those relationships. How dare you presume that you do?"

"As I said—"

"Yeah. You studied me. I haven't studied you, at least not in any depth, so tell me, what would be the point of this marriage? Obviously not eternal bliss, since you're already discussing a marriage counselor."

"Eternal bliss is unlikely in any relationship, but I would hope we could live out our lives together."

"Because we could have good sex?"

"It's also for your safety."

He wasn't making sense. "This is the stupidest conversation I've ever had."

"If we were married, you would not fight to remain here, because you would have no reason to worry about your business."

"Why not?"

"I'm wealthy."

She stared at him, stared until her eyes burned, stared while her hand twitched to slap him. "You rich guys think the same damned thing every time—that a woman can't say no to money. Has it occurred to you my second fiancé was probably as wealthy as you are, and I broke it off?"

"He was older. I assumed—"

"You assumed he couldn't get it up? Not a problem! He was Italian. He was a great lover. But like you, he thought that if we got married, I wouldn't care whether I worked at a job that challenged and excited me."

For the first time, Kennedy broke out of his self-centered pride and noticed her agitation. "If you wished, you could start over again in California."

She stood up—she was so angry, she didn't notice any aches or pains—and pulled on her jacket.

He stood, too. "What are you doing?"

"I'm leaving."

"You can't leave. *He's* out there."

"*You're* in here. Anyway, you don't believe he's as scary as I do, and according to you, you must be right. And"—she shook her finger in his face—"if he wanted to take me out, he could merely firebomb this house!"

Her outrage seemed to astonish him. "What did I say wrong? It wasn't a romantic proposal of marriage, I realize that, but in such grim circumstances—"

She turned on him. "*Romantic?* You think I'm concerned about *romantic?* Today I was almost killed by a falling tree. Two weeks ago, a woman who looks like me was hit by a car. Ten months ago, I almost died of hypothermia. Right before that"—she lifted her hand and showed him—"I cut off my own finger to escape a murderer. Before that I lived almost four months in some of the most brutal, primitive conditions on earth. You think I need to get married to survive? You think the fact that I value my business is some ploy to trick you into marriage?"

"Not at all, but—"

"You think you've had a tough life because your parents are career criminals and you had to get out and make yourself into the great American success story. You think you're doing me a favor by honoring me with your hand in marriage. At least you've got two whole hands. You don't know jackshit about survival." She tapped her chest. "I will survive. And if I don't, if Michael Gracie kills me, you don't need to feel responsible. Tell yourself you offered me marriage and I was too stupid to recognize the honor you bestowed upon me." She stalked toward the back door.

He followed her. "It would be easier for me to keep tabs on you if you are in my custody."

"Yes, it would be awful if Summer was *in your care* and lifted the mayor's wallet or stole some old lady's diamond wedding ring." Summer opened the door, then flung herself back to face him, to confront his prejudices and his assumptions. "By the way, I broke into houses *to survive*. If I hadn't done it, I would have died. You might have had a tough childhood, but you've never had to face a choice like *that,* so how dare you judge me?" She should have shut up then, but she couldn't. She finished with a flourish: "You are a pompous, bigoted ass."

She slammed the door. Really hard.

And she wished she could do it again.

So she did.

CHAPTER FIFTY

The dream started easily, pleasantly. Summer found Kennedy was walking on the beach, barefoot, bare-chested, and handsome as sin. She ran up to him, caught him from behind, and hugged him. He turned in her arms, and kissed her, one of those marvelous deep, wet kisses that taught her heart how to beat. They fell on the sand and rolled, and she was on top, still kissing him. He said, "I love you, please marry me."

She was so happy. This was what she wanted. *This*. His asking not because it was his duty, but because he loved her.

She whispered, "Yes," and he caressed her until she was on the verge of orgasm, straining, reaching . . . and as climax took her, he rolled her beneath him and laughed. "Summer, you'll be happy with me," he said.

She looked up—but it wasn't Kennedy. It was Michael Gracie, looming, smiling, looking deeply into her eyes . . . holding her while she struggled. A wave washed over them, and he pushed her into the sand, into the dark. She was buried in the earth, in a cave, she couldn't *breathe*.

Summer woke up, sweaty and tangled in the twisted blankets. Gasping, she fought her way free. She sat up, knees bent, and cupped her head in her hands.

Her subconscious was not exactly subtle. It told her the thing she already knew, but had not acknowledged. Kennedy and Michael Gracie were both brilliant, charismatic, handsome, focused. They were two sides of the same coin.

Kennedy stood in the light, did everything in full view of the world, and fiercely disdained any criminal activity. She suspected he would fire a man for stealing a pencil. So he was the good guy—except that he made no attempt to understand human weakness. He was stiff-necked, unyielding, uncompromising.

Michael lived in the shadows, hid the truth about himself and his activities, murdered with impunity. So he was the bad guy. Yet his people were dedicated to him. Those men in the wine cellar had been willing to do anything he asked, and not just out of fear. He had been kind to Georg's kitchen staff. His party had raised a hundred thousand dollars for breast cancer research, and he had personally matched the amount. He did good things, maybe not for the right reasons, but they were still good.

Both men were attractive to her.

She did not really trust Kennedy McManus—if driven into a choice among her and his sister and nephew, Summer knew she would lose—yet she had kissed him the first time she met him. Had been tempted to hit the sheets with him.

But having the hots for Michael Gracie? What did that say about her? She had seen him shoot a man in the head. She had cut off her own finger to get away from him. Yet the memory at that moment in the kitchen when he had touched her cheek, and she looked into his eyes, had stayed with her. She felt as if she had caught a glimpse of his tormented soul.

Even more than that, she felt as if he had seen something in her that called to him. Why else would he have singled her out? Had he seen her loneliness? Had he somehow glimpsed the terror and the privation drove her to steal, to live in isolation? That moment when he touched her with compassion had branded her as his, and no matter what stark and terrifying truths she told herself—about kidnapping, extortion, and murder—could not sever that spiritual connection.

Logically, she shouldn't—didn't—care if he was tormented.

But emotionally . . . she cared. She wanted to help him.

My God. She had walked away from her last fiancé because he had tried to reduce her to a decoration on his arm. It hadn't been easy, but in the end, she had felt pretty good about that.

Then she threw herself into danger to save a child's life, survived a long-term ordeal that would have killed most people, escaped, built a life . . . by damn, she was a goddess in every way!

Except in this matter of Michael Gracie, the guy who wanted to reduce her to a grease spot on the highway. Apparently she was a sucker for a man with a tormented soul. Obviously she was a woman who cherished a belief that a woman's love could transform a psychopath. What kind of self-destructive female had she become?

The kind who wrote love letters to serial killers in prison.

She was disgusted, humiliated, haunted . . . and yet, she could not shake her mental conviction that she and Michael Gracie shared a connection.

A knock sounded at her front door.

She jumped, lifted her head from her hands. Had she summoned *him* with her thoughts? And which *him* did she mean?

She slid out of bed and through the tiny living room. She looked through the peephole, and sighed in relief. She opened the door. "Kateri. What's up?"

Kateri used her walker to shove Summer aside. She trekked in, turned on Summer. "We need to get our costumes for the party."

Wow. That was a change. "Are we going?"

"I'm having visions about my Coasties dying in some horrible costume party cataclysm and I'm not there, so yes, we're going."

Summer inspected her. Kateri's dark hair stood up in clumps. Shadows ringed her eyes. She hunched over her walker as if it was the only thing keeping her upright. They took Kateri's visions seriously because sometimes they came true. "You do look sort of rough."

"You should talk."

Summer rubbed her face, then headed into the bathroom, leaned over the sink and splashed cool water over it. "Nightmares'R'Us, babe. I can't go."

Kateri followed. "Because *he'll* be there?"

Summer's mind jumped between the two men in her dream. "Who?"

"Michael Gracie. Who else is giving you nightmares?"

"I'm giving them to myself." Summer used a towel to dry herself off.

"Look, the way I see it, he knows you're here. If he's going to kill you, is he going to do it at the party?"

"No. That would cause a fuss, and possibly lead the police back to him." Summer opened her drawer and got out underwear.

"Right. He'll sneak in and kill you while you're alone."

"Thanks, that's reassuring."

"I'm not trying to reassure you. I'm trying to make you weigh the odds and come to the right conclusion."

"And be your ride to the party."

"That, too."

Summer shut the door in her face, dressed, and came out in jeans and a T-shirt. "Michael's conceited. As in, his murders are clean—he gets away with them all—unless he's trying to scare the bejesus out of you."

"Is that what he's doing with you?"

"Yes. It's working. I hate that. I'm tired of having him control my life." With Kennedy and Michael tugging her in different directions, Summer felt as cranky as a child. "I'm not comfortable in a crowd, but with half the town at the resort, I won't feel safe at home by myself, either."

"That's the way I look at it. Stay at home and Michael Gracie has a clear shot at you. Go to the party and he hasn't got a chance."

"Are you having a prophetic moment?"

"No, I pretty much feel as if both choices suck. It's just . . . going to the party sucks less."

"Then we should go to the costume party."

Kennedy finished tinkering with the house alarm, and reset the code. He had made it—not invulnerable, that was impossible—but more secure. Then he looked around for something else to do.

There was nothing. He had spoken to his office, jerry-rigged the Wi-Fi to be impossible to access for any but the most skilled hacker, fixed a broken wire in one of the motion sensors. That left him to pace toward his computer and stare as his identification program flicked through photos of Jimmys-he-had-known and compared them to the official business-face-forward photo of Michael Gracie.

He didn't need to watch the monitor. But the blue light focused his mind, and right now, his mind needed to be focused. On Summer. And on himself.

In his business, he was known as a master negotiator. So how had he mishandled a marriage proposal so badly? Summer had been livid. And all because he had supposed she enjoyed money and the luxury it brought—after studying her background, that seemed to be a safe assumption.

He had pointed out she could move her business—what difference would it make? He could help her with the start-up.

Most of all, he had speculated on her emotional health. That had made her blow up like a Roman candle. Which made no sense. He thought women wanted to be understood. That's what they said.

The software program had worked its way through two-thirds of the Jimmys, with an estimated time of twenty hours to get him back through the earlier years of his life, right back to his birth.

Another twenty hours . . .

Inevitably his mind returned to the problem at hand.

Summer had a skewed sense of what would keep her safe. Certainly, seeing someone shot before her very eyes would scar her, and the fact that Michael Gracie seemed to have a body disposal system in place was disturbing. Yet to attribute omnipotence to Gracie was an exaggeration at best and full-blown paranoia at worst. She should trust Kennedy to keep her safe.

Why didn't she?

He looked longingly at his computer. Computers, he understood. If only the answers to his questions were there. But from cold, hard experience, he knew they were not. So he did what he always did in situations regarding human emotions.

He called his sister.

A few hours later, a chastened Kennedy heard a knock at the front door. He stood at once, went to the window and looked out. He expected Girl Scouts selling cookies or grade-school kids selling Christmas wrap. Instead a skinny teenager with a handful of cream-colored cards stood on the porch.

Kennedy opened the door.

"Mr. McManus?"

"Yes?"

"For you." The kid handed him one of the envelopes, ran down the stairs, and headed toward a new-model Volkswagen Bug. He got in and drove off like a man on a mission.

Kennedy opened the envelope and read the elegant handwriting:

Mr. McManus,

Tomorrow night, I'll be hosting a Halloween party. I would be delighted to have you attend. The time is eight o'clock. The place is Virtue Falls Resort. Costume required. Don't be late.

Best,
Margaret Smith

No one knew he was here.

Who was Margaret Smith, and how had she found out he was in town?

He grabbed his tablet off the coffee table and found Margaret Smith and the Virtue Falls Resort right away.

Thank God. He could still do one thing right.

CHAPTER FIFTY-ONE

Garik sat in the mostly empty Oceanview Café and watched a blustery wind rip the yellowed leaves off the bigleaf maples and twirl them down the street. The first winter storm was right on schedule, coming onto shore around midnight. It would bring sheets of rain to Virtue Falls, feet of snow to the mountains, and according to the weather service, the temperatures would plunge.

The howling wind, the lashing rain, the threat of lightning, would also give meaningful atmosphere to tonight's Halloween party . . . and make everything from setting up to the transportation of guests more difficult. Which is why Garik planned to stay away as long as he could.

"Warm it up, Sheriff?" Rainbow stood over him with the coffee-pot and a handful of silverware.

"No, thanks."

"Okay." She topped off his cup.

"Um . . ."

She gestured toward the chair across from him. "Mind if I sit? It's time for my break, and these dogs are barking." She tossed down a trivet, put the coffeepot on it, tossed down the silverware, and sat.

He lifted his brows. Now *this* was different. Ever since he could remember, Rainbow Breezewing had waited tables at the Oceanview Café. But also, she was a free spirit, a woman born in Haight-Ashbury to famous hippie artists, a woman known to disappear without a word and return when she pleased. And of course, for all that she had known Garik since he was a kid, and liked him, she did not officially approve of the authoritarian arm of society he represented.

In other words, as far as Rainbow was concerned, he was a cop and not to be trusted. So why was she sitting across from him fidgeting like a guilty child?

"Didn't pay your parking ticket?" he asked.

"Yeah, I did. Most of 'em." She leaned forward and looked earnestly into his eyes. "You know I go wander around the hills now and then? Get in touch with Mother Nature, sleep under the stars, get the stench of civilization out of my nose."

"I know." For the most part, he believed that was what she was doing.

"Sometimes I stumble on some stuff I shouldn't know about. But pretty much, I leave well enough alone because I figure if someone's growing something the state wants to tax, it's none of my business."

"Right. Got it." And if she stopped and smoked a little illegally grown weed, it was none of his business. "Make sure you don't get shot stumbling onto stuff you shouldn't know about."

"Right. Because Virtue Falls needs me at the Oceanview Café." She looked more serious than he ever remembered. "But this isn't like that. Remember those bodies dumped in the forest?"

He went on alert. "I wish I could forget them."

"Any word from the feds about where they come from?"

"No one has a clue." But he guessed Rainbow was about to give him one.

"Okay, so." She poked at the silverware. It clattered and skittered across the table. "When those tourists reported that body, I started thinking. A couple of years ago, this couple came in for breakfast. They looked like shit, like they'd been up all night. I heard them talking and I figured out they were pilots."

"How did you do that?"

"I eavesdropped. Also, I've got a thing for pilots, so I know their jargon. These two weren't in uniform, so I knew they flew private planes, and they were arguing about what was in the locker and whether it was their responsibility to deal with it. They wanted to refuse, but they were . . . I'd say they were skittish."

"Okay."

"Anyway, I love me some pilot, so I hooked up with the guy."

Rainbow *had* figured something out. "Where did they come from?"

Rainbow waggled her finger at him. "Exactly. At the time, I didn't think about that. Occasionally, they would show up in town. He and I would have some laughs. They'd leave. No big deal. Folks come in and out of here all the time."

Garik could see where this was going, but before he went to the feds, he wanted to know every detail. "How often did they show up?"

"Erratically. Honest, I didn't think anything about where they came from or who they were until bodies started falling out of the sky. Even then, it took time to put two and two together. Ya know?" She looked surprised at herself.

"Works that way sometimes."

Now she got to the meat of the matter. "Do you recall that old airport south of here inside Olympic National Park? Built in World War Two when they thought the Japanese were going to bomb the West Coast?"

Excitement began a slow boil in his veins. *She had nailed it. Rainbow had nailed it.* "About a mile off the main highway? In high school, I used to take girls there. It was quiet and creepy. Abandoned ever since I can remember."

"In the past, when I was out wandering, I've stayed in the building. It was pretty decrepit. I mean, you know, World War Two and all, but if it's snowing, it's better than the outdoors."

"So that's where you went this time?"

"Right. It still looks abandoned. But man. Those pilots."

From behind her, one of the regulars yelled, "Hey, Rainbow, how about warming up my coffee?"

Without turning, she acknowledged him with a flip of her middle finger.

Muttering ensued, but nobody had the guts to yell at her again.

"Anyway," she said, "I went and took a look. At first I thought I was wrong. The building looks as ramshackle as ever. But when I walked along the runway, it had been repaved."

Garik wanted to grab her and tell her to hurry. But he knew better. The trouble with civilians was that they couldn't give a straightforward report, and interrupting them either made them forget details or they started over. He couldn't afford either delay.

Rainbow continued, "I figured it was one of two things. Either it was the government—it's still their airport, at least as far as I know, and they're always doing some dumbass surreptitious thing to spy on us."

"Hmm. Yes." Rainbow was convinced the government was out to get them.

She continued, "Or it was our body-dumpers."

He couldn't resist. He had to ask. "You don't think the government is dumping bodies in the forest?"

"No. They have a facility in Utah where they incinerate the people they want to disappear."

He shouldn't have asked.

"I set up camp, out of sight, and I waited. Sure enough, one night this private jet drops out of the sky so fast it looked like someone had shot it down." Right there under the fluorescent lights of the Ocean-view Café, Rainbow pulled off her shirt and showed him her ribs. "See that? That's where the bullet grazed me."

He supposed he should be glad the restaurant was relatively empty. He supposed he should be glad Washington State was so casual about nudity. He *was* glad when she put the shirt back on.

People were staring. Listening.

He did not need them to hear this. He leaned forward and spoke softly. "So not the government."

"Probably not," she admitted grudgingly.

"They shot you. How did they see you?"

"*He* shot me. I got a little too careless about whether anyone could spot me from above, and that man who came in on the plane—he was a sharp bastard." As Rainbow remembered, her eyes narrowed. "He got off the plane looking like a model from *Gentleman's Quarterly*. Hands in the pockets, posed and glamorous. He talked to his buddies. I was watching. Then all of a sudden, the lights went out. A spotlight lit up the trees around me. I took off running. Bullets sprayed all around." She sighed. "I lost my camping gear."

Not the point. "You're goddamn alive!" Elizabeth would kill him if anything happened to Rainbow. Hell, half the town would eat his liver if anything happened to Rainbow. And if Rainbow was hurt, he wouldn't be too happy about it, either. "So they're bringing passengers and bodies in on a plane. The passengers, probably criminals moving around the country surreptitiously, are dispersing in the state. The bodies, they're loading onto helicopters and dropping in the forest."

"I think that about covers it."

He started making plans. He would call Tom Perez, his old boss at the FBI, and give him a heads-up. Go to the airport and check it out for himself. In no time, he would have solved the crimes surrounding bodies that dropped from the skies, and nailed this glamorous murderer who remodeled decrepit airports and shot at civilians who happened to be Garik's friends.

"I spent two miserable days taking the long way around to the road and back to Virtue Falls." Rainbow's mouth scrunched in disgust. "I had wondered where she came from."

The change of subject almost gave Garik whiplash. "Who?"

"Summer Leigh. She showed up, this mystery woman. She didn't talk like one of us, she was in shit shape, and she was scared out of her mind. She got on her feet, started a business, charmed some old guy out of his car . . . she's a mover and a shaker. But she's still scared out of her mind."

"You think she was a body to be dumped."

"Only she was still alive. And whoever this guy is, he's still after her."

CHAPTER FIFTY-TWO

That night, the night of the party, Summer turned off the dark coastal highway into Virtue Falls Resort's parking lot. She rolled down her window, showed the attendant the party invitations, and nodded as she listened to him instruct her where to park. Then she ignored every word and drove to the darkest corner of the asphalt. There she wedged her car in between a Hummer limousine and a Volkswagen Bug.

Kateri pretended she didn't know why Summer hid her car from easy view. No use having someone else sabotage the car on purpose. They might need it for a quick getaway.

Summer killed the engine. "Parking lot's almost full. This joint is jumping."

The two of them exchanged looks.

"Do you think *he's* here?" Kateri asked.

"Michael Gracie?" Summer ran her hand over her close-cropped hair. "I don't know. I'm so tired of trying to figure out his game. Sometimes I wish he'd get it over with, you know?"

Kateri rolled down her window. She looked around at the shifting shadows, tasted the wind, smelled the blend of feverish party excitement, abject obsession, and terror. "Something's coming. I don't know if it's him, or the storm, or if the feelings of every person in the vicinity are boiling over into a wicked brew."

"How appropriate for a Halloween party. We'd better go face it, whatever it is." Summer groped at her waist. "I feel naked without my belt."

"It's a weapon, right?" Kateri had always thought so; now seemed the appropriate time to ask.

Summer nodded. "It's a sling. Think 'David and Goliath.' I'm good enough to knock someone out at fifty feet."

"Seriously?" Kateri was impressed. "That's awesome."

"I can *hit* them at a greater distance, but when I don't get to practice often enough, my accuracy suffers. It's the only weapon I know I can always carry and no one knows what I've got." Summer's eyes glinted in the dark. "Handy for dealing with the Michael Gracies of this world."

"I want you to teach me."

"Name the day." Summer worked her way out of the door, dragging her full skirts out with a series of yanks that freed her one inch at a time.

"Would you wait and let me help you?" Annoyed, Kateri leaned across and caught Summer's arm. "You're stuck on the emergency brake, and we don't want to tear this purple silk. We had to pay a costume deposit, you know."

Summer made a guttural, disgusted sound. "How did Maleficent handle these clothes, anyway?"

"She had a raven. And slaves." Kateri eased handfuls of skirt and petticoats out of the car. "You could have worn the black leather Catwoman costume. Less hassle, and you looked great in it."

"I've got enough problems without parading around half naked in leather and a mask."

"Yes, I suppose it would attract attention."

"Yes, I suppose it would," Summer mimicked. "For whatever sense it makes, dressing up like Sleeping Beauty's wicked witch gives me a sense of power. Maybe if Michael Gracie shows up, I'll turn into a dragon and fry his ass." She leaned down, looked at Kateri, and smiled as if the thought thoroughly entertained her.

Kateri pointed at Summer's cleavage. "Yes, God forbid you should wear a catsuit instead of baring your boobies for everyone to see."

"I don't have much in the way of boobies to bare."

"Sure. Every guy inside is going to care about the size. As I understand it from the guys in the Coast Guard—more than a mouthful's a waste."

"That's a motto to embroider on a pillow." Summer got her voluminous outfit out of the car, shook it out and got down to business. She released the bungee cord on her trunk and retrieved Kateri's walker. She pushed it around to the passenger side of the car.

In keeping with the Disney theme, Kateri had chosen a Cruella de Vil costume. Her black slinky dress clung to her like uber-tight Spanx, and Summer laughed as she wrapped Kateri in the oversized, swooping coat. The black-and-white fur did a marvelous job of creating a menacing identity and hiding the walker, which Kateri so desperately needed tonight. "How's my hair?" she asked.

"Freaky," Summer assured her.

That afternoon, they had bleached half of Kateri's shoulder-length black hair white. She wore massive amounts of green eye shadow, red lipstick, red gloves, and her cigarette holder was long enough to poke a man's eyes out. She hoped Landon Adams was here; she wanted the chance to try it on him. "I'll get a head start." Kateri got her walker arranged, hefted herself out of the car, and headed toward the brightly lit resort. Her hips hurt. Her knees hurt. She had taken a pain pill to get her through the evening. But by God, she would have fun.

"Be there in a minute." When Summer caught up with Kateri, she looked dramatically wicked, with a horned headdress, an upturned collar, and an impressive witch's staff.

Maleficent's staff had been cardboard with a Christmas ball glued on top. Summer had laughed scornfully at that, and on the way back from the costume shop they had paid a visit to the Virtue Falls SF/gaming/comic book shop. There she acquired a heavy walnut staff carved to look like Gandalf's. Personally, Kateri thought mixing fairy tales and Tolkien was blasphemy. But Summer said if Michael Gracie and his goons came at her, she could take them out with a swift clip behind the knees.

Kateri couldn't argue with that.

Summer gripped Kateri's arm. "Listen."

Kateri knew that sound, knew it from her days in the Coast Guard, and more intimately from her own rescue after the tsunami. A helicopter was headed their way.

Summer's clasp tightened. "They're coming."

Kateri pointed at the empty spot, rimmed by lights, at the edge of the parking lot. "That's a makeshift helipad. Probably the Hollywood guests are too important to bother with limousines."

"That makes sense. It really does." But still Summer clung to Kateri's arm.

A small helicopter dropped out of the clouds and discharged a couple dressed as Henry the Eighth and one of his wives. They slipped on their masks and headed for the porch. The helicopter rose again.

"That's Gwen LeFavre and Kharabora," Kateri said. "Color me impressed!"

"Yeah . . ." Summer stared at the popular celebrities, and tripped over the hem of her dress. "Damn it!" She kicked at it viciously, glanced up, and tripped again, dropping down on her knees between two cars.

"Summer!" Kateri bent over her. "Are you okay?"

Gradually, noiselessly, Summer got to her knees and peeked through the windows of a Mazda Miata. "He's here," she whispered.

Kateri looked.

A tall, broad-shouldered man in a nineteenth-century military costume with gold epaulettes ran up the porch steps. He came to a halt, donned a simple black mask, and entered the resort.

Kateri lowered her voice. "Is that Michael Gracie?"

Summer got to her feet. "No, it's Kennedy McManus."

What the hell? Kateri slammed her walker in front of Summer. "*Who's* Kennedy McManus?"

"The man Michael Gracie hates with all his heart."

"That sounds like the good guy to me." Kateri deliberately narrowed her eyes at Summer. "So why would you duck when you see him?"

"Because he and I . . ." Summer struggled to speak.

"Were involved in your former life?" Kateri guessed.

"Not exactly." Even in the uneven light, Summer was clearly rattled. "I contacted him with information about Michael Gracie and he came here to meet me. To help me." She tried to walk toward the resort again.

Kateri hadn't been the local Coast Guard commander without learning a few tricks. Again she slammed the walker in Summer's path. "Here? As in, he just arrived in town?"

"Not exactly that, either."

"He's been in town for . . . ?"

"A day. Or two."

Kateri made the next and obvious leap. "He's been in town, the two of you *are* involved but things aren't going well between you."

Summer gave a guilty nod.

Kateri felt completely betrayed. "Way to not tell me!"

"The less you know, the less chance you have of being collateral damage."

Kateri's temper bubbled over. "Don't give me that righteous shit. I don't need to know about the scheme to catch Michael Gracie. I do need to know how you managed to get involved with Kennedy Mc-Manus, a guy you've barely met. You *did* just meet him, right?"

Summer looked around. "Do we have to stand in the parking lot and talk about this?"

"We can go inside and talk about it, but people will overhear."

Summer glanced toward the house. "I didn't think he'd be here at all. He's supposed to stay at the house so no one identifies him. I don't even know how he found out about the party. Although that's stupid. He says he can find out anything, and I believe him. I shouldn't go in."

"He's in a costume. He put on a mask. No one's going to know it's him, except you, and you can avoid him." Kateri's exasperation overflowed. "And *we're dressed.* So what's the problem?"

"Last time he and I talked, things didn't end well."

"Why not?"

"Because he's a sanctimonious prig." Summer straightened, then sagged against the Miata. "I don't know. Is this a good idea?"

"*We're* in costumes. *We've* got masks. From the look of the parking lot, I'd conservatively say there are a couple of hundred guests. I don't know if it's a good idea. But sneaking back home again is for cowards. So we're going in." Kateri stared sternly at Summer.

"Right you are." Summer pulled on her purple, jeweled, cat-eyed mask. "We're going in."

Kateri followed suit with Cruella's black-and-white feathered mask. "And we will have a good time."

CHAPTER FIFTY-THREE

Summer could hear music, laughter, conversation, even before they entered the resort. And it was early; the party had just started. Tony Parnham must be popular. Or successful. Or he served really good liquor. She hoped he didn't serve drugs for, she had no doubt, Margaret Smith would run him out at the point of a sword.

Before they stepped through the open front door, Kateri said, "Chin up. Shoulders back. Remember who you are. You are Maleficent, the baddest Disney villain ever."

Summer looked at her friend, at the all-enveloping white coat, the red gloves, the dramatic makeup, and most of all, that half-black, half-white hair, and grinned. "And you look positively terrifying." Kateri's intention had been to focus attention on *herself*, not her walker or her disabilities.

She had succeeded.

They walked into the great room. Servers gestured them through and toward the restaurant.

Before Summer could bring herself to step into the party, she took a long breath. Even dressed like Maleficent, with the headdress and a jeweled and feathered mask over her face, she felt the crawly fingers of doom up her spine.

Would Kennedy recognize her? She had recognized him easily enough, even in the dim lights of the parking lot, even with his back turned.

Would Michael Gracie be here? Tonight's party could very well be a trap, yet two weeks ago, when Summer had dined at the resort, Margaret Smith had known about the party. Would Michael Gracie have made arrangements so far into the future? He had no reason to believe his first attempts at murdering her would fail.

The logic of that fortified Summer. She adjusted her mask and stepped through the restaurant's wide doors.

The dining tables were gone. The formally dressed waitstaff had been replaced by black-and-silver-clad skeletons who circulated with trays of drinks and appetizers. Pocket doors on the far wall had been pushed aside to open the next room and double the space, and the mirrored and gilded walls reflected a flurry of color. Bold reds and yellows. Bruised blues and purples. Glittering golds and silvers.

Guests in jesters' outfits and royal princess gowns, Superman tights and French-maid miniskirts, laughed loudly, talked shrilly, drank freely. Jewels flashed in sumptuous tiaras, dazzling rings, elaborate necklaces. Everyone wore a mask: of glittering sequins, of birdlike feathers that swept out from the temples, of mannequin-like flesh molded into eerie immobility.

The noise, the colors, the merriment, made Summer want to retreat . . . and that desire alone sent her into the midst of the party.

Kateri was right. Fear could not rule Summer's life.

Besides, somewhere in here, Kennedy McManus disdainfully watched the common dreck of the human race, judging them according to his superior standards of excellence. She would not be him, alone and isolated; she would join the party and be a person who lived rather than stood aside and watched.

One of the skeleton-waiters swooped in with a tray. "Champagne?" On his bone-white face, rotting teeth decorated his upper lip and chin, and black rings around his eyes provided the illusion of death . . . and madness. The costume was effective; perhaps too effective, for Kateri and Summer stared, transfixed, then shook their heads.

"What can I bring you?" The waiter's voice sounded reassuringly normal, with a reassuringly slow and gentle Southern drawl.

"Water," Kateri said. "We don't drink alcohol."

"Coming right up." He disappeared into the crowd.

Margaret Smith rose from a giant thronelike chair beside the door and made her way over, leaning on her cane. "Welcome, my dears." She sounded absolutely gleeful. "Isn't this grand?"

"It really is," Summer said.

Scarlet flowers hung in vases from the ceiling. Streamers fluttered in the draft of the air-conditioning. A live band played in the corner: one guy on a keyboard, one on the trumpet, one with a clarinet, a woman on the drums and another with some zitherlike instrument that slid up and down the scales in a dizzying whirlwind of notes.

"And you look grand, too," Kateri said.

Margaret wore a costume worthy of *Downton Abbey*'s first season, with a small lace hat, ruffles, and a long strand of luxurious pearls. "This is one of the gowns my mother-in-law wore as a debutante," she said smugly. "I debated whether I should sport about in such a relic, then I thought—what else is one to do with it? Shall I let it rot? I think not."

Summer laughed in delight. "You are absolutely right. You're perfect."

The waiter returned with a tray laden with flutes of bubbling water.

All three women took one, then lifted their glasses, clinked, and took sips.

Kateri grimaced. "Flavored," she said disparagingly.

Summer laughed. "You can't imagine they would serve tap water at a do like this."

"I can bring you anything you like," the waiter assured them.

"This is fine," Summer told him.

He bowed and disappeared into the crowd.

Summer noted no one stopped him to retrieve a glass; the flavored water wasn't nearly as popular as the champagne.

Margaret drained half of her drink. "Johnny Depp is here. He kissed my fingers." She showed the wrinkled, veined hand. "I can die happy."

Kateri craned her neck. "Where is he?"

"He's Captain Jack Sparrow," Margaret said.

Summer scanned the ballroom. "Which one? I can see three from here."

"He's the handsome one." Margaret's eyes twinkled beneath her mask.

"Is Elizabeth here?" Kateri asked.

"She's upstairs. She's very ill." Margaret's happiness faded. "Pregnancy does not agree with her."

"I am sorry," Summer said. "Give her my best wishes."

"I will." Margaret glanced at the door. "I did think Garik would be here by now. That's the trouble with having a son who's the sheriff. He's perpetually late. That will have to change when the baby's born. Now, you girls go on." She shooed them. "Remember, you are required to keep your mask on, visit with as many guests as you can, and have a thoroughly good time. If you need me, I am at your service, and will be at my station by the door." New guests arrived, and she turned to greet them.

Kateri and Summer moved farther along the perimeter of the room.

A waiter—*the* waiter?—appeared beside Kateri and Summer with a plate of appetizers and a handful of cocktail napkins. After they had helped themselves, he moved off again.

Kateri shivered. "There is an element of creepiness about that guy."

"That grinning skull. I know. There's an element of creepiness about *all* the waiters." Everywhere Summer looked, a stream of people were in constant motion, like a snake slithering around the room, and the mirrors reflected and magnified the motion. "They move as if their movements were choreographed."

Kateri lowered her voice. "Maybe this wasn't such a good idea, after all."

Summer felt a sense of relief. She had broken out of her shell. She had come to the party. She'd had a drink and a canapé. "So . . . You want to go?"

At that moment, they heard shouts of, "Commander! Commander Kwinault!" and saw four of Kateri's Coasties heading their way.

"I'll check in with them." Kateri placed her drink between two fingers, leaned into her walker, and promised, "Then we'll go."

"Take your time." Summer moved toward the wall, planted her staff, sipped her water, and watched the dancing. Creepy, yes, but she had to admit that it was fascinating to watch so many people hiding behind their masks, behaving with wild abandon and no thought for tomorrow. This party was Mardi Gras, Prohibition, and the end of the world, all rolled into one.

A man spoke near her right shoulder. "You are, without a doubt, the most beautiful woman here."

She turned—and took two steps back. She groped behind her, got rid of her glass on a discard tray, and took a solid, two-handed grip on her staff.

This guy was a little over six feet, slender with broad shoulders, and dressed like a romance hero in a white ruffled shirt opened halfway to his waist, black breeches, and tall black boots. His mask was simple, velvet black on one side and shiny white on the other, and it gave his face an oddly half-bulging look.

He could be Michael Gracie.

She thought he *was* Michael Gracie. Except that his hair was pale blond, and Michael's hair was sun-streaked, and she thought Michael was taller . . . although she wasn't sure, . . . she hadn't really stood beside him, only for a moment, and all her memories were skewed by terror.

Belatedly, she said, "Hello."

"Hello?" He smiled rakishly. "I call you the most beautiful woman at a party filled with beautiful women, and all you can say is hello?"

"I could point out I'm covered from head to toe with a voluminous gown, I'm wearing a headdress and a mask, and—"

"And you could take me out with that staff." He pretended terror.

She grinned. If he was Michael Gracie, he was a very unthreatening Michael. "Thank you for noticing."

A waiter walked by with a tray of drinks.

The romance hero snatched two and offered one to Summer.

Before she could refuse, another waiter came by—or was it the first waiter?—and offered water in a fluted glass. She accepted and sipped, and wondered if she was nuts to stand in the middle of a vibrant, high-end Hollywood party and think with longing about the isolation of the Sawtooth Mountains.

Mr. Romance moved closer. "When a woman wears a mask, what better time to know that she is beautiful? I judge you by your soul."

"My soul is not on display, and you do not know it." No, this man wasn't Michael Gracie. He was too normal, bantering with typical party inanity.

"I'd like to." He offered his hand. "Shall we dance?"

She didn't think twice. "Sure." Because she'd just spotted Kennedy; with a barrel chest, an impatient air, and a scowl. She wished he didn't look so dashing in his military officer's uniform. And she wished he wasn't headed her way.

She would dance with the devil to avoid Kennedy McManus.

Mr. Romance handed her staff to a waiter—the waiter?—and swept her onto the floor. The band played a waltz. Summer caught a glimpse of Kennedy watching her. She laughed as Mr. Romance swung her in dizzying circles, and thought she could learn to like this uninhibited decadence, especially if her behavior irked Kennedy McManus.

Best of all, she knew it did.

CHAPTER FIFTY-FOUR

Kateri's Coasties greeted her with grins, loud appreciation for her costume, and gentle hugs. She hugged them back fiercely, trying to tell them without words that she wasn't f+ragile and knowing they would never believe her.

Ensign Mark Brown, Ensign Keith Dawson, and Petty Officer Tyler Kovavitch had been assigned to the station during Kateri's command. Seaman Layla Monroe was new, on her first Coast Guard assignment, but she'd heard about Kateri and acquired the guys' attitude, a reverence predicated in part on hearing of Kateri's swift and decisive action that had saved two of the three Coast Guard cutters in port the day of the tsunami, and in part because she had survived the tsunami. Kateri supposed she didn't deserve that kind of worship. On the other hand, she didn't deserve being drowned and crippled, either, so she took it all in her stride.

When the greetings were done, she looked around, searching for the rest of the crew. For Luis. "Where are the other guys?"

Silence fell. Looks were exchanged. The four Coasties pulled her into a corner.

Mark pushed up his Frankenstein mask, and in a low voice, said, "Lieutenant Landlubber sent them out on a mission. He waited until they had their costumes on and were ready to come to the party, then he sent them to check out a possible drug-smuggling operation at Catawampus Bay."

"But there's a storm coming in," Kateri said. "They might be needed for a real mission. Like, you know, search and rescue?"

"We know," Keith said.

Kateri continued, "When the wind's from the southeast, Catawampus Bay's got the most treacherous currents on the coast."

"We know that, too," Tyler said.

"Is Landlubber trying to get them all killed?"

Everyone looked down at their shoes.

Layla muttered, "He's the wicked stepsister. He can't stand the competition."

Kateri spotted Landlubber in his dress whites, wearing a small blue mask and talking animatedly to a very tall, very curvaceous young woman in a mermaid costume that looked as if it had been spray-painted on. Kateri pushed up her fur sleeves and turned in that direction.

Mark grabbed her arm. "Don't. Don't say anything. Don't do anything. He got the promotion, he's pissed, and he takes it out on us. Every time Captain Sanchez tries to check him, Landlubber punishes *him*. If *you* said something, he couldn't get to you, so Captain Sanchez would take it in the shorts."

Kateri stared at these men and women, her friends, her people. She could do nothing to help them. The frustration ate at her guts. "Guys, I am so sorry."

"Not your fault, Commander," Mark said.

Everyone said that. Luis said that. But every time one of her guys charged into danger, every time one of them got hurt, she knew again that she should have handled Landon Adams differently, taught him respect for the Pacific Ocean even if it took dunking him in and dragging him behind a cutter.

Of course, what he needed to learn was respect for human life, and if he hadn't learned compassion in his life before the Coast Guard, she couldn't have taught him.

"Commander, listen. Ignore Landlubber. I've got someone I want you to meet." Mark reached out a hand and brought into the circle a new arrival, a pretty, smiling young woman. "Kateri Kwinault, this is Sienna Monahan. Sienna, this is our former commander, Kateri Kwinault."

Kateri shook Sienna's hand and looked between Mark and Sienna. "How good to meet you. Are you two an item?"

The team hooted.

Mark blushed. "I wish. Sienna was supposed to come with Luis. Instead she's stuck with us."

Kateri froze. The Girlfriend? Sienna was the Girlfriend?

Sienna touched Mark's arm. "I would have said *you* were stuck with *me*. Who wants to haul around someone else's date when there are a hundred gorgeous women drooling over the Coast Guard?"

"Truth," Layla said. "I'm tired of women glaring a hole between my shoulder blades. They want a chance with you guys. So go ask someone to dance. Commander Kwinault and I will babysit Sienna."

The men made protesting sounds that swiftly faded as they surveyed the luscious pickings.

In tones of adoration, Tyler said, "I have never seen so many hot women in one place in my life." He headed off in one direction.

Keith and Mark split for opposite sides of the room.

The women stood alone in the corner.

And Kateri came back to life, back to normal . . . if normal was bitterly jealous and thoroughly bitchy. Which, since she was dressed as Cruella de Vil, seemed appropriate.

Sienna wasn't beautiful. But she was pretty. Really pretty in a wholesome, corn-fed kind of way, with wide blue eyes, clear skin marked by a sprinkle of auburn freckles, roses in her cheeks, and straight red hair so bright it looked like fire. She was thin and petite, with a runner's body, and she smiled all the time, showing dimples that pressed into her sweet cream cheeks . . . so from all immediate observation, this woman was young, healthy, and happy.

Kateri wanted to jab her with her Cruella de Vil cigarette holder.

Except that Sienna grasped Kateri's hand. "I hope you don't mind me telling you this, but since I arrived in Virtue Falls, I have heard so much about you, and I admire your bravery and your intelligence. Luis thinks the world of you. All the Coasties do. You're the person I want to be when I grow up."

"Thanks." *I guess.* "I look forward to knowing you better." *Big fat lie.* "How do you two know each other?" Who would have thought she could speak naturally rather than screech like nails on a chalkboard? She should join the Screen Actors Guild.

The girls put their heads together and laughed.

Layla said, "We were roommates our freshman year at Michigan State, and I could not stand her. I mean, I've got dark curly hair, flashing brown eyes, and the well-toned body of an athlete."

"Not to mention an immense ego," Sienna said.

"A well-deserved immense ego," Layla said. "I get attention. Then I moved in with her. Guys lined up around the block to ignore me."

"That is not true." Sienna fake-fluffed her hair. "Once they got over the shock of my beauty, they crawled all over you."

"The ones you didn't want!" Layla was disgusted.

"I didn't want any of them. Pimple-faced, obnoxious guys with big egos." Sienna turned to Kateri. "I'm not being mean. They're all like that at eighteen."

Kateri felt as if she'd been slapped. Sienna told her that because . . . because she thought Kateri couldn't remember that far back. Or, more likely, she could not imagine that Kateri had ever been that young. She had turned thirty, and apparently joined the Older Than Dirt Club. Who knew? Kateri drained her glass. "So you two went to school together . . . you're both twenty-three?"

"Sienna's twenty-two," Layla said. "She graduated from high school early and started college at seventeen."

Michigan State at age seventeen . . . so much for the vague hope Sienna was dumber than a stump. In fact, so much for the vague hope Luis had taken up with Sienna because he was pining for Kateri. The two women couldn't be more different.

A Phantom of the Opera appeared from the direction of the deck. He smiled at Layla and offered his hand. "Wanna dance?" he asked.

Layla almost bounced with joy. "I thought you'd never ask." She went prancing off, moving with the rhythm of the band and her joy in life, leaving Kateri alone with the Girlfriend.

Kateri caught a passing waiter, passed off her empty glass, and made conversation. "So what are you doing in Virtue Falls?"

"In June, I came to visit Layla and fell in love with the town."

"Not just the town, I would guess." Kateri was being sarcastic.

Sienna didn't catch the sarcasm, and her enthusiasm was undimmed. "Right! I love the state, the whole peninsula. I mean, the mountains and the hiking! The beaches and the whale-watching! The resort, the people, the healthy food and fresh air . . ."

"You don't have to sell me."

Sienna blushed. "You're from here?"

"Here. And there." Kateri had a headache. She glanced around in the hope of seeing Summer signal her to go. Instead, she saw Summer on the dance floor twirling in the arms of a handsome buccaneer.

No escape. Kateri turned back to Sienna. "So you moved to Virtue Falls?"

"My parents think I'm nuts. They're in South Carolina and they think that's the only place in the world where it's fit to live." Sienna rolled her eyes.

"When I was in the Coast Guard Academy, we went to South Carolina for spring break. It is beautiful." *Go back.*

"But not like *this* beautiful. Here I feel as if the wild places are calling my spirit to soar."

Maybe Sienna was right. Maybe Kateri *was* old, because she didn't ever remember being that earnest.

"Once I got here, I started looking around for something I could do to support myself. Be independent. I've got a business degree. I knew I could figure *something* out. You know what they say—find a need and fill it."

"I've heard that." With every one of Sienna's chirpy words, Kateri's headache expanded.

"I realized the tourists need box lunches to take on their day trips, and when the tourists are gone, the locals still have to eat. I talked to the Bayview Convenience Store and convinced them to let me use a corner as a deli, and I created—"

"My God." Light dawned. "You're Sienna's Sandwiches."

"You've heard of me!" Sienna beamed. "Not just sandwiches, though. We make salads, cookies, and sides, and we package them attractively in recyclable boxes with the plastic cutlery tied into the bow. Our food is all organic, and we have vegetarian, vegan, and gluten-free."

"Of course you do." Kateri had ordered from Sienna on days when she was working, when cooking was too much of an effort and standing hurt her joints. Mrs. Golobovitch always brought a platter of Sienna's sandwiches and cookies to the quilting group, and claimed she had made them. Everyone pretended to believe her; they wanted those sandwiches.

"I started with me and one other worker, and I'm up to eight people working part- to full-time. I'll probably have to cut back after the holidays, and it remains to be seen if the tourists will return in the spring, but right now . . . I'm hopeful." Sienna's blue eyes gleamed.

"You'll do great." Kateri's head hurt. The room was spinning. Her vision was blurred. Since she was already sick and miserable, she figured, *What the hell,* and asked, "How did you meet Luis?"

"Oh. Luis." Sienna's expressive face changed from optimistic and enthusiastic to adoring. "I went down to the Coast Guard station to grab Layla for drinks, and he was there. He's cute, you know, but grim and intimidating, and I thought he needed cheering up. So I talked to him, and afterward Layla told me I was the only person she knew who could make him laugh." Sienna was animated and sunny. *Of course* she cheered him up.

Kateri turned her walker backward, lowered the seat, and sank down on it.

Sienna continued, "So every time I saw him, I made it my goal to make him laugh, and then he asked me out. I never thought I would be interested in an older man—"

Luis was a year younger than Kateri.

"—but like I said—cute!—so I said yes. And now I can't imagine life without him." Sienna frowned. "I simply don't understand why Commander Adams hates him so much."

CHAPTER FIFTY-FIVE

After her first dance, Summer never stopped. One man after another followed Mr. Romance, laughing, chatting, complimenting her costume, her beauty, her repartee. She felt exotic, mysterious, daring. For the first time in over a year, she fit into society without worrying about the future and how she would survive.

She did *try* to worry; she felt somehow it was wrong not to. She knew she had reason to be careful tonight, for everywhere she looked, she saw Michael Gracie. That man with his arm around his male partner. That man leaning against a pillar, talking to a full-sized, fabulous feminine bird of prey. That man with the glittering skin and vampire teeth . . .

So many men in this room fit Michael Gracie's description, and yet . . . somewhere in the depths of her mind, she was convinced she would know him if she saw him. He was tantalizing. Dangerous. A viper in a crystal vase full of roses.

Less lethal but more immediate, there was Kennedy McManus. If his furious gaze meant anything, he had recognized her. And judged her. Judging was what Kennedy did.

His superior attitude made her more determined to fling herself into having a good time. And it was easy; the spirit of Mardi Gras had possessed the band. They belted out rock classics and whirling waltzes. The trumpet player and the clarinetist took turns on the solos, and a gorgeous flapper in sequins and fringe spontaneously leaped up on the stage, took the microphone, and crooned jazz standards in a voice that could have easily won *American Idol.*

As Summer whirled from one handsome partner to the other, the worries of the last months fell away.

Then, as she was dancing with a young Gandalf, Kennedy plucked her from the wizard's arms and swung her away across the ballroom.

She gaped at him, surprised, appalled, and, oh God, pleased. He had come for her. He had stolen her away.

"What are you doing?" he asked.

"What are *you* doing?" Not the cleverest retort, but for a few moments she had been so happy, so guilt-free. "You weren't supposed to leave the house." *On the attack. Good, Summer.*

Or maybe not. "All your talk about caution, and you're here, and you've been dancing with anyone who asked."

"I wouldn't be safe at home." As they whirled in circles across the floor, he held her close, body to body, leading her in a waltz that left her breathless.

Yet his harsh tone was a counterpoint to the music. "Is your story all a scam, a lie? Was every moment a manipulation of my emotions?"

"No. No! Why do you think that?"

"As my mother proved, I am blind to a woman's machinations."

She was outraged. "I haven't manipulated you! When . . . why do you think that?"

"I offered you marriage, but you were outraged, yet tonight you dance and flirt with any man."

"It's a party. I've been in fear of my life for a *year*. Tonight . . . I'm having fun."

"Just like my mother." He lashed her with scorn. "You make up pretty stories to make yourself look good, to seem vulnerable, to soften the next sucker to your scam. And this time, that sucker was me."

"I don't do that. *I didn't do that.* Why would you believe such a thing?"

"You're lying right now. You told me you didn't drink, and yet you're drunk, or on drugs." Without regard to the couples dancing around them, he stopped and pushed her mask up and off. "You should see your eyes. Your pupils are huge."

"I've been drinking water!"

He dropped her mask and left her in the middle of the dance floor, staring after him, trembling and . . . she was standing still, but the room was spinning around her.

Why? Why was it spinning?

Beneath the sounds of music, conversation, and laughter, she heard the rustling of silks and the pulsing of impatience as everyone flirted and dreamed of romance, money, sex, and success.

She covered her ears.

But still she could hear the feelings, the hopes, the fantasies.

She took a breath. Exotic scents filled the air: passionflowers and lilies, oranges and strawberries, cinnamon bark and gingerroot. She could feel the colors as they brushed past, rainbows that blurred as they caressed her skin, were absorbed into her bloodstream. They whispered to her to run, to fly, to be free . . .

But how could she so distinctly smell those scents? How could she feel the colors? If she didn't know better, she would say she *was* drunk or high.

No. No! She drank only water. She knew it! She remembered . . .

She looked around. Even now, men flocked toward her. All evening, they had laughed at her jokes, complimented her style, fought over the right to dance with her. In all her life, she had never been so popular. She had never been the most-sought-after woman at the party.

Kennedy was right. Something was very wrong. Very, very wrong.

Water. She'd only had water. But . . . but it was bubbly. Flavored. It could have been drugged . . .

She swayed and tried to *concentrate*.

She had picked a glass at random from every tray offered her. If hers was drugged, then every glass was drugged and everyone who drank water from that same tray had also been . . .

An outcry sounded by the entrance.

Summer swiveled to face it.

Margaret Smith had collapsed. She was sprawled on the floor. Guests and staff ran toward her, surrounded her.

Margaret . . . drank the water.

Kateri . . . drank the water.

Summer looked for Kateri, and saw her sitting on the seat of her walker, her eyes closed and an expression of pained concentration on her face.

Kennedy was right.

They all had been drugged.

Who would do such a thing? Who could be so ruthless?

Who wanted Summer dead?

One man. Michael Gracie.

No time. Summer had to do something. Now.

Tell Kennedy. She had to tell Kennedy. He was the only one who could help her. Them.

Summer started toward him.

A waiter—the waiter?—loomed before her. The grin painted on his lips was grotesque. His real grin was even more grotesque. He was a nightmare come to life. "Can I get you something?" he asked. "More water? Another canapé?"

"You . . . you did this!" She tried to walk around him, toward Kennedy.

"Ah. The truth at last." He took her arm. "Come this way." His voice sounded different. Raspy. No accent.

"Michael?" She tried to struggle, to tear herself away. "No. Not Michael. Jimmy."

"Very good, Summer." He leaned close. "You know me. You fear me."

"Yes . . ." It was disorienting to look into this man's face and see nothing real but the dark, hard glitter of his eyes. Disorienting, and terrifying. Her staff was gone. Her belt was home. She had no way to defend herself. So she balled up her fist and took a swing at him. She missed, swung in a circle, stumbled and fell.

She looked up and saw Kennedy observing her. "Please," she mouthed.

He turned his back.

In her hour of desperate need, Kennedy turned his back to her.

Jimmy helped her up. He lifted her hand to his lips. He kissed her little finger. "Poor thing. You tried so desperately to escape me. All you did was postpone the inevitable."

She fought.

Her dance partners surrounded her, only now these men were not suitors. They were security guards. They held her while Jimmy removed her horned headdress. He handed it off, then swung her into his arms.

She screamed, and heard one of the men surrounding them loudly say, "She's hallucinating. These things happen at these parties."

The crowd parted.

She saw Kennedy. She held out her hands to him.

Jimmy walked toward the door. "Don't bother. He is a slave to the memories of his past, to his parents' crimes and his mother's manipulations."

"We're all . . . slaves to our past. You . . . are a slave to your past."

"True. But he's not smart enough to see what's before his eyes. A few years ago, I set up an accidental meeting with him—not accidental at all, of course. And he didn't even recognize me." Jimmy's smile was sharp as a razor blade. "Do you know how that made me feel?"

"Small," she said. "Kennedy makes everyone feel small." And that was his fatal flaw.

"He will recognize me now," Jimmy said.

As they passed through the door, she noted the loud, panicked babble around Margaret.

"How could you have done that to her?" Summer muttered. She didn't even know if she was forming the words correctly. "She could . . . die."

But Jimmy heard, for he shrugged. "She's an old woman." He kissed the top of Summer's head. "Don't worry about yourself, though. I checked before proceeding. You're not taking any prescriptions. The drugs won't be fatal to *you*."

She wanted to slap him. But her arm fell and dangled. Her head lolled against his chest. Jimmy stopped, adjusted her, then strode on.

Crazed thoughts tumbled around her mind. Jimmy cared for her, supported her when Kennedy didn't. Wanted her when Kennedy didn't.

They stepped outside. The wind, the chilly salt air, the sound of the helicopter blades beating the air . . . they revived her. She fought again, but the security men took her, held her while Jimmy climbed into the helicopter, then efficiently handed her over, like a package, like a . . . like a corpse.

They shut the doors.

The helicopter rose.

Jimmy held her cradled against his side. He brushed her hair off her ear and murmured, "If you survive the game, you get to live."

"It's not a game." Her voice was slurred, but she meant what she said.

"I make the rules. And I say it is."

"Kennedy makes the rules."

He ran his hand down her arm and across her breasts. "You're very brave . . . considering how far it is to the ground."

He was going to take her up over the forest—and drop her. She was going to die a horrible death. And she couldn't even lift her head.

CHAPTER FIFTY-SIX

Kennedy had seen Summer fall. He had seen her appeal to him. He had taken a step in her direction.

Then the waiter helped her up, picked her up and held her so easily, they might have been lovers. And Kennedy heard someone say, "She's hallucinating. These things happen at these parties."

That halted Kennedy in his tracks.

He knew what she had done to him, yet all she had to do was look at him and mouth a plea, and he'd tried to go to her rescue.

Why had he come tonight?

Because he thought Summer might be here, and he wanted the chance to see her, explain, apologize.

Instead he realized he had been taken for a fool. He had studied her, analyzed her, offered her marriage. He had debased himself, confessed his humiliation at the hands of his own mother. And now he discovered the truth: Summer was like his mother, using his weakness against him, stage-managing him . . . laughing at him.

He had to get out of here. He had to pack up and go home to California . . . except he'd promised to clear Summer's name. She didn't deserve it, that he should work for her . . .

But she did. She had saved Miles. Kennedy had made her a promise. He would keep it. And what she had done tonight opened his eyes to her true character. He should be grateful for that.

Yet . . . what if she was lying about Michael Gracie, too? What if he couldn't find "Jimmy" because she had concocted the whole story? Then he was back to ground zero on finding Miles's kidnapper.

Something like a shopping cart slammed into his Achilles tendon.

A woman's slurred voice said, "Kennedy McManus."

He turned to see Summer's drinking buddy, Kateri Kwinault, leaning heavily on her walker.

"Where's Summer?" Kateri asked. "Did he get Summer?"

"I don't know where she is. The waiter took her."

"Oh, God. Oh, God." Kateri put her hand to her forehead. She staggered.

He caught her arm and supported her as she moved the walker toward a seat along the wall. As he lowered her into the chair, she grabbed his cravat and twisted it in a stranglehold. She brought him face-to-face with her. "She's been drugged," she said.

"She has taken drugs. For fun."

"You are so stupid," Kateri said clearly.

That was something he had never been called in his life.

She continued, "*I've* been drugged. *She's* been drugged. *He's* here. I don't know what's going on, why he planned this party to take her

and kill her. But this, all this"—she gestured around the ballroom—
"is about revenge. Money. Power. *It's a game.*"

The words sank into his brain. Sank, and illuminated a blaze so
bright, he stood swiftly.

Kateri lost her grip on his cravat.

He faced the ballroom. And *looked*. Observed. Recognized. Realized.

A game. Yes. A game. *The game.* Everything about this party was
familiar. The mirrors, the gold, the whirling dances, the celebrities, the
laughter . . . all in place to confuse the players. Negotiating the ballroom and retaining your senses required concentration on a goal—that
of retaining or taking the prize.

Kennedy stood in a living reenactment of *Empire of Fire*. And
he had been manipulated by the only other player who had ever
bested him.

Kateri was right. He *was* stupid.

Turning, he raced toward the door, through the lobby, outside. He
hit the porch in time to see the helicopter hover, turn, then disappear
into the clouds.

Kennedy raised his fists and bellowed his wrath and his terror,
"Jimmy . . . James Brachler! I know you. I will find you. I will kill you!"

On the helipad, the circle of security men looked around, observed
Kennedy, his upraised fists, his frenzy, his rage . . . and swiftly, silently
dispersed into the darkness.

He ran inside. Goddamn it, someone here knew what was happening.

But in the ballroom, the party was over. The band was packing
up. The faux guests were stripping off their masks, their wigs, their jewels. They exited by every door, and while they walked, they conversed
calmly, like actors who had finished a job. Only the real guests were
left, people who stood shaking their heads, as if the sudden change left
them bewildered.

Then two of the genuine guests dropped to their knees and slithered to the floor. One was a pretty red-haired girl; her Coast Guard

companion shouted for help, then fell unconscious beside her. More guests staggered, or tilted, and one ran from the room with her hand over her mouth.

Margaret Smith's staff lifted her from her chair by the door. Her head was lolling, her eyes unfocused.

The actors—the other guests *were* actors, Kennedy was now sure of it—stepped up the pace of their departures.

Suddenly, a cool wind swept the ballroom. It swept the clutter of masks and streamers to the back wall and made the drugged guests lift their heads. Kateri had flung open one set of the French doors leading to the balcony, opening the room and the people to the incoming storm.

As she struggled with another set of doors, one man went to help her.

Although he had never met this guy, Kennedy recognized him. It was hard not to recognize someone this famous.

Tony Parnham, young, stout, with black hair retreating from his forehead and growing in long, messy sideburns down the sides of his face. Tony Parnham, in a ridiculously inappropriate medieval warrior costume. Tony Parnham, the Academy Award–winning director—and host of this party from hell.

Moving with speed and vengeance, Kennedy hit him from behind.

Parnham gave an *oof* as he fell, a yell as he skidded along the hardwood floor on his face.

Grabbing him by the shoulders, Kennedy dragged him out onto the deck. Turning him, he lifted him by his leather jerkin and hefted him up over the rail, until only Kennedy's grip kept him from a deadly plunge into the Pacific.

Parnham screamed in terror and clutched at Kennedy's hands.

"Don't struggle," Kennedy warned. "I might drop you."

Tony froze.

"Now—tell me who put you up to this," Kennedy said.

"Up to what?"

Kennedy tipped him backward.

Parnham's nails dug into Kennedy's hands.

"Who put you up to this?" It wasn't a question. It was an ultimatum.

"Please don't drop me."

"I can hear sirens, so someone's called the police and the ambulances. If I threw you, who would testify against me? Every person left in there is so drugged they can't even see straight. Some are unconscious. They wouldn't be reliable witnesses, and as sick as they are, they wouldn't care if you died."

From behind him, Kennedy heard someone clap once, twice, three times in encouragement. Kateri was there.

Parnham's eyes bulged with tears and terror.

"You don't have a lot of room to negotiate." Kennedy shook him. Just slightly. Just enough to make the rail wiggle. "Who set you up to this?"

"Please. Please, he'll kill me if he finds out that I told."

"I halfway hope you don't tell me, because right now, dropping you off this cliff is exactly what I want to do." Kennedy had never spoken words so true. "Let me get you started. It was Michael Gracie."

Parnham gasped. "I didn't tell you. I didn't tell you!"

"Why did you do it?"

"I owe him. I owe him everything."

Kennedy pulled Parnham toward him, slid him off the rail, pushed him onto the decking.

Parnham landed hard, but kept talking. "When I started, he saw my movies, said I had talent. He set me up, made sure the right people saw my work, invested in my first big effort. If not for him, I would still be an insurance agent."

Kennedy leaned over. "So you agreed to do this? To drug people, set them up to be kidnapped?"

"I didn't want to." Parnham tried to put his hand on Kennedy's shoulder.

Kennedy took his wrist and tossed it back.

"Right." Parnham continued, "He said . . . when he set me up, he said I owed him a favor, and I promised to do it, whatever he wanted, whenever he wanted. I thought, you know, like put his girlfriend in a role or something. That's bad enough. Can you imagine what it's like putting a no-talent female in a—" Something about Kennedy's expression stopped him. "Anyway, it's been five years, and nothing, not a word. Then a few weeks ago, he contacted me. He's got a scary reputation, you know. When he said . . . when he said he wanted me to host a party here, I was ecstatic. I'm building a house, I thought this would set me up as one of the good guys. Then . . . then . . . then . . ." Parnham was stuck.

"Then he told you what you had to do."

"*He* didn't tell me. It was that scary guy who works for him. He gave me a list of who to invite, and he told me who to hire: actors who could dance the way Michael wanted them to dance, play the scenes the way Michael wanted them played. It was this elaborate setup, I was the director, and I knew whatever was coming down . . . was bad."

"What's in the drinks?" Kennedy asked. "Drugs? Poison?"

"It's a new derivative of the date rape drug. You get high. You get happy. You get horny."

Behind Kennedy, Kateri said, "I'm not happy *or* horny."

Tony Parnham's eyes darted between faces: Kennedy's and Kateri's, Kennedy's and Kateri's. "Sometimes it works like speed, you're wide awake and pissed. Depends on what other drugs you're on."

Kateri was intentionally harsh. "Like if I'm a cripple and on prescription drugs for pain?"

"Yeah. I'm sorry." Parnham's gaze shifted to Kennedy. "So sorry. I was afraid they were going to kill me if I didn't do what I was told. I was afraid."

Kateri said coolly, "Kennedy, you should have dropped him over the edge."

"That would be murder. How about if I do this instead?" Kennedy gripped the front of Parnham's jerkin, pulled him forward, and slammed him back against the railing. Once. Twice. Three times.

Three times Parnham's skull hit the iron. His eyes rolled back in his head. He slumped to the decking.

Kennedy stood and dusted his fingertips.

Kateri inclined her head in thanks.

Kennedy, looking neither right nor left, headed out to his car.

Every Coastie knew that every ocean was different. The smells, the currents, the birds, the heat, the cold, the salt spray, the storms . . . oh, God, yes, especially the storms.

As Kateri stood out on the deck, she listened to the oncoming storm push across chill water and deep swells, driving toward the coast. Beneath the howl of the harbinger wind and the inescapable scent of incipient violence, the Frog God muttered to her. He was displeased, and if his displeasure continued, she would be punished yet again.

She gripped the rails and screamed back, begging him to protect her men, the ones inside struggling against the combination of liquor and drugs, and the ones on the water. She sounded insane; she knew it. Yet the wind kept her on her feet, and the stimulant in her veins wiped her inhibitions.

So she screamed. Again. More.

At last someone touched her arm.

She swung around.

Mark stumbled backward as if he feared her. "Are you okay, Commander?"

"Fine." She saw him through a wavering haze. "You?"

"Okay. This stuff hit Layla and Sienna harder than the guys. Body mass, you know. But I thought you'd like to know—we just heard from Luis. Everything's okay. So you can, um, stop yelling about it."

"Report, Ensign!"

Automatically, he straightened. "Currents were encountered. The cutter was briefly in jeopardy. Men were hurt: abrasions, contusions, one broken wrist."

"Did they locate any drugs?"

"No sign of any whatsoever." Mark glanced over his shoulder at the prone body of Landlubber Adams. "He drank a lot. Not that I hope he dies, but tomorrow I hope he barfs all day."

Tonight, Adams had sent Luis into danger. Him, and a dozen more of her Coasties, men who pledged themselves to protect America's waterways against threats from within and without. Kateri had taken that oath; she was still bound by that oath. "Someone should do something about Adams," she said.

"Yeah. But who?"

She smiled quite pleasantly. "*I'm* someone."

CHAPTER FIFTY-SEVEN

Kennedy found an older-looking gentleman directing the staff as they tended to the sick and brought in the emergency personnel.

The name badge read: HAROLD RIDLEY, VIRTUE FALLS RESORT MANAGER.

Kennedy told him what he'd learned about the drug, then added, "Tony Parnham is out on the deck. Looks like he fell and slammed his head against the railing . . . three times. Send someone out . . . when you get a chance."

In an ugly voice, Harold said, "If Margaret Smith dies from this, Mr. Parnham might not recover."

"That's okay with me." Kennedy pushed his way through the incoming stretchers and ran outside. The parking lot was lit up like a circus, teeming with emergency personnel, two ambulances, two fire trucks, and a hearse.

Kennedy grabbed the hearse driver. "Is someone dead?"

The driver looked grim. "No, but in a town this size, we don't have enough ambulances for this crisis."

"Sure." Made sense. Kennedy ran to his car, a late-model sedan he'd rented in Seattle, put his hand on the door—and stopped.

He remembered all too well the explosion that had destroyed Summer's rental SUV and ripped a hole in the Idaho forest. He took his hand away from the door, stepped back, and circled the car. Everything *looked* normal. The doors were locked. No scratches on the handles. He clicked on the mini-flashlight connected to his key ring and looked under the car. There it was—a puddle of fluid. Brake fluid, transmission fluid, oil, radiator fluid, gasoline. Hell, he didn't know anything about cars except that fluids under the vehicle could not be good.

The game. *Empire of Fire.* Most likely, James didn't want to play the final round. Not yet. He wanted to thwart Kennedy, to remind him that in college James had been the only person who had matched him in strategy, intelligence, and skill. *Fuck you, asshole* was not a mature response. Kennedy said it out loud anyway.

He returned to the resort and spoke to Harold.

Harold nodded absently, his attention on his conversation with the sheriff, and handed over car keys to his own vehicle.

Kennedy went out to the employees parking lot, climbed into Harold's silver Prius, and hit the road at a sensible speed . . . like he had a choice. This car was born sensible.

He knew that if he had taken his rental, he would have made it halfway back to the house and the car would have died. No one would have been available to come and get him, not with the situation at the resort, and by the time he had walked the dark road to the Hartmans', his rescue of Summer would be seriously delayed. And he knew, by the rules of the game, he had until tomorrow night to find her or he would lose the prize, the game, and . . . his life.

And hers? He frowned. Or would she be taken captive? James had always wanted what Kennedy had. Did he want Summer?

If he did, she had a fighting chance. And one thing that Summer had taught him was respect for her ability to survive.

The other thing Summer had taught him was to be recklessly jealous, to be blinded by emotion, to allow his memories of his past to cloud his judgment.

Damn it. Had he really just tried to blame her for his own failings?

He didn't know himself anymore.

When he turned into the Hartmans' driveway, the house was quiet, the exterior lights shining. The alarm was still set. He circled the house, knowing that James had probably installed cameras that observed his every movement. He could do nothing about that—he didn't have the time, nor did he want to step out of the ring of light from the house. But he moved with caution, watched his step, got inside, and shut the door.

By the rules of the game, he was safe inside.

Was James playing strictly by the rules of the game? Probably. He could have done anything to kill Kennedy. Instead he had carefully chosen the setting, had prepared his traps, had forced Kennedy to play defense without even realizing the game had become real. Now that he knew, Kennedy had to trust his enemy would abide by the rules while ruthlessly using his advantage.

What choice did Kennedy have? He *had* to go in. He *had* to prepare for the fight, and for that, he needed information.

He went first to the computer. It had finished the scans and found no matches. So he went searching for James Brachler, past and present.

No connection. And not a coincidence, Kennedy was sure. He checked to see if the house Internet was active. It was, and he had secured it against all but the best hackers. But he no longer trusted that it was safe.

Kennedy fetched one of his unused connectors, fired it up, and sat down to search.

James Brachler did not exist. He had not been born. He had not attended school in Chicago. He had no arrest record. He had not attended MIT.

So James had wiped his former identity off the face of the earth and replaced it with the so-perfect, so-pristine Michael Gracie.

Yes. Kennedy faulted himself for his arrogance. But he diagnosed the weakness in Michael/James—ego. He filed that away for future strategies.

Yet that didn't solve the immediate problem. Kennedy needed a photo of James Brachler as he had looked in college.

He pushed himself back from his desk, pulled out his phone, and called his sister.

Tabitha answered with that cobweb-mouth sound that meant she'd been asleep, and a note of alarm. "You okay?"

"Fine. I need you to do something for me."

A pause. A slight groan as she sat up. "Sure. What?"

"I want you to go down to storage and find the file box marked *MIT*."

"Okay." She was moving, but slowly.

"I want you to get into the last file for my senior year."

"Okay."

"And get out my yearbook."

That stopped her. "You want your yearbook? *Now?*"

"Tabitha, it's important."

She sighed. "I'm sure it is. I'm going. Let me get my robe." He heard shuffling around, then she came back. "So you found something up there?"

"I found everything."

"You found Taylor Summers?" Tabitha's voice rose.

"Yes, and I found James Brachler. He's who I want you to look up."

"James Brachler." Her voice got dreamy. "I remember him. You brought him when you visited me. I had an instant crush."

"I thought he would encourage you to work harder at your schooling."

Tabitha burst into laughter. "Sure. Gorgeous guy. Blondish with chocolate-colored eyes. I was fourteen. First thing I thought was, *Gee, I need to do my schoolwork.*"

"I was an idiot."

"Pretty much. But you were all I had."

"And I was busy. I'm sorry." Regret clawed at him. "That foster home. I should have taken you out of there."

"Child Protective Services wouldn't have allowed it."

"I knew how to live on the run. I could have removed you and they wouldn't have known where we were. I could have found a job, got an apartment, put you in school . . ." At the time, he had thought he was doing the right thing.

"But then you couldn't have graduated and started your business. You had goals. You had plans. I just couldn't stay there any longer." Before he could apologize again, offer his regrets that she had had to live as a runaway, her tone changed back to brisk. "No big deal. I survived. I got my street creds. And I've got Miles. He's worth it. But . . . James. He was nice to me. Afterward, I dreamed he would rescue me, carry me away and marry me. He was, like, my first serious crush. Except Justin Timberlake, of course."

"Why?" Kennedy had never understood why women flocked to James.

Tabitha sounded bubbly, almost as if she were still fourteen. "He was *such* a bad boy. That voice. Those eyes. He looked like he knew his way around a woman's body."

"What made you think that?" Kennedy had to know, because he had a niggling fear in the back of his mind. About Summer. And about James.

"Oh. Well." As Tabitha descended the basement steps, her voice echoed across open spaces and concrete walls. "He really looked at me. Listened to me. It was like he could see into my soul, like he appreciated what made me unique."

Kennedy paced across the living room. "Did he *do* anything?"

"Make a move on me?" She laughed. "Not a chance. I offered, but he idolized you. He told me he wished he had a sister like me." Kennedy could hear her moving boxes around, shuffling through papers. "Here it is," she said. "Your yearbook. What do you want me to do with it?"

"Find his photo, scan it, send it to me." Kennedy's hand tightened on the phone. "And one other thing. You say he idolized me, and he said he wished he had a sister like you. Well . . . he took Miles. He took Summer. And I'm afraid—"

Tabitha made the logical leap. "That he'll take me. Because then he *does* have your sister."

"Yes. Someone in my organization works for James."

"Who?"

"I don't know yet. Do you still have that pistol?"

"It's upstairs, loaded. And I've got a few knives stashed around the house."

Her years as a runaway had taught her well. "Keep them close. Keep Miles home. Until I give you the all-clear."

"Right." She shuffled around in the boxes again. "I've got a knife now, and I'll get you this photo right away."

He relaxed a few degrees. "While I wait, I will make contact with someone who was at the prison when James served his time. The warden, perhaps."

"That won't work. Whatever happened concerning Jimmy, we can assume it would reflect badly on the warden. Try a guard. Or one of the repeat offenders."

"Good point," he said. "And Tabitha—thank you."

Tabitha locked the basement door—she had a horror of Miles falling down the stairs and breaking his neck on the concrete floor—and turned into the kitchen. And screamed.

The head of Kennedy's development team stood there. Brandon Wetzel was tall and handsome, with melting blue eyes, a body he worked hard to maintain, a big ego, and a wife Tabitha felt sorry for.

She suspected she was about to feel a lot sorrier for Brandon's poor, cheated-on wife.

Brandon put his finger to his lips. "Shh. Kennedy sent me. There's trouble brewing, and he wants me to take you and Miles to a secure location."

She noted that he kept his other hand at the small of his back.

He was carrying a pistol, and at the slightest defiance, he would bring it out, point it at her, and frankly . . . the man was a computer geek. She no more trusted him to know his firearms than she trusted him to keep his promises.

So she widened her eyes in make-believe horror and moved swiftly toward him. "I'll wake Miles right now. Do I have time to pack clothes? I hate to leave in my nightgown." She stood in front of him and loosened the belt to her robe.

His gaze dropped to her cleavage. He lost focus. He reached for her.

She stabbed him in the thigh, and she never even dropped the yearbook.

CHAPTER FIFTY-EIGHT

Summer woke to a single icy snowdrop melting on her cheek.

Where was she?

Stiff with dread, she opened her eyes. Without moving, she cast her gaze around and saw . . . a rock. A gray, granite boulder set into bare dirt, about ten inches from her face. She blinked. A single thought blazed through her mind.

Get up. Escape!

She fought to stand, but she was wrapped, trapped, unable to move. Like a dark tide, panic overwhelmed her. She flipped over. She stared through a snowy curtain down a mountain, into the lonely wilderness.

How did she get here?

The ten months in Virtue Falls had been a dream. She was still in the Sawtooths, isolated, starving, and mad. Stark, staring mad.

No. No! That was wrong. Wherever she was, it was not the Sawtooths. Everything about this was wrong. The air was different. The snow was different. She was above the tree line, where she never went.

She twisted around, looked down at herself. She was wrapped in a sleeping bag, a mummy bag, zipped up so high only her face was showing. The granite boulder . . . she had been placed under its overhang. Someone had placed her here. Someone . . .

A face drifted out of the fogs of her memory.

Michael Gracie . . . Jimmy.

She groped for the inner zipper, slid it down as fast as she could, and flung the bag aside. In a frenzy, she stood up and looked around.

Yes. She was somewhere high in the mountains. Patches of old snow alternated with bare ground, and all of it was being covered by new snow that shifted out of the air and whirled in the wind.

She stared, mesmerized, at the dancing, twirling flakes.

Gold walls and bright mirrors. Glittering, masked dancers circling and spinning. And the waiter with his terrifying face and dark brown eyes. Then his face had melted away, and Michael Gracie had been revealed. Jimmy . . .

Now she remembered. She'd been drugged. He had drugged her. He had planned the party for the purpose of taking her and putting her . . . here . . . to die?

That didn't make sense. Why not just kill her?

Because of the game. He had spoken of the game.

Her cold hands held out in trembling appeal to Kennedy.

Kennedy turns away.

Jimmy's smug, razor-blade-sharp smile . . .

She turned, leaned over the edge of the boulder, and vomited until she had nothing left in her stomach. The drugs, and the memories, made her sick.

She didn't want to be sick. She needed to get out of here, wherever here was. She needed to concentrate on the task at hand—finding her way back to civilization. She could do it. She knew the mountains. She knew how to survive, and if she could get down the slope in time, she *would* survive.

She assessed her situation.

First—she was warm. She wore clothes she had never seen before, outdoor winter clothes designed to keep snow out and body heat in. Boots and dry socks sat wrapped in plastic, waiting for her. She slid under the overhang and pulled them on, and an unwelcome thought caught at her mind.

Last night she had been in costume, in purple silk. Sometime, during the lost hours of the night, she had changed her clothes. How? Who? She rubbed her forehead and tried to think.

She could see the helicopter blades through the glass bubble; they slapped at the clouds, slicing them, then slicing them again. A futile operation; the clouds always re-formed, yet sometimes she glimpsed bright stars in the midnight heavens. "Beautiful," she murmured.

A man knelt beside her on the floor, and she laughed as he found the hidden zip in her costume and pulled it down. "Are we going to have sex?" she asked.

"If you want to," he said.

Summer stood up too fast and slammed her head against the overhang. The impact dropped her to her knees, and she cradled the bump in both hands and moaned, "No. Oh, no." Whatever had happened last night, whatever Jimmy had done . . . she could not remember. She didn't want to remember.

And it didn't matter. The sky was light gray and flat. She didn't know what time it was, only that she needed to get down the mountain before nightfall, when the temperatures dropped and she would be lost in the trackless wilderness.

A small backpack leaned against the boulder.

She pulled it toward her and rummaged through the contents. A canteen of fresh water. Breakfast in the form of fresh strawberries, granola, and milk. Dehydrated-food packages for lunch and dinner.

Jimmy had given her a day's worth of supplies.

A whole day's worth. Wow, thanks, no pressure.

A down coat and gloves.

"Compass . . . Where's the compass?" She sorted through the supplies with increasing desperation.

That bastard. She didn't know where she was—the Olympic Mountains, most likely, but as drugged as she was last night, she could be in the Swiss Alps. She didn't know which direction to go. Assuming these *were* the Olympics, west and to the coast would probably be best. Yet without a compass or a chance to see the sun—and the storm showed every sign of increasing in intensity—she had no way of knowing which way was west.

She scrunched under the overhang. She ate her granola and milk. The strawberries were out of season, yet as ripe and sweet as springtime. The advanced planning for this operation unsettled her, made her realize she was outmaneuvered and outflanked.

Jimmy said it was a game. Okay. Then she was a pawn. A pawn with a mind and a heart of her own. If he thought she could be moved around this chessboard and she wouldn't strike back, he would soon be surprised.

As she finished the strawberries, at the bottom of the small recyclable paper container she found parchment-thin paper sealed in a small plastic bag. She unfolded the paper and read:

> *Darling Summer,*
> *Before dark, you have to make it down the mountain and to the right spot to be rescued. Those are the rules. Cruel, I know, but I didn't make them up. Kennedy McManus did.*
> *Believe me, my dearest, I have faith in you. You know what you should not know. You live when you should be dead. You recognize the real me when no one else does. My darling, I have faith in you. This day requires strength, determination, knowledge and luck, and you have all four. You can do this. Confirm my faith, and I will see you soon.*
> *I am your faithful servant, Venom (or Jimmy, or Michael, as you prefer. I am the man you wish me to be.)*

Was she supposed to be thrilled? Flattered? Encouraged? She was none of those things. She was angry.

She knew the prevailing winds came from the west. The wind was blowing in her face. So she stood and moved toward the tree line, into the teeth of the storm.

Summer trekked downhill. She stepped again, and again, and again, through the snow falling at inches an hour, across paths empty of hikers, through a foot of fresh powder, eighteen inches, two feet, more. The hours rolled along. She paused long enough to choke down the second meal. She had stumbled down this mountain for what felt like forever and she had yet to see anything to indicate she was going the right way. Whatever way that was.

A spot between her shoulder blades itched. She felt as if a sniper held her in his sights. If she didn't get down this mountain by dark, somehow, Michael Gracie was going to kill her. She kept herself motivated by imagining the ways he could do it: the bullet from a rifle, a trip wire, or maybe the dinner she would eat next was laced with enough poison to take her out of this world.

Maybe if she was lost long enough, she would gladly eat it.

Then she stepped in a hole and fell face-first. She put her arms down, yanked her face up and wiped at it, and she wiped away some tears, too.

She stood up. She had to keep going.

The light was so flat and gray, she couldn't even guess at the time. When had she started? How long had she been walking?

But . . . She blinked through the snowstorm. She stood on a flat spot, a long flat spot that wound around the curve of the mountain. And the hole she stood in wasn't a hole, but a rut, matched by another rut about six feet out . . .

She stood on a road! She had stumbled across a road! And someone had driven this road recently! He, or she, had to have come from somewhere, had to be going somewhere. Which way was civilization? Which way should she turn?

She saw no reason to change course. She turned into the wind and walked. Whatever vehicle had come through here was big; the tire tracks were wide, and even with snow filling them up, walking was easier in the ruts.

She had to survive this. She didn't want to die an irony, the woman who had lived through solitary months in the Sawtooths and died on a one-day excursion in the Washington mountains, the dupe of two adult men playing a deadly game. When she got her hands on Kennedy

McManus, she was going to wring his neck, among other things. Because she did not appreciate . . .

Wait.

What was that? In the road ahead of her. What was that?

A tent. A tiny, one-man, fluorescent orange tent set up right on the road.

She rushed toward it . . . Okay, she plowed through the snow as rapidly as she could.

There were footprints around it, a man's footprints by the size of them. She batted the snow off the sloped sides, brushed the snow off her snowsuit, unzipped the door and crawled in. Inside there was a thermos, a small insulated bag, a devise of some kind . . . and a note.

A note. Like the one Jimmy had left her. For the first time, she realized this could be a trap. She snatched up the note; the font was Helvetica, plain and unadorned. She glanced at the signature, and clutched the paper to her chest.

It was Kennedy's signature.

Signatures could be forged.

Then she read:

> *Summer, if you're reading this, you found the tent with the GPS. Activate it immediately and we will come to get you.*

It was Kennedy, all right. Compared to Jimmy's flowery style, there could be no doubt.

She snatched up the GPS, followed the instructions, and activated it. And poured herself a cup of hot coffee.

If Kennedy got back here soon enough, she might live through this day.

Then she only had to worry about tomorrow.

CHAPTER FIFTY-NINE

In the distance, Summer heard the dull sound of a motor.

No, it was the wind in the trees.

She heard it again, louder this time.

An avalanche? Oh, that would be humorous in a good-bye-cruel-world way.

At last, she was sure. That sound was a motor. She fastened her hood and crawled out of the tent.

A silver Hummer rounded the corner toward her.

She waved her arms and jumped up and down. She hoped it was Kennedy inside. She prayed it wasn't Jimmy. But honestly, she didn't care who it was. That Hummer had a heater in it.

The vehicle slowed down.

A man jumped out even before it stopped.

Black hair. Vibrant blue eyes surrounded by freakishly long black lashes. Long stride. Square jaw. Yep. That was Kennedy.

The driver got out, too. She recognized the short, wide man in an orange gimme cap as John Rudda. Nice guy. He lived outside of town, had lost his wife in that serial killer thing a couple of years ago, and more to the point, he was a long-haul trucker. She guessed that was why he was driving—snow and a Californian like Kennedy did not mix.

John headed toward the tent.

Kennedy headed toward her.

Both men stopped short when she started peeling off her clothes and discarding them. "It's a long story," she said. "Did you bring anything for me to change into?"

Kennedy's eyes narrowed. She could almost see his clever brain chugging away, putting the facts together. Then he turned back to the vehicle and opened the back door for her. "Dry clothes inside."

John muttered something about city folks, and continued toward the tent.

As she brushed past Kennedy, he grabbed her. In one quick, tight motion, he hugged her.

She suffered the embrace—she was glad to be rescued, and pissed that she had to be rescued—then she climbed in the Hummer. The lovely, clean, luxurious, warm Hummer.

Oh, God, it was so warm. Essential, since she was going to get naked. "In or out," she said. "Just shut the door."

Kennedy climbed in after her and went to work pulling her new clothes and a blanket out of the backpack where he had stashed them.

He did not try to hug her again.

"We'll dump the clothes out here," he said.

John opened the tailgate in time to hear. "Can't do that," he said in a disapproving voice. "This is Washington. We don't litter in our mountains." He flung in the tent and shut the tailgate.

Kennedy waited until John got in. "According to the rules of the game, we only had until dark to find her or she would die. Therefore Summer is afraid there is an incendiary device in her clothes, set to go off when the sun sets."

"Wait. You mean you think this guy who is playing this game with you put a bomb in her knickers?" John started the Hummer.

In unison, Kennedy and Summer said, "Yes."

John looked at the clock—it was three thirty. Sunset was coming on fast. "As soon as you can, hand that stuff up, and I'll toss it out. When we get the first good spell of weather in the spring, I'll come back and see if I can find the clothes. I wouldn't bet on it. But I'll try."

"I'll pay you," Kennedy said.

"Fair enough," John agreed.

Kennedy held the blanket to block her from John's view as she stripped down to nothing, then he tossed the clothes into the front seat.

John slowed, opened his door, and threw them into a snowdrift.

Summer shivered in the frigid breeze, grabbed the panties from Kennedy's outstretched hand, and shimmied into them.

A quick glance up showed Kennedy's gaze fixed on her breasts.

In exasperation, she asked, "Really? Would you have even bothered to rescue me without a shot at my boobs?"

His gaze jerked up to her face. "I didn't know I was going to get a shot at your boobs."

From the front seat, John said, "I helped rescue you. I could handle a shot of your boobs."

She bobbed her head up over the edge of the blanket. "Not this time, John."

When she seated herself again, she glanced at the frowning Kennedy. She wanted to tell him to get a sense of humor, but he touched her chin with one finger and turned her head away from him. "What?" She touched her hair, her ear, her neck, her shoulder. "What's wrong?"

He let her go, and when she looked again, he looked positively grim. "Later."

John gradually accelerated to about twenty miles an hour. The Hummer held the road without slipping. The guy really could drive.

But within a few minutes, he slowed, stopped, got out, and slammed the door.

She grabbed the blanket, wrapped it around herself, slid down on the hump in the middle of the floor and huddled in front of the heat vent. "What are we doing?" she asked.

Kennedy pulled off his ski pants and parka, leaving him clad in a long-sleeved plaid wool shirt and jeans. He looked good in them. Natural. Like the guy on the Brawny paper towel package. "Because we didn't know where you would descend the mountain, we brought multiple tents and GPS trackers, and placed them every mile along the road. They have to be picked up."

Summer hadn't even considered the machinations they'd gone through. "How did you even know where to start?"

"We're playing the game."

"Tell me something I don't know."

"All right, I will." Kennedy was serious. "I first made the assumption that we would play the game here, in Washington. I also made the assumption that James wouldn't want the game to end too quickly, and would place you somewhere I could retrieve you. In the game, the highest peak plays a part as one of the first challenges. In Washington, the tallest mountain in the Olympic Mountains is Mount Olympus. But in the game, that wasn't the name of the challenge peak. So I researched other peaks. I found that the west peak of Mount Anderson is the hydrographic apex of the Olympic Mountains."

"Of course. I knew that. I was saying that only yesterday." She watched him digest that, decide she was kidding, and smile mechanically. She *thought* he had a sense of humor, yet he also had that intense focus on the subject at hand. Right now, she should be glad of that focus. It had saved her bacon.

He continued, "From West Peak, rivers flow outward to the Pacific Ocean, the Strait of Juan de Fuca, and Hood Canal. That mountain also has the wrong name, but it has the right characteristics. So I chose West Peak. I was right."

"You gambled," she said.

"I chose wisely," he answered.

John opened the tailgate and shuffled stuff around.

"How many setups are there?" she asked.

Kennedy fished his tablet out of his jacket and consulted it. "We left this morning before dawn, and we've placed fourteen."

Summer's vision of a quick rescue faded. "How long until we get back to town?"

John climbed back in the front. "In this weather, with the number of setups we have to grab on the way back, we're going to be driving all night."

Kennedy said, "But we're not going to Virtue Falls. We're going to the Hartmans'—you and I have things we must discuss."

"We can discuss everything right here," she said.

Kennedy flicked a glance at the back of John's head.

John looked as if he was leaning back for a better eavesdrop.

She asked, "John, you got headphones in this thing?"

"Sure do." He reached forward, grabbed them, and held them up. "You want me to put them on?"

"That would give us some much-needed privacy," she said.

He put them on and said loudly, "I'll crank it up!"

She nodded at Kennedy. "There. I'm not waiting all night to hear why I'm sitting naked in a Hummer after being drugged and kidnapped and almost killed. So explain this to me. And this!" She waved at herself, then out at the snowy mountainside. "What am I doing out here? How did I get stuck in the middle between you and Michael? Jimmy? Whatever his name is. *Who is he?*"

CHAPTER SIXTY

"He is James Brachler, an underclassman I knew at MIT. At the time, a friend." Kennedy handed Summer a bra.

She let the blanket drop, slid her hands through the straps and pulled the elastic around. "How did you figure that out?"

"As soon as I realized we were playing the game, I knew." Kennedy reached around her and fastened the hook.

"I can dress myself."

"I need to touch you."

She did not care what he needed. She snatched a long-sleeve navy blue T-shirt and pulled it over her head. "I gathered it was a game."

"No. *The* game. *Empire of Fire.*" Kennedy held her long underwear in front of his heat vent to warm them. "As soon as I looked him up on the Internet, I had a positive ID, for Jimmy Brachler did not exist. He was a man I knew personally, and all record of him had vanished from the face of the earth. So I called my sister and had her find his yearbook photo, and when I received the scan, I ran it through the software. The match was positive."

"Out of all the Jimmys you knew, how did you miss this guy?" She took the underwear and pulled the tight material over her legs. As the heated black silk slid over her chilled thighs and butt, she hummed with delight.

"As far as I was concerned, when James Brachler went into prison, he was dead to me. But more than that, I was told by one of my senior executives, a man who knew us both, that Jimmy had died in prison. I trusted Brandon. I believed him."

"Those are your excuses?" She stretched out her legs. Ah, yes. Long underwear, guaranteed to kill a man's desire.

Except Kennedy didn't seem repulsed. Those blue eyes were alive with appreciation—and apology.

Goddamn right, he should apologize. Yet she would bet he was apologetic for all the wrong reasons.

He was sorry to have involved her in Jimmy's vendetta. But etched on her memory was that moment at the party when she had reached out to him, and he turned away.

He told her, "When you said I had a selective memory—you were right."

"I was right, you say?" She pretended astonishment. "Here's a moment I will hug to my bosom and put in the treasury of my memory."

"You're being sarcastic."

"Damned straight I am." She got the jeans off the seat and worked her way into them.

The car slowed. "Got another tent and another GPS," John said loudly. He removed the earphones and jumped out.

"What are you going to do with your senior executive?" she asked Kennedy.

"Right now he's been neutralized. Brandon tried to kidnap my sister and my nephew. She stabbed him." Kennedy smiled unpleasantly. "Don't screw with my sister. She's a lot like you. She's not afraid to defend herself."

Summer relaxed a little. "So Tabitha and Miles are safe?"

"They are. Brandon's in the hospital under arrest. I have already started backtracking his activities. I expect to find other betrayals." Kennedy took a breath. "I promise he will spend a lot of years in prison. Loyalty is my number-one requirement in an employee. But if you wish to be sarcastic about my unwarranted trust in this man, you would be right there, too."

"We all trust people who don't deserve it," she said meaningfully.

He winced.

"Yeah," she said. "Anyway, how would you recognize the signs of betrayal? You have fewer people skills than most."

From the open tailgate, John said, "Lady, you're rough on him, considering what he did to find you."

She pulled the blanket back around her and shivered. "I'm grateful to *you*, John. But Kennedy's the reason I was kidnapped in the first place. At the first sign that I didn't meet his standards, he decided I was weak and treacherous." Her voice rose. "*Like his mother*. He doubted me immediately. So he owed me a rescue."

"Yes, ma'am." John flung the tent in and slapped the tailgate shut.

When John hoisted himself into the front seat, Summer locked eyes with Kennedy and said, "Besides, John, I wouldn't be here if it wasn't for him and this damned . . . game."

"Yes, ma'am," John said again.

In an overly reasonable voice, Kennedy said, "While I can't argue with that, I would also like to point out that you wouldn't be involved at all if, rather than rescue my nephew, you had remained hidden in the woods. And you did tell me you took responsibility for your actions."

Okay. He got to win this one. "Tell me about the game," she said.

"When I was in college, I had goals—primarily, before I was thirty, I wanted to be wealthy. To do that, I intended to own a successful business." His already firm jaw firmed even more. "I had plans, ways to achieve those goals. I knew with the world proceeding as it was, the need would be for a business that could interpret and investigate the changes in business and government. I also knew I needed a team who would be sufficient to the challenge. So I developed a role-playing game."

"Empire of Fire." She took the faded red sweatshirt out of Kennedy's hands and warmed it with the vent. "I read about it in your bio. You and your friends played it while you were in college, and when you graduated, you sold it and used the proceeds to finance your business."

"That's right—as far as it goes. I attended MIT, probably the most prestigious technical institution in the world. My friends were all highly intelligent and focused. But not all of them had the skills I required for my business, and of those who did, I wanted the best."

"I never doubted it." Of course. That explained so much.

He continued, "So we all played *EoF.* I was able to see firsthand who comprehended the *EoF* world and its ever-changing challenges, and who was the best and fastest strategist."

She was appalled. "You used the game to interview them."

"Yes."

"My God. You're a ruthless bastard."

Kennedy looked surprised. No doubt he *was* surprised. "Why do you say that? It was a logical, intelligent plan on my part, one that has reaped great rewards."

"But you didn't tell them, did you?" She pulled the sweatshirt over her head. "That you were interviewing them?"

"That would have defeated the purpose."

"I'll bet you also used them to refine the game." The T-shirt sleeves had bunched at her elbow. Of course.

"Yes."

He didn't even get it. The immorality of using a game to test his comrades, his friends, to judge them worthy or not, to discard those who were undeserving and gather the ones who excelled. What he said was a lesson, one she intended to remember. "Tell me more about the game, the parts we're playing. You're a warrior, of course, in opposition to all the other warriors."

"Yes." Without a single sign of impatience, he helped her wrestle the sleeves down to her wrists, and when he was done, his touch lingered.

She removed his hands. "And what is my role in this game?"

"You are the Prize."

What bullshit. "The *pawn*."

"At times," he agreed. "But the Prize was not—is not—a thing. It is a person. The game chose the Prize randomly from among the players, and as the person played that position, that gave me the clearest view of the value of a player."

"Because?"

"The Prize is the game-changer. By any means at its disposal, the Prize can take control of the game. The Prize can make alliances, break them, trick the warriors into fighting among themselves, defeat all opponents and ultimately win. Because the Prize is up against the warriors, it is the most difficult role."

"So as the Prize, I'm playing in opposition to you and Jimmy."

"Yes."

She contemplated that. "Interesting." Then she regained her senses. "But also not the point. How did the game become real?"

"That is Jimmy's doing. Apparently—and I am interpolating the facts I learned last night from a prison guard—in prison, he was beaten and cut, his face destroyed."

"Which is why you didn't recognize him." She hated to abandon the heat vent, but her butt hurt. So she eased herself up on the seat, fastened her seat belt, and set to work putting on her socks and shoes. "Why was he in prison?"

"He was convicted of running the drug and prostitution trade at the university and the surrounding area."

"Ohhh." Now she understood. "You discovered his crimes and reported them."

"I did not *discover* them. The university asked me to determine who was behind the massively increased on-campus drug and prostitution problems." Kennedy stared out the window, where the snow swirled and danced its way into the oncoming night. "I had no suspicion at all. I admired Jimmy. He was brilliant. He was my only competitor."

"In the game."

"In . . . everything! I hoped I could hire him. I imagined he had intentions of starting his own business." He turned back to her. "I did not realize he already had."

She looked at Kennedy.

After a moment, he said, "Yes, I reported him."

"Then you washed your hands of him, and forgot about him."

"Yes."

"Did you ever see him after turning him in?"

"Once. He wanted to know why I had betrayed him. Why *I* had betrayed *him*. He didn't seem to understand that what he had done was illegal and immoral. I had badly miscalculated—he was, and is, a psychopath."

"You spit on him."

"I did not."

"Metaphorically."

No hesitation this time. "Yes."

Sometime during one of the stops, John had failed to put on his headphones, and now she met his eyes in the rearview mirror.

They both shook their heads.

She waved her hand at Kennedy. "Okay, back to the story of how you talked to a guard from the prison where Jimmy was incarcerated."

"Jimmy had disappeared off the public records, so what I needed was someone who remembered him. It was not as easy as one might have hoped. He's eliminated or intimidated everyone who knew him."

An image flashed through Summer's mind, of Jimmy peeling off his face.

She screamed, hid her face in her hands and sobbed with fear. Monsters were real, and this one was going to toss her out of the helicopter.

He laughed. He took her wrist and said, "Look at me."

In trepidation, she did.

He looked like Jimmy again, sexy and alluring. He had revealed his true features. He leaned toward her, kissed her . . .

But they weren't his true features. He was a chimera, a creature of many faces, and the soul behind those faces was rotten with corruption.

Yet his kisses had not tasted like corruption. They had been sweet, chaste, then as she warmed to him, skilled and elegant.

She felt ill.

"Are you all right?" Kennedy asked. "You're flushed."

She busied herself arranging the blanket over her legs. "The drug . . . I'm still fighting off the effects."

"No barfing in my Hummer!" John said in alarm.

Kennedy found her a bottle of water and handed it to her.

"Thank you." She took a sip. The water helped subdue the nausea, gave her an excuse to avoid Kennedy's gaze, helped steer her away from unwanted memories. Such a powerful little bottle of water. "The prison guard told you Jimmy had killed people for talking about him?"

"Yes."

Yes. Of course. She had kissed a cold-blooded murderer. She knew that. She had seen him kill a man, his friend. She had seen Jimmy blow Dash's brains across the wine cellar . . . *No! Don't think about that.* Firmly she put her mind to work on the conversation at hand. "Then why did the guard talk to you?"

"He is dying. Cancer. It's expensive. I paid off his medical bills and agreed to give his wife a stipend every month."

"He had nothing to lose." Summer knew that feeling. Yet here she was fighting for her life. Again. And this time . . . her sanity? "You must have been up all night."

"Yes." Yet except for a heaviness around his eyes, he didn't look tired.

Not fair, especially when she was rapidly descending into depression and exhaustion. "What happened after Jimmy was almost killed?"

"When he recovered, he eliminated the competition and took over as the director of the rampant corruption that plagued the prison. When he got out, he had business capital, a business plan, and within the prison, he had vetted his future employees by using them as delivery boys and gang bosses." Kennedy met her gaze. "I don't know that he explained he was interviewing them, either."

She laughed. Reluctantly, but she laughed. "I already knew you two were opposite sides of the same coin."

"You are looking pale," Kennedy said. "We brought soup. Would that help?"

Would soup push the memories away? No. But despite the fact she wanted to know more, she was suddenly trembling and on the verge of collapse. "I think so."

He rummaged behind him, produced a thermos, and poured out chicken broth. "Then perhaps you should stretch out across the seat and sleep."

She examined the size of the seat. "Will you move up front?"

"You can put your head in my lap."

She eyed him skeptically.

"You know I won't take advantage of you."

She did know it. She needed to remember who she was dealing with, and why.

She drank the broth, then reluctantly, awkwardly reclined on the seat. His thigh was too well-muscled to be a good pillow, but he was warm and she was tired. "When Jimmy carried me out of the ballroom, he said you didn't recognize him. But that you would recognize him now."

Kennedy arranged the blanket over her shoulders. "He was right."

"He also said you were stupid."

"In that, he was wrong. I may have blind spots, but when we played *EoF*, we were evenly matched." He petted her hair in a slow, soothing motion. "I will win this match."

"If you were evenly matched, how do you know that?"

"The Prize is on my side."

"You're wrong." She closed her eyes. "The Prize is on nobody's side but her own."

CHAPTER SIXTY-ONE

Kateri shooed the last patron out the library door, flipped the "Closed" sign around, and turned off most of the lights. A good day: one fight between twelve-year-old girls, one four-year-old who vomited on the floor, and one new mother bursting into tears because her breast milk hadn't come in.

Kateri considered it one of the ironies of her life that she, motherless, sisterless, and infertile, gave advice on how to breastfeed. Actually, all she did was find a book on breastfeeding, but the poor woman was so exhausted from caring for her constantly hungry newborn that Kateri had had to read it and explain the process step by step. If she ever found a different job, she couldn't imagine what it would be. Counselor? Know-it-all? Servant to the Frog God?

Oh, wait. She already had that one nailed. Or so her people believed. And today, she would prove it, one way or the other.

She hoped nobody was injured.

"Come here, Lacey." Kateri lifted the dog onto the library table and looked her in the eyes. "I have an unpleasant half hour ahead. I don't want you to feel like you have to protect me, so you need to go in your crate."

Lacey's head drooped.

Kateri stroked her soft ears. "Don't pull that sad-doggie look on me. I know you. You're a survivor, like me. Now, go on." She put Lacey on the ground and followed her into the office.

Lacey went inside her crate, snuggled into the lambskin throw, and put her head on her paws.

Kateri covered the crate with a blanket, creating a den where the dog would feel safe during the upcoming cataclysm. Kateri wasn't sure how this meeting with Landon Adams would come out, but she was betting on . . . not good. It all depended on whether he was reasonable or not. Because *reasonable* was his middle name.

She went back to the table and worked on a list of library needs—when dealing with the city council, she had to justify every broken crayon. She had just finished when Adams came through the door. "Good," she said, "you at least can obey an order to be on time."

His flush lit him up like a traffic light.

Ah, the travails of having a lily-white complexion.

But he was smooth, damn him. "I didn't want to be obstructive to a woman with your physical disabilities."

Score to him. Of all the people in the town, Adams understood how much she hated her broken body.

What he didn't understand was that he could only strengthen her resolve. "Thank you for your kind expression of concern. Now, sit down." She pointed at a chair where just this afternoon, Michelle DeRosa's baby had blown out his diaper in an impressive poop. The chair had been cleaned, of course, but still, Kateri felt a petty satisfaction in watching Adams lower his strong, perfectly formed body onto the scarred red plastic. When he was seated, she folded her hands on the table before her. "As the former commander of the Virtue Falls Coast Guard unit, it has come to my attention that you lack the proper care for the lives and good health of my men."

As she had known he would, he sputtered, "*Your* men? They are not *your* men anymore."

"You're not concerned about my accusation of negligence? Only that I continue to lay claim on my Coasties?"

"I don't have to put up with this shit." He stood and stormed toward the door.

She stood, too, and in a voice that lashed at him and spun him around, she said, "I wouldn't leave if I were you." She limped around the table. "In less than a year, you have permanently disabled one man, and seriously injured another."

He looked her up and down. "Now you're going to accuse me of causing *your* problems."

"Not at all. I was in command, so the loss of the cutter and my injuries are my own fault. But now I must take appropriate action to deal with you—unless you promise to use due diligence in any future Coast Guard missions." Because as much as she didn't want to be fair about this, she had to give him the chance to straighten up.

A smirk flitted on and off Adams's face. Mostly on. "Or what?"

"Or I will be forced to make you."

"You're going to go to my commanding officer and convince him to discharge me? He doesn't dare. My uncle would make his life difficult." He strolled toward her. "Or maybe you want to go to the newspapers and sing your sad song about Kateri, the poor broken Indian maiden, who lost her command to someone with a better pedigree?"

"Neither of those things had occurred to me."

"Face it, you're helpless and you're crippled, and you can't do anything to help your beloved Coasties."

"I wouldn't say that." She wrapped her hand around his wrist. "I can do this." Taking a breath, she grew still and quiet. She called on the earth and the wind, the sea and the power of the Frog God . . . and she made the earth move.

At the first tremor, Adams looked around wildly. "Earthquake!" He yanked himself free and dove under the table.

As soon as he broke the connection, the tremor died away.

She offered him her hand. "You seem spooked by earthquakes."

He ignored her. He climbed out and dusted his knees. "Who isn't?" He saw her still standing, coolly watching him. "You ought to do some cleaning in here. The floor is filthy. What is this white stuff? Chalk?"

"Might be. Might be the compound I spread on the floor when the children vomit."

He blanched and held out his fingers as if they needed to be disinfected.

She didn't laugh. But she came close.

She took his wrist again. "Will you swear that you will behave responsibly when it comes to the lives of my men?"

He looked around, scanned the walls, paid particular attention to the corners. "You're filming this, aren't you? You're trying to get me to say something incriminating so you can use it against me."

"I have no need for such cheap tricks." In her mind, she slipped away again, touched all the elements of the earth and sky—and the ground shook.

This time he rode it out, too embarrassed to climb under the table. When it was over, he asked scornfully, "There's a bunch of weird rumors among the Indians that you're all woo-woo and cool with the gods."

"Just one god," she said, "the Frog God, who lives in the ocean, and when he wishes, he leaps up to the sun, and all the world shakes beneath our feet."

"So you're pretending that you made those tremors? Because they weren't that big, so if I was supposed to be scared, it didn't work." He gestured and rolled his eyes.

"I'm not *pretending* to do anything."

"Let me tell you the truth, lady." He leaned down until they were nose to nose. "I don't give a damn about those Coasties, and they don't give a damn about me. They all whine about how much they loved you. They all blame me for what happened to you. And every time they do, I send them out to get killed."

"You're sick."

"No. I'm in *charge*. In fact, you know what? Right now I'm going back to the station and pick out your very favorite Coasties—ooh, ooh, especially your sweetheart Luis—and send them on the most hopeless mission I can devise to bring in some hopped-up drug dealer, and if I'm lucky, they'll all die, and I can start over with some new boys." Adams was so pleased with himself. "What do you think of *that*?"

She kept her eyes fixed on his. She reached out and took his wrist. And she brought power up through her legs, her gut, her heart, her mind . . . The metal bookshelves rattled first. The glass in the windows undulated like a flowing stream. The cinder-block walls creaked in protest.

The earthquake built.

Books walked off the shelves. Children's artwork fell off the walls.

The earthquake built.

Dust shook off the open trusses, dispersed through the air and into the whirlwind of power she had created, the whirlwind that surrounded them.

The earthquake roared like a beast.

Adams tried to break away and crawl under the table again.

She held him effortlessly.

His eyes got bigger. And bigger. He trembled—shook because the earthquake rattled him like a baby's toy, and shook because he was afraid.

She dug deeper, deeper, bringing up fire from the center of the earth, cold from the depths of the ocean, rage from the center of her being that this man who had everything could be so spitefully, cruelly malicious. She mixed the elements into a lethal brew and in one final gesture, she tightened her fingers and sent a shot of fire and ice through his wrist and into his whole body.

He flew backward and slammed against the wall.

The power of the earthquake diminished and died.

But she was stronger than ever. She walked to stand over him as he lay crumpled on the floor. "I warned you." Her voice sounded funny, deeper than normal. "Now, will you do as you should and have a care for my men?"

He scrambled to his feet. He looked at his wrist. A dark mark encircled it. "You did that."

"The earthquake? Yes. I did that."

"You burned me. Or froze me. You . . . made the earthquake."

"Yes. Swear to care for my men, or I'll make another that will take you out."

He pointed a shaking finger at her. He backed away. "Your eyes. Your face. You did that."

She followed. "I did that."

He looked at his wrist again. "I . . . I'm going to press charges!"

She stopped stalking him. "Press charges?" It was so ludicrous, so petty, she blinked in surprise.

"I'm going to tell the sheriff that you made the earthquake."

"I'd like to hear *that*," she mocked him. "Do you really think anyone will believe that someone with my *disabilities* could make an earthquake?"

"I will swear out a warrant for your arrest. I'm a Coast Guard officer." He tripped over books, kicked them aside, and continued his exodus. "I'm a gentleman from a good family. They'll believe me. And if they don't—I'll show the sheriff my wrist."

Humor curled up in her. "You're going to tell the sheriff I hurt your wrist?"

"He'll look at your eyes, and he'll believe me. I will have you thrown in jail for a million years." As Adams backed out the door, he never let her out of his sight. "You'll be sorry you did this to me, Kateri Kwinault." He slammed the door, leaving her alone among the scattered, worn books.

"Huh." This was an ending she hadn't considered. She would be interested to see how it played out. But she wondered at Adams, and at the terror on his face when he looked at her.

She walked into the miniscule library restroom and looked into the old, speckled glass. From her own face, the green and gold eyes of the Frog God glared back at her.

Whoa. That *was* scary.

As she watched, traces of the god faded, leaving her eyes the same deep brown they had always been.

She laughed softly.

This was shaping up to be a very interesting evening.

On the snow-covered road in the mountains, the ground shook, and shook again.

"Son of a bitch!" John pressed his foot on the gas. "Earthquake!"

The Hummer leaped forward, fishtailed, then gained speed.

Summer woke, grabbed at Kennedy's leg and held on. "John, should we be going this fast during an earthquake?"

"We have to get out of here," John answered.

She looked up, wide-eyed, at Kennedy.

Kennedy, of course, had drawn the correct conclusion. "Earthquakes cause avalanches."

That made deadly sense. She said, "Drive fast, John. Drive faster."

CHAPTER SIXTY-TWO

Two hours later, someone knocked on the door of Kateri's apartment.

Lacey barked, leaped off Kateri's lap, ran to the door and stood wagging her stump of a tail. So whoever it was, was no threat.

Kateri turned off the TV, went to the door, looked out the peephole, and grinned. She opened the door. "Hi, Sheriff."

Garik stood there, holding his ticket book and a pen.

"I feel like you've caught me pushing my walker too fast."

"Ha. Ha." He was patently not amused.

She stepped back. "Come on in."

Garik leaned down to pet the dog, then followed them into the living room.

"How's Margaret?" Kateri asked.

"She's recovering. And spitting mad at Tony Parnham."

"Between Kennedy's beating and Margaret's temper, I wouldn't want to be Parnham."

"Serves him right," Garik said.

"How's Elizabeth? I heard she wasn't feeling well."

"She's sick. Really sick." Garik sounded weary. "Dr. Frownfelter's worried about dehydration. If things don't improve soon, she'll have to check into the hospital for intravenous liquids."

"Oh, no! Give her my love."

"I will." At a wave from her hand, he sat on the couch.

Lacey joined him, leaned on his leg, and smiled smugly at Kateri.

Garik petted the dog's head. "Kateri, do you know why I'm here?"

"You're here because I called Landon Adams into the library, and I irritated the dear boy. He said he was going to report me, but I thought you'd be too busy to visit tonight, what with the earthquakes and all." She thought she handled that well and without actual lies.

"I *am* too busy to visit you tonight. The quake damage is minimal, but after the big one a couple of years ago, the good citizens of Virtue Falls freak out every time the earth moves." He scratched behind his ear with his ticket pad. "I can't blame 'em."

"True. Can I get you a beer?"

"I'm on official business." Too rapidly, he recited, "According to Adams, you threatened him, then when he wouldn't comply with your unreasonable demands, you created today's tremors to coerce him into obedience."

"I created today's tremors to coerce him?" She lifted her eyebrows. "Of course I did. Anything else?"

"You burned his wrist with your freezing touch."

"Sure. Men are always complaining about that." She offered her arms. "Are you going to take me away in handcuffs?"

"I should. Or maybe I'll ask you not to fry anybody else."

Kateri flopped down on her chair. "You have to admit, if I had to fry somebody, Landon Adams is a good candidate."

"He's a jerk." Garik sounded disgusted.

"There are a lot of jerks in the military." She grew cold with rage. "The problem with him is, if he isn't stopped, he's going to get one of my men killed."

Garik's eyebrows rose. "So you *did* do something to him?"

The dog watched the two of them, back and forth, and finally decided she needed to change allegiance. So she hopped down and joined Kateri.

Kateri said, "I asked him to come to the library and I talked to him. The earthquakes rolled through. When he climbed out from under the table, he was pretty insane. Psychotic break or something. Madness run in his family?"

"A question I wisely did not put to him. Kateri, if you did create the earthquakes, I don't have any charges I can press, so I ask as a friend—please, cease and desist."

"I promise I won't make any more earthquakes to intimidate Landon Adams."

"Thank you. As I told Landon Adams, earthquakes are out of my jurisdiction, but I did suggest that they are a matter of national security. I suggested he go to his Coast Guard commander and explain your powers, and if the military deemed it necessary, they would take you into custody."

"I'd love to be a fly on that wall."

For the first time, Garik smiled. "Wouldn't you, though?" He looked her over. "Making earthquakes must agree with you. You look great. You're walking well, and even your hair is all"—he wiggled his fingers by his head—"shiny."

"Thank you. I feel great. Almost better than I did before I drowned."

"Good." He stood. "The weather must agree with you."

She smiled. "Something does."

Lacey escorted him to the door.

He faced Kateri. "You know, I don't want to be sheriff forever. What with Elizabeth's difficult pregnancy, I might be leaving sooner than I'd planned. I keep thinking—if your physical condition keeps improving, *you'd* be good in the position."

"Me?" Kateri was taken aback. "As sheriff?"

"Sure. You've got military training. You know firearms and you know what to do in an emergency. You're a natural leader. You're part Native American, and most of them seem to think you're some kind of . . ." He hesitated.

She helped him out. "Seer."

"At the least. So maybe you could alleviate some of the hostility from that direction. Plus there's the other side of you—you work at the library, you know everybody in this town. You know everybody's problems. Most people like you."

"Except Mrs. Branyon."

"I said *people*."

They both grinned.

"Anyway. The salary sucks and the hours are crap, but it sure pays better than Virtue Falls librarian." He opened the door. "Think about it."

She didn't say anything.

He stepped out and shut the door, leaving her alone.

And she couldn't help it. She did think about it.

CHAPTER SIXTY-THREE

Summer came out of a sound sleep, fist swinging even before she got her eyes open.

The blow went wild, glancing off Kennedy's shoulder.

He grabbed her arm. "Hey, it's okay. It's me."

She stared at him, not quite comprehending. "Kennedy."

"Who else would it be?"

Jimmy.

Slowly she sat up and looked around.

While she slept, the sky had cleared. The sun had risen. It was a crystal-clear early autumn morning . . . and the Hummer was parked in front of the Hartmans'.

"We're back, safe and sound," Kennedy said.

She rubbed her eyes and groaned. "I, um, wanted to go to my apartment."

"We've got to go over our strategy." Kennedy still looked alert. "And your apartment is too small for the two of us."

She was still groggy, but she managed a good glare before she scooted toward the open door.

"I'll get you." Sliding his hands behind her, Kennedy pulled her to his chest and lifted her out of the vehicle.

"Not necessary." Her mouth was dry. She'd probably been lying on his lap for hours, snoring. And drooling. Not that she cared. After the day she'd had—was it yesterday?—he deserved to see her at her worst.

John stood beside the car, heavy-eyed and exhausted. He'd been on the road for twenty-four hours in difficult driving conditions, and she cast him an apologetic glance. "Thank you," she called.

"You bet. Glad you're safe. Try to stay that way." He gave a wave, got in, and drove off.

Kennedy continued to hold her in his arms and strode toward the back porch.

The welcoming house, the sunshine, the dried plants in the flower-beds: they felt surreal, as if something dangerous watched from far too close. "Are we safe here?" she asked.

"As safe as we can be anywhere. Game-wise, Brachler got a head start on us. But he'll play by the rules. He wants to think he can beat me fair and square." Kennedy climbed the stairs, let her slide to her feet—although he kept his arm around her waist—and checked the security system. He entered a sequence of numbers—a different sequence than she had set up—and opened the door.

"Can he? You said you were evenly matched."

He picked her up again and headed inside, and slammed the door shut with his foot. "I think so. If I can convince the Prize to throw her lot in with me."

"A good strategy. How are you going to do that?"

He looked down at her. A lock of dark hair hung over his forehead. He smiled, a sexy, world-weary tilt of the lips.

Oh, God. That single smile reminded her of their first kiss, of irresistible attraction and fierce lust. But she had morals. And principles. Principles that he had mortally offended. "Look," she said, "I hope you don't expect sex."

He strode down the hallway into the living room.

She continued, "Because I am not soon going to forget that moment when I asked for your help and you turned away from me and let Jimmy kidnap me and load me onto his magical helicopter of death—"

Kennedy put her down hard and fast, pinned her to the wall, and kissed her.

She pushed against him.

He pulled back a bare inch. The world-weary smile was gone, replaced by savage fury. "Did he hurt you?"

Taken aback, she said, "Hurt me? You've seen me. All of me. I'm fine."

"I mean . . . did he . . . ?"

She got it now. "Rape me? I don't remember much"—more than she had before; more than she wanted—"but no. He didn't rape me."

"Then what's that?" Kennedy pointed at her neck.

Uneasily, she shrugged. "I don't know. What is it?"

He took her shoulders, moved her into place in front of the decorative mirror, and pushed her sweatshirt aside.

On the soft, pale junction where her neck and her shoulder met, she had a small, round, black hickey. She pushed her neckline back farther, looked harder, unable to believe what Jimmy had done.

That bastard. Rage rose like the tide. Rage, and horror, and dread. As hard as she could, she smacked Kennedy on the arm. "What is it with you guys? Are you teenage boys using me to score off each other?" She smacked Kennedy again, pointed at her neck, and said, "What role does a hickey play in your goddamn game?"

He caught her fist. In a staccato voice, he said, "No role. James always wanted what I have. He wants me to know—"

"That he raped me? First of all, he didn't. I haven't had sex." She maintained eye contact. *"Okay?"*

"Okay." Kennedy's savagery faded. A little.

"Second of all—don't you ever say that again." She let the rage overflow. "You do not *have* me. I am not yours!"

She could see the response that hovered on the tip of his tongue. She doubled her other fist, ready to smack him again.

Finally Kennedy settled on, "He believes you are mine."

"Or maybe he admires me." Her voice rose. "Maybe he thinks I have strength, determination, knowledge, and luck. Maybe he has faith in me because I live when I should die, I know what I should not, and I recognize him when no one else does."

Something must have been off about her delivery, for Kennedy stepped back and watched her as if he could see more than she meant to show him. "Why do you think that?"

She had been quoting Jimmy's letter, of course. Unwisely quoting it, for it was better not to have to show that to Kennedy. She didn't think he would be pleased about the message, and regardless of the fact that Jimmy mattered nothing to her—*nothing*—she would still be embarrassed and uncomfortable. "I don't know," she snapped. "Probably I'm delusional."

Solemnly, Kennedy said, "He's right. You have all those qualities. I'm sorry I insinuated otherwise."

"I'm sure you are. I am thoroughly disgusted with you both. Two little boys playing deadly games." She tugged at her sweatshirt. "I need a shower."

He followed her toward the bedrooms, and when she tried to enter the one that was not the master, he caught her arm. "Please. I need . . . I need . . ."

She would have pushed him away.

But his fingers trembled.

"All right," she said. "Spit it out. What do you need?"

"I need you. I need you like I need my heart to beat, my lungs to breathe. I need you, or I am not alive." Tears wet his lashes. "Summer . . . I love you."

She slapped her hand over his mouth. "Shut up," she said in a whisper. "Just shut up."

Those big, blue, damp eyes pleaded with her.

Still whispering, she said, "I heard him. In the wine cellar. I heard him. He said, *I'm going to destroy his family, his friends, his business, everything he's fought for and loves.* Kennedy, you can fight for me. I need you to fight for me. But don't love me. Please, don't love me. It's a death sentence."

Kennedy took her hand away from his mouth and entwined their fingers. "It's too late."

"No, it's not." She looked around. "Maybe he didn't hear you."

"Whether James is or isn't listening doesn't matter. He knows. How could he not? He's been watching me, and for over a year I have been obsessed with you. Why do you think he chose *you* to be the Prize?"

"One year is nothing for Jimmy. He has been patient for so long, waiting for his revenge." Like everything else about Jimmy Brachler, that made her very nervous.

"I've been patient, too." Kennedy wrapped his arm around her waist. He leaned close. His lips brushed her ear. "You don't have to forgive me. You don't have to love me. But let me make love to you."

"No."

"Let me carry you away from this place, this time. Let me help you forget yesterday and tomorrow. Let me make you happy."

She stood stiff and resisting. "No."

"I can make you happy, you know. You want a shower. I can serve you. I will service you. You'll stand naked under the warm gush of water. I'll kneel at your feet. With soft, scented soap and my own bare hands, I will wash you, starting with your toes and working my way up." His voice grew deeper and richer. "As I slide my hands over your slick, bare skin, I will massage each muscle, I will kiss you, lick you, pleasure you. No place will go untouched. The soles of your feet. The sensitive backs of your knees. Between your thighs . . ."

She swallowed.

"I will move slowly. So slowly. I know how to wait for my gratification. My pleasure will come from the chance to pamper you. I will glut myself on the sight of you, the scent of you. I will wash your clit, use the handheld shower to rinse you. I will taste you, use my tongue to bring you to orgasm."

His conversation proved how very talented his tongue could be.

"I will service you with my fingers, lightly at first, barely brushing your skin"—with his fingertips, he circled her ear—"then with greater and greater intensity until you scream out my name, and beg for more. Do you know what I will do then?"

She shook her head.

This time, his tongue circled her ear, then he whispered, "I will obey you. I will give you more. You'll put your hands against the wall and bend over. I'll glide my hands over your beautiful, taut ass and between your cheeks. I'll be washing you, of course, like a dutiful servant. But really, I'll be preparing you. Tormenting you with the promise of sensual satisfaction."

"Oh." She was breathing. But raggedly. Barely.

"I'll wash your spine, follow each vertebrae from bottom to top. I'll rub your neck and your shoulders. I'll fill my palm with shampoo. I'll knead your scalp, easing away all the tension, replacing it with"— he leaned into her hair and inhaled, and whispered—"desire."

She wet her lips with her tongue.

"By now, you'll beg me to take you. But I won't yield, will I?" He waited as if he expected an answer.

So she shook her head.

"No. Because I promised to bathe you. All over."

"You could . . . wash me . . . afterward."

"I could. I will. But not yet. First I turn you to face me. I'll soap my chest, and I'll rub myself against your beautiful breasts. We'll be warm and wet, slippery with bubbles. I'll slide my hands between us. I'll cup you here . . . and here . . . and I'll indulge you, make you gasp, make you scream, make you fall from the cliff of desire."

She could hardly breathe.

He drew back, his blue eyes vivid with promise. "So. Would you like me to shower with you?"

Reaching down, she grabbed the hem of her sweatshirt and pulled it over her head. She dropped it on the floor and walked toward the bathroom. "Follow me."

At noon, Kennedy crashed, flat on his back on the bed, one arm flung out, one wrapped around Summer, as he tried to recover from two anxious nights with little sleep and one morning spent in a slow bacchanal of sex that promised and teased. And delivered.

But last night in the car she had slept. Now she stretched languorously, and eased away from his embrace. She had things to think about. Things like . . . Kennedy said he loved her.

She didn't want it to be true. She didn't want to believe it. But how could she not? He was a man of cool intelligence. Surely he knew if he was in love for the first time.

Did she love him?

No.

Yes.

She didn't know.

Her feelings for Kennedy were as tangled as a cat's skein of yarn. He had spent a year researching her, searching for her, and when she contacted him, he had immediately come to Virtue Falls. He had believed her story. He had sworn to rescue her. Then at the first sign of trouble, he had doubted her.

She understood why Kennedy saw the world in black-and-white. The stories of his parents and their larcenous lives: they were wrenching. Those people had damaged young Kennedy's ability to completely give his trust. But he made promises with his words and his body; he had no excuse for abandoning her.

How did she forgive that kind of betrayal? Because of Kennedy's undeserved contempt, she had spent one more fearful night and one more desperate day, a pawn in a destructive game she had barely known existed.

And it was so much worse than that.

Jimmy hadn't raped her. No. But because Kennedy turned away from her, Jimmy Brachler had seized the chance to replace Kennedy as a lover. In her mind only; she'd told Kennedy the truth when she said they hadn't had sex.

Yet high in that helicopter, Jimmy had stripped her out of her costume. He had taken advantage of her drugged quiescence to touch her breasts and between her legs, and to her eternal humiliation, while she clung to him, he had brought her to orgasm. Violently. Twice.

Each time he had laughed.

Now Summer rolled away from Kennedy, curled into a ball, hid her head against her knees. But she couldn't hide from the memories that bit into her soul and mind and tore away confidence and self-respect.

She could give excuses for her own behavior. The drugs, of course. They removed every inhibition. But more than that, she had believed she was going to die. She had believed that this man who manipulated her body intended to throw her from the helicopter. Visions of falling from the helicopter into the forest blended with the old, black fears of falling from the ledge in the bottomless cave.

Supplies for survival. A flowery note. Whispered words of support.

Humiliation. Nightmares. Death.

Those were the two sides of Jimmy Brachler.

He terrified her. She *knew* he was a murderer, a thug, a thief, the worst human being she had ever imagined. Yet . . . he drugged her, hypnotized her, seduced her, made her want him. More important, she remembered those moments when he had let her touch him. He had whispered that he wanted her to win the game. He wanted her to live. She was the only woman who was his equal. He wanted *her*.

Kennedy had done as he had promised. For a few hours, he had made her forget. But nothing could keep the fear away for long.

In *Empire of Fire*, Jimmy's name was Venom, and she knew why. He had marked her, poisoned her world with dark fantasies and cruel fears.

No matter what, Kennedy couldn't help her vanquish those. She would have to do that herself.

She was the Prize. She had two choices.

She would win. Or she would die.

CHAPTER SIXTY-FOUR

In a rush of appalled adrenaline, Kennedy came awake. He sat up in the bed he had shared with Summer.

He was alone.

He threw off the covers and dashed out into the living room. He skidded to a stop in the entry . . . Summer sat at the computer desk, dressed in his sweats, sipping coffee and jotting down notes.

She looked up. She surveyed his naked body with appreciation. "Happy birthday to *me*."

Off balance and confused, he asked, "Is it your birthday?"

"No. But we can pretend it is." She smiled. Then she looked back at her notes. "I've been researching *Empire of Fire*, wondering if I can see something you've overlooked. Why don't you get dressed? I'll make us a late lunch and we can talk."

Sensible. Logical. But affectionate? Or even casually lustful? No.

He went into the bedroom.

As he dressed, he recalled the times when, during one of his affairs, the woman had told him that she loved him. He had always thanked her. Finally, she had said, *Can't you just tell me you love me, too? Can't you lie?*

He couldn't, and he didn't understand why she would want him to.

Now, despite a gallant effort to resist, he had to admit to himself that what he felt for Summer was more than obsession. It was love. All-consuming, blazing-fire, shattering-stars, euphoric love. So he hadn't been able to help himself—he had told her.

She hadn't even thanked him.

Worse, she was remote. He had spent the morning making love to her, hours poring over her body, assuring himself she was all right, unharmed, and if not his, then at least not Jimmy's. Kennedy had made her happy. They had gone to sleep together, and now . . . this.

He came back in jeans and a black T-shirt, carrying his running shoes, to find canned tomato soup and toasted cheese sandwiches waiting on the coffee table, and Summer in the easy chair polishing off the plate of food she held in her lap.

His stomach growled; making love for hours had a way of working up an appetite. "You have a bright future as a chef." He dropped a kiss on the top of her head, sat on the couch across from her, and tore into the sandwiches. When he looked up, she was watching him and grinning.

He relaxed a little. There was the affection he'd been looking for. "Did you find anything out?"

"A few things. As I understand it, to win the game, we have to find Jimmy's den and defeat him. So I've been making a list of possible lairs garnered from my concierge responsibilities."

"That's good. The soup." She'd added a touch of basil. "And your plan. Any luck?"

"More than you'd think. More than we'd like. There were some pretty eccentric houses built along the coast in the early part of the twentieth century. Most of them are gone. Some are still there and in ruins. And there's a castle or two. We need to narrow it down somehow."

"Before we can guess at possible lairs, we need to know what role he's chosen."

"Venom."

"He *told* you that?"

A hesitation. "Yes."

Was she lying? "Venom is the snake under a rock, the viper who waits to strike the unwary warrior. He kills with guile and poison." *Had Jimmy somehow poisoned her mind against Kennedy?*

"I read the online description." She held her mug clasped between both hands. Sourly she contemplated her soup, then placed her mug and plate on the table. "But who are you?"

"I'm the Celt."

"Always?"

"Yes."

She frowned. "Isn't that a weakness, to always play the same role?"

"In the hands of someone who doesn't understand the role, it is. The Celt is a barbarian leader who plays the lute and sweetly sings the ballads of war and lost love." He waited to see if she would grasp the significance.

"I know. I read the online description," she said again. "But . . ." She thought. "Ah. The Celt is a dichotomy. He has a warrior's brutality hidden under a veneer of civilization and melody."

"Not brutality. Ruthlessness."

"Call it what you want. I'm the pawn and the Prize. To survive, I need knowledge."

"I can tell you everything you need about the *EoF* world."

"I'm depending on that. From what I can see by observing the game—did you know people still play it?—the world is too vast for me to comprehend without months of study and participation. No. What I need to understand is you. The real you. And *him*. The real him." She leaned forward. "Who was Jimmy Brachler before you knew him? How did he get to MIT?"

Kennedy couldn't keep his disdain hidden. "You mean . . . was he a poor, underprivileged boy from the wrong side of the tracks?"

"I don't mean anything," she said sharply. "I'm not leading the witness. I mean—who was he? Where is he from?"

Oddly, her impatience reassured him. "He was raised by his grandparents on a small Illinois farm south of Chicago. I met Harry and Ruth Brachler once, after the trial. Good, churchgoing Christians. They were grieved and bewildered about the way Jimmy turned out."

"They're dead?"

"I don't know." As he imagined what could have happened to them, his skin crawled. "He wiped them out of existence."

"Like he wiped Jimmy Brachler out of existence?" Summer put her hand over her heart. "There's no record that they ever lived?"

"They're gone." He stood, gathered the dishes, and took them to the kitchen.

She followed and leaned against the door frame.

As he loaded the dishwasher, he said, "His mother was an advertising executive, very successful, who wanted a baby. She had no husband and no desire for one. She conceived James . . . somehow. She died when he was three. His grandparents told me they taught him to work on the farm, but James hated it. They said his mother was the same way. Restless. Ambitious. Always looking to the horizon."

Summer gathered the pans off the stove and handed them over. "So he was brilliant, driven. He had a tragedy in his background—his mother died of breast cancer and when that happened, the only person who understood him was gone. He was alone."

Surprised, Kennedy faced her. "How do you know that?"

"I heard him talk about her. He was . . . sentimental." Actually, remembering the speech Jimmy gave at that fund-raiser still broke her heart. Whatever he was—killer, drug smuggler, pimp, madman—he had loved his mother, and his loneliness had touched Summer in ways she couldn't define. Maybe . . . maybe because her own mother had failed to provide love and support. Maybe because the loss of her father had scarred her more deeply than she had ever realized before.

And she didn't want to talk about it with Kennedy. She didn't want him to put that razor-sharp mind to work, to analyze Jimmy's weakness and how it could be used against him. Jimmy deserved to have the memories of his mother untainted by Kennedy's manipulations. "Jimmy might not have liked living with his grandparents on a farm, but it means he came from a stable environment."

"Probably. The Brachlers seemed like nice people, but it's hard to see the truth about what goes on behind the scenes in any household. My parents didn't lose custody of my sister and I until I was old enough to make it happen."

She mulled that over. "You say Jimmy was from a farm. But he was reminiscing with Dash about when they were kids, stealing cars in Chicago."

"I know that by the time he was a teenager, he had worn his grandparents down. He spent winters in Chicago going to high school and summers on the farm." Kennedy shut the dishwasher and hung up the dish towel. "I didn't know about the stolen cars. I'll bet his grandparents didn't, either."

"So he never got caught."

"Or he got caught and erased the evidence before he could go to trial—he was always a gifted hacker."

"He would only be caught once. He would never make the same mistake twice." With skill and insight, she was building a portrait of Jimmy Brachler.

"You are good at this," Kennedy admitted. "I had never considered the possibility of defeating him by using his own personality as a weapon."

She inclined her head. "It's the technical versus the intuitive. You're the technician. I'm doing what profilers do in the FBI. The more I know about him, the better chance I have of surviving—and winning." She walked to the refrigerator, got a couple of bottles of water and handed one to him.

He took it, and her hand.

She let him keep her hand, but she didn't intertwine their fingers, or give his a squeeze, and after a moment she pulled away to open her bottle and take a long drink.

His first intuition was correct. Something was very, very wrong.

Should he ask? Should he not? Never in his life had he been confronted with this kind of emotional dilemma. All he knew was . . . he needed *not* to chase her away.

He headed back into the living room.

She followed. Probably not because she was drawn by the need to be near him, but because she wanted the information he had. But still . . . she followed.

"How did he get to MIT?" she asked.

"The same way I did. He *aimed* for MIT. He tested well. His grandparents didn't have that kind of money, so he got scholarships. Not enough, though. He was paying his own way, too. He had jobs; he worked as the host at a local restaurant and at the university at the library." Bitterly, Kennedy said, "I thought he needed those jobs to pay his tuition. Actually, he was using them to find his buyers, to keep in touch with his suppliers."

"You said that you admired him."

"I thought he was upright and honorable. I didn't suspect a thing was out of place." Kennedy seated himself, put on his shoes and tied them firmly, as if Brachler's neck was in the knot.

She stood beside him and watched without seeing. Her voice was distant and reflective. "He has a different face now. But he has always lived in disguise—on the farm, in Chicago, at MIT. I wonder if even *he* knows who he is."

"Venom is evil, using stealth and terror to kill. When you think of the drugs he pushes and the lives he has poisoned . . . I don't even know why I'm surprised."

"But Jimmy views himself in a glamorous light, a man who lived through the worst life could give him, a man who survived and thrived through intelligence, deception, and determination." She almost sounded as if she admired him. "If he is a snake, he's a coral snake, decorated with brilliant colors, and each movement is designed to distract from the real, deadly purpose."

Kennedy was tired of her apparent fascination with that little shit James Brachler. "I can't argue with your insights. But what I can say is—I don't care how he views himself. He tried to kill my nephew. He tried to kidnap my sister. He penetrated and attempted to sabotage my corporation. I don't want him captured. I don't want him discredited. I don't want him imprisoned. I want him *dead*."

Fiercely, she replied, "Don't kid yourself. I do, too. I understand the stakes. If he went to prison, it would be nothing more than a short, profitable recruiting expedition. He would be out in no time, and never again would you and I and your family be safe." She put her hand on Kennedy's shoulder as if to comfort him. "He's not going to leave us alone."

"No." He glanced out the window. They had three hours until sunset. "We need to start the search now."

"All right." She hitched up his sweatpants. "I need to go to my apartment to get ready. So what's he going to do next?"

Kennedy got his leather gloves and donned his black leather jacket. "I believe he's fast-forwarded to the end. To finish the game, his castle must be taken and razed to the ground. If a warrior is harried into the castle, he can lose in a frontal attack or because the other warrior sabotages his defenses. He can also lure the opponent into the castle with the appearance of defeat and into the arms of a well-prepared attack. Or he can circle around while the opponent is attacking an empty castle and take the other castle, and win. There are variations of those strategies, but that about covers it."

"Why doesn't he attack here?"

"Venom is the snake you step on unaware. He wants us out, seeking him. Then he'll surprise us, destroy us."

"That's hopeful." She sighed. "Kennedy, how is this going to end?"

"In the game, only one of the warriors can survive."

"So it does end in death. Obviously. Yours or his. And what happens to the Prize?"

"The Prize goes to the conqueror."

"And . . . ?"

Yes. Of course she had thought this through. "The Prize can be retained, or sacrificed." He caught her and pulled her into his arms. "But the Prize can vanquish both warriors, and by any means, no matter what I have to sacrifice, I promise I will save you."

"I believe you. And I promise I will save you, too." She searched his eyes as if wanting to impress him with her sincerity. "Now come on. Enough talking. Let me get my backpack, and we can go. Let's do this thing now."

CHAPTER SIXTY-FIVE

Summer and Kennedy hotly debated whether to start looking for Jimmy's lair now or first go into town so Summer could change.

Kennedy believed the search would be lengthy and would require as much time as Brachler could engineer into the problem. He wanted to start now.

Summer knew she couldn't defeat Jimmy wearing Kennedy's sweat suit. Since it was her car, her beloved, trusty, worse-for-wear but still speedy 1969 Pontiac GTO, and she was driving, she won the fight.

They turned onto the highway and headed north, toward town. She was just getting into the drive, preparing to take Kennedy into another dimension involving a great car, a winding coastal road and her own daredevil spirit of acceleration when—an explosion blasted their ears and rocked the ground.

Summer slammed on her brakes. She looked at Kennedy in disbelief. "He did not do that." She whipped a U-turn, drove back to the Hartmans', and arrived in front of the burning, leveled remains of the house in time to see the detached garage blow up, sending charred debris thirty feet into the air.

She stomped on the gas, driving back to the highway and toward town.

When the speedometer read ninety, Kennedy pressed her shoulder. "Shouldn't you slow down?"

"Trust me, someone's seen the smoke and called in the fire. Trucks will be headed this way as fast as I'm headed that way." As she took the corners, her knuckles tightened on the steering wheel. "How did he do that?"

"The house wasn't wired to explode. I checked." Kennedy was sure of himself. "So did Jimmy lob bombs at the house?"

Summer slowed to a more reasonable speed. "Yes! I was staring at the burning house so hard, and there was so much debris flying, I almost missed it. But something slammed through the garage roof right before it exploded."

"Destroying the opponent's lair is a brilliant move, but was Brachler sitting with a grenade launcher waiting until we left?" Kennedy answered his own question. "Unlikely. So his lair is close enough for him to keep an eye on us."

Summer's eyes narrowed. "That tricky bastard. I'll bet I know where he is . . ." They drove past O'Hara's Pub. She glanced into the parking lot, then turned in. "Let's find out for sure."

It was just past three, and the place was packed with construction guys. *Her* construction guys. Pitchers of beer and tumblers of wine rested on the tables, and most of the men were staring glumly into their drinks.

She walked over to Berk Moore and slapped him on the shoulder.

He peered at her blearily. "Oh, hey, Summer." He sized up Kennedy, silent and stalwart. "He looks like he's got money. At least *you* landed on your feet."

"Thanks. I guess." She pulled up a chair and sat down. "Why are you here this time of day? Why aren't you working on Parnham's house?"

Berk reared back in his chair. "Didn't you hear? He fired us. My whole crew." He waved an arm around at the hopeless-looking guys. "Fired."

"Who's working on the house now?" she asked.

"Nobody. He's not going to finish it." Berk muttered, "Right from the beginning, goddamn job was snakebit. We covered the whole outside to protect it from the weather. What for? I mean, really—what for? So it could rot."

Kennedy asked, "Did he have you finish any of the interior rooms?"

"Yep. I got extra men in to do it on his schedule. Worked day and night. Then . . . *you're fired.*" Obviously, Berk still couldn't believe it. "Just like that."

Summer recognized a force at work that could only be Jimmy Brachler. "Which rooms?"

"What does it matter?" Berk drank the last of his beer and stared into the glass as if surprised to see the bottom.

"Which rooms did you finish?" Kennedy's voice held a touch of the whip.

Berk snapped to attention. "That goddamn black hole of a wine cellar."

Kennedy nodded at Summer. "The Dungeon." He obviously had his suspicions, too.

"Right. It was like a dungeon," Berk agreed. "The tower room."

"The Watchtower," Summer said. "And on the ground floor, the office that faces the cliffs."

"Command Center," Kennedy said. "Anything else?"

"Inside the building, we completely covered a couple of the corridors and the stairway in plywood. When you're inside there, it's like a maze. A maze." Berk stroked his stubbled face. "Who the hell would want a maze in their house?"

"Someone who is playing a game," Summer said.

"He's a goddamn idiot, then," Berk said.

"Can't argue with that." Summer turned to Kennedy.

But Kennedy was no longer behind her. Instead, he was leaning over the bar, talking to the bartender. He handed over a wad of bills, then joined her.

As they headed for the door, the bartender shouted, "That fine gentleman ordered pizzas and drinks for every one of you sorry out-of-work sons a bitches. So give him a hand!"

Summer and Kennedy walked out on a resounding cheer.

Summer didn't know if she loved Kennedy. But she sure did like him. "That was good of you," she said.

"It's the least I can do. It's my fault they're unemployed."

"A few hours ago, just to be a bitch, I might have agreed with you." She grinned at him savagely. "But it's Jimmy's fault, and Jimmy has pissed me off."

"Took him long enough."

"I'm a real even-tempered gal."

He laughed. "I've noticed that about you. Anyway, beer and pizza is cheap. I'm going to have to buy Harold a new car."

"Harold?"

"At the resort. Harold loaned me his Prius to get home from the party. It was parked in the Hartmans' garage."

Kennedy paced Summer's tiny living room and listened as, in the bedroom, Summer and Kateri argued.

"I can't handle a forty-five automatic repeating pistol," Summer said. "It's too unwieldy for me to carry when I climb."

"I can come," Kateri said. "I can carry it!"

Kennedy had just been formally introduced to Kateri. He remembered seeing her at the party, but he could not reconcile that Cruella de Vil with this woman, tall and well built, with snapping brown eyes and straight glossy hair, half black, half bleached white.

"On some level, what I'm about to say to you might sound stupid . . ." Summer took an audible breath. "But we're not allowed to bring reinforcement into the game."

"On *some* level?" Kateri asked.

Sarcasm. He recognized it.

"I know." Summer sounded both resigned and exasperated. "I know."

"That little popgun of yours is not going to stop anything," Kateri said.

"If I aim well—and I will—it'll put a hole right through Jimmy's stone-cold heart."

"Unless he's wearing a Kevlar vest."

"I'll shoot him in the nuts."

"Even if you miss and hit his leg, that's a good strategy. I wonder if I could lift explosives from the Coast Guard and pass them off to you." Kateri sounded thoughtful.

"I think between losing the cutter and being investigated for causing earthquakes, you're in enough trouble with the government."

Kennedy stopped pacing. In trouble with the government? Who was this Kateri?

Summer said, "Anyway, don't worry about a weapon. I've got this . . ."

Kennedy could imagine Summer gesturing. But at what?

"And," Summer said, "I've got an idea."

Kennedy moved closer to listen, but all he heard was Summer's voice say, "Mr. Szymanski," followed by a wild burst of laughter from Kateri.

"My God, girl." Kateri was all admiration. "That's diabolical."

Arm in arm, the two women came out of the bedroom.

If it hadn't been for Summer, Kennedy would have viewed Kateri with interest. But Summer commanded all his attention. She wore dark, tight-fitting jeans, a black tee, and hiking boots. She had her pistol strapped to her side and a carpenter's tool belt loaded with a framing hammer, a grappling hook with a length of rope, a utility knife, and two screwdrivers. She wore one of her woven leather belts, this one with a large, round, blue stone the size of a baby's fist in the middle and two smaller stones on either side. She had a black jacket slung over one shoulder, and she looked tough, capable—and coolly angry.

"I'm ready." Summer handed him her jacket.

He held it as she slipped it on. "Leave your cell phone," he said. "We don't need Jimmy tracking our movements."

She laughed nastily. "I left my phone at the Hartmans'. He blew it up."

Jimmy wasn't smart enough to be scared of Summer Leigh.

Jimmy was a fool.

They walked out to the car.

Summer turned to Kennedy. "I forgot my climbing gloves on the bed. And my iPad—Parnham's house plans are on my iPad. Would you get them for me?"

His eyes narrowed. "You won't try to leave me here?"

She was startled, then outraged. "Do you think I'm going to run now?"

"No," he said. "I'm afraid you want to tackle Brachler on your own."

"The Irish have a saying—better a coward for a few minutes than dead for the rest of your life. Without you I don't have a chance. I'll wait."

He cupped her chin, slid his thumb possessively over her lower lip. "See that you do." He was always trying to be the politically correct, humble supplicant for her heart. Then he did something like that, and blew it all to hell.

Kateri watched him walk away. "Kennedy McManus is a very interesting turn of events for you."

"Yes. He is." Wretched with embarrassment, needing a friend's opinion, Summer said, "He told me he loves me."

"A *very* interesting turn of events," Kateri repeated.

"I could love him, I think, but other factors come into play . . ." Summer couldn't explain the two enemies/two suitors thing. Not when she didn't understand it herself. Not when she couldn't think about it without humiliation. "It doesn't matter. Kateri, here's what I want you to do. An hour after we leave here, call Garik—it's got to be Garik, not one of his deputies—and tell him we're out at the Parnham construction site and have cornered a killer. He's to come in with all guns blazing."

"What about the rules of the game?" Kateri was mocking her.

"I never agreed to play. So I'll follow the rules to get what I want." Summer leaned closer. "If law enforcement shows up too early, they'll arrest Jimmy and give him another chance to run the world from a prison cell—if he ever got that far. I would guess evidence would pop up to show he was innocent, and he'd be released. I can't allow that."

"You plan to kill him?"

"Yes." She had to.

"Honey, I admire your intentions, I really do. But there's a world of difference between thinking someone should be dead and taking a life. They train soldiers to kill people, and they do it, but trauma destroys a lot of them." Kateri put her hand on Summer's shoulder. "I'm not trying to discourage you. I'm trying to prepare you—you have to be mentally strong to stand up to the horror of doing something you cannot undo."

"I know. But I've had over a year of pain and fear to steel my resolve." Summer shrugged. "That's the other reason I want the cavalry to show up to save the day. In case I fail. Or Kennedy fails. Or, God forbid, Jimmy wins."

"Is this the guy Rainbow was talking about?" Kateri asked. "The one who's using the old airport?"

"Rainbow's got it figured out."

"I'll give Garik the message." As Kennedy returned with the gloves and the iPad, Kateri stepped away from the car. "Report in as soon as you can."

As they drove away, Kennedy asked, "Now where?"

"We're going to go talk to a man about a bomb."

Old Mr. Szymanski leaned on his canes, looked at the smashed trunk of his beloved GTO, and trembled with rage.

Summer hoped he didn't have a stroke, so she talked fast, trying to ease his distress. "The guy who dropped the tree was trying to kill me, and the car got in the way."

Mr. Szymanski's cheeks grew mottled and red, and the veins beneath the thin skin on his forehead throbbed.

She glanced at Kennedy.

Kennedy hovered, arm half-extended as if to catch the old man when he collapsed.

She talked *faster*. "But I know who hired the guy, and Kennedy and I, we're hunting him down. The thing is, I know you were in World War Two, and I was wondering if you brought home any—"

Mr. Szymanski swung around and pointed one cane at her face. "If I fix you up, do you promise to kill the vandal who would do this to a classic Pontiac?"

She nodded. "That is our intention."

"Then follow me." He headed toward his tiny, tightly packed house. "I've got exactly what you need."

She and Kennedy drove away from Mr. Szymanski's home carrying two World War II grenades cradled in a towel in a cardboard box, and with Mr. Szymanski's advice ringing in their ears: "Remember, kids, five-second fuses only last three seconds, so pull the pin, throw, and *duck*."

CHAPTER SIXTY-SIX

About a half mile from Parnham's construction site, Summer and Kennedy parked and hiked in, then skulked through the underbrush, from tree to tree, from cypress to Douglas fir, around the perimeter of the lot, surveying the situation.

The house surprised Summer. Berk wasn't kidding that his crew had been busting their butts. Construction was considerably farther along than when she left it. The roof was finished except for a few places where special work was needed to custom-fit the plywood over the trusses and against the walls. All the walls were closed in with plywood and white Tyvek house wrap. With no holes for windows, the place looked like a prison. Two ground-level, steel-plated, riveted doors furthered the impression.

When they got to the northern edge of the lot, Summer put her hand on Kennedy's arm. He stopped, and she pointed up at the tower, where one large window opening had been cut through the plywood. "How much do you want to bet Jimmy's got a view of the Hartmans' from there?"

Kennedy turned and looked behind him. "Since someone cut the treetops in a straight line toward the house, I'd say you nailed it. And that he's got some kind of high-end observation device with attached electronic weapon aimed at the house."

As she remembered the blast that took out that beloved family home, she got angry all over again. "That bastard. I loved that house."

"So you said." Kennedy eyed her curiously. "Brachler kidnapped my nephew, chased you into the mountains, blew up your car, executed a man in front of you, killed the man who employed you, and because of him, you cut off your own finger. But what you're really pissed about is the Hartmans' house?"

"All that other stuff is in the past. My position as concierge is my future, and I have just lost one of my first clients." She stared forbiddingly at Kennedy. Then her professional indignation deflated, and wretchedly she confessed, "The house had a feeling to it, of continuity, of family, of summer vacations on the beach, and a long history of good memories. What am I going to tell the Hartmans? How am I going to explain their family's beloved beach house is gone, blasted to oblivion in a silly, deadly game?"

"Do you want me to—?"

"No. I'll do it. But believe me when I say this—I am bringing Jimmy down."

Kennedy grinned. "Have I told you recently how much I love you when you're a badass?"

She grinned back. "Then at least for the rest of the day, I will endeavor to earn your love." She pulled out her iPad and fired it up. "Here are the plans."

"You're going to set the grappling hook here"—he pointed at the screen, then back at the house—"and climb onto the roof over the window seat. Then you're going to retrieve the grappling hook and set it here." He pointed at the highest place on the steep roof over the master bedroom. "There the framers didn't get the framing fitted. You can squeeze through the hole."

She put her hand on her framing hammer hanging from her belt. "If not, I'll make the hole bigger."

"Once you're inside, all you've got to do is find that weak spot in the maze, and follow it to Jimmy."

"And together we will take him out. Nothing to it."

"You've got ten minutes until I lob the grenade at the entrance to his command center." Kennedy indicated the steel-and-rivet outer door Jimmy had installed.

Summer teased him. "I love it when you're a badass."

"Well, that's something."

That made her look down at her toes. He meant that she'd confessed to loving him for any reason. "I hope the grenades still work," Summer mumbled.

"I'll get in, one way or the other." His eyes were crystal clear and cold as a glacier.

They had about an hour and a half until sunset, two hours until full darkness. They had no time, yet she had to say it. "From the way you reacted to my housebreaking, I wouldn't have thought you'd be so good at this."

His smile was nothing more than a chilly upturn of the lips. "My parents taught me what they knew. At one time they had both been brilliant, but by the time I was seven, ego and a grand contempt for authority had reduced them to jail time waiting to happen. I realized I needed to handle the heists, concoct the strategies, coordinate the timing. If I didn't, my parents were going to get us killed."

"Oh." Summer suddenly understood a lot. "So it's not your first time handling this end of the break-in."

"As a kid I had no morals, no reason to think life should be anything but a game, one that pitted my wits against the best minds in security technology. I enjoyed beating the system. I knew I was the best." He wavered as if he could not bear to reveal himself, and yet was compelled to show her his shame. "I was ten when Tabitha got caught stealing, ten when my mother made my baby sister feel guilty and miserable for every honest impulse. I realized—I decided—that Tabitha couldn't live like that. I was determined she should grow up in a better environment than I had. I figured a foster home would be better for her, for us both. So I designed a bank heist with a fatal flaw, and because of me, my parents were captured, sent to prison for five years, and Tabitha and I were removed from their custody."

"You did it for Tabitha." An admirable impulse, but still, Summer was shocked that he had been the brains behind his parents' larcenous successes, and even more shocked that he would so coolly betray them.

"I didn't understand that Child Protective Services were understaffed and overworked. I didn't realize they would separate me from Tabitha. When they did, I didn't realize how bad some of the homes were. Tabitha was a pretty little girl. She never stood a chance."

"She was abused."

"Oh, yes. And I am to blame." Kennedy touched Summer's cheek. "So you see, you were right. I had no right to criticize you for breaking into houses to survive. Nothing you could ever do would be as bad as what I have done. So, no matter what happens to me, you must live through this. If I can't join you, go to Tabitha. She knows about you. The money all goes to her. She will help you."

Summer hadn't really thought past the moment when they would confront Jimmy—and she killed him. Or Kennedy did. Or they both did. Kennedy had, and he must not like the odds. "Wait." She gripped his sleeve. "Promise me you'll survive."

"I intend to try."

Not the answer she wanted. "Promise me—"

He leaned down and kissed her, hard, and said, "I love you."

She touched her mouth, looked down at her fingers as if she could see the kiss there, then looked up—and he was gone. "Wait. I love you, too." But she only whispered.

She stood there, stupid with longing, confusion, and the terror that she would never see him again. Then she set the timer on her watch. She had only ten minutes; she'd work out her emotions later. She ran toward the corner of the house. She threw the grappling hook up onto the roof, set it, and climbed. And as she did, she asked aloud, "What are the odds we're going to survive?"

Probably a good thing Kennedy couldn't hear her. It was undoubt-edly not a statistic she wanted to know.

Summer found her way inside the house, in the eerie, echoing, win-dowless second story, quietly racing through the partially framed rooms and toward the steps. The rat's maze of closed-in corridors zigged and zagged and gave the place the feel of a labyrinth; somewhere in here, a monster lurked, waiting to rend her, break her, feast on her bones. She feared him. She sweated in the still, cool air and wished her heartbeat didn't thunder in her ears.

Yet she was glad for this, glad they would at last confront Jimmy and end this madness.

The second-story loft abruptly ended twelve feet above the cavern-ous living room. There was no way down; a rough-framed stairway led down to the ground floor, but Jimmy had had the construction crew build his corridor to wrap the steps like a cocoon. Since she was not inside the corridor, she was cut off. She had no choice; she set the grap-pling hook in the chipboard floor and climbed down the rope to the first story. Which worked great, except that she'd lost a powerful tool in her limited arsenal; she had no way to retrieve the grappling hook, and she wondered if she was dancing to Jimmy's tune, if he had made a plan to fit every circumstance. If that was true, and she feared it was, he had manipulated her . . . again.

Did cameras track her every move? If they did, she couldn't see them in the dark. Anyway, she didn't expect to surprise Jimmy.

That was what that grenade was for.

When her feet touched the floor, she veered toward the covered corridor. With one hand on the plywood, she followed it and came to that place where the covered corridor met the wall of Jimmy's office. There was no way in except from inside the corridor. She would have to come through the wall.

She found a seam in the plywood wall, and laughed silently. One nail. Berk's guys had set the plywood with one nail. She hooked the straight claw end of the hammer and dug in. The nail popped.

The silent alarm on her watch vibrated.

In two minutes, Kennedy would pull the pin on the first grenade.

She popped the nail on the other end and pulled the plywood free from the studs. And she realized Berk had cheaped out. The walls were thin one-quarter-inch ply. By the time they framed this, he must have had his suspicions about the job. Villains of the world, beware. No one could foil your evil plans like a disgruntled construction superintendent.

And . . . damn. Between this side of the wall and the inside of Jimmy's office were a whole bunch of upright studs and . . . Sheetrock. Sheetrock was heavier, tougher than cheap one-quarter-inch plywood. She could only hope a single nail held it in place, too.

Another vibration on her wrist.

One minute until the blast.

She ran the razor edge of her utility knife down the Sheetrock, scoring once, twice. She would wait thirty seconds, then thump her hammer against the seam of the Sheetrock, and while Jimmy was distracted, trying to figure out what was going on there, the grenade would blast the door open and—

Boom! The Sheetrock trembled in the explosion.

Summer staggered back.

Early? Kennedy had thrown early? No wonder he'd told her to survive. He was going in without her.

She slammed her hammer against the corner of the Sheetrock hard enough to pop the nail. Again on the other corner.

Inside the room, Kennedy shouted.

She heard an ungodly shriek of fear.

Kennedy laughed, loud and hard.

What the hell was going on?

She picked up a short length of scrap two-by-four and punched the Sheetrock. The Sheetrock broke open along the score line. White dust flew. She slid through the studs and into the office.

Jimmy, in a business suit, stood by his desk, white-faced and trembling.

Kennedy was doubled over, bellowing with laughter as he picked up one of Mr. Szymanski's grenades off the floor. He saw Summer, tossed the grenade in the air, and said, "Dud!"

She swung the two-by-four like a baseball bat and slapped the grenade out of the air and into the wall.

Everyone flinched.

It did not explode.

"Goddamn good thing!" she shouted.

Kennedy laughed again. "Game over!" Before Jimmy could confirm or deny, Kennedy strode over and smashed his fist into Jimmy's face.

Summer heard Jimmy's nose break.

He spun and fell facedown.

Abruptly, Kennedy stopped laughing. He stood, legs braced, above his enemy. "The grenade was for trying to kidnap my sister. The broken nose is for Miles."

Jimmy rolled over. Crimson covered his face, but his bloodshot eyes coolly sized Kennedy up.

"Stupid!" Summer was talking to Kennedy. And, "Snake!"

Kennedy didn't listen. He wanted the fight, and when he leaned down to grab Jimmy's shirt collar, Jimmy yanked him off his feet.

Kennedy adjusted in midfall, landed as hard as he could on Jimmy's prone form.

Jimmy grunted.

The two men rolled, punching and kicking, snarling obscenities.

Summer dropped the two-by-four, pulled her pistol, and waited for her chance to take Jimmy out with a single shot.

Kateri was wrong. Summer's hand was steady. She could do this.

Kennedy stood and yanked Jimmy to his feet.

Jimmy stumbled into him.

And just like that, Kennedy's knees gave way. He collapsed, unconscious, on the floor.

Snake. Venom. Summer swung the pistol and aimed at Jimmy's chest.

He lifted his hand toward his mouth and blew.

Something stung her on the neck.

Her vision blurred. She shot. She hit him, she knew she did.

Jimmy staggered backward, then ran forward and caught her as she fell. "You'll be all right, my darling," he crooned. "Remember, I'm rooting for you to win."

"Already won," she muttered.

"Not yet." He eased her to the floor. "We're not quite done yet."

CHAPTER SIXTY-SEVEN

Summer came awake frozen with cold, staring into the darkness.

It wasn't a nightmare. It was real.

She was in the cave, on the ledge, utter darkness pressing on her chest like a weight. Her limbs were heavy, so heavy. Her mind was confused. She was going to fall. She was going to . . . *wait*. Something was biting her neck . . .

She slapped at herself and cried out in pain, then reached again and discovered a thick needle, two inches long, stuck in her throat to the right of her trachea. In a panic, she plucked it out.

She cried icy tears.

Yet almost at once, the confusion in her mind cleared.

Jimmy had done that. He had used a straw to blow the poisoned needle into her neck and feed drugs directly into her bloodstream. Brilliant. Savage. Effective.

Who did he think he was?

He'd done the same to Kennedy. That's why Kennedy had collapsed.

Kennedy . . .

She wasn't in the Sawtooths, flat on her back on the ledge of a black, bottomless cave. She was in Parnham's wine cellar. She *had* to be in Parnham's wine cellar. The wine cellar was better than the cave, because there was no drop. And Kennedy was here somewhere. He had to be here . . . somewhere.

She threaded the needle into her shirt, then ran her fingers over the concrete floor, stamped to resemble brickwork. Definitely the wine cellar. She sat up and put her hand on her chest to calm her rapidly beating heart, and realized her holster was gone.

Damn it! Her holster was gone. Her pistol was gone. Her jacket was gone. Her tool belt was gone. The framing hammer, her utility knife, her screwdrivers, were gone.

She felt for her leather belt, for the stones that pressed against her waist, and smiled. Her sling was still with her. She was armed, and Jimmy didn't have a clue.

Jimmy, you aren't nearly as smart as you like to think.

Of course, if he had locked her in here and left her, her belt wouldn't do her a lot of good. She would die of thirst, starvation, and madness. Aloud, she said, "Summer, you should be so lucky."

Off to her right, someone—something?—faintly groaned.

"Kennedy?" she whispered. "Kennedy, is that you?"

No response.

Just like her, he'd been drugged. He was a big guy, and Jimmy really had it in for him, so Kennedy probably had received a bigger dose. Yeah. That noise wasn't some wild animal Jimmy had stuck in here with her . . .

He wouldn't have done that to her. Not unless he had the lights on bright so he could watch as the tiger ate her.

Getting to her hands and knees, she crawled and reached into the cool darkness.

Nothing.

She crawled and reached again.

Nothing.

She crawled and reached—and banged her knuckles into a wall.

She screamed a little. Only a little. Then reached again and cautiously felt the dry, rough texture of sloped walls.

Final confirmation, if she needed it. This *was* the wine cave.

She started searching again, and screamed again, when she put her knee on the warm body stretched out on the floor.

It flinched, and groaned again.

"Kennedy?" She groped.

He was dressed in jeans, a T-shirt, and a leather jacket. He was unmoving. He smelled of gunpowder, as if he'd set off a World War II grenade.

Yes. This was definitely Kennedy. She ran her fingers over his neck, then his face. She found a two-inch-long needle embedded in his cheek.

What a bastard Jimmy was.

Summer pulled the needle and threaded it, like the other one, into her shirt.

Kennedy stirred, and in a rush of movement, he grabbed her and smacked her hard onto the floor.

She gasped for breath, then groped toward his face. She cupped her hands around his cheeks. "Kennedy? It's Summer. I'm here."

He was immobile, unspeaking. Then in an abrupt motion he pulled her close. He held her in his arms. His lips touched her forehead. "I dreamed you were dead."

"I'm fine. I told Kateri . . ." She trailed off. She couldn't tell Kennedy that Garik was on his way. Not when she believed Jimmy was listening. "I'm fine," she repeated. "Are you?"

"I'm stupid," he said.

"I did say that." Which was a version of *I told you so,* and one he richly deserved.

"You did. I thought, no matter what, Brachler would honor the rules of the game."

"Because he was a car thief, drug dealer, and a pimp, and has moved on to become a master criminal and a murderer." She kept the sharp edge of her fury well honed. "So you thought he would—"

"Yes." Kennedy sounded earnest. "It's illogical that he would start the game unless he thought he could play and win."

"There's winning, and then there's cheating. And what do I know?

Maybe it's your fault, because you didn't give him time to declare his surrender."

Kennedy started laughing as loudly and as heartily as he had in Jimmy's office. "He pissed himself."

"What?" She had seen Jimmy, white-faced and trembling. But . . . he'd wet himself? And Kennedy had just admitted he saw it? When she knew—she *knew*—Jimmy was listening? God. There was no hope for either of them.

How could Kennedy be so oblivious? Did he not care whether he lived or died?

Kennedy reined in his glee. "When I was outside. I counted down—"

Summer remembered her indignation. "You threw early!"

"Yeah, I did."

"After all that crap about synchronizing our entry and all that talk about honoring the rules of the game—you lied!"

"I intended to save you." His voice was grave. "Now I've made the situation worse."

"He had the needles and the blowgun. He always meant it to end this way."

"So it doesn't matter that I threw early."

They stood at the precipice of death. And he irritated her enough to want to push him over.

He continued, "The first grenade was a dud. It rolled back toward me. I thought we were screwed. I pulled the pin and threw the second one at his oh-so-impressive iron door. It blew right before it hit, slammed that studded monster flat on the floor." Kennedy's voice was vibrant with enjoyment. "I headed in."

"But first, you grabbed the dud grenade."

"Yes." Kennedy was audibly smug. "When I ran into Brachler's command center, I tossed it at him. He saw the grenade flying through the air toward him and—"

"And he wet himself."

"Yep." Kennedy laughed again.

She wanted to *kill* Kennedy. "You laughed, and you can't imagine why he didn't concede defeat? Not even *you* are that clueless about human nature."

"No." Kennedy's voice lost its humor. "Pissing himself was exactly what I had hoped he would do. In fact, I hope he evacuated his bowels, too."

She pushed against Kennedy. "If he did, he will seal the entrance to the wine cellar and no one will ever find our emaciated bodies." She hoped to scare Kennedy into shutting up.

Instead, with keen interest, Kennedy asked, "Are you sure that's where we are? The wine cellar, aka the Dungeon?"

"Yes."

"You're *sure*?"

"*Yes.* I was the construction inspector. Yes!"

"Where's the door?"

Sarcastically she said, "I would point it out, but—"

He sat up. "Stop wasting time. Let's find it."

As she bumbled along through the pitch dark after him, she reflected on how incredibly annoying men were, especially intelligent men who seemed more intent on insulting their enemy than actually living through the ordeal. "It's not actually a game," she said softly. "You understand that? We could die. We could never escape and wither and starve and dehydrate and *die.*"

"Do you still have the needles he stuck in us?" Kennedy asked.

He wasn't listening. Or maybe he wasn't impressed. "Yes."

"Great. Because I found the door, and there's a lock that needs to be picked."

CHAPTER SIXTY-EIGHT

Summer pushed Kennedy aside, knelt beside the door, and went to work. The lock mechanism was simple; she had picked this kind of lock before. But her tools were nothing more than two long needles; even a professional would be challenged.

Each time she reached in with the needles, she touched the right posts, but she couldn't manipulate the internal system at precisely the right speed and just the right moment, and time after time, she slipped and failed.

When she stopped, trembling with frustration, Kennedy said, "Let me." Gently, he moved her out of the way—and within five seconds, he had the door open.

He really *had* learned his parents' trade.

She blinked at the dim light from the stairwell. A great weight lifted off her chest. They weren't entombed. They were free. They still had to face Jimmy Brachler, but she was out of the oppressive darkness, so reminiscent of that cave in the mountains, and that was the first step. She stood up.

Kennedy blocked the door. Turning to her, he took her hand and wrapped it around the two needles. "You can do this."

"Do what?" she asked stupidly.

"Pick the lock." Kennedy kissed her. "I know you can." He shoved her back into the wine cellar, stepped out, and shut her back inside.

"What? No!" She flung herself at the door. "No. Kennedy. Listen, don't. Don't face him alone. He hates you so much. No, Kennedy!"

On the far wall, a twenty-seven-inch flat-screen TV lit up, illuminating the bare walls of the wine cellar with the camera feed from Jimmy's office. She turned. She looked. She saw the office in a way she had not seen it when she burst through the Sheetrock.

Shop light fixtures hung tight against the ceiling. A giant map of

Washington's coast covered the back wall, pierced by red pushpins that created the illusion of a military chart recording battle plans. Above the map was a large, schoolhouse clock. The time read five twelve. P.M.? Had they been unconscious for so short a time?

If that was true, and Garik had not yet arrived, they might yet be saved.

On the right wall, a heavy iron table was bolted to the floor. A polished walnut desk sat against the left wall with a computer, a monitor, a keyboard, a can of paper clips, a container of pens, a worn sci-fi paperback cracked open and lying facedown. A white calendar desk blotter lay on the surface. On top of that was her pistol, her holster, the dud grenade, and her tool belt.

Jimmy sat in his black leather desk chair, facing the camera, staring at her.

His nose was taped. Yay, Kennedy had broken it good.

She stood and faced him in return, not knowing if Jimmy could see her, aware only that his eyelids drooped in sleepy-eyed menace, his black turtleneck sweater looked expensive—and that she wanted to know if he wore pee-stained trousers. Because if he did, Kennedy had no chance of surviving this encounter.

Kennedy came up and into the room, his back to the camera. He inclined his head. "James."

Jimmy mimicked him. "Kennedy."

"What are your terms?"

Jimmy lifted his hand from his lap. He held a Glock 18 automatic pistol in his grip, and he gestured toward the table. "Go over there and lock yourself up."

Summer looked; at first glance, she had missed the handcuffs. No, not handcuffs—a medieval iron manacle with a short chain welded to the table.

"Don't do it," she whispered.

But what were Kennedy's choices?

Kennedy walked over, calm and dignified, a warrior about to sacrifice himself for . . . for what?

She could hardly take her eyes away from the manacle. Or from him.

He faced Jimmy. "Why should I do this? What do I get in exchange?"

"I won't kill your sister."

"And my nephew. And Taylor Summers."

"It's only one manacle. You only get one deal." Jimmy sounded nasal, the result of the broken nose.

Kennedy shrugged. "Then no deal. Shoot me."

"God, no." Summer slid down onto her knees and clasped her hands.

Jimmy faced the camera and smiled.

Yes. He was definitely miked into the wine cellar.

Jimmy swiveled his chair back to face Kennedy. "I'll never touch Tabitha or Miles for as long as I live. I'll let them be. I'll cheer when they thrive. They are no longer part of our fight."

"We don't have a fight. I don't fight with criminals."

Jimmy came to his feet. He wore dark blue, sleek jeans that fit him as if they had been tailored for him. He'd changed his clothes; no pee stains.

"Really?" he said to Kennedy. "Will you *bargain* with criminals?" He pulled a length of half-inch iron rebar out of the belly drawer and set it with a thump on top of his desk. "What are you willing to do to keep Summer alive?"

"No No No No No. NoNoNoNoNo!" Summer turned and flung herself at the door.

The needles. Kennedy had used the needles to open the lock. If he could do it, she could do it.

"You know the answer to that." Kennedy sounded disinterested, like a divorce lawyer negotiating the custody of a set of sheets. "To keep Summer alive, and free to live her life as she wishes, I'll do whatever you want."

Frantically, Summer worked on the lock and listened to the conversation. She didn't want to. But she couldn't shut it out.

"Ever since those inmates held me down while Shel beat my face in, sliced me to pieces, I have dreamed about, obsessed about, imagined one thing." Jimmy's voice was both anticipatory and venal. "I've wanted to do it to you."

Summer's hands shook. Taking a breath, she steadied them and continued her work on the lock.

"That's the agreement, then," Kennedy said. "Summer lives her own life, without fear from you or anyone else. And you beat my face with rebar and slice it with . . ."

"A utility knife." Jimmy picked it up off his desk and clicked the mechanism, exposing the razor blade. "While you're handcuffed."

Summer froze. She listened.

Loud and harsh, the manacle clicked shut.

The needles slipped off the lock.

"Consider yourself lucky," Jimmy said. "I'm not going to rape you like they did me. You don't appeal to me at all."

Summer took another breath. Steadied her hands again. Started again.

"There's a blessing." Kennedy rattled the chain.

Jimmy laughed. "I am going to love this so much."

The needles were in position. The work was precise, delicate; she almost had it . . .

The rebar slammed into Kennedy's face.

He screamed.

She jumped and shook in horror and terror.

She didn't want to see this. She didn't want to hear this. Yet she couldn't stop herself; she glanced toward the screen.

Kennedy was on his knees, hanging from the manacle around his wrist. His cheek had been shattered. Blood spurted from his nose.

No time left. No time to fail.

She visualized the interior of the lock. She took a breath. And she went in again. She applied a delicate pressure. She listened and moved with delicate precision.

The lock clicked open.

Behind her, the rebar descended again, smashing flesh and breaking bone.

Again Kennedy screamed.

Summer slammed back the door, ran up the stairs and into Jimmy's office. As he raised his arm to strike again, she caught his wrist. "Stop."

He turned, his arm still raised, his face alight with anticipation and pleasure.

She looked him in the eyes. "Stop. Right. Now."

CHAPTER SIXTY-NINE

Jimmy surged toward Summer.

She flung up her other arm to protect her face.

He stopped himself in time. "You're . . . you're Summer."

Cautiously she lowered her arm. "Yes. I'm Summer."

"I wouldn't hurt you," he said.

"I know." She believed it. He wouldn't hurt her—as long as he was in his right mind. She simply didn't have a lot of faith in his sanity.

She stood in awe of him. She pitied him. And something about him beckoned her, one kindred spirit to another.

Softly she said, "Jimmy, it's time to stop. You've hit Kennedy twice. You've probably killed him."

"They hit me over and over. They cut me. They peed on me." Jimmy sounded robotic. "*I* didn't die."

"You were young," she said. "You were strong. Now you have satisfaction."

Again with a robotic-like motion, he turned his head and looked at Kennedy. "I would beat him to a pulp and never have enough satisfaction." Each word was dipped in poison.

Jimmy Brachler was a handsome man, with brown eyes that

warmed with amber glints, a taut face, and generous lips that wordlessly whispered of passion in the darkest night, in the depths of a prison,
at the ends of the earth. With Jimmy, the world swirled with the colors
of glamour, of madness, with the promise of a life lived on the edge of
reason. At the same time, Summer could see the thin white scars that
marked his skin. No wonder malice still burned in his face.

The only sound in the room was the faint bubbling that accompanied each of Kennedy's harsh gasps.

She eased her fingers over Jimmy's hand, grasped the rebar, and
took it away. Turning her back to him—that took courage—she placed
it on his desk, and ignored the smear of blood and pain it left on the
white paper calendar.

She turned back to Jimmy.

Distract him. Get his attention away from Kennedy. "I don't understand," she said. "Have never understood. Why didn't you kill me?
Shoot me? Eliminate me? Why give me so many chances to live?"

"Ah. That." Jimmy's face cleared. He became once again the suave,
attractive man she had seen in the kitchen of his Wildrose Valley home.
He walked over to the desk, seated himself on the top, tweaked his jeans
over his knees. "I should have killed you, shouldn't I? But you had survived winter in the Sawtooths. You'd cut off your finger to escape me,
stowed away on my plane, made a life for yourself in a new town. Those
actions alone were enough to earn my admiration. But when I realized
you'd managed to get self-righteous Kennedy McManus to listen to
you, *a thief,* and promise to help you eliminate me . . . I had to give
you a chance. You're a survivor. You're as smart as he is. You're almost
as smart as I am."

"Thank you. I guess."

Jimmy's eyes glowed with sick enthusiasm. "I had you targeted
in a hit-and-run—and you had already set up a doppelganger to take
the hit!"

"I did not!" Poor Mrs. Dvorkin. The woman didn't deserve to suffer for resembling Summer.

Undaunted, Jimmy continued, "That was so easy for you to evade,

I tried something more original—I dropped a tree on you. You drove your way out of it. So I flew you up in the mountains and left you." He smiled whimsically. "With your survival skills, that one was almost too easy."

How dare he downplay her suffering! "In a winter storm!"

"I left that equipment for you. I was already fond of you. I wanted you to live. That's why I kissed you." He beckoned her. "Remember that?"

"No."

He glanced toward Kennedy.

Kennedy, who had struggled into a kneeling position. One hand rested on his thigh. The manacle and chain held the other on the tabletop. His face was crushed, and blood . . . blood spattered his jacket, his jeans, the floor, the walls.

She couldn't stare. She couldn't cry. She had to keep her attention on Jimmy. She had to play this exactly right, or her failure would mean death to . . . to them all.

She looked at Jimmy and lied. "I don't remember you kissing me."

"I do. You were drugged." Jimmy's voice lowered to a croon. "I could have taken you right there on the ground with the helicopter pilot watching."

Kennedy knelt on the floor, his chest heaving. But his breathing had calmed, and he listened.

She didn't want him to hear this. But he *listened*.

"You fought," Jimmy said. "You tried to hit me, but your coordination was off. You bit me and drew blood." He showed her the inside of his lower lip. "You struggled as hard as you could. Struggled! When you should have been unconscious from the drugs."

She shook her head. She didn't want to recall this again. Didn't want to hear him talk about his triumph, and her weakness.

"And then." Jimmy put his fingers to his lips. "Oh, darlin'. You gave in. You kissed me, and it was like you came in my mouth. You wrapped your legs around me. You begged me for sex." He laughed. "You remember now, don't you?"

"No." But she did.

"Too bad." He scrutinized her, and he knew the truth. "Remembering is a great appetizer."

She had to change the subject, before things got out of control and she forgot who he was, and what he was: a brilliant man, warped and broken, a man who raised himself from the dead. A killer. Always, first and foremost, a killer. "So you didn't murder me because I'm almost as good as you."

"Even now, you don't quite understand. I didn't kill you because I knew you were my soul mate."

Horrified, disbelieving, she said, "*No.* I'm not! I'm not your soul mate." *She was not.* Summer wasn't wicked and cruel. She didn't hate and live for vengeance. She didn't care whether her mother had lied about her father, whether her fiancé had sold a bunch of lies about her to the press. She didn't care that Kennedy had turned his back to her when she needed him most. *She didn't.*

Jimmy watched her with eyes that saw her conflicts, her hatreds, her anguish. He tapped his chest. "Choose. Choose me. Go with me. Promise to love me as long as I live. I know you. I understand you."

"You don't!"

"If you go with me," Jimmy said, "Kennedy lives."

"*What?*" That wasn't a choice. That was extortion.

"Choose him . . . and he dies."

"Better," Kennedy muttered thickly.

"That's *stupid,*" Summer said to both of them. "You men and your absurd games and your ridiculous, deadly choices."

"It is your decision," Jimmy said.

Summer didn't take her gaze away from him. She didn't dare. She had no idea what he would do next: knock her unconscious, then kill Kennedy and drag her away, and tell her Kennedy was still alive . . . she could not believe that Jimmy intended to leave Kennedy alive, no matter what choice she made. "You're demanding I sacrifice myself."

"You have already sacrificed yourself once for Kennedy's nephew. You've made sure your Virtue Falls friends were protected. Sacrifice is a pattern for you." Jimmy was mocking her. "You always do what's right, don't you?"

She walked stiff-legged and indignant toward him. "You're a fool if you think that."

"In this case, the sacrifice will not be so dire or so cruel." He smiled, the most beautiful, wicked smile she had ever seen in her life. "Will it?" In slow motion, he stood, reached out to her and wrapped his arm around her waist.

He could not hypnotize her . . . could he? He could not bend her to his will with the force of his gaze . . . could he?

He brought her close, groin to groin. He bent her, caught the back of her head in his hand, held her . . . and still he smiled.

In a thick, halting voice, Kennedy said, "You . . . bastard."

For all the heed Jimmy paid him, Kennedy might not have been in the room. Jimmy was demonstrating, to her and to Kennedy, the control he had assumed over her, how completely helpless she was, and more important, how completely helpless Kennedy was.

But for all that Jimmy was showing off, Summer also knew that his body stirred against hers. He wanted her, wanted to be inside her.

And her body stirred, too. The helplessness she experienced was not from fear, but from need. He was the snake in the Garden of Eden, tempting her with delight. He was the Sawtooth Mountains, isolated and bleak, beautiful and tempting. Deadly. So deadly. And in an odd way . . . there she was home.

She feared him.

She wanted to be one with him.

"You're crazy," she whispered.

"Perhaps I am." He nestled his cheek against her hair. "Perhaps I am sane, the only sane person in the world. And I'll take you with me, show you madness and brilliance, train you in sexual desire and tormented pleasure, teach you to use your magnificent intelligence in a way you never imagined."

CHAPTER SEVENTY

Through the agony, the worry, the anger, Kennedy observed as Summer fell under Jimmy's spell. He didn't believe that she could be so gullible. Yet . . . she watched Jimmy as if entranced. "Don't . . . listen to him." Kennedy's voice scraped with pain—and exasperation. "Don't . . . go with him. Don't even think about it. He's insane. Can't you see it?"

Jimmy lifted his head and considered Kennedy, and in contrast, his voice was low, controlled, elegant and smooth. "You imagined because you were willing to sacrifice yourself for her that she would choose you?"

"She doesn't have to . . . choose me. Or you. She's . . . free." Kennedy couldn't form the words without slurring. Jimmy had struck blows that had broken his cheekbones, his molars. His nerves had been shredded; they could not easily perform the primitive task of speaking. Yet they somehow continued to find pathways to carry pain stimuli to his brain. He was in agony, body and soul, yet he had to concentrate on this—convincing Jimmy to live up to his vow. "You . . . promised she would be . . . free." No. No! He could not lose the power of speech *now*.

"She is free—so she can choose me." Jimmy laughed and shook Summer lightly as if waking her from her trance. "What do you think, my darling? You sacrificed your time, your safety, your finger, almost your life for Kennedy's nephew. Shall we use Kennedy as a blood sacrifice to set the cornerstone of our love?"

Summer swayed slowly back and forth as if hypnotized by Jimmy's words, his voice, his handsome, evil façade. She blinked at him, then looked unseeing at Kennedy. "Jimmy, I don't care about Kennedy. I care about you. And I have to do this." In slow motion, she leaned into him, flattening her breasts against his chest. She placed one hand on his shoulder, the other on his cheek, and she kissed him. She kissed him as she had never kissed Kennedy. She kissed him with undiluted passion and unreasonable dedication.

She kissed wholeheartedly, with an open mouth and such fervent need Jimmy's hands shook as he lifted them to cover hers.

It was only then that Kennedy saw the truth.

Jimmy loved her.

How could he not? Jimmy mocked her generosity, but she was truly good. Not perfect. Not the paragon Kennedy had wanted her to be. But Jimmy was right. She had sacrificed herself for Miles, had set herself on a collision course with death. She had placed herself between Kennedy and Jimmy, jeopardizing her life and her sanity.

Yet despite all evidence, Kennedy hadn't trusted her. He could say he had his reasons, that seldom had he witnessed anything but avarice and selfishness, and that was what he had come to expect from life. But that was an excuse, and he didn't allow excuses for anyone, much less himself.

Now it was too late.

Did she love Jimmy? He didn't know.

But he did know that Jimmy had mesmerized her. Jimmy had enchanted her with the promises he made with his body and his words. She had stopped Jimmy from beating him, yes. Yet now she barely noticed Kennedy was in the room.

She pulled away from the kiss. She stroked Jimmy's ash brown hair back behind his ear and smiled into his dazed eyes. "Don't kill Kennedy. You know I hate killing. You and I . . . we don't need a sacrifice. We're perfect together, just as we are." To Kennedy's horror, the tenor of her voice mirrored Jimmy's—not as deep, of course, but in cadence and tone and creamy-smooth seduction. "I am the sacrifice. You are the sacrifice. Don't you see? Together . . . we will be bleeding and healed, whole and one."

Jimmy nodded slowly, as mesmerized by her as she was by him.

Because—it was horrible to contemplate—he loved her.

Kennedy couldn't bear it. He *could not* bear it. "Summer! Listen to yourself. You're not . . . even making . . . sense."

She whipped around to face him. "Couldn't you let me remember you without all this noise?"

"Huh," Jimmy said. "He can barely talk."

"Shut up, Jimmy! This is my turn." She took a step toward Kennedy. "You didn't want me, remember? Not forever. You didn't trust me. You wanted to *pay* me for saving Miles. Remember? *Remember?* So don't get all noble now and pretend you care . . . although I guess Jimmy is right. You were willing to sacrifice yourself for me only as long as I lived the way you wanted me to—without you, without him. Alone."

"Summer. Please. Don't do this. Leave me if you must, but don't—" For the first time, Kennedy realized what he might have to give to win. And he had to win, or Summer would be gone. He would seek her in every woman's face, but she would live forever in the shadows, dominated by Jimmy. Dominated by evil.

He struggled to get to his feet. "James."

Jimmy's head jerked around, his attention inexorably caught by Kennedy's voice. Kennedy . . . the man he had respected. The man he had hunted. The man who had dominated his life.

"James." Kennedy fought his way past shattered bone and broken nerves to speak the words that would goad Jimmy into a final act of savagery. "We have so much in common. Our intelligence. The game. Our enmity. So . . . do what you have to do to exorcise me. Kill me. Sacrifice me. Do it! Sacrifice me as the cornerstone of your love."

Jimmy took a step toward him. "Why?"

"Then Summer will have no more illusions about who you are, what you are, and she'll be free of you." Kennedy pointed at his own face. "Come on, man. You haven't got much time. A knife to the heart. A bullet to the brain. A garrote around the throat. You've done it all before."

Jimmy's eyes glowed with a sick desire. "I have. In prison, I did it all. It was the only way to survive. You taught me that. You taught me to kill."

"Then use your skills."

Jimmy took a step toward Kennedy.

Loudly, prosaically, Summer sighed with exasperation. "What a drama queen Kennedy is. Come *on,* Jimmy. *They're* going to figure out where we are. We've got to leave."

Jimmy wavered.

She slid a hand around his neck. "Darling, you promised me heaven. How long must I wait?"

Still Jimmy stared at Kennedy, fixated by the chance to finish this at last.

Kennedy stared back. *Yes, motherfucker. Look at me. Do it. Kill me.*

With a snarl of fury, Summer turned, picked up the rebar, and swept it across the desk. Books, pens, and paper clips flew. She picked up the black velvet bag and stuck it in her pocket. Then she swept again. Her holster and pistol toppled off. She sent the keyboard and monitor crashing into the wall. Cables stretched, then snapped. Sparks flew. Glass shattered.

Astonished, the men stared at her flushed face.

Jimmy's Glock 18 automatic pistol remained on the desktop. She picked it up, smiled at it, then grinned unpleasantly at the two men.

They both stepped back.

She checked the safety, then tossed it into the corner. "You two make me sick." She walked toward the door.

Damn her. Kennedy had baited the hook, hooked the fish, had been reeling Jimmy in—and just like that, with a sweep of her arm, she seized Jimmy's attention. She held such power over Jimmy.

And over Kennedy. In a low voice, Kennedy said, "Summer. Please. Before I even met you, I loved your picture. Don't leave me alone, Summer. Don't leave me."

She didn't even glance his way. She kept walking.

Jimmy hurried after her, grabbed her arm, and twisted her to face him. "So you're going with me?"

"Do you promise not to kill him?" she asked.

"I won't kill him," Jimmy assured her. "But you—you're *sacrificing* yourself to save him?"

"Yes, damn you. I'm sacrificing myself to save him." But her body told the truth. She wasn't sacrificing anything. She swayed toward Jimmy, her face upraised, waiting for a kiss.

Jimmy laughed softly, and opened the door for her.

The ocean's wind billowed through the entry and into the office, stirring the papers on the floor, the pages of the books, clearing Kennedy's mind of everything but pain and frozen anguish.

With a last, contemptuous glance at him, Summer walked out of the house, out of the game, out of his life.

He was not so lucky with Jimmy.

Jimmy stayed. He came to within arm's reach of Kennedy. And he gloated. The bastard gloated. In a low voice, he said, "I promised not to kill you. I'll keep my promise to her. But I bought this property. I stopped construction. The place is abandoned. No one knows you're here."

Kateri knew he was here. "You lied . . . to her."

"I didn't lie. I simply didn't tell her all the truth. You'll get an infection from your wounds. You'll die here, screaming in pain. And no one will ever know what happened to the honorable and wondrous Kennedy McManus."

Eventually, Kateri would send help. "Summer . . . will figure out what you've . . . done."

"Don't you get it? She doesn't care about you. Not really. She and I are alike—we survive by any means possible. And you despise us for that."

But it didn't matter what Kateri did. Kennedy didn't care if he lived or died. "I don't despise . . . Summer." Speech became more difficult, but he had to say this. "I love her. Take . . . care . . . her. Treasure . . . as she is meant . . . be treasured."

"Don't tell me what to do with her. She chose me. I know what's best." Jimmy walked toward the door again, and turned. "When you get desperate, try drinking your piss and eating your earwax. I heard it'll keep you alive a little longer. You'll suffer a little longer."

Summer came back and stuck her head into the room. "Jimmy, come *on*. I can hear the helicopter coming for us."

Jimmy offered his hand.

She took it and led him out the door. It shut behind them with a solid *thunk,* leaving Kennedy alone.

He fell to his knees and for the first time since he had seen his parents led away in handcuffs, he cried. Blood and tears mixed on his face and splattered in a bright pink shower onto the rough wood floor.

Yes, he had survived. Yes, he had lifted himself out of the filth of his past and become a man of honor and integrity. And what had that won him? No love. No peace. Only pain, mutilation, and loneliness. His sister was right. If he didn't die here, one day he would be an old man, looking for Summer, sleeping with her photo, always wondering where she was, what had happened to her . . .

His face burned and bled. His lips were swollen. His tongue was swollen. His throat was closing. Maybe he would die now.

Pain pierced his knee and riveted his attention. A shard of glass had cut through his jeans. He jerked it loose, and more blood mixed with the blood from his face . . . he was kneeling on the contents of Jimmy's desktop: the papers, the pens, the paper clips . . .

The paper clips. The paper clips that could be straightened and used to unlock the manacle. No one knew that better than him. No one . . . except perhaps for Summer.

Driven by anger and purpose, he scrabbled through the debris.

Maybe there was more to this than he had imagined.

Maybe Summer had not trashed the desktop by accident.

CHAPTER SEVENTY-ONE

Summer laughed when she saw the house's outer entrance. As Kennedy promised, the iron door had been blasted, warped, and mangled, and rested flat on the floor of the entry hall. The studs around it were shredded, seared and blistered. Mr. Szymanski's grenade had done what she had hoped. Now it was up to her to finish the job, to take out the bastard who had no respect for classic cars. No respect for age. No respect for life.

She leaped over the flattened door and the last rays of sunshine slanting below a low-hanging bank of clouds.

In one graceful bound, Jimmy followed.

To the west, carried by the freshening winds, she could hear a helicopter's blades chopping the sky. She couldn't see it—the low cloud bank concealed its approach. But she knew she didn't have a lot of time. "Which way?" she shouted.

Jimmy grabbed Summer's arm. "This way." He ran over the construction-pocked ground toward the ocean cliffs, pulling her after him with a grip so brutal she could feel the bruising start.

"Stop that. Let go." She twisted away. "I'm *coming* with you."

"To save your boyfriend," Jimmy mocked.

"Yes!" She ran beside him.

The helicopter sounded closer.

"Even if it's true," he said, "even if he wants to believe it, he'll always know you *really* came with me because you wanted me."

"I know." She reached for her belt.

"Because you want excitement, passion, life lived to the fullest."

"He is exciting." She unfastened the buckle. "He is passionate."

Jimmy ran backward, watching her curiously. "He is dull as dishwater."

"You'd be surprised. He massages my feet. He puts the groceries away. He knows how to cook."

"Bor-ring."

"Sometimes, all a woman wants is a man who'll care for her, do the little things that mean he cherishes her comfort."

Clearly, Jimmy didn't get that.

So she added, "Besides—Kennedy can *talk* me to orgasm."

Just as clearly, Jimmy didn't like that.

She twisted the belt in her fist. "You've watched me. You've spied on me. You know everything about me, right?"

He frowned. "I suppose not everything."

"You're right." She stopped.

Finally he realized she was threatening him—and that he should be afraid.

He lunged for her.

Too late. She lifted the belt over her head and whipped it in a single, swift circle.

The stone in the middle of the belt met the middle of his forehead. His skull made a sound like a melon breaking open. His eyes went blank. He fell backward, hard, flat on his back.

Above the sound of the wind and the approaching helicopter, she screamed, "Serves you right, asshole!"

He never stirred.

Yes. He was unconscious. Comatose. With a concussion, she hoped. Or a possible brain hemorrhage. Or hopefully death. Because he might be right—life with him would be a life lived to the fullest. But it would also be a short life, one balanced always on the razor's edge of fear, one of waiting for the moment when he tired of her, or thought she betrayed him, or she failed him somehow . . . he would point a gun, the bullet would crash through her skull, and she would become another undiscovered body tossed like trash into the forest.

She ran toward the house, stopped at a distance, and looked back at Jimmy.

He hadn't stirred.

She ran again, toward Kennedy and sanity.

Funny. She knew how hard she'd hit Jimmy. She'd heard the sound of the stone against his skull. But even now, she feared him.

She glanced toward the sky.

She feared the helicopter filled with his men. So loud. So close.

She ran harder. *Get inside.*

She didn't make it.

A Bell Jet Ranger burst out of the clouds.

She glanced over her shoulder.

The helicopter swooped low, prepared to land.

Two men were in the front, the pilot and, standing at the open side door . . . oh, God. She recognized the other guy. Barry. From Wildrose Valley. The guy who directed operations after Jimmy had shot Dash. Barry was Jimmy's man. And he knew who she was.

Barry surveyed the scene, saw Jimmy lying motionless on the ground and her sprinting toward the house. He yelled something at the pilot, lifted his hands—he held a gun. Not a pistol like hers, but an automatic rifle.

She'd played this scene before, with Dash, but last time she'd evaded a pistol and she'd had a goal—the forest. This time she had no cover, the spray of bullets was inescapable, and to get in the house, she would have to make a leap over the door.

She couldn't hear the sound of the gun firing. Not over the sound of the helicopter. But there was no mistaking the smack of bullets hitting the ground around her.

She dodged from side to side.

She didn't have a chance. This time, she wouldn't escape. She was dead.

More bullets.

Run. Dodge. Stop. Sprint. Swerve. Evade. Escape!

The helicopter moved above her.

She wasn't going to make it—

Out of the house a monster leaped through the broken doorway. Blood covered its face and it roared like a wounded lion.

Kennedy. It was Kennedy, his face unrecognizable, but definitely Kennedy, and he had Jimmy's Glock 18 automatic pistol in his hand.

Barry saw him, too, and changed his target. Bullets skittered away from Summer and toward Kennedy.

Kennedy jerked as if he'd been hit. He went down hard on one knee, teetered for a moment, then regained his balance. He pointed the Glock, and raked the front of the helicopter with a barrage of answering bullets.

The helicopter's windshield shattered. The pilot ducked. He lost control.

Barry shrieked obscenities at the pilot. Grabbed for the door. Lost the rifle. It tumbled, over and over.

Summer flung herself to the ground.

The pilot fought to bring the helicopter level again, battled the wind turbulence that curled over the top of the ocean cliffs.

Kennedy aimed and shot again, aimed and shot again. Summer saw the way he fought the barrel rise, fought to make each bullet count.

Summer leaped up and ran again, toward the house, toward Kennedy.

The helicopter wobbled and spun—and tilted sideways.

Barry fell out, caught himself, clung to the door, dangling and yelling at the pilot.

Kennedy aimed through eyes so swollen he could barely see, ceaselessly putting all his bullets through the windshield.

The pilot convulsed and collapsed.

Violently, the helicopter spun in a circle.

Barry lost his grip. Arms and legs flailing, he plummeted to the ground, screaming all the way down. He landed on the hard-packed ground, and broke into a welter of blood and brains—and that was justice for every body he'd dumped in the forest.

The helicopter swung around again, and again, tighter and tighter, a top spinning out of control. The tail rotor clipped a tall Douglas fir. Jet fuel spilled, ignited, and the tree exploded into flames.

Summer dropped to the ground and curled into a ball, her arms over her head.

With a roar, the engine detonated with blistering heat and a flash of light she could see with her eyes shut.

Stunned and deafened, Summer looked up in time to see the helicopter bounce off the edge of the cliff and plunge into the ocean. Flames leaped so high they seared the brown salt grasses and made sea birds scream with fear.

She touched her fingers to her ears, massaging them, hoping to ease that broken, stuffy feeling the great explosion had caused.

Gradually, her hearing returned. The tree crackled and burned. New, smaller explosions came from the helicopter as it submerged. Yet . . . no gunshots. No screaming. The helicopter no longer ripped the air with its blades. Jimmy was still flat on his back, unspeaking, unmoving . . .

She wasn't afraid anymore.

No. More than that. She was thrilled. Exalted. They had won. She and Kennedy had won. They had beaten Jimmy at the game he had fought so deceitfully!

"We did it," she yelled. She looked at Kennedy, still kneeling on the hard-packed earth. She stood. She raised her fists to the heavens. "We did it! We beat Venom. We won *Empire of Fire!*"

Kennedy nodded. He mumbled . . . something. The pistol drooped in his grasp; he dropped it as if it had become too heavy. Sluggishly, he toppled over, landed on his side, writhed in agony.

Summer's brief, meaningless triumph was transformed into abject fear.

Kennedy had been almost killed. With the injuries he had sustained, he could still die. For a game. For a grudge. To satisfy the vengeance of a madman.

"Kennedy, no, please!" She ran to him.

His face was shattered: swollen, broken, bruised. Blood pumped from a wound in his hip—at least one of Barry's bullets had found its mark.

In the distance, she could hear sirens.

With frantic efficiency, she pulled off her shirt and made a pad, then pressed it against the gunshot wound. "The cops are coming," she told him. "Stay alive, my love. Please. Stay alive."

Kennedy looked up at her through a face so shattered she knew no one could ever quite put it back the way it was. "Love?" he muttered.

"Yes." She was fierce. Desperate. "You're my love. Please. Stay with me. Stay here. Stay alive."

"Will . . . try." He slurred his words.

He was so hurt. For her. He had saved her. From darkness. From terror.

From Jimmy.

Two police cars and an emergency vehicle pulled in and parked close. Garik got out first, shouting instructions to his heavily armed troopers.

EMTs shoved her aside and went to work on Kennedy. She hovered, watching helplessly as they fought to stabilize him.

He lay panting, crazed with pain, but when they tried to give him drugs, he pushed them aside. Opening his swollen eyes a mere slit, he gestured her close. Through battered lips and broken teeth, he asked, "Jimmy?"

"I knocked him out. I may have killed him." Summer turned and gestured toward Jimmy's resting place. "He's right over—"

Jimmy was gone.

CHAPTER SEVENTY-TWO

Impossible.

Not impossible. Not for Jimmy.

Summer grabbed the Glock 18 automatic pistol off the ground. She leaped to her feet.

Law-enforcement officers shouted at her, *"Put the gun down, lady, put it down!"*

She ran a few steps. She held the pistol out straight, swept the area with the barrel, searching, seeking, ready to protect Kennedy. Ready to kill for Kennedy.

"Put it down, ma'am. Put it down now!"

Then she saw him: Jimmy, standing on the edge of the cliff, highlighted against twilight's golden sky, looking at her. Staring at her.

He watched her aim. He touched his forehead in salute, then his lips in a gesture of affection. He turned. And he jumped. Like an Olympic diver, he hung for one moment, arms outstretched.

She aimed. She pulled the trigger. One shot. One shot into Jimmy's heart.

Jimmy plummeted out of sight.

Then . . . there were no more bullets. In his zeal to defend her, Kennedy had left her only one bullet in the magazine.

She ran toward the cliff. She flung herself onto the ground. She peered over the edge.

Far below, ocean waves crashed against the cliff and battered the rock arches. The helicopter burned in pieces, draped across the boulders, lighting the area with a harsh blaze. Seabirds circled and screamed warnings, and in the swells, corpses floated: seals and sea lions, brutally killed in the crash and conflagration.

And there, rolling in the surf, facedown, unmoving, and sullenly aflame—a body. Was that Jimmy? Could it be that the man who had caused them so much grief had spread his arms and embraced his own death?

Jimmy Brachler had enticed her to shoot him. Then he had given his body over to the vast Pacific Ocean for disposal. She supposed he had died on his own terms. "Good for you, buddy. I hope you're happy at last."

She rolled over and sat up.

Garik stood behind her, his hand on his service pistol. He held out his hand, palm up.

She handed him the pistol, butt-first, then allowed him to help her to her feet.

She looked around. Looked for Kennedy to give a report. Looked for Kennedy to know he was still alive.

The EMTs had placed him on a body board and were moving him to the ambulance. Blood and bandages covered him. Tubes went up his nose and into his veins. Pads held his head in place.

"Wait!" she yelled. "Let me tell him!"

The EMTs paused.

She raced to his side. She leaned close to his ear. "Kennedy," she said.

He opened his eyes a slit.

"He's dead," she said. "Jimmy's gone."

He nodded once, a tiny jerk of the chin.

She thought he smiled.

"Gone," he whispered.

Then the EMTs loaded him into the ambulance, and he was gone, too.

CHAPTER SEVENTY-THREE

Two Years Later

Kennedy and Summer entered the foyer of their San Francisco penthouse and dropped their bags, and groaned in unison. And laughed in unison.

"It was a wonderful trip," she said, "but I am glad to be home."

"I'm glad you liked it." Kennedy's blue eyes twinkled at her.

To celebrate the second anniversary of their victory over Jimmy Brachler, he had arranged for six weeks in Provence, just the two of them. Kennedy rented a lovely chateau, they wandered the narrow roads through fields of lavender, ate good food, drank good wine, and made love at every opportunity.

For the first time they even talked about those dreadful days when they had confronted and overcome the fiend who sought to destroy them, and they congratulated each other for surviving against all odds.

They did *not* discuss the eighteen months of surgeries and rehabilitation Kennedy had undergone to return him to his former quality of life, nor whether Summer's bizarre obsession with the cruel and charismatic Jimmy Brachler had been real, or simply good acting.

Some things were better left unsaid.

The vacation was a delightful break from their usually busy lives; since their marriage at Kennedy's hospital bed, his firm had grown exponentially. Summer's vacation-home-concierge business now employed over seventy people and covered the West Coast from Vancouver to Northern California and included the ski areas of Idaho.

By unspoken agreement, they were uncertain about their desire to have children. Their experience with Jimmy had left a permanent scar; they feared to bring their own child into a world they knew could be so precarious.

But still, their life was good, with homes at Martha's Vineyard and here in San Francisco. They kept a condo in Virtue Falls. They regularly visited Mr. Brothers in Wildrose Valley, and as Mr. Brothers grew more feeble, they helped him with his fund-raiser. Wildrose Valley was becoming a cherished part of their lives.

In secret, Summer had visited the cave that haunted her nightmares, the cave where she had hidden from Dash. With a bright flashlight, she had been able to illuminate the stony walls and floor, and she had discovered her fears were all for naught. The cave was wide and long, but shallow, and the floor was only a few feet below the shelf where she had rested. Yet . . . yet sometimes, even now, in her nightmares, she fell again into blackness and eternity. And sometimes, she fell into the flames . . . with Jimmy at her side.

But she never told Kennedy, and in the daytime, the memory of Jimmy had no power to hurt her.

Now Summer wound her arms around Kennedy's neck and kissed him. "Thank you again. I will never forget the wonderful time we had."

"Nor will . . . I." He glanced toward his office. "Now I need to go . . . see how many frantic messages I have . . . waiting for me." Kennedy spoke slowly, careful as always to form the words as his speech therapist had taught him.

Jimmy's brutal use of the iron rebar had left a lingering souvenir: Kennedy's facial nerves had been demolished, and some had not recovered, leaving him with a drooping eyelid, features that seemed slightly lopsided, and difficulty in speaking.

But as before, in business he managed to get his point across, and in their personal life, he never spoke hastily or in the heat of the moment.

She sometimes wished she would acquire that trait.

"Go on," she said. "But don't stay too long. We're both so jet-lagged we almost fell asleep in our soup."

"Is that . . . what that was? Soup?" He grimaced. "First-class airline meals . . . cannot legally be called . . . food."

"I know. We should have grabbed a sandwich in the airport." She yawned.

He gave her a push toward their bedroom. "I'll be in . . . soon."

She nodded, grabbed the strap on her duffel bag, and dragged it down the hall and into their bedroom.

She had decorated simply, in the Japanese style, making the view the centerpiece of the room. On a clear night, from the wall of windows, they could see the Golden Gate Bridge, and across to Marin County.

Tonight was not a clear night. Rain splattered on the glass and clouds swirled around the building. Good news for a city suffering from drought.

As she walked in, soft lights automatically illuminated the room. One of the spotlights had been shifted to shine directly onto the table on her side of the bed, to illuminate a twelve-inch-long, elegantly wrapped box, and beside that, a tall, cut-crystal vase filled with dozens of long-stemmed red roses.

Wine and roses.

She sighed, and smiled.

Kennedy had arranged to make every moment of their vacation perfect. So she would not tease him for forgetting that she hated those freakishly long-stemmed dark red roses. She always thought they were appropriate for vampires on the prowl and excessively dramatic tango divas. Still, it was the thought that counted—that, and the card, thrusting up from the center of the flowers, and the small gold-wrapped box with it.

Wine and roses *and* jewelry.

"Oh, Kennedy." She reached for the gift, yanked her hand back, and sucked on her thumb. Someone had failed to remove one of the thorns. She looked closer. In fact, someone had failed to remove *any* of the thorns. Kennedy needed to have a word with his florist. She reached more carefully for the card and gift, and when she had them, she just as carefully pulled her arm back.

She opened the card.

Always and forever you, Summer, my darling.

How unlike Kennedy. And it wasn't his handwriting, either. He must have called it in to the florist . . .

The card's sentiment made her wonder if she'd received the right bouquet. Not that Kennedy hadn't sent her flowers—the security in their building was too good to think anything else—but maybe somebody had made a mistake about *which* arrangement he had ordered.

Man, she would be sad if whatever was in this box wasn't hers, either. He loved to send her jewelry. She loved to receive it.

She tore off the wrap.

Kennedy walked in, bag in hand, and stopped. "What . . . are those?"

She faced him. "I knew it. This was a mistake, wasn't it?" She gestured at the vase. "You didn't send flowers and wine, either, did you?"

"I . . . did . . . send flowers." He frowned. "But not . . . those. And not wine. Not . . . for tonight."

"Then this is a mistake, too?" She showed him the box.

He stared at it, his eyes narrowing.

"Oh, well. I already unwrapped it. Let's see what it is." She tore off the wrap. She flipped open the box, and stared uncomprehendingly.

There, nestled in black velvet, was a round gold medal hung on a shiny red ribbon.

Had she somehow won the Olympics?

He placed his bag by his closet. "What is it?"

She read aloud, "'Winner Double Gold . . . San Francisco International Wine Competition.'"

Goose bumps rolled from the back of Summer's neck to her toes.

They looked at each other.

They looked at the wrapped box of wine.

Summer's little finger, the finger that no longer existed, burned with remembered pain.

She untied the satin bow.

"Don't!" Kennedy said, and started toward her.

Too late.

The ends fluttered apart. She pulled off the lid. With eyes half-blinded with foreboding, she stared at the label: a masterly painting of a ruined castle perched high on the ocean cliffs, and from its ramparts, a glorious eagle flying free.

She screamed, and fled toward Kennedy.

But she couldn't run from the terror the name had etched into her brain:

Gracie Wines
Cabernet Sauvignon
Summer Forever